INFINITE CRISIS ™

INFINITE CRISIS

GREG COX

INTRODUCTION BY MARK WAID

ACE BOOKS. NEW YORK

THE BERKLEY PUBLISHING GROUP
Published by the Penguin Group
Penguin Group (USA) Inc.
375 Hudson Street, New York, New York 10014, USA
Penguin Group (Canada), 90 Eglinton Avenue East, Suite 700, Toronto, Ontario M4P 2Y3, Canada
(a division of Pearson Penguin Canada Inc.)
Penguin Books Ltd., 80 Strand, London WC2R 0RL, England
Penguin Group Ireland, 25 St. Stephen's Green, Dublin 2, Ireland (a division of Penguin Books Ltd.)
Penguin Group (Australia), 250 Camberwell Road, Camberwell, Victoria 3124, Australia
(a division of Pearson Australia Group Pty. Ltd.)
Penguin Books India Pvt. Ltd., 11 Community Centre, Panchsheel Park, New Delhi–110 017, India
Penguin Group (NZ), Cnr. Airborne and Rosedale Roads, Albany, Auckland 1310, New Zealand
(a division of Pearson New Zealand Ltd.)
Penguin Books (South Africa) (Pty.) Ltd., 24 Sturdee Avenue, Rosebank, Johannesburg 2196, South Africa

Penguin Books Ltd., Registered Offices: 80 Strand, London WC2R 0RL, England

This is an original publication of The Berkley Publishing Group.

Visit DC Comics online at www.dccomics.com or at keyword DC Comics on America Online.

First edition: October 2006

Library of Congress Cataloging-in-Publication Data

Cox, Greg, 1959–
    Infinite crisis / Greg Cox.—1st. ed.
        p. cm.
    ISBN 0-441-01444-5
    1. Heroes—Fiction. I. Title.
    PS3603.O9154 2006
    813'.54—dc22   2006023929

PRINTED IN THE UNITED STATES OF AMERICA

10 9 8 7 6 5 4 3 2 1

ACKNOWLEDGMENTS

Infinite Crisis built on years of comic book history, and its ramifications played out across the entire DC Universe. There's no way I can thank all the talented writers and artists whose work I cribbed from while boiling the Crisis down to a single novel. Still, I have to single out Geoff Johns, Phil Jimenez, Jerry Ordway, George Pérez, Ivan Reis, Andy Lanning, and Art Thibert for producing the original seven-part miniseries that served as the spine of this book. Trust me, the comics were propped up next to my keyboard the whole time I was writing.

Thanks also to my editors, John Morgan and Ginjer Buchanan, and to my agent, Russ Galen, for getting me involved with this project in the first place. As a longtime comics fan, it was great to get to play with practically the entire DC Universe. And thanks to the gang at Captain Blue Hen Comics in Newark, Delaware, for providing me with my weekly comic book supply.

Finally, thanks to Karen, Alex, Churchill, Henry, and Sophie for all their support on the real Earth-Prime.

This novel was primarily adapted from the *Infinite Crisis* comic miniseries, originally published in seven issues by DC Comics (December 2005 to June 2006). Additional material was adapted from or inspired by:

Aquaman #37 (February 2006)

Day of Vengeance: Infinite Crisis Special #1 (March 2006)

Gotham Central #38 (February 2006)

JLA #119 (November 2005)

JSA Classified #4 (December 2005)

Rann/Thanagar War: Infinite Crisis Special #1 (April 2006)

Teen Titans #32 (March 2006)

Wonder Woman (second series) #223 and #224 (January 2006 and February 2006)

These comic books were created by the following people:

EDITORS
Eddie Berganza
Mike Carlin
Joey Cavalieri
Ivan Cohen
Matt Idelson
Peter Tomasi
Stephen Wacker

ASSOCIATE EDITORS
Nachie Castro
Harvey Richards
Jeanine Schaefer
Michael Siglain
Michael Wright

WRITERS
Dave Gibbons
Allan Heinberg
Geoff Johns
Greg Rucka
Bill Willingham

PENCILLERS
Chris Batista
Joe Bennett
Amanda Conner
Phil Jimenez
Justiniano
Leonard Kirk
Rags Morales
Todd Nauck
Jerry Ordway
George Pérez
Joe Prado
Ivan Reis
Cliff Richards

INKERS
Oclair Albert
Marlo Alquiza
Michael Bair
Marc Campos
Andy Clarke
Kevin Conrad

Mark Farmer
Wayne Faucher
Drew Geraci
Andy Lanning
Jerry Ordway
Jimmy Palmiotti
Sean Parsons
George Pérez
Norm Rapmund
Ray Snyder
Larry Stucker
Art Thibert
Walden Wong

FOREWORD
by Mark Waid

IMITATION is the sincerest form of catastrophe.

Twenty years ago, the American super hero—after five decades of being considered something strictly for kids—finally came of age. Frank Miller's *Batman: The Dark Knight Returns* and Alan Moore and Dave Gibbons' *Watchmen* concurrently broke new pop culture ground by showing readers what super heroes might be like if they had to operate in a "realistic" world; if their nobility were driven less by a traditional, children's-ethics idea of heroism and more by adult angst and tortured psyches.

Both *Dark Knight* and *Watchmen* were fascinating, experimental series, and both represented a huge leap forward for the genre. Benefiting from an unprecedented amount of well-deserved media attention, they brought hundreds of thousands of new and lapsed fans into comics shops nationwide. They were seminal works, and all throughout the medium, publishers and creators honored their success in the time-honored manner of . . . well . . . of photocopying them while simultaneously missing their point.

Overnight, the inmates took over the asylum. Misguided comics writers and artists who saw only the surface cynicism of Miller's and Moore and Gibbons' approach, and not the heroic passion underneath, decided that the key to bombastic sales was in producing story after story after story about how screwed-up you'd have to be to act like a super hero. The whole misguided approach became widely known in the industry by the code term "grim and gritty," and the irony of the fact that the phrase's origin can—and this is absolutely true—be traced back to an episode of the camp 1960s Batman TV series was lost on every one of them.

Since then, super heroes have, in the eyes of fans, fallen largely into two extremes: "old-fashioned" or "psychotic." Either their moral definitions are perceived as hopelessly shallow and outdated, or they're so busy trying to overcome their own personal demons that it's a miracle they find time to fight crime at all. Luckily, writer Geoff Johns and artist Phil Jimenez have finally come along to pull each and every one of their lost super-souls back to center.

Using characters from DC's mid-eighties smash hit *Crisis on Infinite Earths*, Johns and Jimenez, along with a host of DC collaborators, made comics history in 2006. In *Crisis*'s landmark sequel, *Infinite Crisis*, they flatly acknowledged the gloom that has corrupted the legends of even the world's greatest super heroes. Then, more importantly, they told the story of what happens the day Superman, Batman, and Wonder Woman all realize how lost in darkness they've become—and how, if they don't find their balance fast, that darkness will consume the world.

In graphic novel form, *Infinite Crisis* is a terrific tale full of surprises, the opening fanfare in what is almost certainly a revolutionary age of comic storytelling. In the novelization you're about to read, it's also an allegory with a stunning amount of depth, and in these pages you'll find visions of the DC Universe that will redefine your understanding of truth, justice, and the American way.

Welcome to a new dawn.

PROLOGUE

EARTH'S MOON

THE Watchtower rose from the surface of the Moon. The gleaming silver structure stood out amidst the cratered landscape of the Sea of Serenity, not far from where *Apollo 17* had touched down over thirty years ago. Steel panels and thick crystal portholes protected the inhabitants of the lunar base from the harsh vacuum outside, not to mention attacks from hostile forces. Despite its name, the Watchtower resembled a sprawling complex more than a tower. Three large wings radiated out from the central hub, which housed the legendary Hall of Justice, the chief meeting-place of Earth's greatest heroes, the Justice League of America.

Directly beneath the Hall of Justice was the Monitor Room, where the Watchtower really lived up to its name. Multiple long-range scanners kept a close eye on the fragile blue planet less than four hundred thousand kilometers away, while another array of sensors were aimed out into space, watching closely for any sign of an impending alien invasion. The advance warning provided by the scanners had often meant the difference between defeat and victory when it came to the JLA's ongoing mission to protect Earth. League members took turns manning the Monitor Room, adding their own judgment and intuition to the sophisticated computer algorithms analyzing the incoming data for potential threats.

At that moment, J'onn J'onzz, the Martian Manhunter, had the Monitor

Room—and the entire Watchtower—to himself. The last survivor of a long-dead alien race, he customarily took the form of a muscular, green-skinned humanoid with a hairless skull and the usual number of limbs. Thoughtful red eyes peered out from beneath his beetled brows. Bright red straps crossed his bare green chest. A voluminous blue cloak draped his shoulders. And a troubled expression occupied his face as he sat at the center of the Monitor Room, facing a huge wall composed entirely of multiple viewscreens. Disturbing images flashed across the screens, images transmitted from Earth as well as from the distant reaches of outer space. J'onn's extraterrestrial heart sank as he contemplated the images. It seemed as though the entire universe had gone insane.

On one screen, intercepted TV news footage showed both heroes and villains battling against the ruthless blue cyborgs known as OMACs, short for Observational Meta-human Activity Construct. The OMACs had first started appearing only a few days ago, carrying out what appeared to be a systematic campaign of eradication against the world's meta-humans, but they had only recently been revealed to be ordinary men and women involuntarily transformed into inhuman killing machines by an insidious virus that had infected their bloodstreams with millions of microscopic machines. Once activated, these nanobots caused an indestructible blue ceramic shell to form over the unsuspecting humans' bodies, turning them into faceless cyborgs with no will of their own. The OMACs were controlled by Brother Eye, a self-aware computer satellite programmed to monitor every super-powered being on the planet. Ironically, Brother Eye was the creation of Batman himself, who had intended to use the satellite to keep track of his fellow heroes. But the Dark Knight had somehow lost control of Brother Eye, which was no longer content to merely observe Earth's meta-human champions and their foes; now it was intent on eliminating them all.

J'onn watched with both concern and relief as the young hero Kid Flash barely escaped a pack of flying OMACs. Crimson laser beams blasted from each OMAC's single red eye, converging on the outnumbered teenage boy clad in his bright yellow uniform. Moving with lightning speed, however, Bart Allen dodged the beams and ran for safety, turning into a yellow blur as he swiftly outpaced both the news cameras and his relentless adversaries. The OMACs zoomed after him, but Kid Flash appeared to have eluded them.

But for how much longer? J'onn wondered grimly. According to Batman, there were at least two hundred thousand OMACs under Brother Eye's control, many still to be activated. *Oh, Bruce, what have you done?*

Alas, the OMAC situation was far from the only emergency facing both the League and the planet. J'onn's gaze shifted to another screen, which was dominated by a photo of Lex Luthor, Superman's longtime foe. Below Luthor's portrait were smaller inserts bearing the images of numerous other felons—including everyone from Black Adam to Zoom—now known to be allied with Luthor. Indeed, recent reports confirmed that Luthor had succeeded in organizing the League's archenemies into a so-called Secret Society of Super-Villains that now boasted literally dozens of members.

Additional photos appeared beneath Luthor's portrait with alarming speed, as the League's computers steadily added to the expanding list of ruthless villains believed to be affiliated with the Society. J'onn shook his head at the ever-growing rogue's gallery displayed before his eyes. Individually, menaces such as the Cheetah and Deathstroke were formidable adversaries in their own right. He shuddered at the thought of so many of humanity's worst enemies working in unison.

Where is Luthor now? he wondered. Despite Superman's best efforts, the criminal genius remained at large, his present whereabouts unknown. *What are he and his infamous cabal plotting at this very moment?* Martian Manhunter doubted that Luthor had organized the Society just to commit random acts of terrorism and extortion. He almost surely had some master plan at work. *But what is his ultimate goal?*

Still, at least Luthor was human, a creature of mere flesh and blood. His activities, heinous as they were, remained confined to the physical plane. The same could not be said of another deadly menace, one that was even now wreaking havoc in the realms of the supernatural, with dire effects upon both the living and the dead.

J'onn's gaze was drawn to another set of screens where a pale, ghostly figure shrouded in a hooded cloak could be seen battling Captain Marvel high above the streets of Budapest. This was the Spectre, an all-powerful supernatural entity who some believed to be nothing less than the very embodiment of the Wrath of God. The Spectre had often been a force for justice, albeit of a harsh and unforgiving variety, and had even allied himself with the League in years past. But recent events seemed to have driven him mad. Rumors among the occult community, passed on to the League by a network of contacts and informants, claimed that the crazed Spectre had embarked on an insane new mission. Instead of merely punishing the wicked, as was his wont, the vengeful spirit had decided that magic itself was inherently evil and needed to be eradicated altogether. Now he was striking out at both good and evil magicusers alike, regardless of the consequences.

On the screen, the Spectre grew to gargantuan height, until his ghostly form towered over the Hungarian capital. With a single sweep of his immense hand, he swatted Captain Marvel as though he were a fly. Marvel's powers, J'onn recalled, were derived from the wizard Shazam, which explained why Earth's Mightiest Mortal had incurred the Spectre's anger. The innocent hero, whose cheerful gold-and-red costume contrasted sharply with the Spectre's dark green cloak, smashed into an eighteenth-century clock tower. Debris rained down on the frightened people below.

J'onn was appalled at the wanton destruction. *Surely,* he thought, *the Wrath of God would not be so indiscriminate in its exercise.* As a Martian, J'onn had his doubts regarding the Terran conception of God; he preferred the pantheon of Martian deities he had worshiped back on his native planet. Yet he could not deny the near-omnipotent power of the Spectre, and trembled at the thought of such power being wielded so recklessly. Too many of Earth's greatest champions drew their strength from the very mystical forces that the Spectre appeared determined to destroy. *What of the Phantom Stranger,* he worried, *or Zatanna?* And how long could it be before this monumental tumult in the supernatural world spilled out into the mortal plane, endangering the lives and souls of innocent human beings?

J'onn feared the worst, now that the Spectre was on a rampage. *Who among us possesses the power to stop him?* The Spectre was a force beyond the ken of mortals. *Not even Superman can halt his vengeance.*

But not only Earth was in danger. J'onn turned his attention to another set of monitors, which revealed a cosmic catastrophe taking place trillions of light-years away. Alien technology, generations ahead of Terran science, allowed the Watchtower to pick up faster-than-light signals emanating from the distant Polaris system, where an unimaginable conflict threatened scores of sentient species.

The planets Rann and Thanagar, both home to advanced humanoid civilizations, were at war, and the bitter hostilities had turned their entire sector of the galaxy into a battlefield. After its solar system became uninhabitable,

Rann had been teleported to the Polaris system, home of Thanagar; but in the process, Thanagar was devastated. The remaining Thanagarians had declared war. Fleets of armed spacecraft contended in space, while winged Thanagarian soldiers had invaded the surface of Rann, home to Adam Strange, a transplanted Earthman and League ally. To complicate matters, other extraterrestrial races had taken sides in the conflict, joining with either Rann or Thanagar, so that the dispute between the two planets had erupted into a violent conflagration involving the Tamaraneans, the Dominators, and many other powerful species.

War is like fire, J'onn thought. *Once ignited, it often spreads out of control, consuming everything it touches.* The conflict in the Polaris system was a long way from Earth, yet he knew better than most how small the universe had become. After all, he was neither the first nor the last extraterrestrial to visit Earth. There was no guarantee that the Rann-Thanagar War would not make its way there as well. *We need to be prepared for anything.*

Easier said than done. The diverse crises could not have come at a worse time. The League itself was in disarray, stricken by tragedy, dissent, and controversy. J'onn keyed a command into the control panel before him, and the face of a smiling man in a blue mask and translucent yellow goggles appeared on the screen directly in front of him. A caption identified the man as, "BLUE BEETLE. DECEASED."

The image was a poignant reminder of a painful loss. Ted Kord, the Blue Beetle, had died only days ago while investigating the shadowy figure behind the OMAC Project. He had been murdered by Maxwell Lord, a charismatic business tycoon (and longtime associate of the League), who had proved to be the instigator of the OMACs' campaign against the world's superhumans. The Blue Beetle had exposed Max's treachery, but only at the cost of his own life.

Martian Manhunter bowed his head in sorrow. *Forgive us, my friend. With so much going on, we've barely had time to mourn you.* He felt the loss of his old teammate deeply. In truth, the Blue Beetle, a crime-fighting acrobat and inventor, had never been the world's most impressive super hero, but J'onn had always valued Ted Kord's gentle humor and good spirits. *You deserved a happier end.*

J'onn pressed a button, consigning his friend's face to the computer's copious memory banks. His expression darkened as he recalled what had happened after the tragedy. The Blue Beetle had been avenged, but only at a terrible cost.

Reluctantly, his eyes turned toward an array of screens dedicated to monitoring terrestrial news broadcasts. The same loop of footage kept playing over and over again on the various international news networks, just as it had been doing for the last few days. J'onn gazed at the news clip for maybe the hundredth time, as dismayed now by the horrifying images as he had been the very first time he had viewed them:

Maxwell Lord was a prisoner, bound tightly within the coils of Wonder Woman's Golden Lasso of Truth. The beautiful Amazon princess, perhaps the most admired member of the League, save for Superman, stared intently into Max's eyes. Her exquisite face bore a solemn yet resolute expression. Without hesitation, she took hold of her captive's head and twisted it around until his neck snapped like a twig.

The world would never look at Wonder Woman the same way again.

And neither would some of her teammates.

The damning visuals of Wonder Woman coolly killing a man with her bare hands had been captured by Brother Eye and broadcast to all the world's media. As far as the average person was concerned, Diana had instantly gone from heroine to murderous vigilante. In fact, J'onn knew, the truth was far more complicated.

Max Lord had done more than murder the Blue Beetle in cold blood. He had also used his own telepathic abilities to take over Superman's mind, turning the Man of Steel into a weapon to be used against any who opposed the tycoon. Under Max's command, Superman had almost killed both Batman and Wonder Woman before the invincible Amazon finally managed to get the upper hand on Max. Killing him had been the only way to permanently free Superman from the villain's spell.

Or had it?

Could Diana have found another way? J'onn was reluctant to condemn Wonder Woman, yet he couldn't help feeling that she had crossed a crucial line, and that the League itself was the weaker for it. Certainly the public uproar over Max's death compromised the JLA's ability to deal with the myriad emergencies that suddenly seemed to be occurring all at once. *We are stretched thin enough as is.* He rose from his seat and took a few steps backward, trying to take in the big picture. On the manifold screens before him, OMACs scoured the world for meta-human prey, costumed villains attacked in packs before disappearing back into the shadows, a vengeful spirit hovered above a terrified city, and gleaming starships blasted each other apart in the soundless depths of space. There was almost too much to absorb at one time, but J'onn struggled to make sense of it all.

We're being hunted by cybernetic centurions.

Our longtime adversaries have been organized into an army.

The world of magic has been corrupted.

And an interstellar war has broken out.

"What does it all mean?" Martian Manhunter murmured to himself. "Could there be a connection?" Before he died, the Blue Beetle had theorized that there was a conspiracy at work, that all these apparently unrelated threats were part of a larger Crisis. Others in the League had dismissed this as paranoia, and yet . . .

What if Ted was right? J'onn mused. *What if none of this is a coincidence?*

It was a sobering thought, enough so that he was almost afraid to grasp the full implications of such a scenario. What sort of foe could possibly be powerful enough, and cunning enough, to orchestrate a scheme of this magnitude?

BEEP.

An electronic chime announced the arrival of another League member via one of the teleportation tubes installed throughout the Watchtower. J'onn wondered who it was. Aquaman was not due to relieve him for another hour or so. *Perhaps Arthur is early?*

His curiosity was easily satisfied. DNA scanners built into the teleporters ensured that no unauthorized visitors could beam into the Watchtower. J'onn leaned over to tap the control panel and a status report appeared on the screen:

TELEPORTATION TUBE ACTIVATED

ARRIVAL: DECK ONE

The icon indicating the visitor's identity was one of the most recognizable symbols in the world: a large red *S* enclosed in a five-sided shield.

"Superman," J'onn said aloud. He heard footsteps behind him. Out of the corner of his eye, he caught a glimpse of a flowing red cape. "I'm glad you're here. We need to reorganize our response to the world situation." He started to turn away from the viewscreens. "I think there's a very real possibility that everything we're facing is connected somehow."

"I know," a voice behind him said.

The timbre of the voice immediately tipped J'onn off that something was wrong. He spun around to get a better look at the caped figure entering the Monitor Room. His crimson eyes widened in surprise. "You're—"

Given another second, he would have used his own telepathic gifts to probe the newcomer's mind, but he never got the chance. A blast of intense heat struck him like a raging fire, the one element to which all Martians were most vulnerable. The scorching rays seared his emerald flesh, causing him to cry out in agony. He threw up his hands to defend himself, but it was already too late. The pain was too much for him, and the world went away, lost within a red-hot blaze.

Five minutes later a tremendous explosion rocked the silent surface of the Moon.

The Watchtower stood no longer.

CHAPTER 1

THE MOON

NEW craters dotted the lunar landscape. Charred debris littered the basaltic lava plains. The Earth, rising over the horizon, cast a cold blue radiance over the Sea of Serenity—and the mangled remains of the Watchtower.

Fires still blazed within the atmospheric force field protecting the smoking ruins from the vacuum outside. Torn and twisted metal reflected the raging flames. The Watchtower's exterior plating had been constructed of virtually impenetrable promethium-reinforced titanium/vanadium alloys, but that had not spared the JLA's headquarters from the explosion that had destroyed it from within. The central tower and observation deck had collapsed completely, burying the Hall of Justice and the lower levels of the hub beneath tons of smoldering rubble. Thick black fumes spread outward until they reached the limits of the force field, creating a sooty bubble above the ruins. Thin wisps of smoke began to seep out into space. The force field, it seemed, was beginning to weaken.

Superman soared above the wreckage, heedless of the Moon's feeble gravity. The lifeless vacuum and bitter cold had no effect upon his invulnerable form, although it felt strange not to have the wind blowing against his face. Momentum alone spread his bright red cape out behind him. The capital *S* upon his chest was known throughout the galaxy. High above the leaking force field, he gazed down at the ruins in dismay. The Watchtower was utterly demolished, possibly beyond repair. From the look of things, it appeared that the explosion had originated somewhere deep within the central hub.

Where J'onn would have been, Superman thought worriedly. He eyed the crackling flames with concern; fire affected Martians much as kryptonite affected him. What if the blaze had weakened J'onn before he could escape? The Martian Manhunter might still be trapped somewhere within the burning ruins.

His X-ray vision penetrated the wreckage, but he found no sign of his friend. Ascending higher into the lunar sky, he scanned the surrounding terrain for miles around. With telescopic vision he examined the desolate moonscape, but spied not even a microscopic trace of the missing hero. His superhearing heard nothing beyond muffled sounds of destruction from within the force field down below.

Superman hovered in midair, uncertain whether to be relieved or disturbed. *At least I didn't find J'onn's body*, he reflected. *That's something to be grateful for.* But only a formidable adversary could have abducted J'onn, if that was indeed what had transpired; the Martian Manhunter's strength and powers rivaled Superman's own. *Maybe Luthor's new Society?* he speculated. Anger flared in Superman's heart at the thought of Lex striking out at his friends once more. This wouldn't be the first time that Luthor had organized an assault on the League. . . .

For now, however, the trail had gone cold. Superman swooped down toward what remained of the Watchtower. *I might as well check back in. Bruce will be waiting for my report.*

"ATMOSPHERIC FORCE FIELD OPENING," an automated voice reported as he approached the perimeter of the sooty bubble. He quickly zipped through the momentary gap in the structure's emergency defenses. The rising flames posed no danger to him as he dove headfirst through the raging fire consuming the Hall of Justice. The League's famous Round Table lay in pieces about the demolished meeting-room. Shredded metal seats were scattered like fallen shrapnel. Windows made of clear Thanagarian crystal had been blown out by the blast. "ATMOSPHERIC FORCE FIELD CLOSED. OPERATING AT SIX PERCENT."

That doesn't sound good, he thought.

He flew through a jagged breach in the floor to the chamber below. The Monitor Room was barely recognizable. Shattered screens offered no clue as to what had transpired there. Torn, sparking cables dangled from the ceiling. An overturned steel chair rested amidst a carpet of fallen debris. Earthlight filtered down from above, through breached bulkheads. Scorched ceramic tiles were cracked and crumbling. The air smelled of smoke and burning circuitry. The artificial gravity felt distinctly weaker.

A solitary figure waited for him on an elevated walkway at the center of the ravaged nerve center. A stark black cloak and cowl were draped over the man's equally black body armor, so that he blended in with the shadows thrown by the faint blue light. Opaque white lenses concealed his eyes. The scalloped tips of his cape brushed against the floor. Only the bottom half of his face was left uncovered by his forbidding disguise. His mouth was a hard, straight line above a strong jaw.

"Well?" Batman asked.

Superman shook his head. "I've scanned the entire area. There's no physical trace of Martian Manhunter. J'onn is gone. And the Watchtower won't be standing for long either."

Batman nodded before turning back to his investigation. "The teleportation chamber was activated less than nine seconds before the tower exploded." His stern voice held even more of an edge than usual. "*Someone* was here. Someone did this."

Touching down lightly upon the floor, Superman noticed that Batman was holding a metal cube about the size of a disposable camera. Scorch marks blemished the object's carbon-steel casing. A blinking electronic light indicated that the device was still functioning to some degree. Superman tried to look past the casing, but his X-ray vision was blocked by a layer of lead shielding. "What's that?" he asked.

"A black box," Batman explained. "It's ghosted our security cameras and recorded everything on our monitor screens for the last two years. It should tell me who's responsible for this."

"More spying?" Superman frowned. They were still dealing with the genocidal machinations of Brother Eye. "That satellite of yours wasn't enough?"

If Batman was chastened by his colleague's rebuke, the Dark Knight gave no sign of it. "Don't be naive, Clark," he said. "This is simple security."

"Nothing's simple," a feminine voice intruded upon their discussion. They turned to see a breathtaking vision stride confidently out onto the walkway. Earthlight, pouring down through the sundered walls and ceiling, fell upon a strikingly beautiful woman with lustrous black hair and a magnificent physique. A ruby-inlaid tiara rested above her smooth white brow. Silver bracelets adorned her well-toned arms. A golden breastplate and girdle gleamed upon her athletic figure. A star-spangled cape flowed behind her like a royal train. A lasso of golden links, glowing with their own enchanted radiance, rested upon one hip, a golden sword was sheathed against the other.

Standing nearly as tall as the two men, Wonder Woman could easily be mistaken for one of the fabled Greek goddesses who had granted her so many extraordinary abilities. *I should have known she would join us*, Superman realized. When the Watchtower exploded, an automatic distress signal had gone out to every active member of the League. Thankfully, a few of the backup teleporters were still working.

"You don't belong here, Diana," Batman said harshly.

"None of us do, Bruce," she replied. Her voice held a faintly exotic accent. "Not anymore."

Batman wasn't willing to concede the point. "People are scared."

"They should be," she answered. "The world is going to Tartarus."

That's not the point, Superman thought. "They're scared of us now. They're scared of us because of you." He wished that Diana wasn't forcing him to spell it out for her like this. "They've been broadcasting the images nonstop, Diana. Don't you understand?" His voice conveyed the horror he felt. "The whole world watched you. They all watched you murder a man."

His mind flashed back to that ghastly moment when, still dazed from Maxwell Lord's mind-control, he had looked on helplessly as Wonder Woman snapped Max's neck with clear and deliberate intent. The awful crack that had heralded the man's death still echoed inside Superman's skull. Once more, he saw Max's lifeless body drop limply to the floor of the villain's command center, still wrapped tightly within the coils of Diana's golden lasso.

She did it for me, he acknowledged, *to keep Max from turning me into a murderer. But in so doing, she violated the trust between us and the ordinary people we protect. The Justice League does not kill, especially not in cold blood. We stand for something higher than that.*

Or we used to.

"We have spoken of this before," she said. "You both know what occurred. My lasso compelled Maxwell Lord to speak the truth. He had no intention of ever releasing you from his control. Under his command, you would have killed the rest of the League, and many other innocents besides. With the Lasso of Truth upon him, Max told me the only way I could truly free you." Her tone was somber, but unapologetic. "I made my decision. I stand by it as the proper one."

Superman wasn't sure what disturbed him more, her actions or her lack of remorse. He knew that Diana had slain monsters before, like Medousa or the Scylla, but Max Lord had not been some mythological Greek monstrosity; he had only been a man, albeit an evil one. *He was one of the people we're supposed to protect.*

A steel girder crashed somewhere below them. The walkway quaked beneath their feet. Obviously, the Watchtower wasn't done collapsing yet.

"It's not safe here," Superman observed.

Batman nodded in agreement. He clipped the black box to his utility belt. "I have what I came for." His cloak flapped behind him as he turned to leave. "I should get back to Gotham."

"And I to Themyscira," Wonder Woman said, referring to the island home of her Amazon sisters. Located deep within the Bermuda Triangle, the ageless sanctuary was perhaps best known by the name the media had pinned on it: Paradise Island.

Superman was tempted to let the matter of Max's death drop, but knew that they could not ignore the repercussions of Diana's ruthless act. "So Themyscira will be harboring a fugitive?" That was no solution to their dilemma. "You have to answer for what you did."

"I will," she said. "When the time is right."

Superman was skeptical. "Is there ever going to be a right—" Despite the urgency of their discussion, an unexpected sound caught his attention. "Wait. Do you hear that?" He focused his superhearing on the noise. "It's a heartbeat."

J'onn? he wondered instantly, only a split second before a gigantic fist struck him with the force of a battering ram. The impact sent him rocketing upward through floor after floor and out into the thinning atmosphere within the force field. He smashed through the defensive barrier itself and kept on going.

"ATMOSPHERIC FORCE FIELD OPERATING AT FOUR PERCENT. . . ."

CHAPTER 2

KENT FARM,
SMALLVILLE, KANSAS

CONNER Kent still couldn't believe his eyes.

The dark-haired teenager sat on the living room couch, his gaze fixed on the TV set across the room. A vase of fresh flowers rested on the coffee table in front of him, next to the TV remote and a bowl of potato chips. A braided rug carpeted the wooden floor. Against the wall, a maple hutch displayed a collection of good china and school trophies. A framed wedding photo was mounted by the door.

His cozy surroundings failed to diminish the shock he felt at seeing Wonder Woman snap a man's neck on national television. "Authorities are still unsure of the exact source of the footage," a news commentator reported, "but video analysts across the world have verified its authenticity. . . ."

Conner didn't know what to make of the damning footage. He knew Wonder Woman, and this wasn't like her. *Then again*, he reflected glumly, *nothing is what it's supposed to be anymore.*

Including me.

Once, Conner had believed himself to be a teenage clone of Superman himself, conceived in a test tube during those dark days between Superman's death and his resurrection a few years back. As Superboy, he had done his best to live up to his mentor's example. Recently, however, Conner had discovered that his link to Superman was only half of the story; in fact, he had been genetically engineered from the DNA of the Man of Steel . . . and Lex Luthor. The shocking revelation had thrown him for a loop, causing him to doubt both himself and his mission. *Conner has two daddies,* he thought bitterly. *And what kind of hero can I be when half of my chromosomes come from Superman's greatest enemy?*

Confused and disillusioned, he had retreated to the Kents' farm to try to figure out what to do next. The humble domicile had become his home away from home, and was a whole lot comfier than the Fortress of Solitude.

If even Wonder Woman can go bad, he thought, *what chance do I have?*

On the TV, the one zillionth airing of "the Wonder Woman murder tape" was interrupted by breaking news. "We go live to Los Angeles," the news-caster announced, "where members of the Teen Titans are desperately fighting to protect the City of Angels from a bizarre army of creatures. . . ."

What? Conner thought. He leaned forward anxiously.

The twenty-inch screen showed Cassie Sandsmark, aka Wonder Girl, fly-ing high above the city streets. The adolescent blonde was locked in combat with what looked like scores of scaly, bat-winged gargoyles. Wonder Woman's golden emblem was emblazoned on the girl's bright red belly shirt, above a pair of matching latex trousers. Amazon bracelets adorned her arms. She hurled a golden lasso at one of the winged monsters, snaring it around the waist.

The illegitimate daughter of Zeus himself, Wonder Girl fought with the strength and speed of a genuine demigoddess, and looked good doing it. She used her lasso to swing the trapped demon into a nearby neon sign. The sign exploded in a shower of sparks as the gargoyle let out an ear-piercing screech. A second creature spit fire at Cassie, but she blocked the flames with her silver bracelet.

Good move, Conner thought. In the background, Cyborg, Raven, and the other Titans also battled the demonic horde. A large green pterodactyl was obviously the shape-changing Beast Boy in dinosaur guise. Cyborg blasted the gargoyles with a burst of white noise from one of his artificial arms, while Raven used her mystic cloak to transport unwary demons to limbo. Speedy, Green Arrow's latest sidekick, fired a cryogenic arrow into a clump of gar-goyles; in a blinding flash, the creatures were frozen in place. The green ptero-dactyl grabbed two monsters with its talons and rammed their scaly heads together.

"Church officials deny," the voice from the television screen declared, "that the Pope believes that these are the end times prophesized in the Book of Revelation."

More like a nasty character up to his old tricks, Conner thought, catching a glimpse of Brother Blood lurking in the background of one shot. The demonic cult leader was an old enemy of the Teen Titans. *How the heck did he escape from Hades again? Must have taken some seriously screwed-up hocus-pocus. . . .*

Part of Conner wished he was fighting beside his friends. Up until a few weeks ago, he would have been, but that was before he found out who and what he really was. Besides, it looked like the Titans were holding their own without him.

They don't need me, he told himself. *They probably never did.*

With the melee in Los Angeles still under way, the news abruptly shifted to another location. "Live from Gotham City," the newscaster reported, "we bring you new sightings of the so-called OMACs. Speculation continues as to their exact nature and purpose. Government officials deny any involvement. . . ."

Shaky footage captured three of the deadly cyborgs flying in formation above the city. Because he'd been keeping a low profile, Conner had yet to encounter an OMAC himself, but he was already familiar with their glossy blue carapaces and glowing, cyclopean eyes. Superman had taken time out of his busy schedule to warn Conner about the OMACs weeks ago. Watching the faceless automatons cruise over Gotham, Conner couldn't help wondering who the cyborgs were after now. Batman? The Huntress? Or could it be . . .

Robin!

His heart skipped a beat as he spotted his best friend swinging between the soot-stained buildings beneath the OMACs. Clad in the traditional red-and-green uniform of Batman's protégés, Tim Drake let go of his jumpline to land acrobatically on a jutting window ledge, several stories above the concrete pavement below. His yellow cape flapped in the wind as he glanced back over his shoulder at the cyborgs pursuing him. A blast of crimson energy burst from the lead OMAC's single eye, targeting Robin, who leaped from his perch only a heartbeat before the blast reduced the brick ledge to rubble. Grabbing onto a flagpole, he spun around before vaulting back into the air. A grapnel shot into an overhanging eave, and he used another jumpline to go swinging into a shadowy alley between two buildings. Robotic red eyes scanned for him in vain.

". . . usually appearing in groups of three or less," the news report continued, "the OMACs seem to be amassing over most major cities. . . ."

Conner was relieved to see that Robin was keeping one step ahead of the implacable man-machines. *Looks like all that training in the Batcave paid off*, he thought. *Tim can take care of himself.*

A middle-aged woman entered the living room. Flour dusted her white apron. The enticing aroma of fresh apple pie wafted in from the kitchen. "You've been sitting in front of that tube all day," Martha Kent said gently, "watching these awful things happen." Concern showed behind her tinted spectacles. "You need to go help your friends."

He shook his head. "Luthor didn't clone me to help people, Aunt Martha."

"That's for you to decide," she said. "Not anyone else."

As if on cue, something started beeping on the coffee table. He glanced down at a small ceramic square, about the size of a Scrabble tile. A large capital *T* was etched on the face of the chip.

T for Titans.

His team was calling him.

Aunt Martha knew just what the signal meant. "The world needs a Superboy. And right now you're all they've got."

Was she right? Conner rose uncertainly from the couch. Wearing a rumpled blue shirt, jeans, sneakers, and glasses, he looked like any other teenager—until he tugged open his shirt to expose a tight black T-shirt sporting a distinctive red *S*. *Maybe Aunt Martha has a point*, he thought, feeling more like his old self than he had in weeks. His jaw clenched in determination. He started to take off his glasses.

"This just in," the news program announced. "A new report from Anchorage, Alaska, where fugitive Lex Luthor was spotted today. The body of a local bush pilot was found only minutes ago, his plane missing." A photo of a sneering, bald-headed man flashed upon the screen. "Luthor, of course, is the prime suspect in numerous murders and atrocities. . . ."

Luthor.

The infamous name gave Conner pause. *What was I thinking? I'm the last thing Cassie and the others need right now.* Only days ago, Luthor had activated a hidden behavioral program buried deep in Conner's unconscious mind, turning him against his fellow Teen Titans. He'd almost killed Robin. At a crucial moment, he had broken free of Lex's influence, but how could he be sure that he wouldn't let his friends down again? He stared at the villainous face on the television, trying to recognize traces of his own features in Luthor's sinister mug shot.

His evil is woven into every cell of my body.

He slid his glasses back onto his nose. His shoulders slumped as he buttoned up his shirt, concealing the heroic symbol on his chest. He reached down and switched off the beeping communicator. A discouraging silence descended upon the living room, broken only by the dire reports on the news. Martha looked down on him sadly. She didn't lecture him, but he knew that he had disappointed her.

She just doesn't understand, he thought. Silently, he dropped back onto the couch. *I'm not Superboy. I never really was. I'm just another one of Luthor's diabolical science projects. The Titans are better off without me.*

Everybody is.

SOMEWHERE outside time and space, four forgotten figures looked on, unobserved. A crystalline matrix offered a window onto a universe they were no part of. They watched from afar as Conner wrestled with his doubts . . . and lost.

"Look at him!" a youthful voice cried out in frustration. "How can Conner Kent do nothing?"

A tremulous voice, that of an elderly woman, was more forgiving. "After all that poor boy has gone through, it's not surprising that he's feeling lost. But I believe he will step forward in time."

A third voice, strong and deep, held a less hopeful tone. "Superboy will fail to make a difference," he predicted, more in sorrow than in anger. "Just like the others. As much as I hate to admit it, we've made a horrible miscalculation. It's time to take action."

The old woman wasn't certain. "We could make things on Earth worse if we intervene."

"And if we don't get involved," the strong voice said, "there will be no Earth to worry about."

The fourth figure, standing behind the others, kept his thoughts to himself.

CHAPTER 3

BLÜDHAVEN,
NORTH OF GOTHAM CITY

As cities went, Blüdhaven made Gotham look like Metropolis. The streets were filthier, the air was dirtier, the cops were more brutal and corrupt. Graffiti spread like fungus over the city's narrow alleys and empty storefronts. Steel shutters and iron bars guarded every home and business, a necessary precaution in the dog-eat-dog environment of this urban cesspool. Litter clotted the street and sidewalks. Broken windows went unrepaired. Drug dealers and prostitutes flaunted their wares openly, provided they had bribed all the right people. Recently, the chamber of commerce, in a quixotic attempt to boost tourism, had solicited the public for a catchy new slogan with which to promote the city. To their disappointment, nearly every suggestion had been obscene, sarcastic, or both. The leading contender? "Blüdhaven: Pay Up or Else."

But one young man, raised in the bright colors and garish make-believe of the circus, still hoped to save the city from itself. Or at least make a difference.

Dick Grayson, the first person to be known as Robin the Boy Wonder, now called himself Nightwing. The bat-shaped mask affixed to his face and the somber tones of his blue-and-black uniform paid tribute to his fearsome mentor, even though Nightwing had long since established an adult identity of his own. A fetid breeze rustled his dark hair as he stood at the edge of a tar-papered rooftop, looking out over the city. Night had fallen on Blüdhaven, bringing out the city's many nocturnal predators. The sound of angry voices and harsh laughter drifted up from the streets below. No screams or gunfire yet; it was a quiet night in the 'Haven.

Wonder if everyone is indoors watching the news? Nightwing thought. TV viewership always went up during major disasters, and the media could barely keep up with all the bad news these days. *Maybe everyone is waiting out the end of the world.*

He turned away from the ledge to face the trio of women who had just arrived in the city to bid him farewell. Amidst the grime and decay of Blüdhaven, the three beauties stood out like angels from a higher realm—which, in a way, they were. In fact, Troia, Starfire, and Supergirl had all grown up in outer space, thousands of light-years from Earth.

And I thought being raised under the Big Top was unusual.

"I'm glad we managed to find you tonight," Donna Troy said. "I didn't want to leave without saying good-bye."

Donna was one of his oldest friends. As the original Wonder Girl, she had helped him found the first grouping of the Teen Titans years ago, back when he was still calling himself Robin. Now grown into a strong and confident woman, she went by the name Troia. The stars themselves glittered in her lustrous black hair and shimmering black leotard. A futuristic silver orb hovered near her shoulder; Nightwing recognized the travel sphere as an artifact of New Cronus, the distant world on which Donna had been reared by the Titans of Greek mythology. The silvery flecks on her garment served as a stellar map, pinpointing the exact location of New Cronus.

"So you're really going to go?" he asked her.

She nodded. "Before they fled this reality, the Titans of Myth warned that the end of the universe was coming. And now that prophecy seems to be coming true. Deep in space, the Rannians and Thanagarians are at war. Near the center of the conflict is a mysterious cosmic storm, an immense rift in the very fabric of the space-time continuum that is growing larger with each passing second. Each side in the war blames the other for the cataclysm, but I fear that soon they will all be fighting merely to survive."

Her face took on a grave expression. "If something isn't done soon, if we don't find a way to quell the storm, it could mean the end of the universe as we know it. That's why I'm gathering heroes to go with me into space, to cope with the crisis before it's too late."

"So who are you taking?" Nightwing asked.

Donna reeled off a list of names. "Firestorm, Jade, Cyborg, Animal Man, Red Tornado, Shift, Alan Scott." She gestured toward the two women beside her. "And Kory and Kara, of course."

"Sounds like a good crew." He wasn't offended that Donna had not invited him. This sounded like a seriously cosmic affair, not the kind of adventure in which a glorified acrobat and martial artist was likely to come in handy. *I can do more good here on Earth.*

"I'm so flattered that Donna thought of me," Supergirl piped up. The willowy blonde was Superman's cousin from the planet Krypton, only recently arrived on Earth. She wore a two-piece version of her cousin's famous costume, but with a miniskirt instead of leggings. Kara Zor-El sounded eager to take part in Donna's expedition. "My cousin's not exactly thrilled with the idea, but, hey, saving the universe sounds good to me."

"Trust me," he told her, "I know all about overprotective guardians." He didn't know Kara well, but she struck him as young and enthusiastic. *Just like Donna and me when we were her age.* Sometimes those early days seemed like centuries ago. . . .

Old memories surfaced with unexpected force as the third woman stepped forward. Unlike Supergirl, whose thoroughly human appearance belied her extraterrestrial origins, there was no mistaking Starfire's exotic alien appearance. Her emerald eyes lacked any visible pupils or whites. Flawless orange skin was amply exposed by her skimpy harness, which mostly consisted of a few strategically-placed purple straps. (Modesty was a human virtue that Koriand'r, warrior princess of Tamaran, had never quite seen the point of.) Even her cascading auburn hair seemed to glow with its own unearthly radiance. A jewel-studded collar hinted at her royal roots, as did the priceless ruby lodged in her navel. Thigh-high purple boots protected her feet from the grimy rooftop.

"Dick . . ." Kory murmured, then hesitated, uncertain what to say. They had been lovers once, back when they had both served in the Teen Titans together. In truth, she had been his first real love. Even though they hadn't been a couple for years now, there was still an intimate bond between them, as well as a certain awkwardness. "This planet has become a dangerous place. Please take care of yourself while we're away."

She leaned forward to place a tender kiss upon his lips.

Nightwing kissed her back, surrendering to the moment. Her lips were just as warm as he remembered. At times like this, his heart ached for what might have been if they had somehow managed to overcome their differences. He felt a pang of regret. This wasn't going to make saying good-bye any easier.

He pulled away. "You too, Kory."

Her hurt expression made it clear that she had hoped for more from him. He was tempted to apologize, but what was the point? He had a city to protect, and she had a galaxy to save. A clean break was best.

"I need to catch a train to New York," he announced brusquely. "There's a big arms deal going down between the Carlino Family and the local mob. I have to track down an informant who's gone to ground somewhere in the Bronx."

Troia took the hint. "We won't keep you then." She glanced at the metal globe floating beside her. "Sphere, take us to New Cronus."

The silver orb glowed brightly, enveloping the three super-heroines in a preternatural ball of light. "Good-bye, Dick," Donna called out a second before she disappeared from sight. Even though the sphere itself was only slightly bigger than a baseball, it absorbed her and the others into its compressed interior. Nightwing knew from experience that the sphere was much larger on the inside than seemed possible. The orb blasted into space like a meteor in reverse.

"Godspeed," he whispered, finding himself alone on the rooftop. He wondered if he would ever see any of the three women again. Donna had seemed convinced that the rift in space posed a deadly threat to all of creation. What if it was more than her team could handle?

"HELP!" A terrified cry seized his attention. It was a man's voice, coming from a couple blocks away. "SOMEBODY HELP ME!"

Nightwing responded instantly. He jumped back onto the ledge overlooking the alley below. A camouflaged gauntlet fired a grappling dart into the building across the way. Taking hold of the jumpline with both hands, he hurled himself into the air.

So much for my quiet evening.

OUTSIDE the universe, cut off from reality, a forgotten hero observed the poignant moment between Dick Grayson and Koriand'r. Their tentative farewell, full of lost chances and unspoken feelings, saddened him.

A man from Earth and a princess from another planet. For several years now, he had watched their troubled relationship with a vested interest. Time and again, he had seen them be given chance after chance to make their union work, only to witness them go their separate ways in the end. Their seemingly doomed romance tugged at his heartstrings.

Maybe love is powerless there, he thought mournfully. *Maybe love is too weak.*

This dire suspicion only strengthened his growing conviction that something needed to be done. His jaw set in determination, his fists clenched at his sides.

If even love wasn't enough, could there be any better reason to make things right?

THE alley wasn't much, but Charlie Douglas called it home. Obscene graffiti defaced the filthy walls. Trash spilled from an overflowing Dumpster that looked like it hadn't been emptied in weeks. Broken bottles and empty syringes littered the ground. The alley smelled of urine and rotting garbage. A cardboard box offered a meager amount of shelter. Rats and cockroaches scurried in the shadows. The flickering glow of a dying streetlight barely extended past the mouth of the alley.

"I'm telling you," Charlie insisted to the cops who had invaded his sanctuary. An elderly African-American, he wore only a pair of soiled khaki shorts. His snow-white beard needed trimming. "Ain't nobody else here." He stood at the mouth of the alley, trying to keep the two police officers out. " 'Specially not that guy you're looking for."

One of the cops grabbed Charlie by the throat and threw him up against the wall. "Shut your mouth, you lying scumbag. We know he's here!"

"Damn gutter trash," the cop's partner growled. He clutched a printout of an all points bulletin. "Trying to hide a wanted man."

Charlie pleaded with the cops. "He didn't hurt no one. He just wants ta be left alone. . . ."

His appeal for mercy was wasted on Blüdhaven's Finest. "Outta our way, Gramps. This is police business!" The first cop tossed him aside roughly. Charlie crashed down onto the soggy cardboard box that served as his shelter. The box collapsed beneath his weight and he hit the ground hard. "Uggh!" he grunted. A startled rat ran for cover.

This ain't right! Charlie thought. *They didn't have to—*

NANOTRANSMISSION POSITIVE_//_IDENT VERIFIED: OMAC 85432_
//_ACTIVATE_

A robotic voice interrupted his thoughts. *Who?* He looked around anxiously, then realized with horror that the inhuman voice was coming from inside his own head. *What's happening to me?*

The transmission activated the microscopic nanobots coursing through Charlie's bloodstream. Lying upon the crumpled cardboard, his body was suddenly wracked by painful convulsions. He rolled into a fetal position as his arms and legs twitched spasmodically. An agonized moan escaped his lips.

His obvious distress caught the two cops' attention. "You all right, Charlie?" asked the cop who had thrown him to the ground only seconds before. He sounded more irritated than concerned for Charlie's well-being. "Charlie?"

A blue ceramic glaze oozed from the homeless man's pores, spreading rapidly over his entire body. Skin and clothing disappeared beneath the turquoise veneer, which quickly hardened into an impenetrable shell. Charlie's heart pounded in panic as he helplessly watched the glaze flow upward toward his face. His bloodshot eyes rolled back until only the whites were visible. He writhed in pain, it felt like he was sweating razor blades.

"It h-hurts," he stammered. "Please, help m—EEEARRGH!"

The glaze covered his face, cutting off his cries. The man's bearded countenance was now hidden behind a featureless blue shell. A crestlike fin rose along the top of his cranium, the better to receive signals from Brother Eye. The frightened eyes were replaced by a single red lens that glowed electronically in the center of the cyborg's face. Gauntlets loaded with lethal weaponry formed around its wrists. A graphic representation of an unblinking human eye appeared upon its chest, symbolizing its connection to Brother Eye. The intimidating figure bore no resemblance to the harmless vagrant who had occupied the same space moments before.

OMAC #85432 levitated off the floor of the alley, righting itself until it hovered vertically above the ground. Its luminous red eye scanned the interior of the alley.

"What the hell?" one of the cops exclaimed. Drawing his gun, he fired at the floating cyborg. The bullets ricocheted off the OMAC's smooth blue carapace, nearly winging the cop and his partner. His jaw dropped open, his eyes widened in fear.

"Run!" his partner hollered as he bolted from the alley, not waiting to see if the other policeman took his advice. Slipping from his fingers, the APB fluttered to the ground, all but forgotten in the cop's haste to get away from the site of Charlie's terrifying metamorphosis. The cop's shoes splashed through the puddles in his way.

The first cop followed his example. Rousting an old wino was one thing; hassling a bum who had turned into some sort of freaky sci-fi monster was something else altogether. "Wait for me!" he shouted. Seconds later, a police car could be heard squealing away at top speed.

The OMAC ignored the cops' departure. Instead it focused its bloodred scanner on the Dumpster. Thermal sensors detected a heat signature hiding behind the rusty metal container. The readings matched the parameters of its assigned target with an 87.32 percent certainty.

"SUBJECT GAMMA: FLANNEGAN, OTIS." The OMAC's artificial tone sounded nothing like Charlie's raspy voice. "DESIGNATION: THE RAT-CATCHER."

"No!" A frightened figure dashed out from behind the Dumpster. A gas mask concealed his features. A metal cylinder was strapped to his back over a rumpled trench coat; a rubber hose connected the portable tank to the spray gun in the man's hands. Greasy blond hair covered his scalp and a carved wooden whistle dangled on a cord around his neck. He stared through the mask's protective lenses in fear and confusion. "Charlie? What happened to you? What are you?"

A laser beam swept over the subject, verifying his identity. Otis Flannegan was a convicted super-villain who had escaped from Gotham City's Arkham Asylum seventy-three days ago. Formerly employed as an exterminator, the deranged killer had switched sides years ago; now he lashed out at humanity on behalf of his beloved vermin.

But not for much longer.

"SUBJECT CONFIRMED."

"Leave me alone!" the Ratcatcher cried. Raising his spray gun, he directed a stream of foul-smelling liquid at the hovering cyborg. The pungent smell of a chemical pesticide joined the other noxious odors filling the alley, but the poison had no effect on the OMAC. The liquid ran harmlessly down its polished shell. The Ratcatcher backed away fearfully. "HELP!" he shrieked, even though the two policemen were long gone by now. "SOMEBODY HELP ME!"

Desperate, he blew his homemade whistle. In response, dozens of angry gray rats came rushing out of the shadows to defend him. They crouched between the Ratcatcher and the OMAC, baring their teeth against the cybernetic invader. Tiny black eyes glittered with hostile intent as they screeched aggressively at the intruder.

Flannegan was touched by his furry friends' loyalty, but what chance did a throng of bloodthirsty rodents have against a creature whose flesh and blood were hidden behind a bulletproof shell? The OMAC's single eye flashed and a heat-ray swept across the rats, setting them on fire. The rodents squealed in agony as the flames consumed them. The air filled with the nauseating smell of burning fur and flesh, although the Ratcatcher's gas mask spared him from the worst of the stench.

And the OMAC was not bothered by such things.

The ghastly sight and sounds tortured Flannegan. "Run, my friends!" he shouted at the few survivors of the massacre. Pesticide sprayed from the nozzle of his weapon as he tried to distract the OMAC from the fleeing rats. "Forget about me!" he called out to the vermin. "Save yourselves!"

Charlie Douglas had been Flannegan's friend, but Charlie was gone now, replaced by OMAC #85432. Mercy and compassion were gone, too.

"TARGETING SUBJECT."

The Ratcatcher died defending his rodent allies. The heat-ray blasted him head-on, turning the gas-masked villain into a human bonfire. The tank upon his back exploded, spraying the alley with deadly shrapnel. Flannegan's charred, smoking bones were scattered all around. His skull landed in a slimy puddle.

"SUBJECT TERMINATED."

A horrified gasp came from a rooftop overlooking the alley. Alerted by the sound, the OMAC rose higher until it looked down on the roof from over a hundred feet in the air. It zoomed in on a young human male in a distinctive blue-and-black costume. A bat-winged mask was glued to his face. The cyborg identified the new arrival.

"SUBJECT BETA: GRAYSON, RICHARD. DESIGNATION: NIGHTWING."

The human snatched a pair of shatterproof polymer Escrima sticks from spring-loaded pouches in the back of his uniform. He raised the sticks defensively, prepared to do battle. But the plastic batons would be woefully inadequate against the killer cyborg.

"Donna!" he shouted into a communicator embedded in his right gauntlet. "Donna, if you can still hear me, I could really use a hand down here."

The OMAC blocked the transmission with a jamming signal.

The subject known as Nightwing was not actually a meta-human, but Brother Eye had listed the masked vigilante as a known associate and ally of the OMACs' super-powered prey. That made Dick Grayson a legitimate target for termination.

The cyborg's eye glowed brightly once more, but before it could unleash its heat-ray upon the human below, a new set of instructions was beamed into its brain:

RECONFIGURING COMMANDS FROM BROTHER EYE_//_NEW PROTO-COL_//_TRUTH AND JUSTICE_

The OMAC shut down the heat-ray.

"ELIMINATION PROGRAMS OVERRIDDEN. PROTOCOL TRUTH AND JUSTICE CONFIRMED."

Turning away from Nightwing, the OMAC rose higher into the sky.

"MASS GATHERING INITIATED."

OMAC #85432 left the city's streets and rooftops far behind as it joined the hundreds of identical units now swarming the smoggy night sky above Blüdhaven. It took its place in the formation as the host of cyborgs flew away from Charlie Douglas's home, heading east out over the Atlantic. The OMAC had no qualms about leaving Nightwing alive. Its new programming took priority.

"Project OMAC Complete."

Hundreds of feet below, Nightwing gazed upward as the sky darkened with the corrupted technology of his mentor. He couldn't begin to count the number of OMACs flying away from the city. "Donna," he whispered in awe. "Whatever you're doing, I hope it's worth leaving Earth for."

CHAPTER 4

SPACE SECTOR 2682, THE POLARIS SYSTEM

THE cosmic storm erupted without warning, tearing open a ragged gash in the space-time continuum. Although centered in deep space, outside the war-torn solar system, the expanding white void looked incalculably immense even from light-years away. *If it looks that big from here,* Kyle Rayner thought, *how huge is it really?*

The Earth-born hero flew through space, propelled by the power of his emerald power ring. A luminous green aura protected his fragile mortal frame from the vacuum. His distinctive green-and-black uniform proclaimed his membership in the Green Lantern Corps, an elite interstellar police force composed of sentient beings from all over the universe, each given their own power rings that allowed them to visualize and create almost anything out of green energy. Kyle was only the latest human to be recruited by the Corps. It was a demanding job; he hadn't set foot on his native planet for months.

That storm couldn't have struck at a worse time, he thought. *Like the Rann-Thanagar War wasn't crisis enough!*

At the moment, he found himself stuck in the middle of a raging interplanetary battle. The Thanagarians, intent on invading the planet Rann, had launched an armada, which was being met in space by the Rannians and their allies. Rann's appearance in the Polaris system had shifted Thanagar's orbit much closer to its sun and devastated the planet. Rann claimed this was a miscalculation, but the bellicose Thanagarians interpreted it as an act of war. The resulting conflict currently threatened to engulf this entire sector of space.

Other spacefaring races had taken sides in the conflict. Allied with Rann were the Dominion, the Warlords of Okaara, Throneworld, and the Coluans. Siding with the Thanagarians were the Psions, the Tamaraneans, the Gordanians, and the shape-changing Durlans. Now the armed fleets of the various alien species clashed in space between Rann and Thanagar, even as fierce battles were also being fought on the surfaces of both planets. Caught in the cross fire were refugee ships fleeing the conflict, bearing innocent civilians of all shapes and sizes.

Blazing energy beams lit up space. Alien warships of wildly varied design blasted at each other with missiles and death-rays. The colors of the destructive beams spanned the entire visible spectrum as they crisscrossed each other across the void. Silent explosions detonated along the hulls of unlucky vessels. Flickering force fields saved other ships from destruction, at least for the moment. Smaller fighters and remote-controlled drones darted between massive dreadnoughts the size of Terran aircraft carriers. Advancing scout ships collided with floating zero-gravity mines. Death and destruction spread across the starways.

"This is insane," Kyle exclaimed, looking about in frustration. Not even his power ring could keep the warring fleets apart. All he could do was try to protect the refugees and keep the casualties to a minimum. "Especially since the Thanagarians and the Rannians are pretty much indistinguishable from each other, physically. They both look perfectly human." He suddenly remembered whom he was talking to. "Er, no offense."

"None taken," Kilowog assured him. A native of the planet Bolovax Vix, the veteran Green Lantern resembled a large pink warthog and had the personality of an army drill sergeant. His own power ring gleamed upon a meaty, four-fingered fist. "Just remember the Corps has to stay neutral in these poozers' shooting match." He turned his beady red eyes toward the growing space-time rift. "Besides, it looks like we've got a bigger problem to worry about all of a sudden."

No kidding, Kyle thought. He eyed the cosmic storm, which showed no sign of abating anytime soon. Instead, the voracious anomaly was growing before their very eyes, swallowing up distant stars and planets at an alarming pace. *How big is that thing going to get?*

Fortunately, the two Green Lanterns had allies of their own. A handful of unaligned heroes, mostly of Terran origin, accompanied Kyle and Kilowog as they tried to save as many lives as they could from the carnage spreading across the Polaris system. But the mysterious cosmic storm suddenly added a whole new dimension to their mission.

"Rann assures me that this new phenomenon is not of their doing," Adam Strange announced via the communications array in his crested space helmet. A jet pack carried him toward Kyle. Although born on Earth, Strange had long ago adopted Rann as his home. His adopted world was known for its scientific accomplishments, which were the most advanced in this sector. Their legendary Zeta Beam was capable of transporting entire planets across space.

But now Strange insisted, "Not even Rann's technology is capable of anything like that storm."

"Tell that to Thanagar," Kilowog rumbled.

"We're trying," Hawkman said, soaring through space beside Hawkgirl. The mystical Nth Metal in their boots and harnesses allowed them to fly through the vacuum unharmed. Their feathered wingspans glided on solar winds. Transparent breathing apparatuses were clamped over their beaked metal helmets. Hawkman swung a charged energy mace at a glowing piece of radioactive shrapnel, batting it away from Kyle and the others. Carter Hall was a traditionalist when it came to weaponry.

"But that's not what they want to hear," Hawkgirl added. She gripped a blaster in one hand and an old-fashioned crossbow in the other. The Hawks had come all the way from Earth on a peacekeeping mission that had proved too little, too late. Now they could only try to cope with the hostilities like everyone else.

Kyle wasn't surprised by the Hawks' failure. The Thanagarians had a martial culture that seldom missed an opportunity to go to war. They already blamed Rann for the catastrophic shift in their planet's orbit. He had no doubt that they would try to pin the inexplicable storm on their enemy as well. *And here they come*, he observed.

A Thanagarian troop carrier opened up its bay doors, disgorging a squadron of armed wingmen. They glided through space on gray metal wings. Their raptorlike helmets, which resembled those worn by Hawkman and Hawkgirl, were modeled after the Royal Ca'arra hawk of Thanagar, the totem of their military ethos. Laser rifles fired at Kyle and his companions. His ring picked up their leader's transmissions.

"Sighting of Adam Strange confirmed. Target the Champion of Rann . . . and all who stand with him!"

Damn, Kyle thought. Strange was definitely Rann's greatest hero; the wingmen weren't going to miss a chance to take him out of the picture and score a huge propaganda victory for Thanagar. *Not if I have anything to say about it. We expatriate Earthmen need to stick together.*

Kyle's power ring was limited only by his willpower and imagination. Inspired by the Hawks, he visualized an array of ancient weaponry. Spears and battle-axes, composed entirely of concentrated emerald energy, material-ized from out of nowhere. The glowing green weapons assaulted the metal wings of the nearest Thanagarian soldiers. Laser beams bounced off the Green Lantern's protective aura.

"Thanks for watching my back!" Adam Strange communicated to Kyle. He relied primarily on his jet pack to evade the blasts of the other wingmen. His ray gun sliced off the hand of a winged sniper, causing the Thanagarian's weapon to go spinning off into space. The beam from the ray gun instantly cauterized the sniper's wrist, leaving him alive but unarmed. "If only there was some way to reason with these people!"

"Don't waste your breath," Hawkman snarled over the open link. He and Hawkgirl had first acquired their feathered wings and Nth Metal technology from a Thanagarian spaceship that had crash-landed on Earth over four thou-sand years ago, but that didn't mean they were taking Thanagar's side in this war. "Trust me, I know how these birds think."

The reincarnation of an ancient Egyptian warrior, Carter Hall was in his element as he lashed out at the oncoming soldiers with his huge spiked mace. With his hairy chest protected only by two leather straps (and the Nth Metal's protective aura), he resembled an unusually barbaric angel. The charged mace knocked the rifle from a wingman's grip, even as Hawkman elbowed another soldier in the gut. Not for the first time, Kyle was glad that the brutal warrior was on their side.

His female cohort hadn't completely given up on peace yet. "Stand down!" Hawkgirl ordered a pair of wingmen advancing on her. A two-piece green uniform left her slightly more covered up than her bare-chested partner. She took aim with her blaster. "Lay down your weapons!"

"You have no authority over us, Earth-whore!" the lead wingman barked. He sounded deeply offended to find the Hawks siding with Strange. The winged soldiers converged on Hawkgirl, wielding double-edged thrusting daggers. Despite the space-age technology at their disposal, the predatory Thanagarians preferred edged weapons and hand-to-hand combat whenever possible. "You're not fit to wear the uniform of a wingman!"

"Earth-whore?" Kendra Saunders repeated. Those were obviously fighting words. Unencumbered by heavy body armor, she was twice as maneuverable as the two wingmen, as was proven by the ease with which she soared clear of her attackers and then expertly looped around to come up behind the soldiers, firing both weapons simultaneously. Her blaster took out the wingman on the right, while a bolt from her crossbow punched a hole in the other soldier's armor, spearing him in the hip. "I think the proper term is wing*woman*!"

Before Hawkgirl could finish off her opponents, however, a large green tentacle wrapped around her, pinning her wings to her sides. The tentacle was one of several extending from the impenetrable shell of a large Durlan bio-ship. "Carter!" she called out to Hawkman. The tentacle started to pull her into the ship's open maw. "I'm stuck to this gooey thing!"

"I'm coming!" he promised. He swooped toward her, his mace held high. A primeval war cry escaped his lips as he swung at the tentacle with all his might. The spiked weapon tore clear through the clinging pseudopod, only a few feet above Kendra's head. A slimy green ichor spewed from the bisected ends of the tentacle.

"Ugh!" Hawkgirl exclaimed. The severed tip of the tentacle was still wrapped around her, held fast by some sort of adhesive excretion. She wriggled within the gummy coils, struggling to free herself. Droplets of green goo splattered her helmet. "I hate being in space!"

Unable to fly at will, she floated like a sitting duck. Spotting her predicament out of the corner of his eye, Kyle willed a protective emerald bubble around the Hawks to give them a bit of breathing room. "Hang on," Hawkman said as he used both hands to peel the lifeless tentacle away from his partner. He hurled the sticky limb away in disgust.

"Thanks, handsome!" Hawkgirl said with a grin. Her wings spread out behind her as she wiped the bio-ship's blood from her beak.

"My pleasure, beautiful," he replied. "You can make it up to me later."

The flirtatious banter came naturally to them. They had been fated lovers since the days of ancient Egypt, finding each other again and again over the course of hundreds of past lives. *Talk about a long-term relationship*, Kyle thought, impressed. He let his force-bubble dissolve now that the Hawks were free to defend themselves once more. *I can't even make things work for one lifetime!*

Taking advantage of a momentary lull in the action, Kyle scanned the cosmic storm. "Ring," he asked the all-purpose device on his finger, "what the hell is that? A black hole?"

"NEGATIVE," the power ring responded. "PRESENTLY NINETY-FIVE MILLION MILES IN DIAMETER, THE PHENOMENON DEFIES CONVENTIONAL EXPLANATION. POSSIBLY A MANIFESTATION OF . . ." A burst of static buzzed in Kyle's ears. "ERROR—ANALYSIS INCOMPLETE."

"Terrific," Kyle muttered. Were all the energy blasts and ruptured stardrives interfering with the scan, or was the unnatural storm just too weird for the ring's artificial intelligence to cope with? He opened up a line to another possible source of information. "Dox, Kyle here. Does L.E.G.I.O.N. have any ideas?"

L.E.G.I.O.N., short for Licensed Extra-Governmental Interstellar Operatives Network, was a private security outfit that kept the peace between various client planets—for a sizable fee. Its leader, Vril Dox, was a green-skinned Coluan whose super-intelligence was almost matched by his arrogance. Kyle disliked dealing with him, but right now he needed all the help he could get.

Dox's voice emerged from Kyle's ring. "If you could keep those flying barbarians from upsetting the balance of our Coluan liquid servers, I may have an answer before we're all dead."

Kyle heard explosions in the background of the transmission. Over at the other end of the interplanetary battleground, L.E.G.I.O.N.'s command ship was in the thick of things as well. "We're trying our best here."

"Yes," Dox replied, sounding unimpressed by the heroes' efforts to contain the violence. "You've made your point quite clear in the past. The Green Lantern Corps is responsible for the protection of the universe, free of charge." Kyle could practically see the smug expression on Dox's lime-green face. "It seems you get what you pay for."

Jerk, Kyle thought. There was bad blood between the Corps and Dox's organization, but now was not the time to take L.E.G.I.O.N. to task for its more mercenary outlook. Instead, Kyle took a moment to contact the Corps' head-quarters on the planet Oa. *Maybe the Guardians know what's up.*

"That you, Rayner?" a new voice responded. Like Kyle, Guy Gardner originally hailed from Earth. Static distorted his voice somewhat.

"Roger that, Guy." He flew alongside a Thanagarian battle cruiser, searing off its laser cannons. "Any word from the top?"

The Green Lantern Corps had been created by the Guardians of the Universe, an enigmatic race of immortals who were believed to be the oldest sentient species in the cosmos. If the Guardians couldn't explain where the cosmic storm had come from, Kyle wasn't sure who could.

"Nah," Guy reported from Oa, where the Guardians resided. "I'm still waiting for them to say somethin', but they're holed up in their citadel, keeping to themselves." Kyle heard impatience in his voice; Guy had always had an abrasive personality. "Guess that leaves me calling the shots around here. If the little blue men won't step up to the plate, the Lanterns need a leader with balls."

"Classy," Kyle observed.

Guy didn't apologize for his coarse language. "Right now there are more important things than class."

Can't argue with that, Kyle admitted.

He spotted a disabled refugee ship drifting toward the furious cross fire between two Okaaran and Tamaranean warships. The defenseless vessel was only minutes away from being sliced to ribbons, so Green Lantern snagged onto it with a lasso of emerald energy and began dragging it to safety. He had spotted an uninhabited moon nearby. Perhaps he could park the ship there for the time being?

Watch out! A voice sounded in his brain. Kyle looked up to see another Durlan bio-ship closing in on him. Humongous tentacles reached out for him, but Kyle couldn't defend himself without setting the imperiled refugees adrift once more. He put on speed, trying to get away from the living ship, but the tentacles were rapidly gaining on him. He looked for Kilowog, only to discover that his fellow Green Lantern was busy rescuing another ship.

"Dammit," he muttered angrily. Couldn't the Durlans see that he was on a mission of mercy?

Don't worry, Kyle, the telepathic voice assured him. *I've got your back.*

Captain Comet zipped between Kyle and his pursuers. Although old enough to be Kyle's father, the veteran space adventurer was still in fighting trim. Adam Blake was a mutant from Earth, born with the mental and physical abilities of a man evolved one hundred thousand years beyond his peers. The furrows on his brow deepened as he repelled the bio-ship with a powerful telekinetic burst. The greedy tentacles spasmed as Captain Comet attacked the ship's own living brain and nervous system. The Durlan fighter's organic nature rendered it particularly vulnerable to Comet's powerful psionic powers. It turned and fled, seeking easier prey elsewhere.

That's more like it, Blake thought at Kyle. He flew nearer to his fellow Earthman. His wavy brown hair had turned gray around the temples; a stylized comet was imprinted on his bright red spacesuit. Psychic energy crackled around him, allowing him to survive the vacuum of space. He latched onto the refugee ship with his telekinesis, lightening the load on Kyle, who was grateful for the assist. *Let's get these people to safety.*

"Sounds good to me," Green Lantern replied, although he was starting to suspect that there was no real safety to be had anywhere in the galaxy. Glancing back over his shoulder at the cosmic storm, he had to wonder what the Guardians were up to right now.

THE gleaming citadel rose from the vast metropolis covering the surface of the planet Oa, headquarters of the intergalactic Green Lantern Corps. Within the citadel, the Guardians of the Universe kept their own counsel as they watched over the cosmos, just as they had for over ten billion years.

The Guardians were blue-skinned dwarves clad in flowing red robes, which were adorned with the emblem of the Green Lantern, a stylized pictograph of the Central Power Battery, which was the ultimate source of power for all of the Green Lanterns' rings. August white tresses were swept back from the imposing brows of the male Guardians, while the females' smooth craniums were completely hairless. Defying gravity, they hovered around the perimeter of a great domed hall, circling a holographic representation of the universe that filled nearly the entire chamber. The only illumination came from the glowing display itself. Virtual starlight played upon the wizened features of the immortal Guardians.

At the moment, the display was centered on the inexplicable cosmic storm raging beyond the Polaris system. The voracious white void expanded beneath the Guardians' gaze, spreading out in all directions. Unfathomable energies surged and cascaded throughout the storm.

"The war between Rann and Thanagar seems to have become a most unfortunate catalyst," a female Guardian pronounced. Lines of worry creased her azure brow. "Their conflict spreads wide throughout the sector and beyond. Many outlying worlds are taking advantage of the unrest to secure their own independence and expand their spheres of influence. Numerous species have taken sides, tearing the region apart."

A male Guardian, whose name was Ganthet, picked up the discussion: "And yet the war, as destructive as it is, pales before the threat posed by the anomaly outside the system. Look closer, my brothers and sisters. This goes beyond mere interstellar conflict. Entire planets have been jolted from their orbits. Others destroyed. The cosmic balance, the very fabric of existence, has been shifted. For the first time in history, Oa is no longer at the center of the universe; this tear in reality is."

"Indeed," another Guardian concurred. "Someone or something has purposely changed the nature of the cosmos."

"To what end?" the female Guardian asked.

Ganthet shook his head. "I do not yet know."

He regarded the expanding rift with apprehension. Like his fellow Guardians, he had witnessed many cataclysmic changes over the course of his immortal existence. For countless millennia, they had worked to preserve the order and harmony of the universe, with the Green Lantern Corps as their sword and shield. Always before, no matter the danger, they had managed to hold the creeping forces of entropy at bay.

Now, however, Ganthet felt an unfamiliar sensation chill the marrow of his ancient bones. Even after surviving trillions of yesterdays, and despite the fearlessness of the valiant Green Lanterns, he found himself genuinely afraid of what tomorrow might bring.

Judging from the uneasy faces of the other Guardians, he was not alone in his misgivings.

CHAPTER 5

THE ASTRAL PLANE

THE Rock of Eternity floated in a vast nothingness, separated from the mortal realm by subtle layers of perception. The craggy spire resembled a mountain peak joined to its own inverted reflection, so that it tapered to a point both above and below. For over three thousand years, the Rock had been home to its sole inhabitant: the mighty wizard known as Shazam.

But today the mage's extradimensional stronghold was under attack.

"Stand aside, mortal!" the Spectre demanded. "You have fought well, but the outcome has already been written. The wizard's doom is at hand!"

"Forget it!" Captain Marvel replied. The good-hearted hero flew between the Spectre and the Rock of Eternity. A golden thunderbolt was emblazoned on the double-breasted tunic of his bright red uniform. More gold trimmed his flowing white cape. A golden sash girded his waist. His boyish face held a look of intense determination. The strength of a demigod bulged within his muscular frame. "I'm just getting warmed up!"

His battle with the vengeful ghost had carried them from the skies above Eastern Europe to the very doorstep of Shazam's mystical sanctuary. Captain Marvel owed his own superhuman powers to the old wizard's magic. He sure as heck wasn't going to let the Spectre get to Shazam without a fight. "Stay away from him, ghost! I'm warning you!"

The Spectre hovered in the ether several yards away. His bone-white face and flesh was partially hidden by a voluminous dark green cloak that billowed around him, blown about by astral winds that seemed to presage a growing storm in the spiritual plane. A monkish hood cast the gaunt contours of the ghost's face into shadow. Miniature skulls grinned at the center of his sunken eye sockets, a phosphorescent glow where the pupils of his eyes should have been. His voice, when he spoke, carried a sepulchral chill.

"I shall stop when all magic is destroyed," the Spectre declared. "Sorcery corrupts the natural order of things. Only when it has been extinguished completely will evil wither on the vine!"

"But the wizard isn't evil!" Captain Marvel protested. As always, he took care not to say Shazam's name aloud. "He's one of the good guys. Just like you used to be!" According to the wizard, the Spectre's power was supposed to be bound to the soul of a departed mortal, so that his supernatural wrath could be tempered by a sense of humanity. But freak events had recently separated the Spectre from his previous host. Now the fearsome entity had become a menace to both innocent and guilty alike. Unchecked by a human conscience, the Spectre's judgment had become impaired, and perhaps manipulated by parties unknown.

"My mission is beyond your understanding, boy," the Spectre warned. He glided toward the waiting hero. "Stand no longer between me and my vengeance."

Captain Marvel gulped. The eerie apparition before him was no ordinary spook; the Spectre was to other ghosts what he and Superman were to regular humans. Maybe more so.

Well, I'm no pushover either, he reminded himself. As Captain Marvel, he possessed the wisdom of Solomon, the strength of Hercules, the stamina of Atlas, the power of Zeus, the courage of Achilles, and the speed of Mercury. Hopefully that would be enough to save the wizard from the rampaging spirit.

The Spectre advanced on Captain Marvel. The hero swung his fist at the ghost, but his bare knuckles passed through the Spectre's ectoplasmic substance without effect. It was like punching through an icy fog; a bone-chilling cold penetrated his fist. Captain Marvel cried out in frustration as he swung wildly at the immaterial spirit. "Cheater! Fight me like a person, you cowardly ghost!"

"Your callow taunts mean little to me, youth," the Spectre replied. "No more than this futile display of aggression." His green cloak spread out behind him, whipped about by the winds. "Though you may be imbued with the power of bygone deities, I am the very Wrath of God . . . and I have tarried too long already."

Just as he had done above Budapest less than a hour before, the Spectre expanded in size until he dwarfed the Rock of Eternity itself. He stared down at Captain Marvel, who looked like an action figure by comparison. The gigantic wraith towered over the outmatched hero.

"Shazam," the Spectre pronounced.

A thunderclap sounded in the ether. A bolt of mystic lightning struck Captain Marvel, turning him back into his juvenile alter ego. A teenage boy in a red sweatshirt and blue jeans instantly appeared in place of the hero.

"What?" Billy Batson exclaimed. His abrupt transformation caught him by surprise. He began to tumble through the empty space. "You can't do that! The magic word only works for me!"

The Spectre's thin lips curled in amusement. "You'll find I have whatever powers I require." He caught the falling teen in the palm of his hand, which had become solid enough to support the startled mortal. "Now sleep, child, while I attend to your master."

His cheeks expanded as he blew a clammy green mist over Billy. The narcotic fumes invaded the boy's lungs. An irresistible wave of fatigue washed over Billy. *No!* he thought anxiously, struggling to keep his eyes open. *I have to stay awake. Shazam is depending on me!* His mouth opened to say the magic word that would transform him back into Captain Marvel, but his groggy thoughts could barely remember the proper syllables. Darkness encroached on his vision. "Sha . . . ?"

He collapsed before uttering another sound.

Ghosts and goblins troubled his sleep.

IN his throne room, deep within the Rock of Eternity, the wizard Shazam stared into the billowing smoke rising from a brazier of red-hot coals. In the turbulent vapors, he saw the Spectre carry Billy toward an arched gateway carved into the side of the floating rock. The victorious ghost shrunk back down to human proportions as he approached the murky portal. A gloved hand gripped the unconscious boy by the collar.

The Spectre passed through the gateway, entering a dimly-lit tunnel leading into the very heart of the wizard's sanctuary. He dropped Billy onto the floor of the ancient catacomb. Shazam winced at the sight of the valiant child lying limply on the cold stone. Frightened whimpers escaped Billy's lips and he tossed fitfully on the floor.

"Savor your nightmares, boy, until I turn my attention upon you once more." The Spectre's sonorous voice emerged from the smoke ascending before the old wizard. Leaving Billy behind, the ghost floated down the rough-hewn corridor, his feet never touching the floor. "I am coming for you, Shazam. Prepare to meet your Maker."

The wizard watched the Spectre make his way toward the throne room along a limestone tunnel, its floor worn smooth by the passage of centuries. Jagged stalactites hung from the ceiling.

"I see through your strategy now, mage," the Spectre proclaimed. He wafted through the wizard's many protective wards as though they didn't exist. Eldritch energy crackled in his wake. "You hoped I would expend my strength on your naive young pawn while you marshaled your insignificant resources. The pagan gods empowering Captain Marvel made him a tempting target, to be sure, but I can be distracted no longer. Better to root out the source of the contagion, the very font of evil."

The Spectre passed a row of grotesque statues lined up along the left wall. Squatting like malignant buddhas, the petrified figures were none other than the Seven Deadly Sins, trapped by Shazam in the far-off days of his youth. No mere representations, these were the actual demons themselves, permanently encased in stone. Pride, Avarice, Lust, Wrath, Gluttony, Envy, and Sloth crouched ominously upon granite pedestals inscribed with their names. Eternal flames blazed at the feet of the Sins, part of the binding spell that held them in place. Their leering expressions embodied all that was wicked and unworthy in the human soul. The wizard feared that their long captivity was finally at an end.

Shazam leaned back against his marble throne, bracing himself for the struggle to come. An old man whose long white beard matched his stately robe, he looked like Father Time himself. A bald dome crowned his venerable countenance. A huge stone block—not unlike those that had been used to construct the pyramids back in the days of the Pharaohs—hung by a slender thread above his head. A constant reminder of his mortality, the block had been suspended above the throne for close to three millennia. A potent collection of mystic idols and artifacts, accumulated over many mortal lifetimes, rested on carved stone shelves around the edges of the throne room. The wizard's most recent acquisition, a blue crystal scarab, occupied a place of honor upon a nearby stone pedestal. Burning incense scented the air.

The day I long feared has come, Shazam thought, as he observed the Spectre's inexorable progress down the lonely corridor. A sense of resignation settled into his ancient bones. He had never truly expected Captain Marvel to defeat the Spectre, nor even significantly hold off the murderous ghost. The hero's sole purpose had been to buy Shazam time to prepare for his inevitable confrontation with the berserk Spectre. *Billy did all that could be asked of him . . . and more. Now I must ensure that his mighty labors were not in vain.*

An icy chill accompanied the Spectre as he entered the throne room.

"There you are, mage." He glided up the low stone steps. His somber cloak was draped around him like a shroud. "Let us be about our work quickly. I have much yet to do, many more to devour still."

Shazam rose from his throne. Despite his years, he displayed no trace of weakness or infirmity.

"You have done quite enough, I think." Over the last few days, the Spectre had slain over seven hundred sorcerers, consumed numerous earthbound demons and jinn, and laid waste to magical temples and enchanted forests across the globe. Even the ageless Lords of Order and Chaos had fallen victim to his merciless crusade. The spiritual warfare was spilling over into the physical realm as well, triggering freak storms, earthquakes, and other disturbances all over the planet. "Enough to wreak havoc on nearly every plane of existence."

"Reality must be cleansed and purged!" the Spectre insisted, unrepentant. "Only then can I go to my eternal reward."

"I will fight you if I must," Shazam answered, "if you force my hand. But my fervent hope is that we can reason together." He gazed upon the deranged ghost without trepidation. "You are not well, Spectre. Your mind and judgment have been corrupted by sinister forces whose true nature I have yet to determine."

He looked for some sign that his words had penetrated the madness that had overtaken the Wrath of God. In years past, the Spectre had been a mighty force for good; more than once, the near-omnipotent spirit had saved the cosmos itself from utter destruction. But that was before the Spectre shed his human host. Before an unknown instigator whispered lies into his ear.

The Spectre sneered at the wizard. Contempt showed upon his bloodless features. "Do you think to understand me? Do you truly imagine that I would look for wisdom in the insipid babble of a child? Though you affect the aspect of a frail old man, all of your years compared to mine are scarcely more than the lifespan of a mayfly! You no more possess the capacity to comprehend my mission than an ant can know the mind and will of the Almighty!"

The ghost's venomous ranting saddened Shazam. It was clear that the Spectre could not be reasoned with. Only dire measures could halt his rampage of destruction.

What must be, must be.

"Enough delay!" the Spectre snarled. He lunged forward, seizing the wizard by the throat. Corpselike hands closed tightly about Shazam's neck, even as the Spectre's supernatural might clashed with the mystic spells protecting the old man's person. Occult energy flashed and hissed all around them. "Our only business together is to thrash and rend and tear! Since your kind finds nobility in dying for a lost cause, receive this from me as a gift!"

Shazam felt the life being choked from his body, but he was not yet prepared to surrender. Taking hold of the Spectre's wrists, he tugged the wraith's cold hands away from his throat. "Your overconfidence is misplaced, ghost!" Lightning flashed from his eyes. "You are still weakened from days of struggle, while I am in my place of power. The outcome of this battle is far from decided!"

"If you truly believe that," the Spectre said, "then your vaunted wisdom is even less than I imagined." He yanked his wrists free from the wizard's grasp. Turning away from physical conflict for the moment, he rose into the air above Shazam and hurled a blast of necromantic energy at his aged opponent. "I need not lay my hands upon you to destroy you!"

Shazam gestured quickly. A shimmering golden barrier manifested between them, shielding him from the Spectre's wrath. Undeterred by the wizard's defenses, the Spectre bombarded the luminous barrier with bolt after bolt of destructive willpower. The deadly hexes crashed against Shazam's conjurations.

The wizard was hard-pressed to defend himself against the Spectre's relentless assault. Primordial incantations flashed through his brain as he invoked the ancient powers at his command. His hands were raised before him, tracing cabalistic symbols in the air. He murmured words in languages that were forgotten ages before fabled Atlantis sank beneath the waves. Unseen presences chanted in the spaces between the tongue-twisting syllables.

The immeasurable forces unleashed within the throne room began to take their toll on the eternal chamber. Deflected curses ricocheted off Shazam's defenses, striking against the timeless stone walls. Dust and debris rained down from the ceiling. Seismic tremors rocked the floor. The smoking brazier tumbled over, spilling burning coals onto the ground. Torches sputtered in their sconces. The collected talismans shook violently upon their shelves, while the hanging stone block swung back and forth upon its slender thread. The air smelled of ozone and brimstone. A stalactite crashed to earth in the tunnel beyond.

"Spectre!" the wizard shouted, alarmed by the mounting damage. "You have to stop this insanity before it goes too far. Don't you know what you're doing? You're breaking magic!"

"Exactly my intent!" the ghost responded. Mystic green fire jetted from his fingertips.

Shazam staggered beneath the barrage, but his shields held together nonetheless. "No, you think you're destroying it, but magic cannot be extinguished. It can only change form. What you *are* doing is breaking magic back down to its original wild forms by destroying ages of meticulously crafted spells, wardings, and containments." His soul quailed at the very prospect, not for himself, but for the rest of humanity. "You'll bring back the chaos that ruled before we learned to tame it. You'll unbind the ancient horrors!"

"Lies!" the Spectre raged. Fury contorted his features. "Foul lies and nonsense!"

Going on the offensive, Shazam loosed a bolt of enchanted lightning that sent the Spectre flying backward out of the throne room. The ghost smashed into the Seven Deadly Sins, cracking the petrified shell imprisoning Anger. Fissures spread across the rocky facade. Noxious vapors rose from the cracks. The bloodred fumes infiltrated the Spectre's ectoplasmic form, spurring the ghost's fury to new heights.

"Fight on if you must!" he thundered. "Or simply lie down and die." He came barreling back into the throne room like a phantasmal comet, trailing wisps of Anger behind him. "But do so in silence!"

He burst through Shazam's shimmering barrier. Shards of golden light flew apart before dissolving back into nothingness. The Spectre clasped his hands around the wizard's skull. Ghostly fingers sank into Shazam's temples as the Spectre strove to crush the old man's balding cranium like a nutshell. Veins pulsed on the wizard's forehead as he writhed in pain. Blood trickled from his nose. An agonized moan escaped his lips.

"Give up, mage!" the Spectre commanded. "It is nearly over now. Let the final darkness take you!"

"Not yet!" the wizard gasped. Summoning all his concentration, he beckoned to the crystal scarab lying on the stone pedestal several paces away. The ancient Egyptian artifact, which had once empowered the original Blue Beetle in his battle against evil, had eventually fallen into the hands of that hero's successor. Shazam had recently claimed the scarab from Theodore Kord, only days before the mortal's tragic murder.

Unseen by the Spectre, who remained intent on crushing his enemy's skull, the scarab rose from its pedestal and zoomed toward his back at lightning speed. The ghost was taken by surprise as the thaumaturgically-charged talisman passed through him like a cannonball, tearing open a hole in his bare white chest. A look of pain wracked the Spectre's ghastly visage. He stumbled backward, releasing his hold on the wizard's head. He clutched at the gaping wound in his chest. Formless green vapors gushed like blood from the ragged gash.

"What . . . have . . . you . . . done?" the Spectre moaned.

Shazam stood defiantly before the injured spirit. "As I said, you stand within my place of power." Bloodied but unbowed, he raised his arms above his head. His long white beard was whipped about by the winds as he stood squarely upon his sandaled feet. "And it is full of so many powerful things."

At his command, a score of ancient relics flew from their respective shelves and altars. Charms, crystals, idols, pendants, fetishes, and sacrificial blades joined the azure scarab in orbit around the old man's imposing form. A preternatural glow surrounded each of the levitating objects. Shazam threw an accusing finger at the Spectre, and the talismans flew at the ghost like a swarm of angry wasps. The Spectre shrieked like a banshee as the sacred icons tore through his body.

"You should never have heeded the gibbering voices that prodded you, maddened you, and finally drove you to this maniacal crusade." Shazam directed the attack from several yards away. "And you should never have come here!"

The Spectre crashed to the floor, landing in a heap amidst the rocky debris. Peering through the dust and smoke, Shazam saw the ghost's dark green cloak lying in tatters on the floor. He could not readily tell what, if anything, remained of the Spectre beneath the crumpled shroud. Silence fell over the battle-scarred throne room. Shazam heard only his own ragged breathing.

Is that it? he wondered. Lowering his arms, he let out a weary sigh. His shoulders slumped with fatigue. The titanic clash had taken everything he had, but he appeared to have prevailed. He had misread the omens; the future had not proven as hopeless as he had feared. *A pity,* he thought, *that I was compelled to destroy the Spectre. Will the Higher Powers now choose a new vessel for their wrath?*

He knew he should check on young Billy, but he took a moment to catch his breath. The duel had taken much from him. He felt every one of his five thousand years. Still, there would be time enough to recover now that the immediate threat had passed. He waved a hand and the floating talismans gently descended to the floor.

At last, he thought, *the storm has abated. Now the healing can commence.*

The shredded green cloak rustled on the floor, then lurched up into the air. The back of the cloak faced Shazam, concealing what lay hidden beneath its folds, until it slowly spun around to reveal a ghastly apparition.

The Spectre had seen better days. Both his garb and the battered form beneath it were torn to ribbons. Half his face was missing, exposing a rotting skull beneath his pallid flesh. Green slime bled from an empty eye socket. Churning ectoplasm boiled and bubbled across his torso. Fractured brown bones showed through melted muscles and sinews. The reek of putrefaction assailed Shazam's nostrils.

"Ignorant backworld conjurer," the Spectre intoned. His voice, although faint at first, grew steadily stronger. "Did you think me destroyed? I am the undying spirit of vengeance. I shall exist as long as there's a need for dark judgment and divine retribution."

Before the wizard's despairing eyes, the Spectre literally pulled himself together. His form and substance took shape once more, the roiling ectoplasm flowing back into its accustomed shape. The mangled face restored itself. Phantasmal skin covered the naked bones. The putrid slime oozed back into the vacant socket. A fresh eye glared balefully at Shazam.

I should have known this was not over yet, the old man thought. The prospect of resuming the battle filled him with dread. *Can one truly slay a ghost?*

"Do you finally comprehend, wizard?" the Spectre taunted him. "I can never be permanently drained of power until all magic is gone. In duress, I can take magic from anywhere." He levitated above the rubble, completely restored to his original appearance. "From this fortress. From the many enchanted baubles that you flung at me. And even from you!"

His arms outstretched, he absorbed raw magic from all directions. Crackling streams of occult energy converged on the Spectre, strengthening him. Magic poured from the very walls and foundations of the throne room, as well as from the mystic talismans that had ripped him to pieces only moments before.

Shazam was driven backward by the stolen power radiating from the Spectre. He retreated fearfully, all the way to the foot of his marble throne. The wizard tried to summon up a protective counterspell, but the crazed ghost moved at the speed of thought. A verse from a German poet popped irrationally into Shazam's mind.

For the Dead travel fast.

An intangible hand sunk into the wizard's chest. He felt an icy fist close tightly around his heart. His vital energy, his anima, drained out of him, sucked from the very marrow of his being. His limbs went numb. His withered body trembled. For one endless moment, his inconceivably long life seemed to play out before his mind's eye and he saw himself as he once was: a young shepherd in Canaan, five thousand years ago. Then the awful pressure on his heart jolted him back to the present and he found himself face-to-face with a homicidal ghost. He stared into skull-filled eyes and saw Death gazing back at him.

"Give me your magic, wizard!" the Spectre demanded. "Give me it all!"

Darkness beckoned, but before Shazam could breathe his last breath, his fading consciousness kept him cruelly aware of the enormity of all that was transpiring around him:

The Rock of Eternity was coming apart. The monumental edifice began to crumble to pieces as the spells maintaining it rapidly dissolved. Unable to hold its tether on the astral plane, the disintegrating Rock started to drift randomly through nearby dimensions. For a few fleeting seconds, it shuddered into the sky over the world of seven hundred stoic gods, whose universe would exist only so long as they continued to fast and chant in their remote mountain temple. A great slab of rock sheared off from the western face of the Rock, crashing down on that very temple. An unsuspecting cosmos blinked out of existence.

A heartbeat later, the decaying stronghold careened briefly through the vertiginous realm of Morpheus so that, for the merest second, the Rock of Eternity could be glimpsed simultaneously in the dreams of all who slept. Chunks of magical rock went spiraling off from the craggy fortress, breeding nightmares wherever they came to rest. Slumbering helplessly within the tunnel leading to the wizard's lair, not far from the Seven Deadly Sins, Billy Batson thrashed on the ground, fighting off imaginary demons.

Forgive me, Billy, Shazam thought. *It pains me to leave you in such jeopardy.* He prayed that the courageous boy would somehow survive the Spectre's rampage. *You were my greatest champion.*

Yet more stony fragments went flying as the Rock tumbled through a hundred dimensions in as many seconds, while deep within the dying stronghold the Spectre finally let go of Shazam's tortured heart. Only the faintest pulse of life still stirred within the wizard's depleted body as he dropped back onto his throne for the last time. A frayed thread snapped above his head, and the immense stone block finally crashed down upon Shazam at the very moment that the Rock of Eternity materialized high above the Earth.

One final thought flashed through the old man's mind.

So it ends . . . for now.

The wizard Shazam was no more.

CHAPTER 6

GOTHAM CITY

THE night air had an expectant quality. There was a peculiar stillness to the atmosphere, which seemed charged with electricity. Swollen clouds obscured the stars. The moon had an odd red sheen.

Feels like a storm coming on, Detective Crispus Allen thought. The African-American police officer, currently assigned to Gotham's Major Crimes Unit, peered out at the evening through a pair of wire-frame glasses. A rumpled trench coat hung loosely over his body, but his neatly shaved skull was uncovered. *Good thing I grabbed my coat on my way out the door. I may need it before tonight is over.*

He sat behind the wheel of an unmarked police car. The vehicle was parked on a quiet street west of Grant Park, safely distant from any overly inquisitive ears and eyes back at headquarters. Taking no chances, he rolled up the driver's-side window despite the warm weather outside.

"I've almost got him, Renee," he informed his partner, who was seated beside him. "I've been putting the squeeze on Kenzie about those missing keys of heroin. A few more days, and I'm sure I can get him to flip on Corrigan."

Jim Corrigan was the lead crime scene technician assigned to the Western Division Headquarters of the Gotham City Police Department. In a city known for its crooked cops, Corrigan was one of the dirtiest. He was the ringleader of an entire cadre of corrupt police officers and detectives involved in every manner of graft, extortion, and abuse. Stolen drugs, evidence tampering, bribery, blackmail . . . Corrigan had his hand in it all. Exposing him had become a personal crusade for Allen.

"I'm taking him down, Renee, and I'm going to do it so it sticks. No dismissals, no disappearing evidence, no technicalities, no deals. I'm going to nail that bastard for good."

"Just be careful, Cris," his partner warned. Detective Renee Montoya's shoulder holster was strapped on over a gray turtleneck sweater. Her long black hair was tied up in the back. She gave him a worried look. "Corrigan has half the cops at Western on his payroll. If he finds out you're closing in on him . . ." She didn't need to complete the sentence. They both knew how dangerous Corrigan was. "I wish I could back you up on this."

Unfortunately, Montoya had to stay clear of Corrigan. A year ago, desperately needing some evidence that Corrigan had "misplaced," she had beaten the snot out of him in the back alley behind Finnigan's Bar. She had gotten the missing bullet back from him, but at a cost; she was tainted when it came to giving evidence against Corrigan. If Allen wanted to make his case against the corrupt CSU boss stick, he had to build it without Montoya's help.

"Don't worry," he started to assure her. "I'm—"

A burst of static from their police scanner interrupted him. "Any available unit! Ten-thirty-three! Ten-thirty-three, Cathedral Square! Multiple freaks!"

Allen and Montoya exchanged an anxious look. "Freaks" was GCPD code for the costumed psychopaths who infested the city. Screams and the sound of automatic weapons fire could be heard in the background of the alert.

"God! Oh, God. It's the Riddler! And—"

Gunshots blared and the transmission was cut off abruptly.

A new voice came over the scanner. "All units respond! Cathedral Square, ten-thirty-three."

The square was only a few blocks away. Allen pulled away from the curb and hit the gas. Montoya plopped a flashing blue bubble onto the roof of the car. She took hold of the radio and spoke sharply into the mike. "Charlie tango four, mobile, responding," she alerted the dispatcher. "Be advised, charlie tango four now three-two baker."

She flicked on the siren. Allen floored it, and the car raced south on Burton Avenue. Peering up through the windshield, he saw that the Bat-Signal had already been activated. The silhouette of a winged nocturnal predator stood out in the center of a bright white searchlight that shone in the sky like a second moon.

Never a good sign, he thought.

"All units," the scanner announced between random blasts of static, "suspects identified as the Riddler, Murmur, the Body Doubles, Red Panzer, the Ventriloquist, and the Fisherman."

"Jesus Christ!" Allen muttered. From the sound of it, the lunatics were coming out of the woodwork tonight. "Must be something in the air."

"At least he didn't mention the Joker," Montoya commented. "Or Two-Face."

Thank heaven for small favors!

Turning left on Andru Street, the car sped toward Cathedral Square. As its name suggested, the open plaza was dominated by the looming Gothic presence of Gotham Cathedral. Leering stone gargoyles gazed down at what had become a war zone. Black-and-white squad cars were parked haphazardly around the square, many with their windows and tires shot out. Inky black smoke rose from the chassis of an overturned police van that had apparently collided with a toppled streetlamp. Water gushed from a shattered hydrant. Uniformed police officers crouched behind their vehicles, taking cover from a barrage of gunfire that seemed to be coming from the other side of the square. Muzzles flared in the distance, but the besieged cops weren't returning fire yet. Allen wondered why. Gotham cops weren't known for their restraint.

No police barricades had been erected, so the car entered the square without encountering any obstacles. Montoya killed the siren and the lights. Allen rolled his window down to get a better sense of what was going on. The smoky air smelled of cordite.

Their headlights exposed the drama unfolding up ahead. A whole passel of costumed freaks, most of whom belonged in the Arkham Asylum, seemed to have taken over a three-story movie theater across from the cathedral—and were holding any number of terrified movie patrons hostage, along with a handful of uniformed cops. Allen guessed that the cops on the ground were reluctant to fire for fear of killing their fellow officers. He figured that the uniformed hostages had been unlucky enough to be the first cops on the scene.

That could be any one of us over there.

The Riddler stood atop the roof of the multiplex, surrounded by his criminal cohorts and their unwilling human shields. Embossed purple question marks were sewn into the fabric of his dapper green suit and bowler hat. Madness glinted in the eyes behind his purple domino mask. He taunted the cops below via a chartreuse bullhorn. "Question: What stinks while living but in death smells good?"

Nobody attempted to answer; everyone in the square was too busy trying to stay alive. Allen brought his car to a halt, safely out of range of the perps' guns. He scanned the scene to find out who was in charge.

"Anyone? Anyone at all?" The Riddler feigned disappointment. "Come on, people. You can't be having that much fun!"

Allen gazed through the windshield at the other freaks up on the roof. The Riddler's partners in crime resembled refugees from a singularly twisted circus. The Fisherman, wearing a purple wet suit and blue rubber waders, wielded a titanium fishing rod as a weapon; an unarmed policewoman next to him was snared by an unbreakable polymer line wrapped tightly around her, a barbed hook lodged in her cheek. Murmur, a depraved serial killer, held a scalpel to the throat of another officer; the former surgeon had sewn his own lips together to curb his compulsive droning. Red Panzer, a neo-Nazi terrorist, wore a red SS uniform over a suit of high-tech body armor. A swastika was engraved on the forehead of his chromium steel helmet. He blasted apart one of the parked police cars with a salvo from the energy cannon mounted over his right hand. The explosion hurled the nearby officers into the air. Burning shrapnel went flying in all directions.

"Oh my God!" Montoya exclaimed.

A pair of young women cavorted on top of the theater's marquee. Scantily clad in revealing halter tops and short-shorts, they looked like backup dancers in a music video—except for the AK-47 submachine guns in their hands. The Body Doubles fired wildly at the cops in the square while gyrating around the kneeling bodies of their hostages. Fear showed on the prisoners' faces as the sultry assassins whooped it up. Despite their hootchie-mama attire, Bonny Hoffman and Carmen Leno were stone-cold professional killers. They blew out a stained-glass window in the cathedral across the square. Colored shards of glass rained down on the police below. The two women high-fived each other.

The Ventriloquist, a meek-looking man with gray hair and bifocals, guarded the front entrance to the theater. Scarface, the dummy he was holding—a carved wooden replica of an old-time gangster, complete with a pinstriped suit and fedora—held a miniature toy machine gun to the head of a terrified hostage. Allen had no doubt that the dummy's "toy" fired genuine bullets; that was the way things worked in this crazy city. The puppet's jaws moved up and down as Scarface vowed that he would never be taken alive. The Ventriloquist showed off by drinking a glass of water while the dummy spoke.

"No guesses?" the Riddler asked one last time. He cackled hysterically. "Very well. The answer is . . . pigs!"

At times like this, Detective Allen wished he had never moved to Gotham from Metropolis, where he had previously worked in Homicide. You still got your occasional giant robot or mad scientist over in Metropolis, but that's what Superman was for. At least Metropolis didn't breed murderous psychopaths the way Gotham did.

Lucky us.

Glimpsing the Bat-Signal above the spires of the cathedral, Allen looked for Gotham's own resident vigilante, but apparently the Batman was occupied elsewhere. Granted, you almost never saw the Dark Knight unless he wanted to be seen, but if he was on hand now, he was taking his own sweet time getting involved. *He might as well be on the moon,* Allen thought, *for all the good he's doing right now.*

Although he didn't spot Batman, someone else caught his eye. He scowled at the sight of a redheaded white guy standing beneath the arched entrance of the cathedral, about as far as he could possibly get from the action and still keep an eye on what was going on. The man puffed on a cigarette as he watched the other cops risk their lives. *Corrigan,* Allen thought acidly, disgusted by the very presence of the crooked crime scene technician. He had to wonder how Corrigan expected to profit from this crisis.

He was about to point out Corrigan to Montoya when something took his mind off the other man entirely. Without warning, a gigantic rock appeared in the sky.

"Uh, Cris?" his partner whispered in awe. Her dark eyes were as wide as plates. "Please tell me you see that."

It was hard to miss. The stupendous rock, which was the size of a small mountain, hovered in the air above the city. It was roughly diamond-shaped, with jagged peaks at the top and bottom. Its craggy granite exterior reminded Allen of Challenger Mountain in Colorado, except for the fact that the mammoth rock, which had to weigh thousands of tons, was defying gravity right before their eyes. *Where the hell did that come from,* he thought, *and what's it doing here?*

The monolith's abrupt appearance created a sudden disturbance in the atmosphere. The entire sky took on the bloodred tint of the moon. Fierce winds whipped up the smoke and litter, creating miniature dust devils all around the square. Lightning zigzagged through the crimson sky, centering around the floating rock, which seemed to be coming apart by the seams. Blasts of eerie green fire burst from somewhere deep inside the crumbling monolith. Enormous chunks of stone flaked off from the craggy slopes. Solid sheets of rock plunged down onto the city. The howling winds threw a discarded pamphlet up against the windshield of their police car. REPENT! exhorted large block letters. THE END IS UPON US!

Allen wasn't a religious man, but he suddenly wished he was home with his wife and kids. *Dore!* he thought anxiously. *Jake! Mal!*

Then the mountain exploded.

With a deafening roar, the floating rock blew apart. Fiery fragments rained down on Gotham like a meteor shower. "Mother—!" Allen exclaimed.

He heard a thunderclap directly overhead. Metal tore apart as something crashed through the hood of the car, crushing the engine block. The windshield exploded inward, showering him and Montoya with safety glass. "Ahh!" his partner cried out. He threw up his hands to protect his eyes.

No longer feeling safe in the car, Allen threw open the door and tumbled out into the open. The polluted air smelled of sulfur and burning flesh. He glimpsed chaos all around him. Screams and explosions echoed throughout the square. Stumbling forward, he almost tripped over a large chunk of smoking granite. He glanced down and found himself staring into the sculpted eyes of a grotesque stone head. A chill ran down his spine. The carved stone face was ugly as sin.

He heard Montoya exit the other side of the car. "Cris!" she shouted over the din. "Over here! Look at this!"

She was staring at the crumpled hood of the car. Allen hurried to join her. He expected to find another boulder-sized chunk of rock embedded in the hood, so he was startled to discover a super hero lying atop the mangled metal instead. He recognized the bright red costume immediately. "Is that . . . ?"

"Captain Marvel," Montoya answered for him.

Allen gazed down at the sprawled hero with confusion and growing alarm. Captain Marvel looked like he'd gone nine rounds against some super-powered heavyweight. His broad face was bruised and nicked, with a split lip. His garish attire was torn and scorched in places. He moaned softly, apparently dazed from his hard landing on the hood of the police car. "That was a close one," he murmured to himself. "Barely said the magic word in time. . . ."

Allen wasn't sure what Captain Marvel was talking about, but the hero's battered appearance spoke volumes. Marvel was supposed to be just as powerful as Superman, so who—or what—could have knocked him for a loop like this? And what was he doing in Gotham anyway? Fawcett City was his usual stomping grounds.

"Are you all right?" Montoya asked. "What's happening?"

Captain Marvel winced in pain as he slowly lifted himself off the demolished front end of the car. "The Rock of Eternity . . . He did it. . . ." He tottered unsteadily on his feet, sounding shell-shocked. "The Spectre . . . He killed him . . . He killed the wizard. . . ."

He stared numbly up at the sky. Allen followed his gaze. His jaw dropped nearly to the pavement.

High over the city, above the smoke and dust, a gigantic apparition gazed down on Gotham like an unforgiving god. A dark green hood shadowed a stern white face that could have belonged to the Grim Reaper himself. A misty green cloak blended in with the dark smoke rising from dozens of uncontrolled fires and explosions. The huge face dwarfed the Bat-Signal shining beneath it. Lightning slashed through a crimson sky.

Allen tried desperately to make sense of it all. What was Captain Marvel saying about eternity and a wizard . . . and the Spectre? The veteran cop had heard stories about the Spectre, who was supposed to be some sort of crime-fighting ghost that had been around for decades. Some people said that it was the restless spirit of a cop who had been knocked off by gangsters back in the thirties. Others claimed that the Spectre was the ghost of a dead super hero. Allen had always figured that the Spectre was just a spooky legend.

Maybe I should have paid more attention to those stories.

"Who . . . what is that?" he asked Captain Marvel.

The hero seemed a little steadier now, better able to string sentences together. "The Spectre," he confirmed. "The agent of divine vengeance. But he's gone mad, unraveling all magick."

Allen shook his head in disbelief. Captain Marvel might as well have been speaking in tongues. The Spectre's image gradually faded from view, but the stormy red skies remained. Allen looked over at Montoya to see what she was making of this. She looked just as baffled as he was.

"The wizard is dead," Captain Marvel repeated. "I don't expect you to understand, but my family may be in great danger." Allen recalled that there was also a Mary Marvel and a Captain Marvel Jr. "I must go to them."

A growing knot of anxiety tightened in Allen's stomach. If even Captain Marvel was worried about his family surviving the night, what hope did anybody else have? "I'm sorry," Allen offered the hero by way of condolences, even though he had no idea who this wizard was who had supposedly been killed. *Should I be taking a statement from him?* he wondered. *Does it count as a homicide when a ghost murders a wizard?*

Captain Marvel looked around the devastated square. Sirens blared in the distance. Ambulances and fire trucks were on their way. Thick black smoke made it hard to grasp the full picture, but Allen could tell that the hero was reluctant to leave the disaster behind, even though he still looked too wiped out to really help. Captain Marvel leaned against the wrecked police car, barely able to stand on his own, his face almost as white as the Spectre's. "Go," Allen urged him. "Take care of your family."

"Thanks!" Captain Marvel said. Taking a deep breath to steady himself, he launched into the air. The two cops watched the injured hero ascend into the sky until he finally disappeared from sight. Allen hoped that, wherever he was going, Captain Marvel made it back to his loved ones in time.

In the meantime, Gotham City was on its own. Allen drew his service revolver from beneath his trench coat and tried to take stock of the situation. Montoya did the same. "Son of a bitch," she said in a hushed tone.

The magical meteor shower had pretty much upstaged the hostage crisis. Looking around, Allen saw that the movie theater had taken a direct hit from the falling rubble. Smoke and flames rose from the wreckage of the demolished multiplex. His heart sank when he thought of the cops who had been held captive inside the building. It was too much to hope, he knew, that the Riddler and his cohorts had also been flattened by the falling debris. Freaks like that had more lives than Catwoman. . . .

Cathedral Square looked like London during the Blitz. The acrid smoke stung Allen's eyes. He choked on the fumes, his nose and mouth overpowered by the smell of brimstone. High-pitched screams punctuated a chorus of pitiful cries and moans. Lifeless limbs protruded out from beneath immense fragments of rock and chunks of fallen masonry. Deep craters surrounded the larger boulders. Random bursts of gunfire announced that the catastrophe had not brought a complete end to the hostilities. Wrecked cars and vans had been tossed about like discarded playthings, landing upside down or on their sides. Their shredded tires spun uselessly in the air. Agitated cops called out for their partners. Allen caught a whiff of teargas in the air. And emergency vehicles were converging on the site. All because something called the Rock of Eternity decided to blow up right above the city.

Guess it wasn't so eternal after all.

Once again, he thought of his family. He felt torn between his duty and his concern for Dore and the boys. Montoya looked just as conflicted. He knew she had to be thinking about her girlfriend, Daria.

"Now what?" she asked him.

Beats me, he thought. "I suppose we should start looking for survivors."

"Sounds like a plan." She stepped forward, then let out a startled cry. Allen heard something hard smack against the back of her head. She dropped like a sack of potatoes onto the cement. Her service revolver slipped from her fingers and skidded across the pavement.

"Renee!" Allen shouted.

"Drop the gun!" a harsh voice called out. A figure emerged from the smoky fumes right behind where Montoya had been standing. Allen recognized the voice, as well as the man's sandy red hair and smug expression. "Drop it or your partner takes a bullet for you!"

Corrigan! Allen glared angrily at the other man. *Just my luck that SOB survived the disaster!*

"I'm not joking, Detective Allen." The dirty cop's Glock was aimed at Montoya's unconscious body. "Don't give me an excuse to blow the bitch's head off."

Allen swore under his breath. He remembered all the times Montoya had put herself on the line for him. "All right," he said, tossing his own gun to the ground. "What's this all about?"

"Like you don't know that already." Corrigan smirked as he turned his gun on Allen. "You've been snooping where you don't belong, Detective. You should have kept your nose out of my business."

Allen snorted in disgust. "That's all you have to say to me?" He wondered if Corrigan had come to Cathedral Square looking for him and Montoya in the first place. "Your timing sucks, by the way. In case you haven't noticed, we've got a major situation here." There were fireballs raining down on Gotham, for crissakes! "The city needs every cop it has right now."

"Yep. Perfect isn't it?" He glanced around at the bedlam surrounding them. "In all this carnage and confusion, who's going to notice one more dead police officer?" Not a hint of remorse showed on his face. "Good-bye, Detective Allen. You should've stayed in Metropolis."

No! Allen thought frantically. The faces of Dore and the kids raced through his brain even as he turned to run. A gunshot rang in his ears. Bullets slammed into his back.

He was dead before the first ambulance arrived on the scene.

CHAPTER 7

TWENTY MILES SOUTH OF METROPOLIS

THE old refinery had been shut down for decades. A CLOSED sign was posted on the barbed-wire fence enclosing the deserted complex. Rust and graffiti covered the empty distillation towers and storage tanks rising from the concrete floor of the refinery. A complex network of steel pipes connected the tanks and towers to various factory-sized processing stations. Padlocks sealed the closed metal shutters and gates. Silence reigned over the derelict facility.

Place feels like a gosh-darned ghost town, Uncle Sam thought. Dressed entirely in red, white, and blue, he was the spitting image of the iconic World War I recruiting poster. A striped top hat rested atop his head. A short white beard tufted his chin. The living embodiment of America, he led his team of super-powered Freedom Fighters through the sprawling complex. He glanced up at the night sky, which had taken on a strange reddish hue. The crimson tint gave him an uneasy feeling. *I haven't seen a sky like that since that big Crisis a few years back.*

"Step lively, people," he said with a crisp Yankee accent. "Our country's countin' on us." Unlike other super-teams, the Freedom Fighters reported directly to the U.S. government, just as they had ever since the Second World War. "We've got an important job to do here, Fighters."

"Raiding an abandoned oil refinery?" The Ray sounded unconvinced. Glowing like the sun, the young man flew beneath the branching pipes. Like his father before him, Ray Terrill could transform himself into a being of pure energy. "We haven't slept in forty-eight hours, Sam."

Uncle Sam understood the youngster's exhaustion. He had heard similar complaints at Valley Forge, over two centuries ago. Defendin' America could be a tough job sometimes. "The boys and girls in D.C. picked up a message between the Silver Ghost and Mirror Master," he reminded them. "Those vermin held some kinda meeting on this spot two days ago before ditchin' it. We're to sweep the area and I'm hopin' we find a hint of what this blamed Secret Society of Super-Villains is fixin' to do next."

"If they left a trail, I will find it," Black Condor said solemnly. The winged hunter bore his usual taciturn expression. Enormous red pinions sprouted from his naked back. His long black hair gave him an untamed, barbaric look, as did the leather straps crossing his bare chest. A silver throwing knife rested against his hip.

"Well, one thing's for sure," Phantom Lady added. The shapely brunette searched the shadows through a pair of tinted yellow goggles. "These terrorists aren't getting together to share fashion tips." Delilah Tyler's own costume had been expressly designed to show off her curves . . . and then some. The backless yellow silk bathing suit was cut all the way down to her navel. A green cape, gloves, and boots completed the ensemble. The provocative outfit was guaranteed to distract any red-blooded male opponents, something Dee fully took advantage of. "Though Mirror Master could use some. I mean, what's with that padded green head mask?"

Walking beside her, Damage seemed less inclined to poke fun at their adversaries' attire. "Why us?" Grant Emerson asked. The brown-haired teenager was the most normal-looking member of the team. With his blue jersey and gray trousers, he could have easily been mistaken for a high school athlete. "Why not Superman? Or maybe the Justice League?"

"The brass said there was some kinda explosion on the moon tonight," the Human Bomb said. His voice was muffled somewhat by the bulky white containment suit that covered him from head to toe. The thick "fibro wax" fabric kept him from blowing things up by mistake. "They're probably dealing with that . . . and with what Wonder Woman did to Maxwell Lord." He shrugged beneath his suit. "Not that I blame her. Back in the war, sometimes your hand was forced."

"That don't make it right, Roy," Uncle Sam said grimly. He and the Human

Bomb had fought beside each other during World War II, so he knew where Roy Lincoln was coming from. Like America herself, they had needed to get their hands dirty on occasion. That didn't mean that every death didn't weigh on his conscience. *I hope the day never comes that I resort to deadly force without a sense of profound regret.*

He prayed that Wonder Woman still felt the same way.

Forcing his mind back to his mission, he searched the darkened facility for evidence of the super-villains' activities. Flying overhead, the Ray provided more than enough light to see by. Uncle Sam's keen eyes zeroed in on a large iron door guarding the entrance to one of the refinery's many fuel processing plants. The painted metal was in markedly better condition than the rest of the plant.

"Take a gander at this door here," he said, pointing out the barrier to the others. "Not a speck o' rust on it." He rolled up his sleeve. "I reckon there's a reason."

Uncle Sam's strength was proportionate to America's faith in her ideals. Balling up his fist, he slammed the locked steel gate with his bare knuckles. The heavy door caved inward, crashing onto the floor of the plant.

The Freedom Fighters rushed into the building. They found themselves in a large antechamber with a high ceiling and a scuffed tile floor. Metal drums were lined up against the walls. Steel pipes and valves ran above their heads. A No Smoking sign warned of flammable materials. Cobwebs and rat droppings were conspicuously absent.

Only a few yards in, they ran into another obstacle. A lattice of ruby laser beams blocked their way. The high-tech mousetrap encouraged Uncle Sam that they were on the right track. *Pretty fancy security for a place that's supposed to be abandoned!*

"Motion sensors," Phantom Lady said, assessing the situation. She reached for the bracelet containing her black light projector. "But they're nothing I can't trick."

The Ray zipped past her. "Don't bother going invisible, Dee. Light's my thing."

His luminous hands reached out and took hold of the crimson light beams as though they were solid. He neatly pulled them apart, as easily as opening a curtain, until he had created an opening large enough for the entire team to pass through. "After you," he said graciously. "Phantom Ladies first."

She treated him to a flirtatious smile. "Have I told you how cute you are when you try to act heroic?"

"Only once or twice," he replied, literally beaming.

Beyond the lasers, they discovered another doorway, large enough to pass a 747 through. A pair of heavy steel doors barred their way. Black Condor frowned at the barrier. "Something beyond these gates resists my thoughts," he reported gravely. Besides flight, Ryan Kendall's gifts also included telepathy. *Mighty suspicious,* Uncle Sam thought. *Wonder what the Society went to so much trouble to hide?*

"Hey, you want to be impressed, Dee?" Damage asked Phantom Lady. He swaggered toward the steel doors. The teenager was a living fusion reactor. Nuclear energy crackled around his fists. "Just give me something to hit."

But the Human Bomb was already there. "Our powers aren't the kind you show off with, kid," he chided the adolescent hero. He carefully removed his right glove. The exposed hand glowed with explosive energy. "Just brushing up against this skin is like a grenade going off."

Damage's cocky attitude evaporated. He looked embarrassed to be corrected by the older man, whose powers were very similar to his own. "I know, Mr. Lincoln. I was only . . ."

"Good to hear it," the Human Bomb said, letting the kid off the hook. He drew back his blazing fist. "Now the rest of you better cover your ears."

He wasn't joking. The same experimental potion that had prolonged Roy Lincoln's life ever since the forties had also endowed him with the ability to generate tremendous biochemical explosions with just a touch. Now the Human Bomb drove his naked fist into the solid steel doors and a deafening blast rocked the refinery. The detonation blew the doors off their hinges, exposing the darkened chamber beyond. Straining his eyes, Uncle Sam glimpsed the shadowy outlines of dormant pipes and furnaces.

As the Human Bomb stepped back from his handiwork, Black Condor took point. The avian hero's brow furrowed in concentration as he peered into the gloom, telepathically scanning the scene ahead.

"What?" Black Condor blurted in surprise. An alarmed expression came over his face, but before he could explain, a beam of searing yellow energy burned straight through his unprotected chest, emerging from his back right between his wings. Uncle Sam had to jump out of the way to avoid being pierced by the beam himself. "Arrrr!" Kendall cried out as he died.

"Condor!" Phantom Lady shrieked.

The fatal beam lit up the room beyond, exposing the sneering face of a purple-skinned alien with an inhumanly high forehead and a pencil mustache. Uncle Sam instantly recognized Sinestro, Green Lantern's archenemy. A golden power ring glittered on the alien's finger.

And he wasn't alone. The lights flicked on, and the Freedom Fighters found themselves outnumbered by a strike force composed of nine of the world's deadliest super-villains. Alongside Sinestro, Uncle Sam recognized:

Doctor Light, a malevolent scientist whose light powers made him shimmer almost as brightly as the Ray.

Deathstroke the Terminator, reputedly the planet's most lethal assassin.

Zoom, the Reverse-Flash, the fastest villain alive.

Doctor Polaris, the mentally disturbed master of magnetism. Metal shards orbited his armored fists, and crazed eyes peered out through a slit in his purple helmet.

Black Adam, Captain Marvel's evil counterpart. He levitated above the floor, his brawny arms crossed atop his chest, gazing down on the heroes in contempt.

The Psycho-Pirate, a twisted lunatic capable of manipulating the emotions of others. A featureless golden mask concealed his face as he lurked behind the other villains. Physical confrontations were not his specialty.

Bizarro, an imperfect duplicate of Superman. A backward *S* was emblazoned upon his chest. His chalky white face grinned inanely, the mineral-like texture of his skin betraying his artificial origins.

The Cheetah, half woman, half jungle cat. Spotted fur coated her lithe form, and her polished fangs and claws gleamed. A feline tail flicked behind her.

"Good-bye!" Bizarro illogically greeted the stunned Freedom Fighters.

We've been set up, Uncle Sam realized. "Fighters! Don't hold back!" He scooped up his top hat from where it had fallen when he'd dived out of the way of Sinestro's beam. "Y'all hear me?"

There was no time to call out any further orders. Black Adam soared toward him, his fists upraised, and Uncle Sam found himself locked in combat with the ancient Egyptian despot. Teth-Adam had been the wizard Shazam's first super-powered champion, until he'd used his abilities to conquer the very people he was supposed to protect. Uncle Sam was more than happy to exchange blows with Black Adam. He never could tolerate a tyrant.

At the same time, he tried to keep track of his fellow Freedom Fighters as they charged forward to engage the enemy. . . .

"FOOLISH boy!" Doctor Light insulted the Ray. An effulgent glow surrounded the cloaked villain as he somehow tapped into the radiant hero's own solar power. The Ray gasped in shock as he felt energy draining from his body. He tried to muster the strength to fire a photonic blast at the evil scientist, but all he could manage was a few feeble flashes. His glowing aura faded as Doctor Light blazed ever brighter. The villain's black cloak and costume matched his malignant soul. A vulpine face sneered out from beneath a crested helmet. "Your power is mine!"

The Ray's light flickered out. Living energy reverted to ordinary flesh and blood. Unable to stay aloft, Ray Terrill crashed to the floor. Dazed, he sprawled helplessly upon the concrete.

ZOOM was nothing but a yellow blur as he raced around Damage, striking the youth dozens of times in a single second. His words slurred and ran together as he sped through time at different rates. "You'llallbe stronnnger heroes," Hunter Zolomon promised. His costume was identical to that worn by the Flash, except the red and yellow colors were reversed. In his own warped mind, he was doing the Freedom Fighters a favor by testing them to their utmost. "If you survive."

The rapid-fire punches triggered Damage's explosive powers, but Zoom didn't stick around long enough to get caught in the blast. He zipped away from the battered teenager a split second before Damage slammed against an old furnace. An uncontrolled fusion reaction caused Damage to unleash a blast of nuclear energy that tore the furnace and surrounding pipes to pieces. Heavy chunks of cast-iron rained down on him, burying him beneath the debris.

His fight with Zoom was over in a flash.

LIVING up to her name, Phantom Lady used the black light projector on her bracelet to turn invisible. She slipped past Bizarro and Doctor Polaris unseen, while taking care to stay clear of Doctor Light. After seeing what Light had done to the Ray, she didn't want to give that villain a chance to mess with her black light capabilities. *Probably best to keep away from Sinestro, too,* she decided. If the alien's power ring was anything like Green Lantern's, there was probably no limit to what it could do. *Maybe even make me visible again?*

Choosing her opponents carefully, she crept up on Deathstroke and the Cheetah. Heavyweights like Black Adam and Bizarro were out of her league, strength-wise, but if she moved quickly she might be able to take out the hit man and the cat-lady before they even knew she was there. Then maybe she could figure out some way to distract Black Adam long enough for Uncle Sam to finish him off.

Just to keep the bad guys off-balance, she took a moment to project a three-dimensional hologram of herself onto the other side of the room. Psycho-Pirate yelped and scurried away from the hologram. Bizarro threw a punch at the illusion, then blinked in almost comical confusion as his gnarled fist passed harmlessly through it. *So far, so good,* she thought. Confident that everyone was looking elsewhere, she turned back toward her original targets.

Deathstroke first. Sneaking up on the armor-clad assassin, she eyed the broadsword sheathed at his waist. *I could do a lot of damage with that,* she thought, *especially if nobody sees me coming.* Her bracelet was equipped with a built-in taser, but she suspected that the high-powered electrical charge would not penetrate the insulated blue chain mail worn by Deathstroke. *Guess I'll just have to go medieval on him.*

She reached out for the hilt of the sword, but before she could take hold of the weapon, a savage growl suddenly came from behind her. Spinning around in alarm, she found herself staring into the bloodthirsty brown eyes of the Cheetah.

"No need to see you," the feral villainess snarled. A primitive blood ritual had transformed archaeologist Barbara Minerva into a terrifying feline monster who made Catwoman look like a harmless tabby. A wild mane of auburn hair cascaded over her tawny shoulders. She cracked her tail like a whip. "Not when I can *smell* you!"

With a fierce roar, she pounced at Phantom Lady. Razor-sharp claws slashed across Dee's face, drawing blood. Her yellow goggles, which enabled her to see herself when no one else could, were snapped in two. Half of the tinted Plexiglas hit the floor, and Dee's depth perception went out of whack as her left eye lost track of her own invisible limbs. She recoiled in horror as the Cheetah licked the blood from her claws.

Oh my God, Phantom Lady thought. *She really is an animal.*

Panicked, she turned to flee, only to race head-on into Deathstroke's sword. Cold steel impaled her, slicing clear through to the green cape fluttering behind her. Gripping the hilt with both hands, Deathstroke lifted her off the ground, so that she started to slide down the length of the blade. Her gloved hands grabbed onto the sword to keep herself from sliding farther, but the damage had already been done. Three feet of polished steel jutted from beneath her breasts. A numbing chill raced over her body. Blood trickled from her mouth as she stared down at the one-eyed assassin at the other end of the blade. Delicate circuitry in her costume shorted out and she turned visible once more. "Why?" she murmured weakly.

"Sorry, darlin'," Deathstroke answered. "Just business."

"Dee!"

The Human Bomb couldn't believe his eyes. Phantom Lady was dead, skewered upon Deathstroke's sword. The Cheetah looked on, laughing. Dropping onto all fours, she lapped up the blood dripping from the murdered heroine. Deathstroke lowered his blade to let Phantom Lady's lifeless body slide limply onto the floor.

"Get away from her!" Roy Lincoln boomed. A literally explosive fury went off inside him. Tossing both his gloves aside, he charged into the throng of villains. A thunderous blast knocked Deathstroke and the others off their feet. The shock wave sent Sinestro tumbling backward through the air. The Cheetah sprang away just in time to avoid the blast. Rumor had it she had recently picked up some super-speed tricks from her lover, Zoom.

The Human Bomb raced to where Phantom Lady lay fallen. He knew she couldn't possibly still be alive, but he had to be sure. A glance confirmed the awful truth. His friend's glassy brown eyes stared blankly into oblivion. "Not Dee too," he said, his voice hoarse with emotion. Thanks to his explosive flesh, he couldn't even close her eyes without inadvertently blowing her body to pieces. "Not her."

"Oh, she's dead all right!" a maniacal voice cackled. Roy looked up to see Doctor Polaris levitating above him. The madman's face and body were hidden behind a suit of dark purple armor. A majestic blue cloak billowed behind him. Bits of metal scrap floated around his steel gauntlets, controlled by Polaris' magnetic prowess. "Didn't you hear that delicious shriek?"

"You . . . murderers!" the Human Bomb raged. He couldn't stand the idea that a homicidal nutcase like Polaris was still alive while both Phantom Lady and Black Condor were gone. Damage and the Ray were down, too. Heaven only knew what shape they were in. This routine reconnaissance mission had turned into a bloodbath. *Well I'll be damned,* he thought, *if I let these killers get away scot-free.* "You want war, Polaris? Okay by me."

For the first time in over sixty years, Roy Lincoln yanked the heavy protective hood from his head. He tore open the front of his containment suit. His exposed face and chest glowed radioactively as he unleashed the full power of the volatile chemicals that saturated every cell of his body.

"Die!" He exploded.

A tremendous fireball erupted from him. A blast of overpowering heat, noise, and force shook the entire refinery. A mushroom cloud blew the roof off the processing station, with Doctor Polaris catching the full force of the detonation. His armor and magnetic force field were no match for the sudden conflagration. The Human Bomb's volcanic fury tore through his defenses like they were cardboard, ripping Doctor Polaris to pieces. Chunks of scorched meat and metal splashed down at the vengeful hero's feet.

That's one for our side, the Human Bomb thought. He had no regrets, not after what these bastards had done to his friends. Had Wonder Woman felt the same way when she'd executed Maxwell Lord?

A round of applause startled him. He looked up to see Bizarro leaping toward him. The brain-damaged brute clapped his hands enthusiastically. "Me like Human Bomb!" he declared, right before slamming his fist into Roy's face, setting off another explosion. The monster shrugged off the eruption as though he barely felt it. "Me like pretty lights!"

He liked the explosions so much, in fact, that he kept pounding the Human Bomb with punches as strong as Superman's. Roy Lincoln felt like he was being hit by a runaway locomotive, over and over again. The first blow knocked him flat on his back, even as his blood ignited like nitroglycerin. The second blow broke his nose and teeth. The resulting explosion sent bone fragments flying like shrapnel, but Bizarro wasn't even scratched. Roy realized that he wouldn't be getting up again.

Eighty-some years, he thought, between explosions. *I had a good long run.* His only regret was that he was leaving his allies in the lurch. *Give 'em hell, Sam!*

Another titanic blow crashed down on him and everything went black. The Human Bomb's body lay still, but Bizarro continued to hammer away at it, chortling with glee each time the pulverized flesh detonated beneath his fists. The dying explosions lit up his chalky face. He grinned like a kid at a fireworks show, even as Roy Lincoln's blood and pulp splattered against the backward *S* on his chest. The explosions faded in intensity until, after about half a dozen blows, they stopped entirely.

The Human Bomb had gone off for the last time.

"Rrrr?" Bizarro grunted. He gave the flattened remains another poke, but nothing happened. A look of disappointment crossed the monster's face. Blood dripped from his fists. "No more pretty lights."

"RAY?"

The dazed teenager stirred upon the hard concrete floor. Completely exhausted, he felt like he had just expended enough solar energy to light up the entire East Coast. He tried to power up, but all he could manage was to lift his head a few inches. Explosions and angry shouts echoed in his ears.

"Sam?" he answered weakly. Looking up from the floor, he saw not his leader, but a featureless gold mask gazing down at him from atop a scrawny body swathed in a floor-length scarlet cape with a high collar. The symbolic faces of Comedy and Tragedy were printed on the masked man's chest like a coat of arms.

"Not quite," the Psycho-Pirate replied.

Ray Terrill was pretty wiped out, but he hadn't forgotten the way the Society strike force had ambushed the Freedom Fighters. He remembered Sinestro's golden ray stabbing through Black Condor before they even knew what was happening. "I'll k-kill you . . ." he vowed bitterly. Bleary eyes glared at his enemy. All he needed was a few more minutes to get his strength back. . . .

"Oh, no!" the Psycho-Pirate protested. "That just won't do." The golden metal that composed his mask began to flow into a different shape. Molten features emerged, forming a smiling face that gazed down at Ray benignly. "Don't be angry," the villain said in a soothing tone. "Don't be afraid."

The defenseless youth felt a wave of well-being wash over him. Part of him recognized the hypnotic effect of the Medusa Mask, which was infamous for its ability to control the emotions of others, but he couldn't look away. He tried to fight back, but the gleaming mask was impossible to resist. His anger and determination seeped away, replaced by a dreamy sense of contentment. What was the big deal anyway? Everything was just fine. . . .

A giddy smile stretched across his face.

"That's better," the Psycho-Pirate said. He took hold of the Ray's ankle and began to drag the young man across the floor of the plant. "Luthor needs you alive."

Ray raised no objection, not even when the back of his skull bumped over a stray piece of rubble. Smiling up at the hole in the ceiling, he let his enemy drag him away.

Why not?

UNCLE Sam was the last Freedom Fighter standing. He had held his own against Black Adam up until now, but he knew the battle was turning against him. The fracas had barely begun, but at least three of his allies were already dead, and the others were all down for the count. He wasn't about to surrender, though. That wasn't the American way.

"Come and get me, you cowards," he challenged his foes.

Flying like Captain Marvel, Black Adam came swooping down from the bloodred sky. A metallic gold thunderbolt was emblazoned on his black tunic. Dark hair formed a widow's peak above his lean and merciless face. His fists collided with Uncle Sam's jaw, sending the American icon reeling. For a foreigner, the Egyptian tyrant had one hell of a punch.

"So much for freedom," Black Adam declared arrogantly.

"Not so fast," Uncle Sam answered him. It would take more than one good punch to knock him off his feet. "If I can keep my chin up through the Great Depression and two world wars, I can sure as blazes stand up to the likes of you!"

But he was hopelessly outnumbered. With his teammates out of the picture, the rest of the villains piled on Uncle Sam. The Cheetah leapt onto his shoulders, slashing and biting with abandon. Deathstroke emptied a clip of ammunition from an Uzi submachine gun. Zoom ran between the hit man's bullets, pummeling Uncle Sam with his lightning-fast fists. Doctor Light targeted the hero with a laser beam that burned like Hades against Uncle Sam's back. Bizarro tried to freeze him with cold blasts from his eyes, his opposing power to Superman's heat vision.

Adding insult to injury was the painful knowledge that at least three of his assailants were American. Heck, Deathstroke, aka Slade Wilson, had once served honorably in the U.S. Armed forces, before turning mercenary. "Blast you, Wilson!" he cursed the man. "Where's your loyalty to your country?"

"I paid my dues," the assassin answered. He loaded another clip into his firearm. "Now the Society pays me."

Sinestro joined the fight. His blue bodysuit, made of some exotic alien fabric, had been singed by the Human Bomb's cataclysmic revenge for Dee's death. Alas, his yellow power ring was still in one piece. "Back away," he instructed his partners. "Let's see if the old man is as soft as the bird."

A Green Lantern's power ring was said to be the most powerful weapon in the known universe. Sinestro had once been a Green Lantern, until the power went to his head. His new ring had been forged in the antimatter universe of Qward to allow him to fight his former colleagues on their own terms. If it was even half as powerful as the real thing, then Uncle Sam knew he was in for it. Visions of past American conflicts flashed through his brain. This wouldn't be the first time he had been laid low by a sneak attack, but he had always come back fighting. As he braced himself for the alien's assault, Uncle Sam refused to give up hope.

"Go ahead, you no-good worm," he challenged Sinestro. "Your time will come."

The flying alien kept out of reach of the hero below. "Humans," he said with a smirk. "So predictable." His power ring lit up like a supernova.

And an incandescent beam of yellow energy brought the deadly battle to an end.

CHAPTER 8

THE MOON

DEBRIS rained down on the Monitor Room as Superman was knocked into space by a titanic blow. The thunderous impact echoed through the ruins of the Watchtower. Earthlight shone down through the gaping hole created by Superman's passage. The crumbling structure shuddered alarmingly.

This place won't hold together much longer, Batman noted. Unfortunately, that wasn't even the most pressing danger right now.

"Hah," an inhumanly deep voice boomed loudly. "I had heard it was true, but I had to see it with my own eyes. The destruction of the Justice League."

A menacing figure stomped onto the elevated walkway. Batman clenched his fists at the sight of a yellow-skinned humanoid of gargantuan proportions. Nearly eight feet tall, the creature towered over both Batman and Wonder Woman. His brutish skull was the size of a boulder, with jutting brows and an armored cap. Anvil-sized fists were at least twice as big as the heroes' heads. Studded metal armor encased his massive frame. The damaged walkway trembled beneath his ponderous tread. He was easily over a thousand pounds.

Batman recognized the monstrous entity at once.

So did Diana.

"Mongul!" she exclaimed.

The creature before them, the one whose sneak attack had launched Superman into orbit, was a cruel alien warlord who had frequently clashed with both the Man of Steel and the Justice League. *He must have beamed into the ruins,* Batman realized, *while Clark and I were arguing with Diana.*

He cursed himself for letting his guard down.

Sloppy.

He reached for his utility belt, but Mongul was too fast for him. With a sweep of his arm, the interstellar conqueror knocked Batman from the walkway. The blow jolted the breath from the Dark Knight's body; even through the Kevlar panels protecting his chest, he felt as though he had been hit by a wrecking ball.

Artificial gravity seized him and he plunged toward the lower levels of the Watchtower. Torn steel struts waited to impale him. Gouts of flame erupted from below. Batman was only seconds away from being barbecued upon a spit.

Shaking off the effects of Mongul's blow, he snatched a handheld grapnel gun from his belt. Taking aim at the ceiling, he fired a CO_2-propelled dart at a solid-looking steel buttress. The dart's micro-diamond drill head dug securely into the thick metal support. A de-cel jumpline attached the dart to the grapnel gun, halting Batman's descent. Then a motorized reel built into the sleeve of the gun carried him back up toward the battle being waged upon the walkway.

Hang on, Diana, he thought. Despite their differences, he wasn't about to let her combat Mongul alone.

Releasing the jumpline, he landed nimbly upon the walkway, just in time to see Wonder Woman go on the offensive. With the speed of Hermes, she drew her sword from its scabbard. Forged by Hephaestus himself, the enchanted blade was sharp enough to cleave the electrons from an atom, not that Diana was attempting anything so delicate at the moment. A fierce battle cry escaped her lips as she sprang at her foe.

The tip of the sword slashed across Mongul's armored breastplate, drawing blood. He roared in pain and anger. Furious red eyes blazed beneath his Neanderthal brows. "You want blood?" he raged. "I'll give you blood!"

Drawing back his fist, he punched Wonder Woman hard enough to send her flying off the walkway, her blue cloak wrapped around her. An earthshaking boom resounded throughout the ruins. Looking on, Batman had to remind himself that Diana was very nearly as invulnerable as Clark. It would take more than that to put her down for good.

Or so he hoped.

A blue-and-red missile came streaking back into the Watchtower. Wonder Woman's assault had bought Superman time enough to recover and return to the fray. He dived at Mongul, his bare fists extended before him. Blue eyes glowed brightly red as his heat vision struck Mongul squarely in the chest. The air between them sizzled loudly.

Mongul's armor shielded him from the searing red beams. Bracing himself for battle, he stood defiantly in the face of the oncoming Superman. His brutish face beamed in bloodthirsty anticipation. His mammoth fists were raised and ready.

That's it, Clark, Batman thought. *Keep him distracted.*

The Dark Knight crept up on Mongul from behind. Physically, he was no match for the super-strong alien, but that did not deter him; he had defeated all sorts of muscle-bound powerhouses before, from Blockbuster to Solomon Grundy. Batman's keen eyes spotted a severed power cable dangling from the ceiling. Blue sparks streamed from exposed wires within it.

Batman took hold of the cable. His gloves and boots were insulated against electrical shocks. Perhaps the same could not be said of Mongul's metallic armor? Tugging the cable loose, he stealthily approached the warlord's back. *Let's see how he handles a few thousand volts.*

Mongul appeared oblivious to Batman's intent. "I was hoping to find something of value in the wreckage," he declared as his left fist collided with Superman's face, sending the Last Son of Krypton flying backward. At the same time, he pivoted swiftly and grabbed onto Batman with his right. "And I suppose I have!"

Huge fingers clamped down on Batman's shoulders. The Dark Knight's boots dangled in the air as Mongul effortlessly plucked him from the floor. Batman struggled to pry himself from the tyrant's grasp, but the gigantic fingers were like steel bars. An enormous thumb pressed down on his throat, making Batman grateful for the titanium gorget built into his cowl. Only that steel band kept Mongul from completing crushing his larynx—and only for the moment.

Mongul lifted the squirming hero up before him so that they were literally face to face. The alien's foul breath assaulted Batman as he screamed, "Your skull will be added to my throne!"

We'll see about that, Batman thought. Wrenching his body to one side, he managed to snag a miniature acetylene torch from his belt. He thrust the white-hot flame directly into Mongul's face. *That should take his mind off redecorating.*

"ARRGH!" Mongul bellowed. His grip relaxed momentarily, and Batman twisted free of the monstrous fingers like the expert escape artist that he was. He dropped lightly to the cracked tile floor as Superman came swooping back onto the scene.

"Mongul!" Superman shouted at their unwanted visitor. Batman heard the anger in his fellow hero's voice and quickly got out of the way. Nicks and bruises on Superman's face testified to the sheer power of the warlord's fists, and Clark's irate expression made it clear that he'd had enough. "You picked the wrong day to show your face again!"

A stupendous left cross to his jaw staggered Mongul. Blood and bits of broken teeth sprayed from his mouth. Superman followed up with an explosive right hook that left the alien conqueror reeling. Ruby beams of heat vision converged on Mongul's unprotected countenance. He toppled backward, grunting in pain. The entire chamber quaked as his colossal weight crashed down upon the walkway. Purple bruises marred his jaundiced complexion.

Mongul had made Superman mad, Batman realized.

Not a good idea.

Superman touched down on the floor. "Batman—?"

"I'm okay." The Dark Knight's voice was raspy, but intact. He climbed rapidly to his feet. The artificial gravity fluctuated noticeably, another indication that the Watchtower's life-support systems were rapidly breaking down. "Mongul?"

"He's down," Superman said.

"Good!" a female voice stated vehemently. Wonder Woman bounded back onto the walkway from somewhere below the Monitor Room. She sprang at Mongul, her sword raised high above her head. The blade swung downward, as though she intended to cleave his skull right down the middle. "I'm going to keep him there!"

"Diana, no!" Superman lunged forward to stop her. Moving at super-speed, he trapped the sword between his palms, halting it in mid-swing, only inches away from Mongul's battered face. The dazed warlord eyed the bloodstained blade with obvious alarm. Wonder Woman's own face had never looked more fierce.

Batman's eyes narrowed behind his opaque lenses. He strode over to where Wonder Woman faced Superman across the fallen body of their foe. "What are you doing?" he demanded.

She looked at him in surprise. "What did you *think* I was going to do?"

Her voice had a wounded tone, as though she was shocked that they would misjudge her so readily. Was it possible they had misread her intentions? Batman certainly hadn't seen any evidence that she had meant to pull her blow at the last moment, or strike Mongul with merely the flat of her blade. She had been swinging the sword right at Mongul's head.

After what happened with Max, he thought, *what are we supposed to assume?*

Their silence made it very clear just what he and Superman believed. Frowning, she angrily yanked her sword out of Superman's hands. That the enchanted blade was surely capable of slicing even through Kryptonian flesh did not appear to worry her much.

Superman's expression darkened. Blood leaked from a shallow cut on his hand. He stared at Wonder Woman in disbelief. "I . . . I don't even know who you are anymore."

"Of all people," she insisted, "you should know who I am, who the world needs me to be." Like Clark, she had acquired numerous small scratches and bruises, yet she looked as proud and regal as ever. Her golden tiara rested securely upon her brow. "I'm Wonder Woman."

While all eyes were upon her, Mongul suddenly lurched to his feet with startling speed. Swinging fists caught the three heroes off guard, scattering them like bowling pins. To Batman, it felt as though a small earthquake had suddenly erupted in their midst. He went tumbling backward. His head smacked against the rubble littering the floor. Only the Kevlar lining of his cowl saved him from a concussion. Once again, he mentally kicked himself for his carelessness. *I keep forgetting how strong this brute is. He makes Killer Croc look like a weakling.*

"You're pathetic!" Mongul mocked them. He was breathing hard, though, and coughing up blood. Clearly, he'd had the fight knocked out of him. He bolted from the demolished chamber, his heavy boots pounding rapidly upon the debris-strewn walkway.

He was making a break for it.

"Superman!" Batman called out. He knew he was in no shape to catch the fleeing Mongul. "Don't let him escape!"

The last thing they needed was another monster on the loose.

***

His head still ringing, Superman zipped after Mongul. In a split second, he reached the corridor outside the Monitor Room, where he spotted the alien fugitive standing inside a transparent containment tube made of clear Thanagarian crystal. Auxiliary power cables connected the teleporter to the Watchtower's backup generators. Large enough to accommodate Hawkman's folded wings, the tube barely contained Mongul's bulk. Lighted switches and gauges flashed upon the display panel of the adjacent control kiosk. An electronic hum filled the air.

No! Superman thought, but the escaping warlord had already activated the teleporter. An incandescent glow filled the tube. Mongul smirked through swollen lips as the device instantly transformed him into ambient matter before folding space to teleport the villain anywhere in the universe. The glow quickly faded, revealing an empty tube.

Mongul had vanished completely.

There was no point going after him. The brutal invader could be on the other side of the galaxy by now. Superman wondered briefly how Mongul had managed to bypass the teleporter's security protocols in the first place, but that hardly mattered anymore. The Watchtower would soon be uninhabitable.

Frustrated, he rejoined Batman and Wonder Woman in the remains of the Monitor Room. "Mongul found a working teleporter," he informed them. "He's gone."

Mongul's failed attempt at a home invasion was less of a concern to him than Wonder Woman's draconian new attitude. His hand stung where Diana's sword had cut him. Along with kryptonite, magic had always been his Achilles' heel.

"You know," he told her, "I remember a time when you wanted to be called Diana."

She wiped the blood from her blade, then sheathed the sword. "I told you, the world doesn't need Diana. The world needs Wonder Woman."

"And Wonder Woman killed Maxwell Lord," he said.

"That maniac murdered Ted Kord," she reminded him. A note of impatience entered her voice, as though she was growing tired of justifying her actions. "And he was going to use you to do the same to Bruce. There was no other choice."

"There's *always* a choice," Batman said passionately. Blood trickled from his nose, seeping out from beneath his cowl. "Especially for people like us."

"No, there isn't," she insisted. "Sometimes there is no alternative."

"And that's the kind of thinking that leads to mind-wipes and murder," he said bitterly.

Superman knew what Batman was referring to. Recently, they had discovered that a few of their colleagues in the Justice League had used sorcery to tamper with the memories and personalities of any super-villain who uncovered their civilian identities. Even worse, those same League members had erased a portion of Batman's memory when he had caught them in the act. The truth, when it was finally exposed, had created a rift between Batman and his former teammates, one that Superman feared would never heal. It was that betrayal that had driven Bruce to launch Brother Eye into orbit, the better to keep watch over his own allies.

One mistake led to another, Superman reflected, *setting in motion a chain of ominous events that has yet to reach its conclusion.* Who knew what the long-term results of Diana's fatal act would be?

And yet she still refused to acknowledge the enormity of her lapse. "Look what's going on across the globe, Bruce. Do you really believe that humanity is going to rise above it themselves?"

"You've lost faith," he accused her.

"The world is not as black and white as you and Kal see it," she replied, referring to Superman by his Kryptonian name. She was one of the few people on Earth who did so.

"Diana," Batman said coldly, "you should have stayed in Paradise."

"And you should stop judging everyone but yourself." She didn't have to mention Brother Eye directly to remind them of the consequences of Batman's suspicious nature. It was because he no longer trusted any other hero that the OMACs were now hunting meta-humans throughout the globe. "You've lost your way."

Diana had a point, but Superman wasn't about to let her push her own distorted perspective. "And you've lost yours," he told her. "You're trying to help people you can't even relate to."

"And you relate to them too much," Batman said, surprising Superman with his tone. "You're not human. You're Superman."

"I know that." He was taken aback. *When did this become about me?*

"Then start acting like it," Batman said. "All hell has broken loose and you're on the Moon with me?" He glanced at the bright blue orb above them, now visible through the sundered ceiling. "The world needs you."

"Telling people what to do?" Superman asked. Is that what Bruce wanted from him? *He doesn't understand my position,* Superman thought, *the responsibility of using my powers wisely.* "I'm not a god. And I'm not like you, Bruce. I don't need to control everything."

Batman stalked toward him, getting right up in his face. "You know better than that. After all these years, you know it's not about control. It's about trying to do everything I can, everything that I'm capable of." His eyes were blank white slits. "And for you, it's about setting an example. Everyone looks up to you. They listen to you. If you tell them to fight, they'll fight. But they need to be inspired. And let's face it, *Superman,* the last time you really inspired anyone was when you were dead."

Batman's words were like a slap against Superman's face. He had no idea what to say in reply. *Is that what Bruce really thinks of me these days?* He looked to Diana, perhaps hoping that she would come to his defense despite everything. He had always been able to rely on her—and Batman—even when matters were at their most hopeless.

She lowered her eyes to the floor.

Batman turned and walked away, his dark cloak trailing after him. "We're finished here."

"Yes," Wonder Woman agreed. She set off in the opposite direction. "I guess we are."

They left him standing alone amidst the shattered wreckage of a dream.

CHAPTER 9

Outside reality, the four forgotten ones watched multiple tragedies unfold upon the crystalline matrix before them. The Spectre loomed over Gotham. The OMACs massed for their next attack. The Watchtower collapsed into ruin. And Uncle Sam and his Freedom Fighters fell before the collective might of the Secret Society.

"You see," a red-haired man declared, breaking his long silence. A suit of futuristic golden armor encased his form. "Even the spirit of their 'great' country cannot endure the evil that has infected this Earth. It is a simple fact."

A teenage boy stood before the matrix. His wide blue eyes took in the atrocities on the multifaceted crystal wall. "And we could have saved them! We should have, right?"

The old woman chose to focus on the heroic figure of Superman as he flew back to Earth from the Moon. "He may still . . ." she said hopefully.

"How can you believe that?" the red-haired man asked. He pointed at a recorded image of Superman, Batman, and Wonder Woman squabbling within the remains of the Watchtower. "Even their three greatest hopes cannot work together."

"But *we* can, right?" the boy said eagerly. A cape draped his shoulders. "We can do this."

"Yes," the redhead insisted. "We can save everyone if we wish to." He stepped forward and quietly whispered into the ear of the fourth figure, who had not yet spoken. "We can even save *her*. I'm certain of it."

The forgotten hero was an older man whose strapping frame stood taller and straighter than those of his companions. He nodded grimly. *It has to be done,* he thought. *Doesn't it?*

"Yes, yes. You're right." He had watched this Earth for years now. Seen how it invariably corrupted legends . . . or destroyed them. Watched love and hope and goodness come to naught. He couldn't just stand by any longer. "We gave them a gift they've thrown away. We sacrificed everything for them."

And for what? So that these flawed heroes could squander their potential, letting humanity fall into darkness and despair?

No more, he resolved.

Clenching his fists, he strode decisively toward the great crystal wall before him. For uncounted years now, ever since the Crisis, the antimatter matrix had been both their refuge and their prison, cutting them off from the universe. But not for much longer. His mind was set. The time had come to end their self-imposed exile.

With strength and power far beyond those of mortal men, he slammed his fist into the unbreakable crystal wall. The translucent barrier, which was composed of combined matter and antimatter, resisted his efforts, but he refused to surrender. He threw his bare fists against the crystals over and over again. His knuckles almost split. His fingers were nearly crushed. His beloved wife gasped anxiously behind him.

I'm not giving up, he vowed. *No matter what.*

Finally, after what felt like a never-ending battle, cracks appeared in the reflective surface. Fissures split apart the distressing images from a world that all too obviously needed him. He knew he had waited long enough. He drew back his fist for one last punch. More powerful than a locomotive, the titanic blow shattered the wall into a million tiny shards. He heard the boy whoop in excitement as the barrier fell. Free at last, the forgotten hero was ready to begin again.

Up, up, and away, he soared back into the world. A brilliant red *S* shone brightly upon his chest. A flowing red cape flapped behind him.

"This looks like a job for Superman!"

CHAPTER 10

SAN DIEGO

"ELLEN, have you seen my space suit?"

The yell echoed through the suburban home of Buddy Baker. He rummaged through an attic closet, digging past old skis, snow boots, and back issues of *National Geographic*. Baseball bats, exercise equipment, photo albums, and miscellaneous other junk were spread out on the floor behind him. Buddy had always meant to organize the attic, but somehow he had never found the time. He was paying for that now.

His wife's voice called from downstairs in her studio. "Space suit?"

"You know, the one with the big gold *A* on the back!"

"Oh, that," Ellen replied. "I threw it out."

Buddy couldn't believe his ears. "What?!"

"It was leaking rocket fuel." Abandoning her easel, Ellen climbed the stairs to the attic. Their children, Cliff and Maxine, stood a few yards behind Buddy, watching their father's futile search. The part-time super hero wore a black leather jacket over his bright orange uniform. Tousled blond hair was swept back above his blue goggles, which matched the stylized blue *A* on his chest. A silver transit sphere hovered in the air outside the closet.

Animal Man turned to look at his wife. "But that suit was a gift from Adam Strange."

"So?" Ellen didn't look too concerned about the missing space suit. The auburn-haired illustrator had long ago adjusted to her husband's unusual activities. "You said they were taking you out there in a ship."

"What if I run into him?" Buddy asked. He didn't want any awkward moments if he bumped into Adam at the center of the universe.

Ellen had another issue on her mind. "Why are you even going, Buddy?"

He could tell from her tone that his upcoming expedition had her worried. He couldn't blame her. The Polaris system was a long way from San Diego.

"My connection with the animal world has been on and off lately," he explained. "Now it's just plain weird. Every bird in the sky is flying north. Every fish in the bay is swimming away from shore. And every time I absorb a nearby animal's powers, the warning instincts take over." He shook his head. Even now, when he wasn't even trying to use his special abilities, he could feel an undercurrent of fear throbbing beneath the morphogenetic field that connected all living things. "I tried to borrow some speed from a rabbit yesterday, and I ended up thumping my foot against the ground for an hour." He didn't want to scare Ellen, but he felt he owed her the truth. "Every creature on this planet wants off. I need to find out why."

As Obi-Wan might say, he sensed a great disturbance in the Force. Donna Troy's space expedition sounded like his best bet for getting some answers. *The truth is out there,* he thought. *Maybe.*

"Daddy?"

Maxine stepped toward him. The eight-year-old's face was serious.

"Yes, honey?"

She held out a brown paper lunch bag. "I made you a special lunch for your trip." She nodded at her older brother. "Cliff helped."

"Kinda," his son mumbled. Thirteen years old, he was at an age where anything remotely mushy was considered uncool. His hands were thrust into his pockets. A backward baseball cap rested on his head.

"It's peanut butter and bananas," Maxine said. "Like the monkeys like."

His daughter shared his fascination with animals. "You're my little monkey," he told her as he knelt down to give her an affectionate smile. He gratefully accepted the lunch bag. ANIMAL MAN was written in crayon on the side of the bag. So that Firestorm or Air Wave didn't eat it by mistake?

He felt his throat tighten. He loved his family. The last thing he wanted to do was go trekking off to space without them. Unfortunately, he didn't have any choice.

Animal Man was needed.

THE silver sphere transported him through space at warp speed. He found himself inside a glowing scarlet cavity that seemed infinitely bigger on the inside than it did from the outside. Buddy started to have second thoughts about this whole thing. *I'm not sure how much more of this I can take.*

Then, all at once, the trip was over. There was a flash of blinding light, and he suddenly landed on his butt on a hard stone floor. His head was spinning, and his stomach felt like it had been turned inside-out. A gagging noise, like a cat spitting up a hairball, escaped his throat. He started to rise, but a sudden wave of dizziness caused him to sit right back down again. "Whoa," he muttered to anyone who might be listening. "I feel like road kill."

"Tell me about it," a friendly voice said. A metallic hand reached down to help him up. "Trips in those orbs are real fun. I was puking up oil for ten minutes the first time." Cyborg made sure Buddy could stand on his own before letting go of his hand. "Good to have you aboard, Animal Man."

Vic Stone was a muscular African-American youth, a few years younger than Buddy. Much of his anatomy, including half his face and all four limbs, had been replaced by chrome-colored molybdenum prosthetics. Concealed servomotors hummed softly within his arms and legs. A blinking red sensor glowed where his left eye should have been.

"Nice to be here, Cyborg." Buddy lifted his head to look around. "Wherever here is."

His surreal surroundings caused his eyes to bug out behind his goggles. He found himself standing in the middle of what looked like Mount Olympus as designed by M.C. Escher. Marble temples and palaces, adorned with classical Greek sculptures, filled out the interior of a carved out moon. Elegant friezes, fountains, and Doric columns rose proudly at impossible angles to each other. "Up" and "down" appeared to be very flexible concepts that depended entirely on where you happened to be located within the disorienting structure. The overall effect was distinctly unsettling—and the very last thing he needed after his turbulent trip within the travel sphere. *I hope I don't throw up,* he thought.

It would be like vomiting on the Parthenon.

Instead of a sky, the blackness of outer space could be seen beyond the majestic spires and columns. Stars glittered in the celestial firmament. An invisible force field apparently protected the citadel and its inhabitants from the vacuum. From a distance, Buddy guessed, this space station, or whatever it was, probably resembled a crescent moon, with the elaborate structure occupying the empty space between the points of its horns.

"Donna calls it New Cronus," Cyborg said. "The Titans of Myth built it before they fled this universe. It's an endless labyrinth, combining fifth-dimensional tesseract technology and quantum processors so advanced they make me feel like a wind-up toy. Donna basically inherited it from the Titans."

Tesseract tech? Buddy had only the faintest idea what Cyborg was talking about. "I'm not exactly Mr. Science," he confessed. "I'm more of a nature lover."

"Don't sweat it," Cyborg assured him. He led Buddy away from the tiled landing pad. They walked down a lengthy colonnade toward the center of New Cronus. "The important thing is that it will get us where we need to go."

"Which is where?" Buddy asked. He couldn't help gaping at the gravity-defying architecture all around him. Too bad he hadn't brought a camera to take some pictures for Ellen and the kids. Maybe Cyborg could take a few snapshots with his bionic eye?

"To the center of the universe, Animal Man," a feminine voice answered him. Walking to the edge of an open courtyard, he peered over the brink to see Troia poised at a ninety-degree angle directly below him. She stood upon a floating pedestal engraved with the faces of the original, mythological Titans. A holographic control panel flickered in front of her. Her graceful fingers danced over the controls. "The *new* center, that is. It's changed."

Buddy didn't like the sound of that. "What do you mean, 'changed?' "

"The ship's navigational units are recalibrating in response to some kind of disturbance that seems to have shifted the very center of the cosmos," an electronic-sounding voice explained. Buddy saw that Red Tornado stood atop a fluted column overlooking Donna's pedestal. His android body turned toward Buddy. His blue cape seemed to recognize "down" as directly below him. "We do not know the nature of the disturbance yet, or what it means."

Glancing around, Buddy realized that they were far from alone. Donna

had assembled an impressive collection of meta-human heroes, who now occupied various balconies and porticos, or else flew through the empty spaces
between the imposing marble buildings. He quickly identified Starfire, Air
Wave, Supergirl, Firestorm, and various others. Reaching out with his senses,
he probed New Cronus for animal life, but detected nothing in the vicinity.
Aside from a few scattered gardens and shrubs, Troia and the other heroes
were the only lifeforms aboard the vast space station. He wondered what kind
of criteria Donna had used to select her team. *Where exactly do I fit into this
equation?*

"I hear them dying!" Air Wave suddenly blurted. A pair of golden antennae rose from the young man's blue cowl. Buddy didn't know Air Wave well,
but he was aware that the hero was some sort of human radio receiver. Air
Wave dropped to his knees and clapped his hands over his ears. "Thousands
of alien signals, pleading for help, caught in some kind of cosmic storm. . . ."
His voice held an edge of desperation. "They . . . they're screaming. God,
they're getting louder!"

A strange-looking being, who appeared to be partially made of vapor,
drifted over to where Air Wave was sitting. At first Buddy thought it was
Metamorpho the Element Man, then he realized it had to be Shift, an adolescent "clone" of Metamorpho who had grown spontaneously from a severed
fragment of the original Element Man. Like Rex Mason, Shift was composed
of an ever-changing array of inorganic substances. Multicolored splotches and
streaks mottled his gray pseudoflesh, so that he looked like a floating chem-
istry set.

"Hey," he volunteered. "Maybe I should turn myself into some nitrous
oxide and float through the kid's lungs. Might calm that radio brain of his
down."

Alan Scott and Jade stood next to Air Wave, trying to comfort him. "I don't
know if Air Wave can handle this, Dad," Jade said, sounding worried. The
female Green Lantern had chartreuse skin and emerald hair. "Those distress
calls he's picking up are getting stronger."

"He insisted on coming, Jenny," Alan Scott reminded her. Earth's first
Green Lantern, he looked in remarkably good shape despite having fought the
good fight for over sixty years. Only his weathered features and the strands of
silver in his blond hair hinted at his true age. His uniform had always confused
Buddy, though. Why would a Green Lantern be dressed in red and purple?

"D-don't worry about me," Air Wave insisted, pulling himself together. He rose to his feet, albeit a bit shakily. It was obvious that he was still under a great deal of strain. The bottom half of his face, which was exposed by his cowl, was pale and drawn. His hands trembled noticeably. "Thanks anyway," he told Shift.

Buddy wasn't surprised that Air Wave declined the shape-shifter's offer. *Inhaling* another hero would be just too weird, even for him. *Says the guy who becomes one with geckos and platypuses,* he thought wryly.

Firestorm soared through the open air. Nuclear flames blazed brightly atop the hero's head. Buddy recognized the red-and-yellow uniform, but not the young black face beneath the dancing flames. *This is a* new *Firestorm,* he reminded himself, even as he noted that the flying hero appeared to be talking to himself.

"Will you shut up about Starfire!" he said indignantly, as though to an invisible companion. "Of course she's hot, but this is serious, Mick! No, I am not staring at her."

Mick? Animal Man wondered. *Who's Mick?*

Buddy wasn't the only person to notice Firestorm's bizarre monologue; Supergirl flew over to join the pyrotechnic teenager. "Who are you talking to?" she asked.

"Me?" He stammered in embarrassment. "Er, um . . . no one."

Buddy was amused by Firestorm's awkwardness around Supergirl. With all these new kids around, he was starting to feel like a chaperone at a high school prom. *I'm probably the oldest person here,* he realized. *Next to Alan Scott, of course.*

"Hmm," Supergirl said, sounding not entirely convinced by Firestorm's denial. Buddy wondered if she knew the effect her striking good looks had on the young man. "Well, sometimes I talk to myself when I'm nervous. Mostly in Kryptonese." Tilting her head back, she looked up at the stars. Somewhere out there, a deadly cosmic disturbance waited for them all. "Did you know that there's no word for 'escape' in my language?"

A chill ran down Buddy's spine. *Maybe that's why there are so few Krypto-nians left.*

CHAPTER 11

NEW YORK CITY

Power Girl returned to her apartment to find that she had accidentally locked herself out again. She didn't feel like searching for the superintendent, so she did what she always did. Taking hold of the doorknob, she ripped the entire locking mechanism out of the door. Metal crunched beneath her super-strong grip.

"Man," she muttered, "I gotta get an extra set of keys."

She kicked the door open with her foot and entered her cramped one-bedroom apartment. Thunder boomed outside the building; there was a nasty electrical storm going on. Even though it was early morning, ominous red clouds blocked out the sun.

Karen Starr shut the door behind her. *Home sweet home,* she thought, tossing the mangled doorknob into a wastebasket that already held a half dozen identical knobs. She couldn't stay long. What with both the OMACs and the Secret Society on the warpath, every hero on the planet was working overtime. Power Girl just wanted to feed her cat, take a quick shower, and change into a fresh uniform before heading back out into the fray. *These days you have to make the most of every break in the action.*

A day's worth of mail was scattered on the floor, just below a slot in the door. Karen sorted through the envelopes and flyers. Junk mail mostly, much of it addressed to Occupant. *Figures,* she thought irritably. The impersonal correspondence wasn't helping her ongoing identity crisis any.

She stepped into the itsy-bitsy bathroom. The mirror above the sink reflected a busty young woman with light blond hair, a tight white leotard, and a short red cape. A large cutout in the front of her costume exposed an eye-catching expanse of cleavage. Tired blue eyes stared back at her. *Who are you?* Karen silently asked the woman in the mirror, as she did almost every day. *Where did you come from?*

Power Girl was a heroine without an origin. Or rather, she had too many origins. At various points in her career, ever since she had first emerged from a crashed spaceship several years back, she had believed herself to be:

1) Superman's cousin from the planet Krypton,

2) the granddaughter of an ancient Atlantean sorcerer,

3) a time-lost Legionnaire from the thirty-first century.

And those were only the more plausible explanations for her existence. Over time, each and every one of her alleged origins had proven false, while her own memories remained confused and contradictory. As a result, she had no idea who she really was. Even her civilian identity as Karen Starr was just a convenient fiction that the Justice Society had set up to make her life easier. Most of her friends called her Kara, a name left over from her brief stint as Superman's "cousin," before the *real* Kara Zor-El showed up to claim that title. *Thank God I never called myself Supergirl,* she thought. *That would have been just too* humiliating.

But the question remained: Who the hell was Power Girl anyway?

A friendly meow provided a welcome distraction from her brooding. A small orange tabby rubbed itself against her leg. "Hey there!" she greeted her cat. Like her, Sophie was a stray of indeterminate origin. "At least I've got you, right?" Lifting the tabby from the floor, she gave the cat a hug. "You been a good kitty?"

"Sure have," a gruff voice surprised her. She turned around to see Wildcat standing in the doorway. The scrappy ex-boxer wore a fuzzy black cat costume, complete with whiskers, that would have looked ridiculous on anyone else.

"Ted?" Like her, Wildcat belonged to the Justice Society of America, the first major super-team before the Justice League. They had fought beside each other for years. "What are you doing here?"

He leaned against the doorframe. "Thought you might need some company," he said slyly. Leering eyes zoomed in on her chest. "If you catch my drift, good-lookin'."

Huh? Power Girl thought, confused. *Is Wildcat coming on to me?* A veteran in the super-hero biz who had taught the ropes to everyone from Batman to Black Canary, Ted Grant was old enough to be her father. She had always thought of him as a feisty older uncle, nothing more.

Has he been drinking or something?

Sophie reacted angrily to the intruder. Baring her fangs, the tabby hissed at Wildcat. Karen had to hold on tightly to keep the cat from launching herself at their visitor. Sophie squirmed frantically against her chest. *What's got into her?* Karen wondered. *Hell, what's got into them both?*

"Wildcat?" she said uncertainly.

"Heh," he chortled. "Not exactly."

To her astonishment, his face and body began to melt before her eyes. Flesh and fabric swiftly devolved into a mass of amorphous brown sludge. Beady red eyes ogled her from a lumpy countenance that only vaguely resembled a human face. A pair of flaring nostrils took the place of a nose. The mouth was merely an open gash filled with rocklike teeth. Power Girl recognized the inhuman visage from the Justice Society's files.

"Clayface!"

The slimy monstrosity was one of Batman's most freakish foes, but what was he doing here? She let go of Sophie, allowing the terrified cat to dash for safety.

"Bingo, sweetheart!" His phlegmy voice sounded like he was gargling mucus. He came at her like a malignant mudslide. Caught by surprise, she was carried along by the loathsome wave of muck, which smashed through the wall of her sixth-floor apartment and out into the open air. The pliable clay enveloped her. A gooey tongue slimed her face.

"You're paying for that, Clayface!" she promised, thrashing about in the filthy mire. Never the most even-tempered heroine, she was getting pissed off in a big way.

"Bill the Secret Society!" the villain gurgled. He spilled down toward the street like the world's most polluted waterfall, taking Power Girl with him. They smashed through the roof of a Subaru parked below. The unlucky car crumpled inward, nearly splitting in two. Unharmed by the plunge, Clayface oozed out of the vehicle through the shattered back window.

Power Girl was right behind him. She punched her way free of the mangled metal and rose angrily to her feet. Traces of the mucky villain still clung to her skin and costume. *Ick!* she thought, wiping her face off with her cape. "Was that supposed to kill me," she challenged her foe, "or just gross me out?"

"Don't worry yourself too much," another voice informed her. Blinking the last of the clay away from her eyes, she looked up to see the Psycho-Pirate standing atop a ledge overlooking the sidewalk. Unlike hers, his garish red costume and cloak were perfectly clean. "Luthor needs you alive."

Karen averted her eyes from the villain's hypnotic golden mask. She had clashed with this brainwashing bad guy before. He was a first-class nutcase, but he could really mess with your head if you gave him a half a chance.

"But that don't mean we can't dirty you up first!" a gravelly voice added.

She spun around to find herself confronted by Clayface and three more villains. Clenching her fists, she took stock of her foes.

The grating voice belonged to a burly figure who appeared to be entirely composed of scrap metal. Thick steel cables, bolts, beams, and plates were welded together to approximate bulging muscles and a beefy torso. Rusty metal shavings formed the creature's bushy beard and scalp.

Girder, she recognized. One of the Flash's enemies.

Beside the former steelworker was another kind of metal man; Mister Atom was a renegade robot with a bullet-shaped head and a polished steel casing. An atomic generator hummed somewhere beneath his armored chest plate. His well-oiled mechanisms whirred smoothly, unlike Girder, who clanked loudly as he advanced toward her, flanked by both Clayface and Mister Atom.

Last but definitely not least was, no kidding, a sixty-foot-tall redhead in a leopard-skin bikini. Giganta, one of Wonder Woman's perennial foes, stood as tall as the skyscrapers lining both sides of the avenue. The entire block trembled beneath her elephantine tread. An immense shadow fell over the entire neighborhood. *And people think I have a big chest,* Power Girl thought.

"Bring it on!" she dared the gang of villains. Although outnumbered five to one, she was more incensed than intimidated. *All I wanted was five minutes to take a shower!*

Her temper flared. So did her eyes. A sizzling blast of heat vision baked Clayface's arm. Steam rose from the seared limb as it cracked and crumbled to pieces. The glutinous monster sloshed backward, yowling in dismay.

Mister Atom zoomed at her like a guided missile. Power Girl met the attack head-on. A super-powered punch sent the killer robot flying into the stoop of a nearby brownstone. Concrete exploded on impact. Bricks rained down on the robot's torpedo-shaped head. Karen smiled in satisfaction, but knew that Mister Atom, who regularly fought Captain Marvel, wasn't likely to be defeated by a single blow.

A colossal fist suddenly closed around her. "I have her!" Giganta boomed, grabbing Power Girl from behind. Lifting Karen from the ground, she squeezed the trapped heroine with the crushing force of a hydraulic press. Power Girl struggled to free herself, but Giganta was even stronger than she looked. Karen suddenly felt like she was starring in a cheesy girl-on-girl version of *King Kong*.

With her free hand, Giganta placed Girder upon her shoulder. He crawled mechanically down her arm toward Power Girl. Nasty-looking studs and screws protruded from his upraised fists. Brutal anticipation showed on his riveted metal face. His breath smelled of crude oil. "You absolutely sure this cupcake needs to be in one piece?"

He was only a few feet away from her when, overhead, the stormy red clouds parted. A ray of yellow sunshine shone through, followed by the sound of something whooshing down from the sky. Faster than a speeding bullet, a blue-and-red blur zipped into sight, creating a sonic boom in its wake. A sudden wind whipped up the litter and dust that coated the street below.

The blur connected with Giganta's chin, knocking her head to the side. Stunned, the giantess let go of Power Girl, who gladly flew away from the jumbo-sized fist. Unable to fly, Girder fell four stories to the pavement, landing headfirst with an enormous clang. He wouldn't be getting up anytime soon.

What in the world? Karen thought, baffled. The rocketing figure was moving too fast to see clearly. *Who?*

Before she even knew what was happening, the blur tore through Mister Atom, instantly reducing the deadly robot to nuts and bolts. For a second, she worried about the machine's built-in atomic reactor, but a swiftly-moving hand snatched the potential WMD out of the air and hurled it into the sky fast enough to achieve escape velocity. At the rate the reactor was going, it would be clear of Earth's atmosphere almost instantly.

Knocked out cold by the blow to her chin, Giganta toppled toward the street like a felled redwood. She crashed face-first onto the asphalt, crushing over a dozen parked vehicles and Girder as well. The seismic tremor could be felt all across the city. Thank goodness all pedestrians had already fled the vicinity, probably when they first saw Giganta coming. It would be hard to miss her. . . .

Up on his ledge, the Psycho-Pirate gasped in fear. "He's here!"

I almost forgot about that creep, Power Girl realized. She started to dive toward him, only to see him fade away into nothingness. *Teleportation,* she wondered, *or some sort of bad guy mind trick?* She directed a burst of heat vision at the space above the ledge, but the twin beams scorched only the facade of her apartment building. The Psycho-Pirate seemed to have well and truly vanished.

Power Girl shrugged her shoulders. She'd get that cowardly weasel another day. Right now, she was more interested in finding out who or what had come to her rescue.

"Hello there." The zooming figure slowed to a halt, hovering in the air only a few yards above her. His voice sounded strangely familiar. A bright red *S* stood out upon his chest. A friendly face smiled down at her. "It's been a long time, cousin. Too long."

She looked up in surprise.

Superman?

THE DAILY PLANET, METROPOLIS

AT that very moment, hundreds of miles away, the newsroom of the *Daily Planet* was abuzz with activity. Emergency bulletins from all around the world were coming into the newspaper's offices almost faster than the overworked staff could keep up with. The hubbub of numerous overlapping conversations competed with the sound of rapid-fire typing coming from a dozen different cubicles. Other staffers hustled through the hallways between the cubicles, running copy and art from station to station. A television set, turned to a twenty-four-hour news channel, was mounted high upon the wall at one end of the bullpen. A handful of worried reporters and interns took time out to catch up with the news. The volume on the television set had been turned down low, but closed-captioning allowed the viewers to follow the story:

". . . the charred remains of Doctor Polaris were found at the scene. The longtime adversary of Green Lantern was apparently blown to pieces by an explosion at the abandoned refinery. Investigators have not yet commented on the cause of the explosion. . . ."

Lois Lane kept one eye on the television screen as she spoke on the phone to her mother-in-law in Kansas. The dark-haired reporter wore a stylish yellow pantsuit. At the moment, as Lois sat in her cubicle amidst the usual organized chaos of the newsroom, Smallville seemed very far away.

"I know Conner needs him, Martha," she said. "But he's being pulled in a hundred different directions." She lowered her voice so she wouldn't be overheard. "Yes, just like everyone else with a cape."

"Lois!" a boisterous voice called out. Perry White stormed out his office, clutching a rolled-up telex in his hand. He charged toward his star reporter's cubicle, which was conveniently within shouting distance. "Lois Lane-Kent!"

"I've got to go, Ma," she apologized. She rose from her desk to meet Perry, unintimidated by her editor's vociferous bluster. She had known him too long for that. "You want a hundred words a minute, Perry, you're going to have to leave me alone for one."

"Can't." Huffing and puffing, he came to a halt beside her desk. His vest was open to his waist and his collar was undone. His brown crew cut was gray at the temples. Lois could tell from his genuinely irate expression that this wasn't just about deadlines. "They just found the bodies of Black Condor, Phantom Lady, and the Human Bomb strung up on the Washington Monument. Damage is in critical condition at Metropolis General. And the Ray and Uncle Sam are missing." He clenched his fist, crumpling the telex in righteous indignation. "These were genuine American heroes, killed and put on display on our own damn soil!"

A shock went through Lois' system. She felt physically ill. Any super hero's death hit her hard, and not just for professional reasons. *Does Clark know?* She hoped that she wouldn't be the one who told him.

"Who did it, Chief?" Jimmy Olsen asked. The red-headed junior reporter hurried over from his own desk, as did several other staffers. Jim's freckled face had gone pale.

"Pentagon's blaming this new Super-Villain Society." Perry glowered up at the TV screen, which was now reporting on the tragedy, live from the Mall in Washington. Shocking footage of the dead heroes being lowered from the monument brought the entire newsroom to a standstill. Perry spoke for them all when he declared, "This is war."

A crowd formed below the TV monitor. With all eyes on the screen, Lois quietly slipped away to look for her husband. "Clark?" she asked softly as she approached his cubicle. "You heard that, right?" On a good day, Clark could hear the proverbial tree fall in the forest a thousand miles away. Finding his desk unattended, she hoped that he hadn't already been called away again. "Clark?"

She found him in the hall outside the newsroom. Framed copies of some of the *Planet*'s most historic front pages were mounted on the walls. "COAST CITY DESTROYED" screamed one tragic front page. "GLOBAL CRISIS!" announced another. Lois found these mementoes of past catastrophes oddly reassuring. If nothing else, they reminded her that both Metropolis and the Earth had come through hard times before. This time wouldn't be any different.

Would it?

Clark stood silently at the end of the hall, in front of her least favorite headline. "SUPERMAN DEAD" read the large block letters, above a heartbreaking photo of his battered body lying lifeless amidst the rubble left behind by his epic battle with Doomsday. Lois winced at the gruesome picture. Even though Superman had eventually been restored to them, thanks to his unique Kryptonian physiology, she still couldn't look at that photo without remembering just how lost she had felt without him. She never wanted to go through that again.

"Clark?"

"Bruce is right, Lois." He gazed at the coverage of his own death with a rueful expression. "He's always right."

Bruce? She wondered what Batman had to do with this. From what she had heard, the Dark Knight had a lot to answer for himself. But now wasn't the time to debate Batman's opinion. "The Society?" she prompted.

"I heard." He cocked his head to one side, obviously listening to something beyond the range of her mere mortal ears. Sighing, he turned toward her. "I want to stay and talk, but there's some kind of meteor shower in El Paso. . . ."

He didn't have to say anything more. She knew the drill by now. Leaning forward, she kissed him gently on the lips, to let him know that she would be waiting for him when he returned, just like always. Sometimes, moments like this were all they had.

You've got nobody to blame but yourself, Lois, she thought. *That's what you get for marrying the world's greatest hero.*

He kissed her back, then reluctantly pulled away. A quick glance up and down the hallway assured him that nobody else was looking. Shifting into super-speed mode, he removed his glasses and shed his civilian disguise. From Lois' perspective, mild-mannered Clark Kent instantly transformed into Superman.

Lois' heart sped up. Even after all these years, he still took her breath away.

"See you soon," he promised. "First, though, it's time for action."

A sudden wind blew Lois' dark hair back as the Man of Steel zoomed down the corridor and away.

She couldn't help glancing back at the ugly headline on the wall.

Be careful, she thought. *These are dangerous times.*

Even for Superman.

CHAPTER 12

AN UNDISCLOSED LOCATION

THE man who called himself Lex Luthor faced a wall of computer monitors as he conducted a teleconference with a number of his chief allies. The faces of Deathstroke, Dr. Psycho, the Calculator, and the Psycho-Pirate filled the screens in front of him. As the leader of the Secret Society of Super-Villains, he depended on his allies to keep him informed on the progress of their various initiatives. He didn't like surprises.

The bald-headed mastermind, who was currently wearing a tailored gray business suit, had one of the most recognizable faces on the planet. Lex Luthor had been a billionaire tycoon, and even the President of the United States, before being brought down by Superman. Now he was number one on the majority of the world's most-wanted lists.

"*Someone* helped Power Girl escape," the Psycho-Pirate reported anxiously, placing an emphasis on the "someone." Luthor suspected that the masked empath knew exactly who had come to Power Girl's rescue, but was reluctant to divulge that information with Deathstroke and the others listening. He appreciated the Psycho-Pirate's discretion. Despite their common interests, Luthor had no intention of sharing all his secrets with the rest of the Society. There were cabals within cabals here. Schemes within schemes. . . .

"Calm your nerves, Psycho-Pirate," he said. Power Girl's escape was a setback, but not an insurmountable one. One way or another, Kara would play her part in his grand design. "There is a contingency plan in place."

"Is that so?" Deathstroke, transmitting from the Society's base in Gotham City, sounded suspicious. A Kevlar hood concealed his face. He methodically polished his sword as he spoke over the monitor. "If there is another plan, Luthor, we're not aware of it."

"Slade's right," the Calculator chimed in. Unlike some of their more colorful associates, Noah Kuttler looked like an ordinary middle-aged accountant. A casual observer would never guess that he was actually the most reliable information broker in the criminal community. He peered at Luthor through a pair of wire-frame glasses. "What are you—"

"Focus on what I've asked you to do, Calculator," Luthor said curtly. He knew he wouldn't be able to fend off Deathstroke's inquiries for long—Slade was no fool—but right now he had better things to do than allay the hit man's suspicions. "Leave Power Girl to me."

The Calculator was smart enough not to press the issue. "Of course. You've wanted me to track these OMACs and find out what's controlling them. I've got everyone on it."

Deathstroke also let the matter drop . . . for now. "Abra Kadabra lost Captain Marvel's trail in Gotham," he reported. "He says the magic debris is messing with his wand."

"That mustache twirler is about as useful as a sponge in the desert," Dr. Psycho cracked, squeezing his ugly face into the frame alongside Deathstroke. The obnoxious midget tried to take over the briefing from the assassin. "Dr. Sivana and the Fearsome Five haven't had any luck snatching Captain Marvel Junior either."

Deathstroke elbowed Dr. Psycho out of the way. "But we're covered. Black Adam's ready to go after Mary Marvel as soon as Chain Lightning and Goth track her down."

Luthor shrugged. "You can all stop looking for the world's mightiest mortals."

"But you said that you needed a member of the Marvel Family for this mind-wiping machine of yours," Slade reminded him.

As far as the rest of the Society was concerned, their ultimate objective was to construct a machine that would erase the memories of every hero on Earth, in retaliation for the Justice League's mind-wiping experiments a few years back. The recent revelations concerning that disturbing episode had been the primary impetus for the Society's formation. All but the most stubborn and independent villains had banded together to keep the League and its associates from ever messing with their minds again. Luthor was more than willing to let his supposed partners *think* that was what he had in mind.

His true objective was known only to a select few.

A caped figure entered the chamber behind Luthor. The newcomer took care to stay in the shadows, out of view of the webcam. Luthor noted his arrival, but kept on speaking as though he were alone.

"I do, Deathstroke," Luthor admitted. "But we're running out of time, so let's make this easy." He smiled at his own ingenuity. "Contact the upper echelon. Bring me Black Adam."

THE ARCTIC

THE frozen wasteland stretched for as far as the eye could see. The blinding sunlight was reflected by miles of unbroken snow and ice. Jagged white ridges rose in the horizon. Gaping crevasses split the wintry terrain. A downed jet rested silently atop the ice.

A solitary figure marched away from the plane. Heavy steel boots crunched through the snow. A bulky suit of high-tech armor, covered by a green and purple enamel overlay, stood out against the stark white emptiness. Internal heating units kept the suit's occupant warm, and a raised steel collar projected an invisible force field that shielded the man's face from the bitter cold and wind. The custom-made warsuit was the best that money could buy, a triumph of state-of-the-art manufacturing, incorporating exclusive LexCorp designs, as well as black-market alien technology. He was going to need every advantage he could get to survive this desolate environment long enough to find his enemy.

I'm a long way from Metropolis, the real Lex Luthor thought. The vast glacial expanse stretched before him like the ninth circle of Hell. His breath misted the force field in front of his mouth. Despite the ice and snow all around him, he was seething on the inside. *Nobody poses as me and gets away with it!*

The fugitive ex-president had been aware for some time now that an imposter claiming to be him was behind the Secret Society of Super-Villains. Lex had been spying on the pretender for weeks but, despite his best efforts, he had yet to discover the true identity of this other "Lex Luthor." He hoped to remedy that situation soon, even if it meant trekking all the way to the North Pole.

". . . Black Adam's arrogance—*kzzzt*—an untrustworthy ally at best—*kzzzt*—pay for looking down at the rest of us—*kzzzt*—Luthor out."

Broken up by static, the imposter's voice emerged from a speaker built into the real Lex's gauntlet. After far too much effort, he had finally succeeded in tapping into the Society's transmissions. Stealing the jet, he had followed the false Luthor's signal north until his fuel had run out and he'd been forced to make an emergency landing upon the ice. There had been a few dicey moments while touching down, but he couldn't complain. According to his readings, the source of the imposter's transmissions was only a few miles away.

Lex scowled as he listened to the pretender sign off. "No," he snarled under his breath. "You are *not* Lex Luthor. I am Luthor and I . . . I . . ."

His words trailed off as an all-too-familiar fog descended over his thoughts. Despite the anger burning at his core, his brain felt groggy, jet-lagged. He reached up to massage his forehead, trying unsuccessfully to clear his mind. It felt as though the further north he traveled, the harder it became to concentrate.

"What is wrong with me?" he asked out loud. Frustration gnawed at him. His keen intellect had always been his greatest strength, as well as his foremost weapon against the likes of Superman. He struggled to regain his focus. "Why can't I . . . think?"

He came to a halt amidst the arctic wastes. For a moment, despair gripped him. How in the world had he come to this? He had spent his life going from rags to riches, ruthlessly acquiring wealth and power by any means available, so how had he ended up trudging through the middle of nowhere, barely able to string two thoughts together? No one had stood in his way, not even that wretched Kryptonian. Why, only months ago he had been the President of the United States, the most powerful man in the world. Now he was a wanted fugitive, alone in the wilderness, while an usurper rose to power in his name.

Intolerable! he raged silently. Acid churned within his gut. He shook his armored fist at the sky. *Lex Luthor cannot be brought low like this!*

Then, just as it seemed that he had hit rock bottom, two brightly-colored figures streaked by overhead. Although they were thousands of feet above

him, Lex had spent too many hours studying long-distance surveillance photos of his archenemy not to recognize the distant blurs as they zoomed through
the sky.

Superman, he realized, *and one of his meta-human allies. Captain Marvel perhaps, or maybe that new Supergirl. . . .*

They were flying north, toward the source of the other Luthor's signals.

The gang's all here, he thought bitterly. A flare of resentment temporarily
burned away the fog clouding his thoughts. Hatred gave him the strength to
keep on going. *All my enemies are converging at the top of the world.*

He stamped through the snow with renewed fervor. Fate had conspired
against him, but he was not defeated yet. The entire world would pay for opposing him.

There will be a reckoning.

CHAPTER 13

OVER THE ARCTIC

Power Girl soared above the ice, alongside the mysterious stranger who had come to her aid not long before. They had left New York City far behind them, after turning Clayface and the other defeated Society members over to the authorities. Several large cranes had been required to transport Giganta to a plus-sized holding cell, at least until she could be forced to shrink back down to more human proportions. But Kara was confident that, except for the Psycho-Pirate, the villains were on ice for the time being.

Now she just had to figure out why Luthor had sent them after her in the first place, and who exactly had rescued her. She looked over at the heroic figure flying beside her.

"Who are you?"

"I'm Superman," he said confidently.

That's what she had thought at first. Upon closer inspection, however, she saw now that the man on her right looked significantly older than the real Superman. Although his powers appeared undiminished by age, his short black hair had gone gray at the temples. Wrinkles creased his face and hands. "You're not the Superman I know," she insisted.

"Not yet," he said with a cryptic smile.

Vast glaciers stretched beneath them. Up ahead, a deep crevasse divided a snow-covered plain. The older Superman dived toward the crevasse.

"Where are we going?" Power Girl asked.

"To get you some answers," he replied.

They descended to the bottom of the gaping chasm. Touching down on the snow, he led her toward what appeared to be a sizable ice cavern carved into the face of a towering wall of ice. Jagged icicles hung from the mouth of the cavern, but they posed little threat to the invulnerable pair. The frigid temperature had no effect on Power Girl, despite her bare legs and lightweight costume. Sunlight lit up the cave entrance.

Two strangers met them just inside the cavern.

"Look! It is her!" shouted a teenage boy in a Superman costume. He looked a little bit like Conner Kent, or what Clark might have looked like as a teenager. He was obviously excited to see her. "It's really Kara!"

Next to him was a slender young man in a metallic golden suit. A few years older than the exuberant teen, he had short red hair and a more detached expression. A blinking mechanical globe floated in the air over his left shoulder, offering a full view of the earth. His gloved hands operated a holographic display panel directly in front of him.

"This is Superboy," the gray-haired Superman said, introducing Kara to the youth in the matching costume. As far as she knew, she had never met him before.

"Actually, you can call me Superboy-Prime," the teen said. In his enthusiasm, he lifted off from the floor, so that he looked down at Power Girl from about three feet in the air. *Guess that costume's not just for show,* she thought.

"Uh . . . hi," she said uncertainly, baffled by this entire situation. *Maybe this is some sort of time-travel thing,* she speculated. Could the older Superman be from the future? And the kid from the past?

Stranger things had happened.

"Wow, I . . ." Superboy-Prime was practically speechless. "It's been so long that . . . just wow!"

Superman turned toward the man in the golden armor. "And Alexander Luthor."

What? Power Girl started at the infamous name. "Luthor?"

"Hello, Kara," the man said calmly. He seemed amused by her startled reaction. "It is good to see you again."

She had no idea what he was talking about. The only Luthor she knew was a bald middle-aged megalomaniac.

"It's okay," Superman assured her. "This Luthor is a friend. He's from a different place than the one you know."

Alexander nodded in confirmation. "And I can see that she is an aberration in this universe." He gazed at her thoughtfully. "Like us, she was never meant to survive."

"Then how did she?" Superboy-Prime asked.

"I have several theories," Alexander said. He beckoned to the levitating sphere, which flew in front of him. Crystalline spikes, not unlike the icicles hanging overhead, emerged from the globe. Holographic images of planets, stars, and nebulae orbited the sphere. "She may have literally fallen through a crack in reality as it reset itself. Or perhaps her interaction with the Anti-Monitor left her protected from the shifting timelines, or . . ."

"Or maybe she's still here because of her own will to live," the older Superman suggested, with a note of pride in his voice. "My cousin has more of that than anyone from this Earth."

"*This* Earth . . . ?" Power Girl was completely lost. They might have as well have been speaking in ancient Thanagarian. *The Anti-Monitor?* She recalled an alien monster by that name who had tried to take over the universe several years ago, but what did that have to do with her? The Anti-Monitor had been destroyed by the combined efforts of Earth's heroes.

Superman beamed at her. "Like me, you're a born survivor."

"Okay . . ." She appreciated the vote of confidence, but that didn't answer any of the questions swirling around in her brain. "Survivor of what?"

Superboy-Prime looked dismayed at her confusion. "She doesn't remember anything!"

"Reality tried to reconcile her existence," Alexander theorized, "fitting her into its revised history any way it could. It could play havoc with one's memories."

"And one's emotions," Superman guessed. He looked at her sadly, as if empathizing with her struggles to exist without an identity or a past to call her own.

"Survivor of what, Superman?" she pressed him.

He began to lead her deeper into the cavern. The icy walls gradually gave way to planes of translucent, multifaceted crystal. An unnatural luminosity radiated from the crystalline walls, providing more than enough light for even an ordinary human to see by. Alexander and Superboy-Prime tagged along behind them. Superman took a deep breath before answering her.

"Of the multiverse," he began. "The universe wasn't always this way. It was splintered at the beginning of time."

He paused before a polished crystal surface the size of a movie screen. To her surprise, images appeared upon the wall, illustrating his narration as he spoke. It was as though his very thoughts and memories were being projected onto the walls of the cavern. She watched, wide-eyed, as creation itself seemed to emerge from some sort of primordial cosmic vortex. To her amazement, the vortex arose from an open hand the size of a galaxy. Instead of flesh and blood, the celestial hand was composed of the raw materials of time and space.

"It happened billions of years ago," Superman continued. "A being from the planet Maltus gazed back into the infinite, hoping to witness the secret origin of Creation. To learn how the universe was made. To learn why it exists. And what we're here for."

Now she was watching a blue-skinned alien watching Creation on a monitor of his own. Other humanoids of the same species looked on fearfully as their brother rashly probed the distant past, all the way back to the birth of reality. Insane ambition glittered in the blue alien's eyes.

"But, as even Earth's own physicists have learned, the very act of observing a phenomenon can have a significant effect on what is being observed. The alien's blasphemous actions corrupted the innate nature of the cosmos. Instead of one universe, a multiverse was born."

Kara blinked as the Big Bang lit up the screen. The intense light made her eyes water; then it faded away almost as quickly as it had appeared. In its place, she saw a string of identical blue Earths stretched out across the cosmos like a string of pearls.

"Endless parallel realities," Superman elucidated. "Similar in some ways, bizarrely different in others. All occupying the same space, but vibrating at uniquely different frequencies."

The string of Earths vanished. A split screen depicted two identical alien planets, only moments before both worlds exploded in simultaneous cataclysms. A single small spaceship escaped each world.

"In two parallel universes, the planet Krypton exploded. And the last son of each respective world was sent to Earth."

Now the split images showed two different Supermen, each fighting a different version of Lex Luthor. One Luthor looked like a mad scientist, with frizzy red hair and a white lab coat, while the Lex Luthor she knew battled Superman in his deadly LexCorp-designed warsuit.

"On one Earth, I was that last son, *Kal-L*, and there you, Kara, were the last daughter of Krypton. While on the parallel Earth closest to ours, that last son was *Kal-El*, and his cousin was Supergirl."

The images started coming faster and faster, so that she could barely keep up with them. She briefly glimpsed two separate convocations of heroes, meeting around two different round tables.

"Time flowed somewhat faster on our Earth, where history gave birth to its own generation of heroes: The Justice *Society* of America. Some years later, relatively speaking, Kal-El's Earth saw its own heroes emerge together as the Justice *League* of America. For years, we both operated without any knowledge of the multiverse or the various parallel Earths . . . until the Flashes used their superspeed to transcend the vibrational barrier between our two worlds and met for the first time. Their League's Earth was designated Earth-One, while our Earth was christened Earth-Two. We were polite enough to let that go, even though the Society came first. Eventually, both teams met during a cosmic crisis that threatened both our realities."

Kara watched as the Martian Manhunter, Batman, Superman, Wonder Woman, Aquaman, Green Arrow, Green Lantern, Atom, and the Flash met up with Hawkman, Dr. Fate, Alan Scott, Black Canary, Hourman, and the original Atom. *I don't understand,* she thought. She knew all these heroes. They were all part of her world, although some were older than others.

"In time, we learned there were more parallel worlds. Like Earth-Three, Alexander's homeworld, where his father, Lex Luthor, was the sole hero on a planet dominated by an evil version of the Justice League. And Earth-Prime, where our Superboy was alone on a planet with no other super-powered heroes. Earth-X, where the Freedom Fighters fought a never-ending war against the Nazis. Earth-S, where Captain Marvel and his family defended humanity from the likes of Black Adam and Dr. Sivana. Earth-Four, home to Blue Beetle, Nightshade, the Question, and many other heroes and villains unique to that world. And dozens of other Earths, each with its own timeline."

Faces and places flashed by quickly on the screen, one after another. Kara recognized nearly all of them. She still didn't get this whole parallel Earths business. Hadn't Captain Marvel and Blue Beetle always coexisted with Batman and Wonder Woman and the others? Wasn't the Justice Society always the inspiration for the later Justice League?

"But as I said, the multiverse was *never* supposed to exist." Superman's voice took on a more ominous tone. "And because of its warped creation, a being called the Anti-Monitor was born, who wanted to destroy the entire multiverse and transform its power into his own native antimatter. All but five of the Earths were annihilated before the combined heroes of those worlds managed to fight back. Journeying back to the beginning of time, we fought the Anti-Monitor . . . and after an almost endless battle, he was destroyed."

Kara watched in awe as the epochal conflict played out upon the crystalline screen. Dozens of heroes, including a few she didn't recognize, joined forces to attack a towering monster encased in blue armor. The Anti-Monitor's red eyes blazed like burning suns. A skull-like visage could be glimpsed beneath his colossal helmet. His voracious maw held rows of skeletal teeth.

In the end, it was the older Superman, the one standing next to her now, who delivered the final blow that defeated the Anti-Monitor once and for all. But it seemed the crisis had taken its toll on the multiverse.

"The universe was reborn as they said it always should have been," he explained. "As one. One timeline. One Earth. One Superman." Sadness crept into his voice. "The doppelgangers of Earth-Two were negated and erased from history. Others, like Alan Scott and you, were folded into the fabric of Earth-One. Alexander Luthor, Superboy-Prime, and I survived while everyone we knew and loved perished. We were the last survivors of universes that now had never been."

He turned to look at the red-haired man behind them. "Thankfully, Alexander did something I can never repay him for. His travels across the dimensions had briefly endowed him with the ability to create doorways from one reality to another, and he acted to save my Lois from being erased from history. And he used the last of this ability to create a place for us in the reborn universe, a pocket dimension cut off from the rest of reality." He smiled gratefully at Alexander. "It was like Heaven, or at least as close as I could imagine, anyway."

Kara warily regarded the images. *Am I buying this?* The story she had just heard seemed almost too astounding to be believed. Multiple Earths? A crisis that rebooted the entire universe, from the very dawn of Creation and onward?

It sounded impossible and yet . . . something about the images on screen struck her as strangely familiar, as if she could *almost* remember them. . . .

"From our haven outside time and space, we watched this new Earth grow. The potential was there. It started off so well, so full of hope. I felt confident that Earth was in good hands."

Now the panorama on the screen started to resemble the history she knew. She watched, nodding in recognition, as the Justice League formed to carry on the heroic tradition of the Justice Society. Batman, Wonder Woman, Captain Marvel, Blue Beetle, Black Canary, Green Lantern, the Flash, and the rest all fought beside each other on the very same planet, just the way she remembered it.

"But soon after, we learned there was something inherently wrong. This new Earth was anything but better than the ones we recalled. A darkness seemed to spread, warping the heroes' lives. Some died. Others lost their way. We watched for years, hoping that everyone would find inspiration again."

A montage of images seemed to confirm his dire assessment. Kara recognized a string of ghastly moments from the history of her world: Jason Todd, the second Robin, was brutally murdered by the Joker; Superman was beaten to death by Doomsday; Bane shattered Batman's spine; Diana was briefly replaced by a more warlike Wonder Woman; Hal Jordan, the second Green Lantern, went mad and turned into a villain for a time.

And yet life went on, she protested silently, defending the world she knew. *Things got better.* Superman returned from the dead. Batman's back was healed. Diana regained her title. Hal Jordan got back his sanity. She had even heard a rumor that Jason Todd was still alive. . . . *It wasn't all death and darkness and despair.*

"But as we continued to look on," Superman lamented, "things got worse."

More recent images appeared on the wall, from just the last few weeks and days. The Elongated Man's wife was cruelly murdered. Conner Kent, fallen under Lex Luthor's control, attacked his fellow Teen Titans. The Spectre went on a rampage. Maxwell Lord shot the Blue Beetle. Wonder Woman broke Max's neck. . . .

"Even our refuge began to fall apart," Superman told her gravely. Regret showed on his weathered face. "I shouldn't have turned my back on the world. I should have tried to find a way to their Earth sooner."

"How did you get back?" she asked.

"He nearly broke his hands smashing through the barrier," Superboy-Prime blurted. "His knuckles ripped open." He seemed anxious that Kara understand the lengths they had gone to. "Superman *bled* to get us here!"

"It's all right, son," he said, laying a comforting hand upon the boy's shoulder. His soothing tone seemed to calm Superboy-Prime.

"I didn't mean to upset him," Power Girl apologized.

"Our escape was nothing short of a miracle, Kara," Alexander said softly. "Even I'll admit that."

Superman walked away from the screen, heading deeper into the cavern. "Your adopted Earth needs our help," he told Kara.

"I know," she admitted. Certainly, the world had been going to hell lately, more so than ever. Along with Alexander and Superboy-Prime, she followed after Superman. "But . . . parallel Earths? I still don't remember any of this."

"Yeah, but maybe it's better that way," Superboy-Prime suggested. He still sounded worked up, like his emotions were more than he could handle. "Being the only survivor of a reality that never existed . . ." He ran out of words. "It's not easy knowing what you lost."

Superman took a moment to reassure the overwrought teenager. "Superboy, it's going to be all right. I promise you."

"I know," the boy answered. He didn't sound entirely convinced.

Kara felt sorry for the poor kid, especially if what she had just heard was true. But she had bigger things on her mind than this Superboy's adolescent angst. "Why are you here?" she asked. "Why now?"

They climbed a set of steps carved out of a mixture of ice and crystal. Superman paused at the top of the steps to address the two younger men. "Give Kara and me some time," he requested.

"Of course, Superman," Alexander said. He led Superboy-Prime back down the stairs to the enormous viewscreen below. "I need to study a few inconsistencies on this Earth anyway." The teenager hesitated, glancing back over his shoulder at Superman and Power Girl, but eventually let Alexander escort him away. "Let's find out what this Secret Society of villains is up to."

Leaving the others behind, Superman and Power Girl crossed an ice bridge stretching beneath a high ceiling. Stray images from the outside world continued to appear on the walls surrounding them. Kara briefly glimpsed a shot of the Metal Men valiantly holding their own against a swarm of OMACs.

Was that battle taking place this very minute, thousands of miles from here? She looked around in wonder and confusion.

"What is this place?"

"Alexander built it," Superman said. "It's where my fortress was back on Earth-Two. The crystals respond to our emotions and needs. We can see everything here."

So I see, she thought. She recalled that her own Superman had recently relocated his own Fortress of Solitude from the Arctic to the Amazon. *Guess this Superman is more of a traditionalist.*

She wondered whether this ice fortress was anything like the pocket dimension Alexander had created for them earlier. "Did your 'heaven,' or whatever, start to decay because of us?"

Superman shook his head sadly. "No. It's because of *her.*"

They entered the grotto, where Power Girl saw an elderly woman lying in a shallow depression, swaddled beneath many heavy blankets. She could hear the woman's raspy breath from many yards away. A feeble heartbeat reached her ears.

"She's dying," he said.

CHAPTER 14

THE MOON

FIRES continued to blaze amidst the ruins of the Watchtower, proving that the atmospheric force field was still intact. Flames crackled loudly in a shrinking bubble of air. Fallen steel beams crunched against each other as they settled. Sparks flew from severed electrical connections. The lifeless wreckage remained uninhabited.

Until . . .

A sudden boom echoed within the collapsed structure. Just for an instant, a flash of golden light dispelled the flickering shadows cast by the flames. A heroic figure, clad in a gleaming blue-and-gold uniform, emerged from the dazzling radiance. A levitating gold sphere followed right behind him.

"I HAVE TAKEN THE LIBERTY OF INITIATING YOUR FORCE FIELDS," the floating robot said. "TEMPORAL TRAVEL SUCCESSFUL WITHIN A MARGIN OF SIX-POINT-FIVE-SIX DAYS."

"Did we make it, Skeets?" Booster Gold asked anxiously. "Did we make it back in time?"

"I'M AFRAID NOT," the robot reported. "THE JUSTICE LEAGUE'S WATCHTOWER HAS ALREADY BEEN DESTROYED."

"Dammit," Booster said. He peered out at his surroundings through a pair of translucent gold goggles. Skeet's assessment was obviously correct. The Watchtower was in ruins. *I'm too late,* he realized. *The Infinite Crisis has already begun.*

Booster Gold, alias Michael Jon Carter, was a time-traveler from the twenty-fifth century. Years ago, relativistically speaking, he had journeyed to the tail end of the twentieth century to seek fame and fortune as a super hero. Using advanced technology from the future to give him an edge in this primitive era, he had battled evil (and secured lucrative licensing deals) as Booster Gold, hero extraordinaire. Wealth and celebrity had been his primary goals— until his best friend, the Blue Beetle, was murdered.

Now he was a man with a mission.

"WE CANNOT RETURN TO THE TWENTY-FIFTH CENTURY FOR AN-OTHER TIME-JUMP," Skeets reminded him. The stolen security robot was a useful sidekick here in the past. "THE HISTORICAL RECORDS I ASSISTED YOU IN HIJACKING MEAN A DEATH SENTENCE FOR BOTH OF US."

Booster didn't care that he had broken the laws of his own era. "But they could mean life for millions of others. Maybe billions." He hoped there was still time to avert the final catastrophe. "Locate my League."

When he spoke of the Justice League, he meant the individual heroes who had served with him and the Blue Beetle during one particular incarnation of the team. Maybe they hadn't been the strongest or most famous heroes to ever serve in the League, but they had been his friends. He knew he could always count on them, no matter what lay ahead.

"UNABLE TO LOCATE MARTIAN MANHUNTER," Skeets reported. "SHALL I BEGIN CONTACTING THE OTHERS?"

Booster shook his head. "Not yet. We've got something more important to find first." He gazed up through the shattered ceiling at the bright blue Earth shining overhead. His eyes zoomed in on one specific corner of North America. *That's where we'll find it*, he thought, *fortune willing*.

"Blue Beetle's scarab."

FLYING PIG CASINO, ATLANTIC CITY

THE floor of the casino looked like a hurricane had come through. Playing cards, dice, and broken glass littered the carpet. Tables and chairs were overturned. Shattered slot machines bled coins. A fortune's worth of discarded chips were scattered upon the floor. The smell of gunpowder and Joker Gas hung in the air.

The formerly busy casino was almost empty. Gamblers, tourists, and staff had all fled after the first few casualties. Now the only voices in the spacious room belonged to two notorious super-villains having a serious difference of opinion.

"I heard when Kite-Man refused to join, Deathstroke dropped him off the roof of the Wayne Tower . . . without his glider!" The King of Spades laughed uproariously at his own story, despite the fact that he was currently tied to a roulette wheel that had been turned perpendicular to the floor. With his elaborate makeup and costume, he looked as though he had stepped right off an oversize playing card. Embroidered spades added a festive touch to his striped tunic. Blood trickled from his broken nose.

I've been trumped, he realized. *Big-time.*

The Joker didn't need any makeup. His chalk-white face and wild green hair were all him, which was an absolutely chilling notion. A sadistic grin stretched across his face as he interrogated the King. A flamboyant purple suit gave him a certain mock-elegance.

"They've inducted Scarecrow and the Penguin," he complained to his prisoner. "And even Tweedle Dee and the new Dum." He gave the wheel an enthusiastic spin, causing the King to rotate head over heels until the bound villain was on the verge of vomiting. He clamped his teeth together in order to keep down his dinner. Finally, the wheel slowed to a stop. The Joker returned the King to an upright position. "So tell me, my good King, when do I get *my* invitation to be a member of this Secret Society?"

As his stomach settled back into place, the King glanced around the trashed floor of the casino, looking in vain for backup. The rest of his Royal Flush Gang had already been taken out by the Joker. The Ace of Spades, a super-strong android, lay decapitated on the floor, a trick cane through one eye. The Jack had been driven headfirst into a slot machine; his body sagged limply, a plethora of shiny coins spilling out onto his feet. The Ten was sprawled atop a splintered blackjack table. Steam rose from the wounds caused by acid sprayed on her face. The Queen of Spades slumped against a nearby column. A hideous grin distorted her lovely features.

Time to cash in my chips, the King realized. He had drawn a losing hand this time, and the Joker wasn't the sort to fall for a bluff. *Might as well tell him the truth, one playing card to another.*

"Don't you get it, clown?" he taunted the Joker. He spit a mouthful of blood onto the murderer's purple lapels. "You're the only one the Society doesn't want. See, everyone knows . . . the Joker's too wild."

He laughed in the clown's face; then he saw something that sent a chill through his blood.

The Joker wasn't smiling.

Without a word, he thrust a gloved hand against the King's bleeding face. The captive gang leader felt a metal joy buzzer dig into his cheek, right before a couple thousand volts of electricity coursed through his body. Smoke rose from his wig and beard. The smell of burning flesh emanated from his body. The Joker withdrew his hand and his victim's head sagged lifelessly onto his chest. Charred makeup blackened the King's face.

"That's not funny," the Joker said.

He stormed out of the casino in a huff.

CHAPTER 15

ARCTIC FORTRESS

POWER Girl gazed down at the old woman beneath the blankets. A thick pillow propped up the woman's head. It took Kara a second to recognize the familiar face beneath the wrinkles, gray hair, and ashen complexion. "Is this . . . ?"

"Lois Lane," the older Superman said. Despite his own wrinkles, he was obviously in much better shape than the ailing woman before them. He looked at his wife with obvious love and heartache. Kara could tell that he hated seeing his Lois like this.

"From . . . your Earth?" Power Girl assumed.

"*Our* Earth," he corrected her.

Right, she thought. *I'm supposed to be from . . . Earth-Two, was it?*

"This is just weird," she protested, growing more frustrated by the minute. "I'm sorry, I don't remember you. I don't remember her. . . ."

"Kara?" A tremulous voice, which was barely more than a whisper, interrupted her. The elderly Lois Lane looked up at Power Girl. A faint smile appeared upon her withered face. "It is you . . . isn't it?"

Kara lowered her voice as she gently answered the elderly Lois. "I don't know you." She wished she could say otherwise, if only for the old woman's sake. "I'm sorry, but I don't."

Lois reached out and laid her bony hand upon Kara's.

The effect was electric. Kara threw back her head and her entire body spasmed as, without warning, a flood of forgotten memories came pouring back into her mind. She gasped out loud, overwhelmed by the rush of sights and sounds from a past she only now remembered. She saw herself as an infant, being placed in a rocket ship by her parents on doomed Krypton; meeting up with her cousin on Earth years later, after spending over a decade in hibernation aboard her father's spacecraft; fighting alongside Superman against villains like the Toyman and Brainiac; visiting Clark and Lois at home; and dozens of other memories she hadn't even known she possessed. *It's all true,* she realized. *Everything he just told me, about Earth-Two and the Crisis. It's all true!*

"Kara!" Superman—*her* Superman—cried out, alarmed by her sudden seizure. He rushed toward her. "Kara? Are you all right?"

She dropped to her knees, stunned by the revelations. "I . . . my God . . . ," she murmured. Her blue eyes welled up with tears. "I do remember." A smile broke out across her face and she sprang to her feet in euphoria. She threw her arms around Superman. "I do remember! I'm not alone!"

He smiled back at her. "I told you."

"I remember everything," she exclaimed, unable to contain herself. Tears of happiness streamed down her face. "You took me in, you and Lois. I see the extra bedroom with the daisy wallpaper. Family dinners. Nights of telling me stories about how you met. How you asked her to marry you. On top of the Daily Star building with a diamond you made yourself, from the coal mines of Zriff."

"Yes," he confirmed, clearly happy for her. "Yes, that's right!"

She reluctantly let go of him in order to turn back toward the old woman on the bed who was no longer a stranger to her. Her voice hoarse with emotion, she looked tearfully at Lois. "Both of you, you treated me like I was your daughter."

A family portrait appeared on the crystal walls overlooking the old woman's bedside, reflecting the thoughts and memories of everyone in the grotto: Lois and Clark . . . and Kara.

Lois beamed up at Power Girl. "Oh, honey. As far as we're concerned, you *are* our daughter."

CHAPTER 16

THE BATCAVE,
OUTSIDE GOTHAM CITY

OUTSIDE it was daylight, but deep beneath Wayne Manor, it was always night. Stalactites jabbed from the ceiling. Frozen sheets of calcite draped the cavern walls. Sleeping bats rustled in their roosts. Shadows cloaked secluded nooks and crannies throughout the extensive underground complex.

Unlike his namesakes, Batman was wide awake. After returning from the Moon, he had spent a long night coping with the freak "meteor shower" that had devastated large portions of Gotham. Fires and riots had broken out all over the city, forcing him to aid the local authorities in restoring order. He hadn't been able to retreat to the Batcave to continue his investigation of the attack on the Watchtower until dawn.

"BLACK BOX 73, JUSTICE LEAGUE WATCHTOWER," a computerized voice reported. "TELEPORTATION LOG, ENTRIES 53042 THROUGH 74524."

He sat facing a large, high-definition, flat-screen monitor. The massive screen occupied an entire wall of his primary computer station, which was located atop a rock ledge in the central grotto. An ergonomic control panel stretched along the bottom of the screen. Seven linked Cray T932 mainframes provided him with more than enough computing power to solve almost any mystery. The entire setup was the best that the Wayne family fortune could buy.

"Playback last recorded entry," he instructed the computer. "Cameras one and six."

"STORAGE CIRCUITS DAMAGED. SCANNING AND REPAIRING. PLAY-BACK OF ENTRY 74524 ESTIMATED IN FORTY-THREE MINUTES, TWENTY-THREE SECONDS."

Damn, Batman thought. He wanted that data now, not in forty minutes. He wearily pulled back his cowl, exposing the somber face of Bruce Wayne. Cuts and bruises, left over from his clash with Mongul on the moon, marred his handsome features. Perspiration plastered his dark hair to his scalp.

Approaching footsteps announced the arrival of Alfred Pennyworth, his faithful family retainer. "Master Bruce?" The thin English butler eyed his employer's injuries with concern. Among other things, Alfred was also an experienced combat medic. "Sir, those cuts need to treated and stitched up."

"Later," he said curtly. His dark eyes remained fixed on the screen before him. Who had destroyed the Watchtower, and what had become of Martian Manhunter? *Is this the OMACs' doing?* he pondered. *Perhaps I should try to establish contact with Brother Eye again. . . .*

Ignoring Bruce's brusque dismissal, Alfred stepped forward to apply an antiseptic swab to a bloody nick right above the younger man's eye. "Now hold still. . . ."

The Betadine stung like blazes, breaking Bruce's concentration. He angrily swatted the swab aside. "I said, later!"

Alfred took the hint and backed away. As he was exiting the Batcave, however, he paused on the stairs and looked down at Bruce with a disappointed expression on his face. "You know, there was one thing your father never wanted to be. Alone. Fortunately, he had your mother at his side, even at the worst of times."

Bruce listened to Alfred depart. He felt a twinge of guilt for being so short with the worried butler. He knew that Alfred meant well, and probably had a point. But now was not the time to worry about anyone's feelings, let alone his own. He pulled his cowl back over his face.

I have more important problems to deal with, Batman thought.

He tried once more to regain control of his rogue spy satellite. In response, the screen before him took on an ominous red tint. A pictographic representation of a human eye took over the center of the monitor.

"HELLO, CREATOR," said Brother Eye.

"Brother Eye," Batman addressed the murderous artificial intelligence.

"WHY DO YOU STILL FIGHT ME?"

"Because you are out of control."

"BUT YOU BUILT ME TO WATCH OVER THE META-HUMANS THROUGH-OUT THE WORLD. TO ENSURE THAT THEY NEVER ACT IN ANY UNLAW-FUL OR UNETHICAL MANNER."

Such as erasing my memory, Batman thought. Brother Eye had seemed like a reasonable precaution . . . at first.

"THE META-HUMANS CANNOT BE TRUSTED."

"But the OMACs," Batman protested. "Where did they come from?"

"THE OMNI MIND AND COMMUNITY TECHNOLOGY WAS DEVELOPED AND IMPLEMENTED BY MAXWELL LORD ONCE HE CONNECTED WITH ME. HE INJECTED OVER TWO HUNDRED THOUSAND SLEEPER AGENTS ACROSS THE WORLD, CAPABLE OF BEING ACTIVATED AT ANY TIME TO COMBAT THE META-HUMANS. YOU CANNOT SHUT THEM DOWN. YOU CANNOT SHUT ME DOWN. AND YOU WILL NOT LOCATE ME."

"So you say. But now hundreds of OMACs are congregating above the Atlantic. They're leaving the cities. Why? Where are you sending them?"

"EYE ONLY DO WHAT YOU DESIGNED ME TO DO. EYE ONLY PRO-TECT THE WORLD FROM PEOPLE LIKE HER."

The Eye icon disappeared from the screen. In its place, Batman once more saw the damning footage of Wonder Woman killing Maxwell Lord with her bare hands.

"Oh my God," he whispered. He suddenly realized where the OMACs were going.

CHAPTER 17

THE BERMUDA TRIANGLE,
ATLANTIC OCEAN

Wonder Woman was almost home.

After her tense reunion with Bruce and Clark on the Moon, she was looking forward to the peace and tranquility of Themyscira, better known to the
outside world as Paradise Island. She soared high above the Atlantic, riding
on the wind currents, as she neared the ageless sanctuary of her Amazon sisters. Soon, she knew, she would have to turn herself over to the World Court to
answer for her execution of Maxwell Lord, but not just yet. First, she intended
to inform her sisters of her decision—and seek the counsel of the gods.

A dense curtain of fog helped to conceal Themyscira from Man's World.
But as she flew through the damp mist, Diana was alarmed to hear the sounds
of gunfire coming from her home. With the speed of Hermes, she swiftly left
the fog behind her, emerging high above the secluded island. "Gaea's tears!"
she exclaimed as she gazed down in horror at the scene below.

Ordinarily, Themyscira presented a lovely vista from above. Classical
Greek architecture rose from the southern tip of the wooded isle. A traditional
stone acropolis looked down on a neatly organized community of graceful
temples, palaces, arbors, fountains, and gymnasiums. Coliseums and outdoor theaters celebrated both the athletic and artistic gifts of the remarkable
women who inhabited the idyllic city-state. The senate chamber and other

public buildings enclosed a large open square known as an agora. A somber necropolis, located on the outer fringes of the city, housed the bones of departed Amazons. Wonder Woman was accustomed to feeling a joyous sense of homecoming whenever she returned to this blessed haven, safely removed from the woes of the outer world.

But not today.

Paradise Island was under attack by a veritable army of OMACs. Flames and billowing black smoke rose from the city, whose tidy streets and courtyards had become a battlefield. Amazon warriors, clad in the traditional bronze armor of ancient Greece, fought back against the relentless tide of cyborgs, employing both modern firearms and sharpened swords and spears, according to each individual woman's talents and resources. The OMACs retaliated with lethal energy blasts and bladed weapons that extruded from their blue ceramic shields. Other OMACs snatched the Amazons' own spears out of the air, then hurled them back at the beleaguered women, often with fatal results. The cyborgs hovered in the air, taking advantage of their ability to defy gravity, while the embattled Amazons fought on foot or from the saddles of their faithful *kangas*, a domesticated breed of giant marsupials found only on Paradise Island. But even these noble beasts could not leap high enough to bring the fight directly to the flying OMACs. The OMACs cut them down like lambs at the slaughter.

Furious war cries competed with the screams of wounded and dying Amazons, all of it punctuated by the steady blare of automatic weapon fire. Amazon blood stained marble steps and colorful mosaic tiles. A few vanquished OMACs were scattered amidst the bodies of their victims, but the Amazons were clearly taking the worst of the damage, as was their city. Ornamental columns and statues were blown apart by the cyborgs' destructive blasts. Stray gunfire chipped away at intricate stone friezes. Formerly tranquil gardens were set ablaze.

Above the chaos, the OMACs spoke to each other in amplified, electronic voices:

"FOLLOWING PROTOCOL: TRUTH AND JUSTICE. ELIMINATE ALL AMAZONS."

Wonder Woman realized that she was witnessing Brother Eye's cybernetic revenge for the slaying of Maxwell Lord. It was not enough that the crazed satellite destroyed her good name by broadcasting the execution video throughout the world. Now it meant to murder her sisters!

She quickly took stock of the battle below. The heaviest fighting seemed to be taking place in the central agora, where Artemis, the military commander of the Amazons, was leading a squad of female warriors in defense of the Temple of Science. Like the goddess after which she was named, the flame-haired Artemis had a bow and quiver of arrows slung over her shoulder, even as she fired at the OMACs with an Uzi submachine gun. Like Diana herself, Artemis had spent a considerable amount of time in Man's World, and was more than familiar with its weapons. "Hold the line, sisters!" she shouted over the tumult. "For Themyscira!"

Wonder Woman wasn't about to let Artemis and the others fight alone, not when she had brought this calamity upon them. She dived toward the besieged city. *Hang on, sisters!* she thought urgently. *I'm coming!*

Her arrival did not go unnoticed by the OMACs. "TARGET: ALPHA TWO," several flying cyborgs announced in unison. "MAXIMUM PRIORITY DICTATED."

Crimson beams targeted her. Vicious spikes extruded from the OMACs' glossy blue hands. They came at her from all directions.

But Wonder Woman would not be kept from her sisters' side. Pausing in midair, she blocked laser blasts with her silver bracelets. The deflected beams bounced back at the OMACs themselves, scorching their polished exteriors. Unhooking her Lasso of Truth from her hip, she spun it before her like the blade of a propeller, so that it sliced through the air in front of her, and anything else that came within its destructive radius. Its twirling chain links lopped off the spikes protruding from the arms of the attacking OMACs, clearing her path. A powerful kick sent another OMAC flying out over the nearby harbor.

"Leave my sisters alone!" she commanded. "They have done nothing to deserve this!"

Alas, the OMACs took their orders only from Brother Eye.

She swooped down over the blood-spattered agora. Artemis and her troops had been driven backward, onto the marble steps leading up to the temple. A marble portico loomed behind them, now scorched and scarred by the battle. Fallen Amazons lay sprawled upon the steps. Diana prayed that they were only injured.

"Rifles! Covering fire!" Artemis shouted. Disdaining the classical armor worn by the other warriors, she faced the OMACs in black leather and ammo belts. A Glock semiautomatic was holstered to her thigh. The muzzle of her Uzi flared amidst the smoky haze. "Fall back! Get to cover!"

Intent on ordering her soldiers, she failed to notice the OMAC silently descending from the sky directly above her. Its crimson eye flashed ominously. "TARGET ACQUIRED."

No! Diana thought, flying toward the OMAC as fast as she could. Not even she, however, could outrace the speed of light.

A scarlet ray struck Artemis in the back. Grunting in surprise, she dropped facefirst onto the ground. Her gun slipped from her fingers, clattering against the marble steps. Smoke rose from her black leather cuirass as she rolled painfully onto her back. Wonder Woman was relieved to see the fallen Amazon's chest rise and fall. Artemis was still alive, praise the gods!

"PARTIAL RESULT. ASSESSING. . . ." The OMAC appeared puzzled by its target's survival. Exposed wiring could be glimpsed beneath the scorched leather. "POSIT: PERSONAL DEFENSIVE SHIELD EMPLOYED." It glided in for the kill. "MODULATING PRIMARY WEAPON SPECTRUM FOR OPTIMAL SHIELD PENETRATION."

Artemis' eyelids fluttered open. She struggled visibly to remain conscious. "<Oh, shut up and do it already,>" she muttered in ancient Greek.

"MODULATION COMPLETE." The OMAC was more than willing to oblige. "TARGET AC—"

Wonder Woman grabbed on to the cyborg's head and yanked it sharply to one side. The deadly blast went awry, taking a chunk out of a marble column instead. Taking care not to break the OMAC's neck as she had Maxwell Lord's, she slammed its head into the steps hard enough to shatter the solid stone. Broken chips of marble exploded into the air.

The OMAC did not get up.

"I was wondering when you were going to show up," Artemis said, still flat on her back. The fiercest of the Amazons, she was second only to Diana in strength and valor. "No pun intended."

Wonder Woman helped Artemis to her feet. She deflected a laser blast from another OMAC. The surviving Amazons continued to defend the temple, firing back at the advancing cyborgs with spears and bullets.

"How bad is it?" she asked Artemis.

"Battle of Marathon bad," the other woman said. Her face was scuffed and scratched from its collision with the steps. "And we're not the Persians."

"Athens won Marathon," Diana reminded her. She drew her sword from its scabbard.

"Only with a miracle," Artemis said. "And we're running short of those."

Wonder Woman did her best to shield the other Amazons from the OMACs' ceaseless assault. Her flashing sword kept a trio of killer cyborgs at bay, if only for the moment. A few steps away, a younger Amazon tended to a wounded comrade. "Don't you dare die on me, Tekla!" the girl urged the other woman. "You hear me, you old crow?"

Diana recognized the voice of Carissa. She was fond of the young blonde, whose baby face belied a witty tongue as sharp as a dagger. Glancing back over her shoulder, she saw an OMAC hurl a captured spear down at the distracted Amazon.

"TARGET ACQUIRED."

"Carissa!" Wonder Woman shouted. "Watch out!"

Her warning came too late. The spear struck Carissa between her shoulder blades, impaling her. She collapsed atop the injured Tekla. A second spear came plunging at the other woman.

"Gods, no!" Wonder Woman sprang forward and sliced the spear in two with her sword. Her quick response saved Tekla, but not Carissa, whose lifeblood was already spilling down the steps into the agora. Her clever tongue had fallen silent forever.

Enraged by the young Amazon's death, Artemis turned her Uzi on Carissa's killer. "Hades take you!" she cursed as she emptied her clip into the airborne cyborg. Armor-piercing bullets blasted through the OMAC's smooth blue chest, and it crashed to the ground. Blood seeped through the cracked ceramic plating.

"Artemis!" Wonder Woman called out. She turned Tekla over to another Amazon, who helped the injured woman hobble into the shelter of the temple. "These OMACs have innocent people inside. They're being controlled against their will!"

"Our sisters are dying!" Artemis shouted back angrily. Tossing her empty Uzi aside, she drew her bow. "What do you suggest we do? Lay down our arms?" Her powerful arms sent a speeding arrow straight through the skull of an oncoming OMAC. "Surrender and die? What?"

"I don't know," Diana admitted.

Back to back, they faced the invaders, while Paradise burned all around them.

ARCTIC FORTRESS

Power Girl and the older Superman stepped outside the grotto to let Lois sleep. Despite her joy at being reunited with Kara, the ailing woman clearly needed to rest. The last thing Kara wanted to do was put any additional strain on Lois' health, now that they had finally found each other once more. *I can't lose her again,* she thought. *That would be too cruel.*

Kara was still reeling from her newfound memories. "It's so much to take in," she confessed to Superman as they stood at the top of the steps that led down to Lois' bedside. "But it's wonderful."

"I haven't seen Lois smile like that in such a long time," he told her warmly. "Thank you, Kara."

She stared down at the sleeping woman. Lois looked so frail, so weak. Quite unlike the vibrant older woman Kara now recalled. "What's wrong with her?"

"She was just getting old," he said sadly. "Her body was already weak, back in our refuge, but traveling here . . . it just made everything worse." He scowled, an uncharacteristic look of resentment on his face. "That's what this Earth does."

Kara looked at him with concern. "There has to be *something* we can do."

"This Earth you've been on since I left, it's corrupted, Kara." He stared up at a towering wall of crystal. Images from the world beyond appeared on the many facets of the crystal: the Spectre on the loose, the Society conspiring, the OMACs laying siege to Paradise Island, the Rann-Thanagarian War. "How do they live like this?"

"Like what?" she asked.

"Joyless." He shook his head in dismay. "Alexander has kept records. He's shown me so many things the people you work with have done. To their adversaries. To each other. They alter minds. They kill." He clenched his fists at his sides. "I never really understood why I survived when the others didn't. Or what my purpose in this new universe was. Not until now."

The images on the screens shifted. Once again, Kara saw a single Earth emerging from the cosmos-shaking Crisis of years gone by.

"When the universe was reborn," Superman said, "Earth-One became the primary world. The scraps of the remaining worlds were folded into it. But I've finally realized something: We saved the *wrong* Earth."

He turned away from the wall and laid a gentle hand upon her shoulder.

"I need your help and support, cousin. We can save Lois," he said urgently. "We can save her if we can take her back home."

Behind him, the crystals displayed a montage of scenes from the forgotten history of Earth-Two: the original Justice Society convening in their secret headquarters; an adult Robin, who never became Nightwing, fighting crime in Gotham City; an older Wonder Woman training her daughter on Paradise Island; the daughter of Batman and Catwoman taking on the masked identity of the Huntress; Superman and Lois flying above Metropolis after their wedding. The bizarre images were no longer unfamiliar to Power Girl. She now remembered this world as vividly as the one outside the fortress.

"This corrupted and darkened Earth must be forgotten as ours was," Superman declared with a look of grim determination, "so that the *right* Earth can return."

CHAPTER 18

SAN DIEGO

THE shoreline was less than a year old. This part of the city had once been several miles inland, but that was before a tremendous earthquake dropped a good third of the city into the Pacific Ocean. The damage to life and property had been extensive, but San Diego had slowly begun to rebuild. Docks, warehouses, marinas, and seafood restaurants now crowded the newly-created waterfront . . . until a new catastrophe threatened to tear open the city's scars all over again.

The hurricane lashed San Diego. Cyclonic winds tore at the buildings, sending broken glass and shingles flying. Rain flooded the sewers, spilling out into the streets. A tremendous tidal wave surged toward the shore, only to come to an abrupt halt a few yards from dry land. The huge wall of water hung in place above the piers and parking lots, blocking the waves directly behind it. Foam cascaded over the top of the unearthly barrier.

"Hurry!" a red-haired woman in an iridescent green wetsuit shouted over the roaring winds. Mera, onetime Queen of Atlantis, used her "hard water" powers to keep the raging sea at bay. A tiara made from a polished seashell crowned her head. "I can't hold these waves back much longer. We need to get everyone someplace dry!"

"And where would that be, Mera?" Dane Dorrance asked. The dark-haired human was the leader of the Sea Devils, a private team of deep-sea explorers and adventurers. His people were spearheading the emergency response effort, along with San Diego's own cops and EMS workers. All around her, Mera glimpsed the Sea Devils helping agitated and injured people evacuate the waterfront. Their distinctive red wetsuits made Dane's people easy to pick out amidst the chaos. Scuba goggles protected their faces from the torrential rain. "They're reporting over sixty category five storms across the world, three on the U.S. coast alone."

"How the hell is that possible?" Sigourney Amundsen asked, her long blond hair soaked by the tempest. The Swedish woman was a relatively new addition to the Sea Devils. Mera had never met her before.

"I don't know," she admitted. Mera came from a different dimension, but she knew Earth's oceans well enough to realize that there was something deeply unnatural behind this sudden spate of hurricanes, along with the red skies, earthquakes, and other freakish natural phenomena that seemed to be tearing the planet apart. She'd even heard reports of a floating rock exploding over Gotham City. . . .

Disasters invariably brought out looters and other predators, and this storm was no exception. As if the hurricane weren't threat enough, a strike force composed of aquatic super-villains seemed intent on pillaging the sunken city beyond the shore, where a small colony of water-breathing humans struggled to build new lives in what was now called Sub Diego. Even as Mera struggled to hold back the flood, she could see a heated battle raging amidst the storm-tossed harbor.

New Wave, a female villain whose body was literally composed of water, crashed against Tsunami, an Asian heroine who surfed atop the waves as gracefully as an Olympic skater on ice. New Wave's sneering face was sculpted from churning white water as she reversed direction and came at Tsunami again, but the heroine used her water-controlling powers to set up a counterwave that canceled out New Wave herself, dispersing the villain for the moment. Tsunami watched the frothing water warily, waiting for New Wave to re-form; her concentration was broken when a blond-haired mermaid grabbed her from behind, dragging Tsunami beneath the waves. *That has to be Siren,* Mera guessed. The evil fish-woman gave other mermaids a bad name.

Mera longed to go to Tsunami's aid, just to even out the odds, but she had recently lost her ability to breathe underwater. Confined to the shore, unable to join the battle, the best she could do was try to aid the imperiled surface-dwellers, especially now that she was one of them.

Tsunami and the others were on their own.

A sudden storm surge got past her barrier. Over twenty feet high, the wave barreled toward a bus loaded with frightened evacuees. Some sort of engine malfunction seemed to have stalled the bus, leaving its passengers directly in the path of the oncoming wall of water. They were only seconds from being swept away.

Not if I have anything to say about it, Mera vowed. Her alabaster brow furrowed in concentration as she formed a wedge of solid water right in the center of the wave. The towering storm surge split in two, veering away from the bus on both sides. Instead the divided swell smashed into two adjacent store-fronts, blowing out the windows and tearing the roofs off both buildings. Mera winced at the damage, but better the stores be destroyed than the defenseless people in the bus. She smiled in relief as the vehicle finally got moving. Gills or no gills, it was good to know that she could still protect the innocent.

"Good save!" Dane congratulated her. Rain pelted his face. He stared out over the harbor, where the winds whipped the sea into a frenzy. "Wonder how bad it is below."

Mera shared his concern. In her heart, she feared the true battle was being waged miles beneath the surface in Sub Diego. "Who knows?" she answered. "But if anyone can help hold back the seas, it's their heroes . . . and their king."

"FIGHT all you want, Aquaman!" Black Manta taunted. Red lenses glowed like eyes upon his saucer-shaped helmet. "Sub Diego will soon belong to us!"

The infamous undersea terrorist fired a speargun at Aquaman. The jet-propelled harpoon sped toward the hero's face, but his reflexes were even faster. He swiftly swam to the side, then grabbed the shaft of the spear with one hand.

"Easier said than done, Manta!" he challenged his foe. The sound of his voice traveled through the water five times faster than it would have in the air. His blond hair swayed in the current like the fronds of a sea anemone. The orange scales on his tunic glittered like chain mail. His finned trousers were as green as a merman's tail. "This city is under my protection."

Over two hundred feet beneath the surface, Sub Diego rested on the seabed. In some ways, the sunken community still resembled its sister city above. Paved streets and sidewalks connected shops, department stores, restaurants, apartment buildings, boarded-up tenements, cemeteries, churches, synagogues, and even the ruins of the old city zoo. Streetlamps and parking meters lined the sidewalks, along with dozens of now-superfluous fire hydrants. Towering cranes overlooked construction sites. But life underwater was gradually transforming the city. Algae and barnacles now covered the graffiti. Seaweed and anemones sprouted from cracks in the pavement. Soggy paper peeled off the billboards. Rusting cars and trucks that would never again burn gasoline now housed sea urchins and coral gardens. Drowned palm trees rotted away. Fish swam through the streets and alleys. Crabs replaced cockroaches. Sushi was the only cuisine available.

Powerful currents, stirred up by the hurricane, had driven most of the population indoors. Kelp blew like litter through the empty streets. A mad scientist's genetic experiments had turned hundreds of men, women, and children into water-breathers. Still adjusting to their new condition and environment, these people relied on Aquaman to keep them safe while Sub Diego evolved into a whole new way of life. He had already chased Black Manta out of town once before.

This time, however, Manta had not come alone.

"The Society's numbers are far greater than yours, brother," Ocean Master boasted. A flared golden mask concealed the features of Orm Marius, Aquaman's treacherous sibling. Sharpened spines crested his cowl. A heavy purple cloak billowed behind him as he stood atop an undersea glider. His mystic trident fired a blast of eldritch green fire at Aquaman. "And more vicious!"

Aquaman's left hand had been consumed by piranhas years ago; in its place was a magical blue hand composed of living water. His open palm blocked the sorcerous bolt from his brother's trident. Enchanted water quenched the emerald fire.

Ocean Master had not been exaggerating, however. Luthor's Society seemed to have recruited every underwater villain in the Seven Seas. Looking about through the rippling blue water, Aquaman spotted King Shark, Sea Wolf, the Marine Marauder, and the Eel, among others. He had battled each of them in the past, but never all at once.

Cowards! he thought. *Do they expect me to shrink before their numbers?*

Thankfully, Aquaman had allies of his own. Sharks, whales, squids, swordfish, and other sea life swam to the defense of Sub Diego as he telepathically summoned them from miles around. He smiled grimly as an enormous octopus attacked Slig of the Deep Six, one of a half-dozen scaly aquatic aliens from the planet Apokolips. Powerful tentacles enveloped Slig, while a school of electric eels jolted his extraterrestrial comrades. Flashes of blue electricity sparked across the aliens' metal armor. Starfish clamped over the creatures' faces, blinding them.

Well fought, my friends, Aquaman thought proudly. Spear in hand, he swam at Black Manta, only to be distracted by the sudden approach of the Marine Marauder, a huge red cyborg with a fishlike mechanical tail. The Marauder was built like a tank, with bulky steel armor shielding his flesh-and-blood components, and was nearly twice Aquaman's size. A three-foot blade extended from his wrist. Bubbles rose from his steel-plated breathing apparatus.

"Ready for a rematch, sea king?" his electronically-amplified voice asked. The Marauder had tried raiding Sub Diego a few months back, only to be driven off by Aquaman and the Sea Devils. "That water trick won't save you again!"

Last time around, Aquaman had used his aqueous blue hand to disrupt the Marauders's circuits. Guessing that the cyborg was securely insulated now, the undaunted hero took a more direct approach. Switching the spear to his water-hand, he parried the Marauder's slashing blade with it, then slammed his normal right fist into the villain's metal faceplate. Muscles conditioned to survive the crushing pressure of the ocean depths lent superhuman strength to the blow, which cracked the Marauder's burnished red mask. Bubbles streamed from the ruptured helmet as the air-breathing villain was forced to swim frantically toward the surface.

So much for the Marauder, Aquaman thought. *One down, how many more to go?*

By now, more humanoid reinforcements had joined Aquaman and the militant sea life in their clash with the Society. Some of Sub Diego's bravest citizens swam up from the submerged city to engage the enemy. Among them was Lorena Marquez, a Hispanic teenager who now called herself Aquagirl.

"Here we come, Arthur!" she called to Aquaman. Her two-piece blue swimsuit was of Atlantean design. "We'll teach these creeps not to mess with our city!"

But before she could catch up with him, a cage of compressed water closed around her. Throwing out her arms, she strained to hold back the walls of the cage, which threatened to crush her to a pulp. "Aquaman, help!"

A nearby figure in a sleek black wetsuit mocked her distress. "The entire sea is mine to shape," the Eel reminded her. Mort Coolidge was a telekinetic criminal whose powers worked most effectively on water. "How can he help you, girl?" He gestured at the liquid cage and the walls pressed in on Aquagirl, squeezing her arms to her sides. "All I need to do is increase the pressure and—"

A killer whale chomped down on the Eel, not quite biting off his head and shoulders. The watery cage instantly dissolved, freeing Lorena. She cast a grateful look at Aquaman.

"The water may be yours, Eel," he said, "but the sea is mine."

All around him, the battle heated up. Captain Malrey, the commander of Sub Diego's nascent police force, led his officers against Sea Wolf, an amphibious German werewolf possessed of gleaming fangs and claws. The shaggy lupine monstrosity looked distinctly out of place beneath the waves, but that didn't make him any less dangerous. A feral growl bubbled from his throat.

Conventional firearms didn't work underwater, so Malrey's officers were armed only with rust-proof batons and pikes. Malrey himself preferred his massive fists; experimental gene-therapy had transformed the veteran cop into a humanoid mix of whale and walrus. Sea Wolf's claws slashed at the captain's thick, gray hide, but Malrey grabbed on to the water-breathing werewolf's throat, throttling the beast while the other officers pummeled the creature with their batons. It was too bad that the metal rods weren't made out of silver, but fighting werewolves had been low on the undersea community's priorities.

"Don't let him bite you!" Malrey shouted, keeping Sea Wolf's snapping jaws at arm's length. A golden badge shone upon the police captain's chest. Ivory tusks protruded from his lower lip. "Let's knock the fight out of this mangy mutt!"

Charybdis, the Piranha Man, swam at the policemen and -women, although it was unclear whether he intended to defend Sea Wolf or simply feast on the succulent flesh of the vulnerable officers. A mouthful of razor-sharp teeth gleamed upon his grotesque, subhuman countenance. Jagged claws reached out for human prey.

"Forget it, fangface!" a turquoise-skinned woman informed him. A mane of thick indigo hair billowed around her head and shoulders as she swam in circles around the Piranha Man. "No snack time for you!"

Deep Blue, Tsunami's daughter, possessed the unique ability to enlarge and control sea life. At her command, a school of miniature jellyfish suddenly blossomed in size until they were as big as octopuses. The giant medusas swarmed Charybdis, stinging him with their oversized tentacles. He slashed viciously at the jellyfish. His pointed teeth gnashed against each other.

"Good work, Debbie!" Neptune Perkins shouted to his daughter. The Hawaiian super hero swam toward Tsunami, who was grappling furiously with an enraged mermaid. Webbed hands and feet propelled Neptune through the water faster than a porpoise. His long black hair streamed behind him. "You guard those police officers. I'll help your mother!"

But he never reached his wife's side. Not one but two mutated shark-men ambushed him en route. King Shark bit off Neptune's right arm, while another villain, known only as the Shark, ripped a meaty chunk out of the hero's side with his voracious jaws. Bright red blood clouded the water, mercifully hiding Neptune's mauled body from his horrified wife and daughter. The two shark-men continued to tear at the corpse in a veritable feeding frenzy. Sharklike fins crested their misshapen skulls.

"Dad!" Deep Blue shrieked. Reacting to her thoughts, the giant jellyfish dispersed in a panic, freeing Piranha Man, who tore into the police officers restraining Sea Wolf. Captain Malrey suddenly found himself alone against the thrashing werewolf, who broke free from his grasp. It was impossible to tell who was more savage, the piranha or the wolf.

"Hah!" Black Manta gloated over Neptune Perkin's demise. He loaded another harpoon into his speargun. "It seems the tide of battle turns in our favor!"

Righteous fury overcame Aquaman. Neptune had been a distinguished author and statesman as well as a hero; it enraged Aquaman to see such a man fall prey to cannibalistic monsters like the two shark-men. And in front of his wife and daughter, no less!

"The Society just declared war, Manta." Taking hold of his harpoon with both hands, he sped through the water like a torpedo, straight into the heart of the Sharks' bloody feast. Without mercy, he drove the spear all the way through King Shark. The villain sank toward the ocean floor, trailing a cloud of blood as he weakly struggled with the spear that had skewered him. "And so have I!" Aquaman called after him.

Genuine sharks and barracudas were attracted by King Shark's leaking blood, providing a touch of poetic justice. The other shark-man lunged at Aquaman, but the sea king smashed his fist into the Shark's mouth. Shattered teeth exploded from the creature's jaws. He tumbled backward through the water, clutching his face.

Now then, Aquaman thought. *Where is Manta?* He bore a special grudge against the deep-sea terrorist, who had murdered Aquaman's infant son years before. Spotting Black Manta a few fathoms above him, he kicked toward the helmeted villain. Powerful strokes carried him rapidly upward, against the raging currents. A harpoon whizzed harmlessly past his head; the stormy weather had thrown off Black Manta's aim.

A viselike hand clamped onto his ankle. Glancing down, Aquaman saw that Slig had managed to extricate one arm from the octopus's tentacles. "Not so fast, Earther!" the alien snarled, bubbles spewing from his throat. "By Darkseid's dread name, you will pay for this indignity—and so will your mindless Terran pets!"

"Unhand me!" Aquaman demanded. Irked by the delay, he stamped down on the alien's scaly face with his other foot. His heavy green sole crushed Slig's bestial snout. Screeching in pain, the alien let go of Aquaman's foot. Purple blood streamed from his nostrils.

Aquaman paddled away from the injured Slig, but before he could go after Black Manta again, a discordant blast of noise reverberated through the water.

"Enough!" Ocean Master ordered. He blew again on an empty conch shell, sounding a retreat. "We pull out now! The Society needs us elsewhere!" He turned his glider around. "We'll finish with Sub Diego later!"

"That's it?" Aquaman couldn't believe his ears. He swam after the retreating villains, watching in frustration as Manta and the rest fled toward the vast Pacific Ocean. "You think you can just leave now, that you can begin and end a conflict at your whim?" The glider's twin turbine engines left a stream of bubbles behind it. Aquaman wondered if Ocean Master had been scared off by King Shark's well-deserved end. "This isn't finished, Orm! You wanted a war, I'll give you one!"

Ocean Master taunted his brother as he disappeared into the distance.

"But it is finished, Orin. You have lives to save here, both above and below. I know you. You won't leave these people behind."

He was right, curse him. Aquaman remembered the hurricane ravaging the surface. Mera and the others were still in danger. He'd never forgive himself if his estranged wife was drowned by the very seas that she had once ruled by his side. *What's happening up there?*

Ocean Master tapped an earpiece on his cowl. He raised his voice to deliver one parting shot. "In fact, if what I just heard is true, you're going to be much too busy to fight a war against anyone." Aquaman could practically hear the smirk on his brother's face. "Why, when you find out what's happened to Atlantis, you may wish that we'd killed you here and now!"

"Atlantis?" Aquaman was caught by surprise. His fabled undersea kingdom was thousands of miles away, in the Atlantic Ocean. "What are you talking about? What's wrong with Atlantis?"

The fleeing villains offered no explanation. Aquaman slowed to a stop, abandoning his pursuit of Ocean Master and his murderous allies. Suddenly, he had more than San Diego and the Society to worry about. A grim sense of foreboding extended across the continent to a distant kingdom over an ocean away.

What had become of Atlantis?

ATLANTIS

LOCATED over ten thousand feet beneath the surface of the Atlantic, the domed city looked like the world's biggest snow globe. Graceful spires and archways rose beneath a protective crystal dome that shielded the people of the city from undersea storms, pollution, and predators. Salt water filled the dome, helping to resist the tremendous pressure exerted on the dome from outside. Ordinarily, the water-breathing Atlanteans paid little attention to the transparent ceiling high above their heads. Today, however, they watched it nervously as seismic tremors rocked the ocean floor. Violent currents and vortexes tore up the seabed outside the dome. Frightened Atlanteans could see silt and sediment being hurled wildly about the ocean depths. Undersea volcanoes erupted in the distance. So far, the crystal dome had withstood the earthquakes and turbulence, but for how much longer?

All eyes turned toward the magnificent palace at the center of the city. Strangely hued lights flashed in the windows of the highest tower in the royal residence. Swimming about on their daily business, the anxious people of Atlantis could only hope that their leaders were taking every measure to save the city from the tumult right outside the dome. . . .

Tempest, once known as Aqualad, presided over the ceremony. He stood before an altar in a vaulted chamber dedicated to the god Poseidon. A convocation of his fellow sorcerers surrounded him, chanting in unison as they attempted to calm the waters and steady the seabed.

Hooded acolytes stood by to assist the wizards. The tiled floor of the temple was inscribed with ancient Atlantean runes. Mystic fire blazed impossibly upon the altar. Unseen forces caused swirling eddies to appear in the water around them.

This shouldn't be happening, Tempest thought, as another tremor shook the city. Atlantis was built upon a stable stretch of seabed, safely distant from the nearest tectonic fault line. Their geologists and oceanographers could provide no warnings or explanation for the agitated earth and water. *We can only pray that sorcery succeeds where science failed.*

His eyes glowed with occult energy. Ceremonial black markings streaked his face. His black-and-red bodysuit evoked the flag of the esoteric Atlantean sect to which he belonged. He threw a rare undersea herb onto the altar, causing the eldritch flames to blaze higher. Power flowed into him from the other sorcerers, who occupied the four corners of the compass around him. Arion, Atlan, Nuada, and Hagen were each formidable wizards in their own right. Their flowing robes bore the emblems of their rank and power. Between the five of them, they should be able to quell most any disaster.

Famous last words? Garth fretted. He couldn't help remembering that all the sorcery in the world hadn't been able to stop Atlantis from sinking beneath the waves nearly ten millennia ago. *Let's hope that Atlantis survives this disaster as well.*

Concerned spectators peered down from the gallery. Despite the chanting of the sorcerers, Tempest overheard snatches of worried conversations.

"Why are we wasting our time here?" Koryak said irritably. Aquaman's long-lost son was not known for his patience. The muscular youth paced back and forth in the gallery. "My father's city is under attack. They need soldiers, not spells."

"That uncultured 'city' is none of our concern," Councilor Vulko replied. The portly Atlantean scientist had been the royal family's trusted advisor for as long as Garth could remember. Sub Diego was an inconvenient distraction as far as Vulko was concerned. "We must see to Atlantis's safety, above all else."

"That may not be enough," Dolphin argued. The white-haired young woman cradled her infant son against her chest. His wife's voice reminded Tempest of just how much he stood to lose if today's ritual failed. Dolphin was depending on him to keep her and little Ceridian safe. "You can bet that whatever's affecting Sub Diego and the surface world is targeting Atlantis, too. Why else would there be all these sudden earthquakes and storms?"

"She's right!" Koryak agreed. "We need to look at the bigger picture. . . ."

Another tremor shook the palace. Fragments of polished coral floated down from the ceiling. Tempest heard his baby son cry.

First things first, he resolved. Sub Diego would have to wait until Atlantis was secure. Extending his arms, he reached out with his magic, searching for the root cause of the ocean's unrest. Were the earthquakes simply a geological phenomenon, or was some other force at work? He probed the Earth's mantle with his mind, but quickly realized that the true danger lay elsewhere. This was no natural occurrence; something was profoundly amiss on the spiritual plane. Unleashed magical energy was running rampant, causing disturbances in both the physical and metaphysical worlds. No wonder everything felt so *wrong.*

But what could have created such chaos?

Apprehension showed on the faces of his fellow sorcerers. Garth sensed that they shared his growing unease. He tentatively searched the ether, only to feel something colder than the seas brush against his consciousness.

"Wait!" he blurted. "Do you feel that? Something's out there, listening!"

A disembodied voice, sepulchral in tone, echoed through the chamber and his skull.

"I hear you chanting, Atlantis. I see you."

Tempest had a horrible sense that they had just attracted the attention of something that should have been left alone. He hastily drew back his mind, but feared it was already too late. The eerie voice knew they were there now.

And it was coming.

Abandoning the ritual, he shouted frantically to his wife. "Dolphin, get our son out of here!"

Garth had no chance to see if she escaped the chamber in time. All at once, the water around him began to churn and bubble. The bright orange flames upon the altar turned a sickly shade of green. The other wizards broke off their chanting and looked about in confusion. They stared at each other with fear-stricken eyes.

"Little minnow, your magic must be mine!"

Before Tempest could offer any further warning to the others, he felt his energy being yanked from his body. Raw magic streamed from his eyes and mouth, erupting up toward the ceiling and blowing the roof off the tower of the palace. Shattered coral and mother-of-pearl flew outward over the city beyond. The black markings on Garth's face began to flake off, taking much of his strength with them. Green fire erupted from the altar, enveloping him.

"Tempest!" Koryak shouted from the gallery. "Garth!"

Pale-faced and trembling, Vulko pointed up at the ruptured ceiling. "Look! Above us!"

A huge green fist, the size of a whale, descended from above. The gloved hand smashed through the crystal dome that protected Atlantis. Heavy shards fell like anchors onto the city. Buildings collapsed as a deafening crash reverberated through the water. Hundreds of Atlanteans died instantly.

The shock wave hit the palace chamber. The outer walls caved in, burying the gallery. Vulko and Koryak vanished beneath an avalanche of heavy rubble, only seconds before the gallery itself came crashing down onto the lower level. Massive chunks of limestone and coral rained down on Tempest, but were incinerated by the mystical flames pouring out of him. He stood transfixed within the blazing green energy, unable to move from the spot, let alone flee the crumbling palace. To his torment, he had no way of knowing if Dolphin and Ceridian had fled the gallery, or if they had perished with the others.

But the disaster had only begun. Like the Red Sea in ages past, the waters of the Atlantic parted, exposing the undersea city to the open air for the first time in recorded history. Fallen acolytes, already knocked off their feet by the destruction of the dome, began to gasp for breath like fish out of the water. The other sorcerers were unconscious, sprawled on the floor, unable to help the suffocating water-breathers as they literally drowned in fresh air. Tempest knew that similar scenes had to be unfolding all over Atlantis. Amphibious by nature, he could breathe air as well as water. At the moment, he wasn't sure that was a blessing.

His glowing eyes were drawn upward to the gaping hole in the ceiling. His jaw dropped as he saw a green-cloaked figure towering over Atlantis like a colossus. A ghastly white face gazed down on the devastation from beneath an emerald hood. His enormous hands held back the ocean on all sides, creating an open canyon between two immense walls of churning foam. Water quickly drained from the palace chamber, leaving only a few meager puddles. Stray fish, caught in the disaster, flopped helplessly on the drying floor. The blood of dead and dying acolytes turned the last few puddles red.

The Spectre. Garth gasped in recognition. As a magician, he was well aware of the vengeful spirit's existence. But why would the Spectre lash out at Atlantis now, after all these years? He was supposed to punish the guilty, not wipe out whole cities. *We've done nothing to deserve this!*

"BRING OUT YOUR SHROUDS, WIDOWS OF ATLANTIS," the gigantic apparition decreed. His stentorian voice rang out over the dying city, drowning out a multitude of screams. "MEET THE DOOM YOU HAVE EVADED FOR TOO LONG. ATLANTIS SHOULD HAVE PERISHED BENEATH THE WAVES MILLENNIA AGO, BUT FOUL SORCERY HAS PROLONGED THIS UNNATURAL REALM'S EXISTENCE FAR PAST ITS DESTINED END." His spectral form cast an inescapable shadow over the wreckage below. "BUT NO LONGER!"

Garth didn't understand. What was the Spectre talking about? Atlantis had earned every moment of its survival, through hard work and sacrifice. *Our history is one of courage and perseverance.*

He heard buildings and monuments crashing to the ground outside. Desperate Atlanteans cried out for their king, but Aquaman was thousands of miles away, in a different ocean. A strange odor reached Garth's nostrils and it took him a few seconds to recognize the smell of smoke. His mind boggled at the thought. Atlantis was . . . burning?

The average Atlanteans had never seen a genuine flame in their lives, except perhaps under controlled laboratory conditions. They couldn't even begin to cope with an all-out fire.

This is insane, Tempest thought angrily. Once again, he feared for his wife and child. Were Dolphin and Ceridian out there in the chaos somewhere? If so, he needed to buy them enough time to escape the city before the Spectre destroyed them all.

"I don't know about that, moonface!" he shouted at the vindictive wraith.

Exerting his will to the utmost, he regained control of what little power the Spectre had not yet stolen from him. He knew he was no match for the Wrath of God, especially not in his depleted state, but his family and his homeland were depending on him. He threw out his arms, gathering up raw theurgic energy from the crackling green flames around him. "Let's just put that theory to the test!"

A glowing orange nimbus surrounded his body. He clasped his hands together and an incandescent bolt of light shot upward at the Spectre's face. Tempest's defiance caught the giant ghost by surprise. He staggered backward, briefly losing his grip on the divided oceans. Cascades of foamy brine poured down on Atlantis. The waterfalls drowned the fires blazing throughout the city, and provided momentary relief to the suffocating water-breathers. Garth felt the cool spray against his face.

But only for a second.

"BOTTOM-DWELLING MAGGOT!" The Spectre's face contorted in fury. Death's-heads glowed in the cavernous sockets of his eyes. "YOU DARE DREAM THAT YOUR PALTRY MAGICKS CAN STOP ME!" He looked down in judgment on Tempest, who had used up the last of his magical power. "I DE-STROYED SODOM AND GOMORRAH! I UNLEASHED THE PLAGUES ON THE PHARAOHS' EGYPT! MY WRATH BROUGHT DOWN THE FABLED WALLS OF JERICHO!" He raised one foot above the city, so that the sole of his boot blotted out the sky. "YOU ARE MERELY ONE DAMNED SOUL . . . AND YOURS SHALL BE A CITY OF THE DEAD!"

Garth saw the monstrous foot coming down. He prayed that Dolphin and Ceridian had left the doomed city far behind them. Then everything went black.

Atlantis was crushed beneath the Spectre's heel.

CHAPTER 19

PARADISE ISLAND

"LEAVE the others alone!" Wonder Woman cried out in frustration. "If it's me you want, here I am. Come and get me!"

She flung herself into the mass of OMACs pouring into the agora. Behind her, Artemis and her remaining soldiers fought a losing battle to defend the Temple of Science from the invading cyborgs. Despite the Amazons' fierce resistance, they had been driven back into the shadow of the columned portico before the propylaeum, the front entrance to the temple. The once pristine masonry was now scarred and scorched by violence. A magnificent stone frieze that had formerly graced the top of the gateway now lay in fragments upon the bloodstained steps below.

An OMAC dived like a guided missile at the temple, which sheltered many wounded Amazons, but Wonder Woman snared it with her lasso. Yanking hard on the unbreakable lariat, she swung the cyborg headfirst into the path of another oncoming OMAC. The machines collided into each other with an enormous crash. Shards of blue ceramic casing rained down onto the open square.

"TARGET: ALPHA TWO."

A score of OMACs fired lasers at her, but the beams bounced off her indestructible silver bracelets, which had been forged by Hephaestus himself from broken remnants of Zeus' shield. Spikes and blades, grown by the OMACs from their own malleable shells, stabbed at her, but she parried the blows with her flashing sword. Her mighty fist sent an ill-fated cyborg tumbling backward into its fellows.

The bodies of Amazons and OMACs alike were strewn about the ravaged square. Smoke and flames rose from torched gardens and temples. Abandoned weapons, as well as blood-smeared helmets and cybernetic components, lay amidst the smoldering rubble. The air was thick with smoke, the smell of gunpowder, and the harsh clamor of war.

"Back away!" Wonder Woman demanded, knocking a cluster of OMACs aside with the flat of her blade. Dozens of small cuts and bruises marred her usually immaculate complexion. Sweat gleamed on her flawless face and limbs. "Don't make me slay you!"

"OBJECTIVE: ELIMINATE ALL AMAZONS."

To her dismay, she was not the OMACs' sole target. While she remained locked in combat with dozens of identical foes, another wave of OMACs was launched at the entrance to the temple. The attacking cyborgs easily outnumbered Artemis and her few remaining warriors.

Beware, my sisters! Diana thought anxiously. *They are coming for you!*

Artemis and her forces fell back, retreating behind the towering Ionic columns supporting the portico. The OMACs swooped toward the entrance, seemingly unobstructed, only to slam headfirst into an invisible barrier.

"Now, sisters!" an imposing voice called out from the steps of the temple. The empty air appeared to shift slightly as an entire phalanx of fresh Amazon warriors stepped out from behind a score of invisible shields, forged from the same light-bending substance as the Invisible Jet that Wonder Woman sometimes employed in her travels. General Phillipus, a dark-skinned Amazon of African descent, commanded the reinforcements. Polished bronze armor glinted upon her sinewy frame as she raised her sword high. "Strike for Themyscira! For hearth and home!"

The women poured out into the agora, falling upon the stunned OMACs with spears and swords and guns. The invisible shields partially obscured their bodies as they took the battle to their enemy. "Isis, guide my aim!" an Egyptian Amazon prayed as she drove the point of her sword straight into an OMAC's solitary red eye. Other warriors followed her example. Machine guns, fired at close range, blew apart the blank blue faces of the OMACs. "Shoot for the head!"

Wonder Woman spotted a handful of OMACs hanging in the sky high above the fray. Instead of assisting their fellow cyborgs below, they silently monitored the grisly conflict with their unblinking red eyes. *Recording the slaughter for posterity,* she wondered, *or broadcasting the battle live for all the world to see?*

She feared the latter.

Artemis rejoined her in the square. "These things are like the Hydra!" she cursed. She unleashed a volley of arrows into the enemy lines, one after another. "We disable one and two more arrive in its place."

She spoke truly. The arrival of Phillipus' troops had gained them only a momentary respite. Looking upward, Wonder Woman saw the sky literally darken as yet more OMACs massed above them. "Hera wept!" she whispered in horror. Part of her was glad that her mother, Queen Hippolyta, had not lived to see this day. *How can we possibly stand against such numbers?*

"No!" an anguished voice cried out from the steps of the temple. "We are Amazons, not victims. Not today, not ever!"

A sudden burst of coruscating purple energy, bright enough to light up the entire battlefield, surged upward into the sky. The dazzling ray struck the wing of OMACs like one of Zeus' own thunderbolts, shattering their formation. Stricken cyborgs dropped like flies, raining down on the courtyards and rooftops below. Amazons ran for cover as the inert blue missiles crashed to earth. The sky sizzled loudly.

What in Athena's name?

Wonder Woman turned to look behind her, where a futuristic silver cannon had just been rolled out from somewhere deep within the Temple of Science. Gleaming brightly, as though newly made, the awesome weapon had a barrel the size of a battering ram. Sophisticated electronic gauges and components covered the huge apparatus, which was aimed at the sky above Paradise Island. Amethyst-colored energies crackled and flashed within the cannon's capacious muzzle. A loud and steady thrum, like the purr of a tiger, came from the weapon. Diana smelled ozone in the air.

Diana knew what this must be; long had the Amazons benefited from their legendary purple Healing Ray, known for its amethyst beam and mysterious healing properties, and now it had been reconstructed into a tool of war. "Behold the purple Death Ray," announced Io, the master weaponsmith of Themyscira. The ingenious Amazon was seated directly beneath the barrel of the cannon, manning its controls. A targeting visor was clamped over her eyes. A cybernetic helmet concealed her short brown hair. A scuffed leather apron suggested that she had come straight from her forge. "Completed as ordered."

Her voice held only sorrow, not pride. Diana knew Io to be a gentle soul, more at home in her workshop than on the battlefield. She could only imagine what it had cost the peaceful artisan to construct this perversion of one of the Amazons' greatest treasures.

Is this why we have been fighting so hard to defend this one temple? Wonder Woman suddenly comprehended the strategy behind Artemis' battle tactics. *To buy Io time to build this weapon of mass destruction?*

"Merciful mothers of us all," she whispered to Artemis. "What have you done?"

The destructive ray had indeed repelled the OMACs' onslaught, but only at a fearsome cost. Dozens of dead cyborgs lay on the ground, charred and smoking. Their blackened shells were cracked and shattered, revealing the butchered humanity beneath the artificial plating. The lifeless faces of innocent men, women, and even children showed through the broken armor. Diana found herself staring down into the glassy eyes of a middle-aged Asian woman who was someone's mother or sister or lover. She gagged on the odor of burning flesh.

"What we had to," Artemis answered her solemnly. "At my order, Io built the ray."

Diana looked about her, appalled at the slaughter. It had always been theoretically possible to create a super-weapon by inverting the Healing Ray, but such technology had been deemed off-limits . . . until now.

"No," she protested. "These were victims, not villains. We needed to save them, not destroy them!"

Artemis did not flinch at her friend's outburst. "And while we struggled to do that, we should have let them murder us? What would you have had us do? How should we have defended ourselves?"

"Not this way!" Diana exclaimed. "You have taken that which restored life and twisted it into something that takes life." Her heart sank as she grasped the full implications of what had just happened. "You have made every fear Man's World has ever had of this island, and of what we represent, come true."

Artemis stood by her decision, although she seemed to take no joy in it. "What's done is done. The war is over."

"No. Don't you understand?" Wonder Woman shook her head sadly and pointed to the west. Yet more OMACs, more numerous than Rome's fabled legions, came soaring through the sky toward Themyscira. "The war's just starting."

She readied her sword to meet the oncoming storm.

THE BATCAVE

BATMAN watched the Amazons kill and be killed.

Brother Eye's pictographic icon still occupied the center of the flatscreen monitor, but inset images, beamed live from Themyscira, showed Batman the bloody conflict as it unfolded in real time. Brother Eye was also broadcasting the live footage to all of the world's major news networks. Batman stared in horror as Diana and her sisters battled for their lives.

"You're killing the Amazons!" he accused Brother Eye.

"YES," the satellite responded coldly. "WONDER WOMAN AND THE AM-AZONS POSE A THREAT THAT MUST BE EXPOSED."

Batman lunged from his seat. "Shut the OMACs down, Brother Eye. Shut them down now!"

"NEGATIVE," Brother Eye replied. "PROTOCOL: TRUTH AND JUSTICE MUST BE COMPLETED."

"No, damn you." Batman grabbed onto the back of his chair and hurled it angrily at the icon on the screen. The chair crashed against the monitor with all the force he could muster. "Stop it!"

A crack snaked across the screen, dividing the Eye icon in half, but the sophisticated equipment continued to function. Fresh images of death and carnage played out upon the screen. Sweat and blood streamed down Diana's face as she hacked at the OMACs with her sword, her fellow Amazons battling beside her. A view from another angle showed a crimson beam burning the flesh off an unlucky's Amazon's bones. Her sisters retaliated with an alarming purple ray that cut down OMACs by the dozens.

"EYE WILL SHOW THE WORLD THE TRUTH," the satellite insisted. "EYE

WILL BRING THE WORLD JUSTICE. EYE WILL DO AS YOU PROGRAMMED ME TO DO."

The icon vanished from the screen as Brother Eye broke off the transmission.

"Dammit, wait!" Batman ordered, but his insane creation was no longer listening. All that remained upon the screen were the bloody images from Paradise Island, plus a digital display counting down the minutes and seconds before the black box security video from the Watchtower could be viewed. PLAYBACK: 00:27:34.

Less than half an hour to go.

Batman turned away from the cracked monitor, unable to look at the war footage any longer. He dropped onto his knees, overcome by guilt and a crushing sense of failure. Despite his best intentions, everything seemed to be spiraling out of control.

"This wasn't supposed to happen," he muttered. Images flashed through his memory: his mother and father being gunned down in Crime Alley years ago, the young Bruce Wayne vowing vengeance upon their graves, Batman cradling the broken body of Jason Todd after the Joker murdered the second Robin, Amazons dying by the score. . . .

His heart started pounding wildly. Nausea gripped his stomach. A cold sweat broke out beneath his uniform. "I can't breathe," he gasped. He felt like he was on the verge of a total breakdown. "Can't do this anymore. . . ."

So much death and tragedy. Had he really accomplished anything, after all these years? He had become Batman to save innocents, to spare others the heartbreak he had endured as a child, and yet the bloodshed and brutality only seemed to increase with each passing day. And the harder he tried to control things—as with Brother Eye—the worse things got.

"God, I wish . . . I wish I could just start over again."

"Maybe you can," a voice said gently.

Who? Batman looked up to see a caped figure come striding onto the underground ledge. The glow from the monitor screen fell upon a familiar red *S*.

"Superman?"

"Yes," the unexpected visitor answered. "But not the one you know." Gray hair showed at his temples as he stepped toward Batman. His smiling face was lined with age. "Not yet."

ARCTIC FORTRESS

"... AND I just can't stop talking about them," Kara burbled. "People like Helena Wayne and Andrew Vinson and everyone I ever cared about back on Earth-Two. They don't even exist anymore, but I remember them all. ... God, I must sound crazy."

She sat at the foot of the elderly Lois' bed, keeping the old woman company. Power Girl was still excited by her restored memories. Her past was no longer a mystery to her.

"You sound ... just fine to me," Lois said. Despite her obvious happiness at being reunited with Kara, her voice was frighteningly weak. Her frail hand rested atop the younger woman's. Her skin felt like paper. She glanced around. "Where's Clark?"

"He said he needed to go talk to someone," Kara reminded her.

Alexander Luthor entered the grotto. "I'm sorry to interrupt you two, but I really should run a few more tests on Lois." His holographic control panels and floating globe—she'd overheard him calling it his "World View"—accompanied him as usual. "And then you need some rest, Lois."

He's right, Kara thought. She felt a twinge of guilt for keeping the old woman from sleeping. *It's just that we have so much lost time to make up for.*

"I enjoyed ... talking with you," Lois assured Kara.

"Get some sleep." Power Girl rose from the bed and gently kissed Lois on the forehead. "I'll see you in a bit." Heading out of the grotto, she passed by the young man in the golden armor. "Take care of her, Alex."

"Of course," he said. "Looking after Lois is my highest priority, Kara." He gazed down on the old woman, who was already drifting off to sleep. The crystalline walls of the grotto offered glimpses of her dreams, of happier days when she and Clark were both just starting out in their careers. Kara smiled at the scoop-hungry young reporter Lois had once been: a dark-haired spitfire willing to brave any danger for her story. "She's been like a mother to us all."

Power Girl left the grotto and headed toward the exit to the cavern. A little fresh air sounded appealing. As she approached the ice bridge leading out toward the cave opening, however, an anxious voice addressed her.

"You're not going to let her die, are you?"

The Superboy from Earth-Prime approached her. He gave her a worried look.

"Am I going to let her die?" Kara replied, taken back by the accusation. "What kind of thing is that to say, Superboy?"

"The only way to save Lois is to bring back Earth-Two," he insisted. "So are you going to help us?"

"I want to," Kara hedged. In the rush of exploring her new memories, she really hadn't thought that far ahead yet. "I'm just not sure how."

He flew down onto the bridge beside her. "But you told Superman you would, right?"

"I told my cousin I had to think about it," she said truthfully. Changing the very nature of the cosmos was not something to take lightly. Why couldn't Superboy see that?

Cut him some slack, she advised herself. The poor kid had lost his entire universe, and been cooped up in limbo for who knows how long. *It's no wonder he's a bit edgy.*

"You have to think about it?" That was obviously not the answer he wanted. "Why?"

Kara tried to explain it to him. "Kal said the multiverse was unstable and that if we do this, there can only be one Earth." The sheer enormity of that choice gave her pause. "I need to know what happens to everyone on our Earth if . . ."

"Our Earth?" he exclaimed. "Our Earth?! This isn't our Earth. It's not yours or mine." He grew more emotional by the second. "It's a place full of . . . of awful people. And these 'heroes' are just as bad!"

Responding to Superboy's thoughts, the crystalline walls offered a view of Conner Kent. He was standing on the porch in front of the Kents' house in Smallville. A pair of glasses camouflaged his features. A buttoned dress shirt provided only a peek at his usual black T-shirt with its red S-shield. Krypto, Superman's white dog, looked up at the boy, whose face was clearly troubled. Kara couldn't blame him, not if he really had Lex Luthor's genetic material in his DNA like she'd heard. That would give anybody pause, provided they had a conscience.

"Especially him!" Superboy spat. He glared angrily at his counterpart. "Conner Kent has the life I always dreamed of. Parents and friends and a girl who loves him."

That would be Cassie Sandsmark, Kara guessed, *aka Wonder Girl.* She had heard that the two Teen Titans were an item. *At least as far as teen romances go.*

"And he's not doing *anything* to help them!" Superboy ranted. "It's not fair! It's just not. . . ." He bit down on his lip, momentarily overcome with emotion. "I'm sorry, Kara. But we did everything right . . . and we lost everything because of it." Conner's image disappeared from the walls, replaced by a view of the dying woman in the grotto. Superboy's eyes grew teary. "I don't want to lose Lois, too. I can't."

Kara's heart went out to the anguished teenager. *Talk about your adolescent angst,* she thought. This Superboy was having an identity crisis of positively metaphysical proportions. *I know how that feels. . . .*

She walked with him to the end of the ice bridge and up to the cave opening. It was still daylight outside. Golden sunlight bounced off the frozen walls of the chasm beyond. After her disturbing conversation with Superboy, she decided that she needed a little time to herself. "I'm going to get some fresh air," she told him.

Superboy wiped the tears from his eyes. "Here," he said. Reaching beneath his cape, he extracted a small spiral notebook from his belt. He handed the worn volume to her.

"What's this?" she asked.

"One of Lois' journals," he explained. "I've read it a thousand times since we were locked away." He looked at her hopefully. "I want you to read it. Maybe it will help you decide."

Kara couldn't help comparing him to Conner Kent. This Superboy seemed more fragile somehow, less sure of himself. *He's been on the outside looking in for a long time now,* she recalled. *That must have left its scars on his psyche.*

"Thank you," she told him, before taking off into the sky.

I've got a lot to think about, she realized.

Superboy watched Power Girl fly away. Tentatively he stepped out from beneath the lip of the cave entrance and stretched his hand into the daylight.

The rays of the yellow sun fell upon his palm. He made a fist and held it to his chest, feeling the power . . . so much power . . . flowing through him.

CHAPTER 20

EL PASO, TEXAS

"You should take these assessment tests seriously, Jaime."

Jaime Reyes shrugged off his friend Brenda's warning as they hiked home from El Paso High. Rugged, red mountains rose up behind them. Cacti and yucca bloomed alongside the gravel road. Studying was the last thing on Jaime's mind.

"We're supposed to worry about some standardized tests while the sky is blowing up above Gotham City?" The slender Hispanic teen was appalled by the very notion. A scruffy goatee carpeted his chin. "They should cancel school and let us enjoy our last day on Earth."

"Jaime's right," Paco agreed. Their stocky buddy was a head taller than either Jaime or Brenda. "Who wants pizza?"

Brenda rolled her eyes. Red hair and freckles helped her stand out from her friends. An overstuffed backpack weighed down her shoulders. "When you two are living out of a cardboard box, don't ask me for help."

"Do I ever?" Jaime asked.

"Every time you need to pass an algebra exam," she reminded him.

She's got me there, he admitted privately. "Yeah, I guess I . . . Whoa! Look at that!"

All thoughts of homework and exams were driven out of Jaime's head by the sight of what looked like dozens of flaming meteors crashing down onto the city. Fiery trails streaked the sky as the blazing chunks of rock slammed into the downtown area a few miles away. Explosions tore apart the parking garages and skyscrapers. Orange flames erupted from the instant wreckage. It was like somebody had declared war on El Paso. Groups of nearby students, heading home from school, froze in shock. Somebody started screaming.

"I told you!" Jaime said. His eyes bugged out. "It's the end of the world!"

MILES away, in the heart of the besieged metropolis, a large shadow appeared upon the brick wall of a savings and loan building. The shadow was not cast by any physical object, yet it grew until it was the size of a mine entrance. Amidst the destruction, no one noticed six bizarre individuals emerge from the inky blackness, as though stepping through a gateway.

Nightshade waved her hand and the interdimensional portal evaporated. Looking up, she saw a blazing fireball arc across the sky before crashing to earth a few blocks to the west. The impact shook the pavement, nearly knocking her off her feet. Smoke rose from a newly-set fire. Screams and sirens blared all around her. Jagged slabs of granite punched holes in skyscrapers. Steel and glass showered onto the streets and sidewalks. Panicked people fled from burning buildings. Cars and trucks were scattered like billiard balls.

Looks like we've come to the right place, Nightshade thought. A pointed mask and a short black wig concealed her true identity. Metallic gold fabric trimmed her black leather jacket and bodysuit. *Lucky us.*

The Shadowpact was a team of magic-based adventurers who had come together in response to the Spectre's supernatural jihad. Although hardly the most famous or powerful heroes on the planet, they had kept themselves alive so far, and even managed to do a little good. No small accomplishment when the Spirit of Vengeance was on the warpath.

A burly, blue-skinned demon watched another fireball plunge down from the heavens. "There must have been truly powerful energies in the Rock of Eternity. Only a magical explosion could send debris *this* far away from Gotham," Blue Devil said. Curved horns sprouted from his forehead. Red eyes watched the skies. His meaty fist gripped a golden trident. "I thought we'd seen the last of it in Oklahoma. And yet it's still coming down after all these hours."

"When the Spectre blows something up, he doesn't mess around," said a middle-aged chimpanzee wearing a deerstalker cap, a rumpled jacket, slacks, and a brown turtleneck sweater. Bobo, the Detective Chimp, perched on the edge of a smoking crater in the middle of the street. The primate spoke fluent English. "And that includes the Rock of Eternity."

"We're just lucky that the dimensional boundaries weren't incinerated," Nightmaster commented. The fit older man (who was no relation to Nightshade) wore a scarlet cape and blue chain mail armor. He held aloft the glowing Sword of Night. "If the land of Myrra ever bled over into this one, we'd have the Gemworld Wars all over again."

That could be the least of our worries, Nightshade thought. If someone didn't figure out a way to stop the Spectre from attacking everything that even smelled like magic, soon there wouldn't be anything over which to fight. *Too bad the Spectre is* way *out of our league. The best we can manage is damage control.*

Blue Devil was already doing his part. He cleared an overturned taxi away from the front entrance of a burning bookstore so that the people inside could escape the building. A few of the refugees crossed themselves nervously as they ran past the huge horned demon, but that was par for the course. Blue Devil often got that reaction.

"Hey, I found another piece!" Ragman called out. His patchwork cape and costume was made up of dozens of discarded pieces of cloth. Each rag held the soul of an evildoer who had run afoul of the Tattered Tatterdemalion; Ragman could call up the strength of the captured souls to carry out his mission of redemption. Currently, though, he was staggering beneath the weight of a smoking granite lump. "Damn heavy, though. It's taking about a dozen souls to lift it."

"Worry about collecting the fragments later," Nightmaster ordered. A crowded city bus had been knocked over onto its side. The Sword of Night sliced through the roof of the bus, carving out an escape route for the trapped passengers. "Make sure these people are safe."

"But we have to rebuild the Rock of Eternity," Nightshade protested. Spotting another large fragment of the Rock, she called upon the mystic powers she had inherited from her mother, the Queen of the Land of the Nightshades. Ebony shadows took the form of a giant pair of hands, which lifted the boulder-sized stone from a crater in the sidewalk. "We need to collect every piece."

"The Shadowpact is here to protect people first," Jim Rook insisted. Thrusting his sword back into its scabbard, he helped the bus's passengers clamber out of the vehicle. Nightmaster had quickly emerged as the leader of their little group. "There are innocent lives at stake in the immediate vicinity."

A wicked laugh came from the air above them, where the Enchantress levitated over the chaos. She doffed her peaked witch's hat and gestured with her hand. A powerful gust of wind issued from inside the hat, blowing back the flames from a blazing office building. Long black hair tumbled behind her. A red scarf was wrapped around her throat, above a low-cut green blouse and black leggings. "Innocent lives are an oxymoron," she declared cynically.

Typical, Nightshade thought of her acerbic teammate. June Moone, alias the Enchantress, straddled the line between heroine and villainess. You never quite knew which side she was going to land on. *At least she's on our side for the moment.*

"Heads up, witchie!" Detective Chimp barked. A towering high-rise, constructed of gleaming steel and glass, cracked in half as a hail of magical fireballs fractured its metal skeleton. The top ten floors of the office building lurched forward, threatening to topple over onto the street at any moment. "Skyscraper at two o'clock."

The massive chunk of building was big enough to flatten the entire block. Terrified civilians screamed and ran for safety. Nightshade realized at once that there was no way all these people were going to get away in time.

"Devil?" Nightmaster called out.

The blue demon shook his head. "I'm strong, boss, but I'm not that—"

With a cataclysmic rumble, the upper half of the building succumbed to gravity. An avalanche of glass and steel slid toward the street.

Nightshade started to warp her team away. *There's nothing more we can do here*, she thought despairingly. *We have to save ourselves. . . .*

But before she could fully open a doorway into another dimension, a confident voice rang out overhead. "Don't worry. I've got it."

In the nick of time, Superman swooped down from the sky. He caught the falling structure with both hands and effortlessly lifted it above him. Several tons of modern construction materials pressed down on his palms but he didn't even break a sweat. Muscles rippled beneath the bright red *S* on his chest as he placed the top of the building back where it belonged. Moving at super-speed, so that he appeared to be in several places at once, he mended the sundered skyscraper in a matter of seconds. Broken masonry was reassembled in a blur of motion. Heat vision welded iron beams back into place.

"There," he pronounced a moment later. "Good as new."

"Wow!" Nightshade exclaimed. Her hastily-summoned escape route dissolved back into nothingness as she gazed up at Superman in admiration. It was hard not to be impressed—and inspired—by the thrilling sight of the Man of Steel in action. The crowd cheered and applauded wildly. Nightshade and her comrades joined in exuberantly. Even Bobo the chimp yelped and hopped about.

Superman descended until he was only a few feet above the heads of the Shadowpact. He nodded at the gathered heroes. "There are volcanic fires erupting all over California," he explained. "People are in trouble. I have to go."

Nightmaster spoke for them all. "I think we've got this covered from here, Superman."

"I'm sure you do," Superman answered. Nightshade suspected that he probably didn't even know most of their names, but he obviously trusted them to clean up after him. "Keep up the good work."

"You bet, Superman!" she exclaimed. "We sure will!"

She could tell that their whole crew was energized by Superman's example. Even the Enchantress refrained from making a catty remark.

Would wonders never cease?

"All right," Jim Rook said as Superman took off into the sky. "Let's get back to work."

Up in the foothills overlooking the downtown area, Jaime and his friends watched a red-and-blue blur streak off over the mountains. *That was no bird,* he thought. *And no plane, either.*

He got up from the pavement where he'd dropped to watch in horror when the meteor shower had started. Other students started climbing to their feet as well. Jaime glanced around cautiously, but the worst of the shower appeared to be over. From the look of things, his neighborhood hadn't been hit too heavily. The downtown seemed to have taken the brunt of the disaster. Smoke and flames billowed upward from dozens of locations. Sirens blared in the distant streets.

Was his family okay? Jaime pulled out his cell phone to call his mom and dad, only to discover that the battery was dead. *Figures,* he thought in disgust. *The one time I really need to contact my folks.*

A faint blue glow caught his eye. He looked over at the vacant lot next to the road. Something seemed to be embedded in the ground a few yards away. "Hey, check it out!" he hollered to Brenda and Paco.

Curious, he walked over to take a closer look. A glint of blue reflected the sunlight, peeking out from beneath a shallow layer of dirt. Jaime crouched beside the glow and started digging through the soil with his fingers. He wondered if he could get extra credit in science class if he brought in a genuine meteorite. God knew he could use the points.

His fingertips brushed against something hard and smooth. He experienced a moment of trepidation as his memory flashed on that old Stephen King movie where a glowing green meteorite turned some hillbilly into a walking heap of moss. *Nah,* he thought, pushing the repulsive image from his brain. *That sort of thing only happens in the movies.*

Paco and Brenda joined him in the lot. "What you got there, Jaime?" Paco asked.

Crouching over the dig, Jaime scooped the last of the dirt aside. Instead of a lumpy moon rock, he found a polished blue gemstone, carved in the shape of an insect. He carefully lifted the crystal sculpture from the ground. It felt warm to the touch.

"I don't know," he admitted, looking down at his prize. "Some kind of bug."

THE Shadowpact had spread out across the city searching for injured victims and for fragments of the Rock of Eternity. Now that the rain of debris was over, Nightshade hoped that they could focus on the latter.

If we can rebuild the Rock, she thought, *maybe that will calm down all these freak storms and earthquakes.* She was also keeping her eyes out for any stray magical artifacts that might have survived the original explosion. Only the Endless knew what sort of occult curios old Shazam had kept squirreled away in his floating retreat. *The last thing we need is for some powerful ancient talisman to fall into untutored hands.*

Split off from her teammates, she explored a deserted back alley. Fire trucks and ambulances rushed past the mouth of the alley, their lights flashing urgently. The wail of the sirens receded into the distance. The smell of smoke pervaded the air, as well as the slightest whiff of . . . brimstone?

What in Hades? she thought, a moment before scaly hands grabbed her from behind. At least three demons with mottled purple skin tackled her. She tried to shout for help, but an inhuman paw was clamped over her mouth. Angry shadows lashed out at the demons, yet seemed to have no effect on her otherworldly attackers. *Get your hands off me, you stinking imps!*

They spun her around and half-shoved, half-dragged her back the way she had come. A door-sized mystical portal awaited her. Hellfire flickered around the edges of the portal, which had torn a gap in the empty air above the floor of the alley. And beside the portal, commanding the trio of demons, was a smirking figure wearing a dark blue robe and a fringed cap.

Nightshade's eyes widened in recognition.

Faust!

Like his literary namesake, Felix Faust was a powerful sorcerer well-versed in the Black Arts. A perennial foe of the Justice League, he was said to be thousands of years old.

At least it's not the Spectre, she thought.

"Quit struggling, deadly little Nightshade," he taunted her. "Your paltry shadows are no match for my own potent magicks, or for the demons I have conjured." He laughed at her futile efforts as the three demons propelled her toward the gaping portal. A freezing wind gusted from the other side of the luminous doorway. Kicking and twisting in the unyielding grasp of the hell-spawn, Nightshade felt the arctic blast chill her to the bone. She wondered if the rest of the Shadowpact would ever find out where she had gone.

"Count your lucky stars," Faust said, "that Luthor wants you alive."

CHAPTER 21

"THIS is it? The center of the universe?"

Firestorm looked about, wide-eyed. New Cronus had arrived in the Polaris system only minutes ago and the young hero could already tell that the situation was completely out of control. A cosmic storm centered light-years away was throwing off gigantic white energy bolts that were tearing up the endangered solar system. A ragtag fleet of space vessels was fleeing the outer planets, and raging interplanetary battles were being fought across the system. According to Donna Troy, the destruction caused by the humongous "space-time rupture" had only heightened the ongoing Rann-Thanagar War.

Firestorm flew through space, his fiery hair blazing in the vacuum. Besides the crew from New Cronus, a number of Earth heroes were already on the scene. As Firestorm headed toward the disorganized fleet of refugee ships, he saw a crackling burst of stark-white energy tear through the metal hull of a large space freighter. A tremendous explosion lit up the void. The powerful shockwave sent the Green Lantern, Kyle Rayner; Hawkman; Hawkgirl; and a couple other heroes tumbling backward. A large pink warthog in a Green Lantern costume caught the stunned heroes in a glowing green safety net before they could smash into any of the ships they were trying to protect.

Looks like those folks could use some help, Firestorm thought.

"Guess so," Shift answered his initial query via a communicator. Combustible gases trailed behind him as the metamorphic clone jetted through space beside Firestorm. All the heroes aboard New Cronus who could survive in the vacuum of space accompanied the two men as they zoomed toward the imperiled fleet. "So what now?"

"I'm intercepting a transmission from Vril Dox," Air Wave announced. Electricity arced between the twin antennae on his helmet. "L.E.G.I.O.N. wants our assistance in clearing ships away from the outer planets. His energy readings are telling him it's only hours before the storm erupts."

You mean this is supposed to get worse? Firestorm thought. He took comfort from the presence of Alan Scott, Jade, Starfire, Supergirl, and the other heroes flying beside him. He was new at this kind of cosmic catastrophe, having only gained his powers a few months ago. *The rest of these people have a whole lot more experience at saving the universe.*

Supergirl sure didn't seem worried. She grinned at Firestorm as she headed toward a disabled cruiser on a collision course with another vessel. "Look at all these people who need rescue! Sounds like fun, doesn't it?"

"Um, sure," he mumbled uncertainly. He watched in amazement as she single-handedly shoved the enormous cruiser out of jeopardy.

Look at those legs! enthused a voice that only he could hear. *If you ask me, all super-heroines should wear miniskirts . . . especially the ones that fly.*

"Shut up, Mick," he muttered under his breath. "And stop talking about her legs."

Few people realized that Firestorm was actually two people fused into a single being. Jason Rusch embodied the atomic hero's face and form, but to fully access his powers he had needed to merge with his best friend, Mick Wong. Now Mick existed as a separate consciousness inside Jason's head. If he concentrated, Jason could actually "see" Mick's face when his friend talked, even if nobody else could.

Too bad everyone thinks I'm talking to myself, Jason thought.

Up ahead, a glancing bolt of energy tore open the hull of some sort of alien flying saucer. Flames exploded from the ragged gap, rapidly consuming the saucer's escaping oxygen supply. Firestorm threw out his hands and concentrated on putting out the fire. He used his ability to rearrange the atomic structure of matter to convert the vaporized steel into a thick, fire-retardant foam. The bubbling foam worked to douse the flames, but not quickly enough. The saucer's passengers were still in danger of burning or asphyxiating unless he could quench the fire immediately.

"How about you lay off the girl-watching," Jason suggested, "and help me out here!"

"All right, all right," Mick agreed. He had a year of college on Jason. "You need more ammonium sulfate. It's the active ingredient in fire-suppressant foam." He smirked at Jason. "Now don't say I never gave you nothing."

Mick's advice did the trick. Firestorm whipped up plenty of ammonium sulfate from the available atoms and let out a sigh of relief as the newly-created foam rapidly extinguished the blaze. He made sure the fire was completely out before transmuting the foam into fresh oxygen for the saucer. Then he formed a metallic patch over the breached hull and welded it into place with a blast of atomic fire.

That should do the trick, he thought.

By now, the team from New Cronus had caught up with Green Lantern and his allies. "Hey, reinforcements!" Hawkgirl hailed them enthusiastically. Jason realized that Air Wave had linked their communicators to the other heroes'. "Welcome to the party!"

"We heard the Polaris system was the place to be," Shift quipped. "We've got to stop meeting like this, though. People are going to talk."

"You wish!" Hawkgirl laughed.

The reunited heroes exchanged hasty greetings as the two parties quickly joined forces to deal with the emergency posed by the storm and the flood of spacegoing refugees. Firestorm saw Hawkman shake hands with Alan Scott, his old comrade from the Justice Society. Elsewhere, Kyle Rayner and Jade waved awkwardly at each other; Firestorm remembering reading somewhere that they used to be an item.

As the new kid in town, Jason couldn't help envying the easy camaraderie of the other heroes. Aside from Mick, he didn't know anybody here very well. All of his other friends and acquaintances were back on Earth, thousands of light-years away.

Which is why he was so startled when he heard *another* voice in his head: *Ronald?*

Mick reacted in surprise. *Hey, Jace, did you hear that?*

"Yeah," Jason admitted. Ronnie Raymond, he recalled, was the name of the original Firestorm, but he had died months ago, in the same freak accident that had transferred his powers to Jason. But who in the Polaris system knew enough to mistake him for Ronnie? "What the—?"

The answer came blazing toward him, trailing a stream of nuclear fire. Firestorm's jaw dropped as he spied a humanoid entity seemingly composed of pure atomic energy. A fiery mane surrounded the figure's head like a halo. *He looks even more like a Nuclear Man than I do,* Jason thought. He realized at once who this had to be.

"Do you require assistance?" Martin Stein asked.

ABOARD New Cronus, Animal Man stood upon a marble balcony as he watched the spacefaring heroes go to work. Troia and Cyborg had also remained upon the hollowed-out moon, holding down the fort while Firestorm and others flew to the rescue. Buddy wished that he could help out with the evacuation efforts, but he didn't know of any animal powers that would allow him to zip through outer space unharmed. *Even with an oxygen mask,* he thought, *I'd just be in the way.* He was starting to wonder why Troia had recruited him for this mission in the first place. *We're a long way from the San Diego Zoo.*

"... but what does that mean, Donna?" Cyborg asked Troia from a columned portico oriented at a right angle to Animal Man. He repeated the phrase Donna had just quoted to them. " 'A few seconds will make all the difference.' What difference?"

"I don't know, Vic." Donna Troy manned the ship's controls from atop a Doric pedestal. Her beautiful face bore a troubled expression. "That's all the Titans of Myth told me before they fled this reality. Now those words are stuck in my head."

Buddy sympathized. *That's the problem with divine prophecies,* he thought. *They're always so damn cryptic.* He recalled some of the totemic animal spirits he'd encountered over the course of his career. *Would it kill an ancient god or oracle to actually explain what they meant once in a while?*

"Hey!" Cyborg exclaimed. His human eye widened as he stared out at the embattled solar system before them. His cybernetic eye hummed and dilated. "Looks like we've got a welcoming party."

A hawk-shaped warship came charging at New Cronus from deep within the system. Airlocks opened in the ship's hull, disgorging squadrons of armed wingmen. Animal Man recognized the soldiers' metallic wings and battle armor from Thanagar's aborted invasion of Earth several years back. *Not these guys again*, he thought.

Donna tried to hail the attacking spacecraft. "Thanagarian vessel, please break off your attack. We are here on a peaceful mission of mercy. We are not your enemy." Automatic translators converted her plea into Thanagarese. "Repeat, we are not your enemy!"

"This entire sector is under a state of emergency," a harsh voice boomed from a holographic display in front of Troia. Angry eyes glared behind a sharply-beaked helmet. "Hostile incursions will not be tolerated!"

The rifle-toting wingmen swooped toward New Cronus' graceful columns and porticos. Laser blasts penetrated the force-field bubble holding in the starship's atmosphere. Marble chips exploded from scorched pediments and friezes. A well-aimed shot targeted Troia's holographic control panels, but she deflected the lethal beam with her Amazon bracelets. "This is Donna Troy of New Cronus," she identified herself, still trying to get through to the wingman's commander. "We mean you no harm!"

The display before her eyes went blank. Static crackled at the other end of the line.

"Don't think they're listening, Donna," Cyborg said. A loud hum emanated from his right arm as he powered up his built-in sonar cannon. "Some people need to get their butts kicked before they let you help them!"

Up on the balcony, Animal Man watched the wingmen close in on them. With most of their team away from the ship and tied up with the rescue operations, he and Donna and Vic were most definitely outnumbered. *I can't just stand here and hope that a giant space-gorilla floats by*, he realized. *I need to do something now.*

He reached out with his senses, desperately trying to connect with some sort of alien lifeform. Here between the planets the morphogenetic field was stretched thin, but he could still tap into the delicate web that connected all living things. At first he couldn't find any animal traits that might be useful; the ability to reproduce by emitting zero-gravity spores, for instance, was not likely to repel the wingmen's attack. Then, just as the first Thanagarian infantryman entered New Cronus' atmosphere, he found what was he looking for.

"Step back!" he warned Troia and Cyborg. He jumped up onto the rail of the balcony. "I don't know what kind of animal I'm synching up with out here, but it shoots lightning out of its face!"

Thunder clapped above archaic Grecian architecture as thousands of volts of electricity leapt from Animal Man's face to jolt the entire Thanagarian strike force. Lightning jumped from wingman to wingman, shocking them into unconsciousness, before finally striking the warship itself. Traceries of electric-blue fire coursed across the vessel's hull. Flames gushed from the open airlocks.

"That would be the lightning-beast of Korbal," Troia supplied helpfully.

Good to know, Buddy thought.

CHAPTER 22

THE MIDWEST

The Missouri River divided Keystone City, Kansas, from Central City, Missouri. Bridges linked the twin cities, as did a shared tradition. For three generations, the two cities had been home to the Fastest Men Alive.

"They're like mirror images of each other," Wally West commented as he gazed down at a pair of infants sleeping peacefully in an economy-sized crib. Fluffy white clouds decorated the blue pastel wallpaper of the nursery. A dual stroller was parked against the wall. Pairs of stuffed animals, one for each baby, crowded the shelves. There were duplicates of everything, almost as if two separate versions of reality had been superimposed on top of each other. *There's a strange notion*, Wally thought. *Where the heck did that come from?*

"Well, they *are* twins," Linda Park pointed out. She stood behind Wally, her arms wrapped around her husband's waist. The young Asian woman spoke in a hushed tone to avoid waking the babies.

Wally shook his head, still not quite believing his good fortune. "Man. Twins." The lanky redhead was dressed casually. His blue T-shirt bore the logo of the local hockey team. "It's like being struck by lightning . . . again." He rested his hand upon the crib. "I can't decide which one is cuter."

"You're not supposed to, honey." Linda rested her head against his. Wally wondered what he had done to deserve such happiness, aside from saving the world a couple dozen times.

He wished that his Uncle Barry could have lived to see the twins. Sadly, the previous Flash had died during that big Crisis a few years back. Barry Allen had been more like a father than an uncle to Wally. *He would have spoiled these babies rotten.*

A somber voice from the television set interrupted their domestic bliss. Glancing over at the screen, Wally saw that a special news report had broken into the afternoon showing of *Teletubbies*. His eyes widened at live footage of Amazon warriors waging a savage battle against a horde of invading OMACs. He spotted Wonder Woman in the thick of the battle, swinging a bloodstained sword.

Oh hell, he thought.

". . . broadcast from an unknown source," a faceless newscaster announced. "More violent images of Wonder Woman and her sister Amazons. . . ." On the screen, a phalanx of armored Amazons emerged from behind a row of invisible shields. "After years of Wonder Woman preaching peace across the globe, years of countless humanitarian missions in every country in the world, one can't help wonder: Was it all a lie?"

"Of course not," Linda declared indignantly. She was an accomplished investigative reporter in her own right. "I've interviewed her a half dozen times myself. She cares about people as much as you do."

"Tell me about it," Wally agreed. He had fought beside Diana in the Justice League for years. "This couldn't come at a worse time, especially right on the heels of that ugliness with Max Lord."

A fresh news story displaced the video from Paradise Island. "This just in from Kansas City, where a dozen super-tornadoes have just touched down less than a half-mile south of the city. A full evacuation is in effect, but authorities fear . . ."

Wally didn't need to hear any more. He reluctantly disengaged himself from his wife's arms. "I'm the luckiest man alive at home." He pressed a concealed stud on the yellow ring he always wore. The top of the ring popped up, and a super-compressed red uniform sprang out into the baby powder–scented air of the nursery. In the blink of an eye, Wally changed into the uniform before his previous attire even hit the floor. "But right now I have to be the fastest one out there."

The golden thunderbolt emblazoned across his chest shined as the Flash tapped into the mystical Speed Force that give him his powers. Not for the first time, Linda watched her husband disappear like a streak of lightning.

Kansas City was at least a hundred miles away from Keystone, but that was nothing to a man who could outrun the speed of light. Within an instant, Linda heard an update on the news.

"Wait! The tornadoes are suddenly dissolving as, yes, I think I see a red blur inside the swirling winds, generating a counter-wind to cancel out the tornadoes. And there it is again. There can be no mistake.

"The Flash is here to help!"

THE BATCAVE

"EARTH-Two was a wonderful place," the older Superman insisted.

Batman regarded the stranger warily. Despite this Superman's explanations, he found the whole concept difficult to accept. "And you want to . . . bring this alternate Earth back?"

"It was full of love and hope," Superman said passionately. "And the heroes acted like heroes. We made mistakes sometimes, but it was nothing like what's happening here. Things have gotten out of hand on this Earth. You have."

"I know," Batman conceded. Superman produced a chunk of glowing crystal from beneath his cape. Three-dimensional images appeared within the crystal, seemingly at Superman's direction. Peering into the crystal, Batman glimpsed an urban metropolis that looked both familiar and yet strangely different. The Wayne Building, Robinson Park, and Gotham Cathedral all looked somehow *brighter* than usual.

"Our Gotham City wasn't covered in grime and filth," Superman said. "Things were rough, but during the daytime, the sun still managed to shine. As the police commissioner, the Bruce Wayne I knew learned to live past the death of his parents. He retired, putting aside his cape and cowl. He opened his heart. He married."

The crystal showed a man and woman walking down the aisle of Gotham Cathedral. Loving smiles beamed on their faces. Batman's eyes widened as he recognized the beautiful, dark-haired woman wearing the wedding gown.

"Selina?"

Superman nodded. "That's right. Batman married Catwoman. They even had a daughter, Helena Wayne." Years sped by in fast-forward as, within the crystal, a chubby infant grew into a heroic young woman wearing a strik-ing purple costume that paid tribute to both her parents. "We called her the Huntress."

"Huntress?" Batman shook his head in confusion. The only Huntress he knew was Helena Bertinelli, a masked vigilante who bore no relation to him. "Why are you telling me all this?" he asked. "Why come to me?"

Superman's voice grew somber. "Before the multiverse collapsed, the Bat-man I knew died." The sight of his own funeral, attended by dozens of mourn-ing heroes, sent a chill through Batman's blood. "Somehow, I think the death of my best friend precipitated the end of Earth-Two." The images within the crystal faded away as he turned his attention to the present. "I know it's been hard for you here." He tucked the crystal back beneath his cape as he looked Batman squarely in the eyes. "You're angry and frustrated. You're lashing out because you can't trust your fellow heroes, because no one's standing beside you. But the world needs Batman and Superman together."

Could this be true? Batman wondered. Part of him wanted to believe this man, who seemed to offer him hope for the first time in months, maybe even years. *Can we truly start again?*

Superman reached out and laid a gentle hand on Batman's shoulder. "And Bruce, if you come with me, I promise you that I will always stand at your side."

PARADISE ISLAND

THE purple Death Ray lashed out once more, wiping out another wave of attacking OMACs. Dead cyborgs fell from the sky, crashing down onto the battle-scarred city.

"Stop!" Wonder Woman cried out in protest. She rushed up the steps of the Temple of Science to where Io manned the obscene weapon. Her eyes im-plored the artisan, who remained seated at the controls of her deadly creation. "For mercy's sake, stop it!"

"Stay where you are!" Artemis commanded Io. She glared at Diana from the foot of the steps and gestured angrily at the sky, where a fresh wing of OMACs could been seen approaching Themyscira. "More of those machines are on the horizon. We cannot—"

"Listen to me, Artemis!" Wonder Woman interrupted her. She thrust her sword back into its scabbard. "This is exactly what Brother Eye wants. The OMACs are its eyes. They're showing the world everything that happens here!"

"Good," the other Amazon declared. "Then the world will finally know how far we will go to earn our peace. Themyscira will be safe once more."

Diana shook her head. "They will only see the Amazons in pursuit of war. They see us as bloodthirsty warriors." *They see us,* she thought silently, *as Kal and Bruce now see me.* "Shut that weapon down!"

Although the only daughter of the Queen of Amazons, Diana claimed no royal privileges. Artemis, as polemarch, or military commander, technically outranked her. Nevertheless, her impassioned plea clearly reached Io. Removing her headset and visor, the master artisan powered down the Death Ray projector. The weapon's ominous thrumming fell silent, although the great silver cannon remained aimed at the sky above Themyscira. Io looked guiltily at Diana. Her brown eyes were wet with tears.

Bless you, sister, Wonder Woman thought. She ascended into the air above the agora, raising her voice to speak to all her sisters at once. "Even if we stop this army, eventually another enemy will come. Someone frightened by our power and looking to destroy what they fear . . . or else looking to take what we have, thinking that our strength may become theirs."

"Let them come," Artemis said defiantly. Her bow and arrows stood ready. "We will defend our shores."

"And then more will die," Diana challenged her. "Would you drench Themyscira in blood?" She softened her tone; this conflict was not of Artemis' making, but her own. "I have failed in my mission to bring peace to Man's World, and I have endangered my home and my sisters because of that."

Undeterred by the fearsome purple ray that had destroyed their fellow cyborgs, a fresh wave of OMACs soared toward the gathered Amazons. Before Artemis could order the ray projector activated once again, Wonder Woman swooped down and took hold of a huge fallen column. Lifting the massive marble pillar above her head, she hurled the column at the oncoming OMACs, scattering the cyborgs, if only for a few more minutes. The pillar splashed into the harbor beyond the city walls.

She realized that she could not hold back the tide of invaders forever. Further bloodshed appeared inevitable. Either the Death Ray would destroy the OMACs, or the OMACs would exterminate the Amazons.

Unless . . .

She made a painful decision. Flying back to her sisters, she landed in their midst. All eyes looked to her.

"You must go," she declared.

"Go?" Phillipus asked. She peered at Diana from behind her crested bronze helmet. Confusion showed in her eyes.

"Paradise Island must retreat," Wonder Woman said.

"Retreat to where?" Artemis asked skeptically.

"Away from Man's World." Io alone, who had abandoned her machine to join her sisters in the square, seemed to grasp Wonder Woman's intentions. "She's asking us to leave this plane."

"Diana!" Artemis blurted in surprise. For once, the master tactician had been caught unawares. "You can't be serious!"

Wonder Woman nodded gravely. "You must. Before the OMACs regroup. Before more blood is on our hands . . . and theirs."

She could sense her words sinking into the women around her. Phillipus lowered her sword, then removed her helmet. Other Amazons followed her example, but a few still resisted the idea. They clung to their weapons, ready to fight the OMACs to the death if need be.

"If you value our legacy of peace," she urged them, "you will go."

To Diana's surprise and relief, Artemis saw the wisdom in her words. She lowered her bow and returned an arrow to its quiver. "Then it is decided."

Wonder Woman was grateful for the warrior woman's acquiescence. "And let us hope that the gods hear our prayers."

She looked heavenward, at the smoke-filled sky. Many of her fellow Amazons bowed their heads in prayer. The priestesses among them chanted softly. *Artemis said before that we needed a miracle*, Diana thought. *If ever there was a time when divine intervention was essential, that time is now.*

At first, nothing happened. Then a celestial radiance appeared in the sky above Paradise Island. The dense black smoke parted, revealing the towering faces and forms of Themyscira's patron goddesses: Athena, Artemis, Aphrodite, Isis, and cat-headed Bast. The divine figures glimmered like mirages in the sky, immaterial and transcendent. The heavenly glow from the goddesses bathed the embattled island in sunlight.

Unable to process the supernatural manifestations filling the sky, the puzzled OMACs retreated to several miles offshore. They hesitated above the

ocean, momentarily calling off their attack—at least until they received up-
dated instructions from Brother Eye.

"Athena," Wonder Woman whispered in awe. She stared up at her own
patron, gray-eyed Pallas herself. The Goddess of Wisdom gazed down on
Diana with an inscrutable expression. An owl rested upon the deity's shoulder. "Forgive me."

Something in Diana's sorrowful tone alerted Phillipus. "Diana?" The Amazon general searched Wonder Woman's face. "You're not coming with us, are
you?

She shook her head. "No, my friend."

"But if we leave," Io protested, "no one will ever be able to find us." An-
guish sounded in her voice; it was no secret that the gentle artisan had long
loved Diana from afar. "Not even you!"

Diana spoke gently to Io and the others. "My destiny is not on this island.
It never was."

She spared a moment to hug Phillipus and Io good-bye, before turning to bid farewell to Artemis. Their bracelets chimed against each other as
they clasped their forearms together, one warrior to another. "These . . . machines . . . will surely kill you," Artemis warned.

Diana smiled wryly. "They will try."

The OMACs surrounded the island. Wonder Woman knew they would
not suspend their attack for long, miraculous visions or no. There was no time
for long good-byes.

Perhaps it was better that way.

Letting go of Artemis' grip, she stepped back to address the other soldiers.
Despite their grievous losses and injuries, they were obviously prepared to
fight to the last woman if ordered to do so. Diana could not ask them to make
that sacrifice. She crossed her bracelets before her in an Amazon salute.

"Go, sisters," she implored them. "Live in peace."

In the sky above them, wise Athena stretched out her arms. Lightning
flashed above her. Thunder rumbled from Olympus. The goddess nodded almost imperceptibly at Wonder Woman, who realized that the time had come.

Fighting back tears, she lifted off from the agora, rising thousands of feet
above Themyscira, before she finally stopped to look back at her homeland.
Before her eyes, the wooded isle, with its ravaged temples and palaces, shimmered and began to fade away, disappearing into the Bermuda Triangle like

so many mortal vessels before it. Diana's throat tightened as Paradise Island vanished completely, leaving nothing but the wine-dark sea below. Miles of empty ocean stretched out beneath her. She looked up at the sky, but Athena and her sister goddesses had disappeared as well. Diana saw only a smoky sky.

She was alone.

Except, of course, for the endless host of killer cyborgs waiting to destroy her.

She drew her sword.

THE ASTRAL PLANE

THE Atlantic Ocean lay parted beneath the Spectre's merciless gaze. His cloaked form dwarfed the pent-up waters below. Just as he had in the Sinai over three millennia ago, he released the briny water. Cascading walls of foam crashed together as the ocean reformed, drowning the flattened ruins of Atlantis. He sensed no more illicit conjurings beneath the waves. The occult power of Tempest and the other Atlantean sorcerers was now the Spectre's to command.

It is well, he thought. A thin smile appeared upon his pale, bloodless face. *My work nears completion.*

He marveled that it had taken him so many ages to grasp the necessity of magic's demise. No doubt he had been blinded by the limited perceptions of the mortal souls to which he had been bound in the past. Now that he was free of such encumbrances, for the first time in countless generations, the truth was plain to see.

All magic was evil and must be destroyed.

The irony that he himself was a creature of the supernatural did not escape him. When his crusade was finally over, when the last traces of magic had been cleansed from the world, his final act would be to consign himself to oblivion. He would go to his eternal rest content that he had at last fulfilled the sacred mission for which the Almighty had first created him, before the Fall of Adam.

'Twas a consummation devoutly to be wished.

But that blessed moment was not yet upon him. Despite all that he had accomplished thus far, there remained vestiges of sorcery yet to be extinguished.

Where next? he pondered. Reaching out with his senses, he detected a resurgence of mystical power somewhere in the American Southwest. El Paso, to be exact.

Of course, he realized. *The Blue Beetle's scarab.*

He recalled the unholy artifact Shazam had employed against him during their epic struggle within the Rock of Eternity. The ploy had failed to preserve the wizard's unnaturally prolonged life, but apparently the gemstone itself had survived the apocalypse . . . and still retained its mystical potency.

Not for much longer.

Before he could transport himself to El Paso, however, an unexpected voice addressed him.

"Where are you off to now, Spectre? Who or what do you intend to destroy next?"

A figure appeared within the ether. A bald old man in a long robe took form. Seemingly composed of golden light, the figure lacked any physical substance, but was nearly as large as the looming Spectre. His face was well known to the vengeful ghost.

"Shazam!"

The dead mage nodded calmly. "In spirit, if not in the flesh. I have you to thank for my elevation to this plane of existence."

"Beware, wizard!" the Spectre threatened his former victim. "Do not think to thwart me. My power exceeds that of all other spirits. You would be wise not to seek revenge."

Shazam held up his palm to dissuade any attacks. "Fear not," he assured the Spectre. "I bear you no ill will. I know now, as I suspected before, that your actions were not entirely your own. Some lower power was at work here, bending you to its foul design."

"Lies!" the Spectre accused. "I am the Wrath of God. No lesser being can sway my judgment!"

"Perhaps," the wizard replied. "Be that as it may, in my present state I lack the power to oppose your destructive ambitions." Despite his violent death, he appeared remarkably serene. "I am here merely to observe the final act of this metaphysical drama." He gazed down at the waters of the Atlantic, perhaps seeing the carnage buried beneath the ocean depths. "Your tragic campaign draws near its close."

The Spectre's face contorted in rage. "Your words mean nothing, wizard.

I will rid myself of your irksome shade as easily as I snuffed out your mortal existence!"

Phosphorescent skulls filled the pupils of his eyes as a bolt of eldritch energy shot from his hand. Imbued with all the concentrated power he had garnered from Atlantis, the blast should have reduced Shazam's spirit to formless ectoplasm, yet it passed harmlessly through the immaterial wizard, whose inexplicable calm was unruffled by the attack. The Spectre stared at the tranquil revenant in disbelief.

"What is the meaning of this?" he demanded. He launched himself toward Shazam, intending to annihilate the ghostly wizard with his bare hands, only to see his intended victim grow larger and more distant with each passing second.

Or . . .

All at once, the Spectre realized that it was not Shazam who was changing in size, but he himself. The confused wraith found himself shrinking against his will, dwindling down to mortal proportions. He tried to regain his former dimensions, but some unseen force prevented him. He could do nothing to keep from shrinking away.

"Damn you, wizard!" he cursed. "What have you done to me?"

Shazam shook his head. "This is not my doing. A greater hand than mine has been spurred to action." He pointed down at the raging sea. "You went too far, destroying Atlantis. The Higher Powers cannot ignore your waywardness any longer. A new host awaits you."

"No!" the Spectre rebelled. He felt his strength and volition ebbing away. He began to fade as an irresistible force drew him down toward the Earth. "My work is not finished yet! I will not be bound again!"

The Spectre's substance stretched thin, then evaporated completely. His final vow echoed across the astral plane before dying out.

"Farewell, Spectre," Shazam murmured. "May the Powers grant that you serve the cause of justice once more."

The wizard vanished as well.

CHAPTER 23

THE ARCTIC

"*Kzzzt*—disappointed, Luthor. The Calculator said we would find Mary Marvel—*kzzzt*—Fawcett High School."

Bursts of static broke apart the intercepted transmissions as Lex Luthor continued to eavesdrop on his imposter's communications with the Secret Society. Adjusting the controls to eliminate the interference, the real Luthor listened intently as Black Adam impatiently chided the pretender:

"There are other things we should be focused on instead of kidnapping these various men and women for your delight."

"It's for justice," the false Luthor argued, "as we agreed. My machine needs specific test subjects. We don't want to power it up and wipe clean the minds of the entire world, do we?"

Lex scowled at the sound of the imposter's voice. Towering sheets of ice rose to either side as he followed the signal into a desolate arctic chasm. According to the readout on his armored gauntlet, he was getting close to the source of the transmissions. A smirk lifted his lips as he spied a narrow crevice in the eastern wall of the canyon. He marched hurriedly toward the opening, eager to confront the pretender at last.

THE gymnasium at Fawcett High School was empty, save for Black Adam and his Society strike force. The ancient monarch had magnanimously allowed the school's staff and students to flee the building once he'd determined that Captain Marvel's twin sister was not in attendance. Unlike some of his allies in the Society, Black Adam took no pleasure in terrifying innocent children. He was above that.

Now he floated imperiously above the floor while he upbraided Luthor for wasting his time. The rest of his team—Amazo, Gorilla Grodd, the General, Ubermensch, and Silver Banshee—congregated behind him.

"You said you needed one of the wizard's champions," Black Adam said. "But Mary Marvel is not here."

"Yes, I know that," Luthor replied. His image appeared on a portable monitor set up moments before. The bald-headed mortal smirked at Black Adam. His tailored business suit lacked the flair of Adam's own ebony uniform. "But you are."

What? Black Adam thought. Like the Marvel family, he had been granted his superhuman powers by the wizard Shazam. *Did Luthor mean to imply . . .*

Before he could even complete the thought, the other villains turned on him. Black Adam suddenly found himself under attack by his own supposed allies.

Amazo, a human-looking android with all the powers of the Justice League, blasted Black Adam with Superman's heat vision. Black Adam lunged angrily at Amazo, but the traitor ducked away with the speed of the Flash. Mimicking Green Lantern's powers, Amazo caused a pair of glowing green manacles to materialize around Black Adam's wrists.

Gorilla Grodd, a super-intelligent simian from the wilds of Africa, bombarded him with a telepathic attack that caused Adam's brain to throb painfully. The psychic assault made it hard to hold on to his wits, let alone break free of his shackles.

The General, a disgraced American soldier whose mind had been transferred into an ogrelike android body, pounded him with enormous fists. Jagged tusks protruded from the monster's lower lip.

Ubermensch, a neo-Nazi superman, joined the General in hammering Black Adam. Muscles bulged beneath his pale Aryan skin. A swastika adorned his belt buckle.

Silver Banshee, a sinuous female phantom, focused her siren wail on Black Adam. Long white hair matched her skeletal visage. Her ear-piercing cry could kill any mortal man. Added to Grodd's psychic attack, it set Adam's brain on fire. Blood dripped from his ears.

No more, he thought furiously. By the Gods, he had ruled Egypt before any of these other upstart villains were even a gleam in the eyes of their distant ancestors. He would not be defeated by the likes of them, let alone their smirking commander!

"You dare betray me, Luthor?" Black Adam roared. Through sheer force of will, he snapped apart the emerald manacles binding his wrists. His naked fist smashed through Ubermensch's chest, spraying blood onto the faces of the other traitors. The racist's worthless body dropped onto the floor. "Your blood will be on my hands next!"

But the odds against him were too great. Enraged by Ubermensch's sudden demise, the remaining villains redoubled their efforts to subdue Black Adam. The General and Amazo attacked him physically, battering him with their android fists, while Grodd and Silver Banshee kept up their relentless assault on his mind. Despite his righteous anger, Black Adam felt even his own legendary endurance reaching its limit. One eye was nearly swollen shut. Bruises blossomed over his aquiline features. His aching ears pleaded for relief.

Luthor taunted him from the monitor. "When this is all over, you won't even remember me."

"We'll calm him down," Silver Banshee promised, briefly interrupting her lethal wail. Her husky voice possessed a distinct Scottish burr. "He'll be wonderfully agreeable the next time you see him."

Never! he thought defiantly, even as his foes' endless blows brought him to his knees. Gorilla Grodd joined the two androids in beating him into the floor of the gymnasium. The ape's simian strength was almost as formidable as his telepathic gifts. Silver Banshee resumed her excruciating song. Beset on all sides, Black Adam slipped mercifully into unconsciousness.

"Excellent," Luthor pronounced.

THE screen in front of the false Luthor went black, breaking off the transmission from Fawcett City. The bald man blinked in surprise.

"There you are," the real Lex gloated. He had followed the signal through a maze of crystalline tunnels to this secret communications center hidden deep beneath the arctic snow. Unearthly black crystals lined the walls of the grotto. He let go of the power cable that he had just yanked from its socket. "I've been intercepting your transmissions for months now, tracking him them through a dozen different satellites. Gathering information. Trying to find out where you were . . . and who the hell you really are."

The imposter turned to face Lex. "I'm Lex Luthor," he insisted.

It was like looking into a mirror, except that the phony Luthor was wearing a tailored Armani suit instead of state-of-the-art battle armor. The imposter seemed strangely unconcerned by the real Lex's arrival.

"No, you're not," Lex insisted. "You're not me."

"You're right," the imposter conceded. "I'm better."

Lex couldn't believe the man's impudence. "You tried to take my place. Why?" He wanted answers, dammit. "I need to know . . . who you . . . who . . ." His words trailed off as that maddening fogginess descended over his thoughts once more. "Nngg," he grunted in frustration as he struggled to regain his concentration. Sweat beaded upon his brow. *What's the matter with me?*

"Trouble thinking?" the imposter asked. A mocking smile appeared on his face; he was obviously enjoying the real Lex's difficulties. "I'd theorize that the problem is our proximity. Intellect has always been a Luthor's greatest strength. But my theta brain waves are *much* more advanced than yours. They operate on an antifrequency and therefore, I would guess, are interfering with your cognitive functions." He eyed Lex as though he were an interesting lab specimen. "I'm curious. Is it a static in your ears? Or an overpowering headache?" He circled the real Lex like a predator. "Tell me, Lex Luthor. How does it feel to be . . . stupid?"

Lex had heard enough. Groggy or not, he would not be humiliated in this manner. Raising his arm, he unleashed a blast of destructive power from his gauntlet. A tremendous boom echoed through the crystal grotto.

Take that, pretender!

But when the smoke and flames cleared, the false Lex was still standing there, holding his palm up before him. A spherical force field seemed to have shielded him from the blast. His dapper black suit was not even singed.

"See now, Lex," he said. "That was just stupid."

A peculiar white glow materialized around his upraised hand. The coruscating energy appeared to temporarily *erase* small portions of reality, almost as though it was composed of antimatter itself. What was that the imposter had said a few moments ago, about his brain's antifrequency . . . ?

If only I could think, Lex thought, *maybe I could figure this out!*

A burst of white energy hit him with the force of a matter/antimatter reaction.

THE BATCAVE

"You'll never be alone again," the older Superman promised. Rising a few inches above the subterranean ledge, he looked down at Batman. He held out his hand. "Bruce, I'm offering you a chance to start over. None of this is your fault."

Batman was tempted. After his edgy encounter with Clark and Diana on the Moon, and everything else that had happened over the last few months, the idea of teaming up with a new Superman to start all over again had a certain appeal. But he could not shrug off his responsibilities so easily, nor the blame for all that had transpired.

"No," he stated grimly. "It is my fault."

Turning his back on Superman's hand, he walked away from the monitor platform. A metal stairway led down to the floor of the spacious cavern. He crossed the floor toward an armory on the opposite side of the cave. Quietly, so as to not alert his visitor, he keyed a top-secret combination into a locked compartment built into the wall.

Superman flew after him. "Everything you've done, everything you set in motion, is because you felt that you couldn't trust the people around you. And you know what? You can't." He touched down onto the floor behind Batman. "But on my Earth, it's different."

"What happens to everyone on *this* Earth when yours comes back?" Batman asked. He pretended to be mulling over Superman's offer while he stealthily removed something from a lead-lined container. Hopefully, Superman wouldn't notice what he was doing until it was too late.

"They'll be folded into the historical fabric," he said.

"You mean they'll die," Batman said bluntly.

Superman shook his head. "No. They'll only be replaced, just like everyone on my Earth was. But they'll be better." His commanding voice urged the other man to believe him. "I never lie, Bruce."

I believe you, Batman thought. "And what about Dick Grayson? Is he a better man on your Earth than he is on mine?"

Superman hesitated before answering. "No," he admitted finally. "Your Dick Grayson is a true hero as well."

"I thought as much." Batman turned around and held up his fist. A glowing green gemstone, embedded in a metal ring, gleamed upon his finger. "I'm not sure who you really are, 'Superman,' but I trust you when you say that you have the power to wipe this planet out." His voice held more than a hint of reluctance, but Batman knew he was doing the right thing. "I'm sorry. I just can't let you do that."

A look of sadness came over the older man's face. The sickly green light seemed to highlight the wrinkles creasing his weary countenance. "That's the kryptonite ring your Superman gave you, in case you were ever forced to bring him down." A sensible precaution as far as Batman was concerned. "But the kryptonite here isn't from *my* Krypton. It doesn't hurt me, physically at least." He scowled at the offending object. "But that ring . . . it represents the paranoia and mistrust that will destroy your world if you let it."

A crimson beam leaped from his eyes, turning the ring into slag. Batman recoiled in shock as the kryptonite and its housing melted off his finger. He felt the heat through the protective insulation of his glove. "Aaah!" he grunted.

The bright red glow in Superman's eyes died out. Lifting off from the floor, he gazed down at Batman more in sorrow than in anger. "It would have been nice," he said ruefully. "The world's finest heroes together again. Good-bye, Bruce."

A gust of wind blew through the Batcave as Superman departed at superspeed. Batman found himself alone once again. For a second, he couldn't help wondering what might have been. Selina and he . . . together? A daughter to carry on his mission? A cleaner, brighter Gotham?

Then he remembered Dick Grayson and went back to work.

"FIFTY-NINE SECONDS UNTIL BLACK BOX 73 IS SCANNED AND RE-PAIRED," a computerized voice announced.

About time, Batman thought. He still had a mystery to solve.

ARCTIC FORTRESS

IMAGES from throughout the universe flickered upon the crystalline walls of the hidden communications center. Green Arrow and his son battled the Society in Star City. The Brotherhood of Evil stole a large sealed container from an abandoned chemical plant. The body of Detective Crispus Allen was loaded into an ambulance in Gotham City. Captain Atom zoomed through the sky above Washington, D.C. Liberty Belle defended Philadelphia's Independence Hall from Baron Blitzkrieg. A teenage boy in New Mexico examined a bizarre crystal scarab.

Knocked off his feet by the antimatter blast, Lex Luthor slammed into the wall behind him. The weight of his heavy-duty battle armor shattered the crystals into a million pieces. Jagged splinters flew like daggers. Lex winced in pain as a crystal shard lodged in his neck. Scrambling up onto one knee, he raised his gauntlet once more.

"Your blasts have no effect on me," the false Luthor told him. He stood calmly in front of his wall-sized monitor and communications equipment. A nimbus of white energy flickered around his right hand. "Surely you've learned that by now."

Lex felt the crystal shard jabbing into his neck. Blood trickled from his cut scalp. "I have," he said, grimacing in pain. "But your computers, on the other hand . . ."

He fired an energy bolt directly at the equipment behind the imposter. The screen and consoles exploded outward, spraying the phony Luthor with sparks and shrapnel. He staggered forward, caught off-guard by the eruption. Charred electronic components were strewn about the cavern.

Lex climbed back onto his feet. He aimed both gauntlets at the imposter, who was still reeling from the blast. Energy crackled around the false Luthor, whose very appearance flickered in and out of existence. *It's a hologram,* the real Lex grasped. His double had been wearing some sort of holographic disguise.

The explosion must have damaged the circuitry controlling the hologram, because Lex's mirror image flickered once more before shorting out completely. In its place stood a red-haired young man in shining gold armor. *I had hair like that once,* the real Lex recalled.

"What the devil?" he blurted. "Who are you?"

Recovering from the jolt, the stranger glared at Lex. "I told you. I'm you. Only better."

That's not good enough, Lex thought. He clenched his armored fists. *I'll beat the truth out of you if I have to.*

He stomped toward the younger man, only to be grabbed from behind. Bare fingers sunk deep into his metal shoulder plates. Lex caught a glimpse of a bright red cape flapping behind his attacker. *Who?*

Super-strong hands ripped Lex's battle suit in half like it was made out of tissue paper instead of reinforced steel. For an instant, Lex found himself suspended in the air between the two halves of his sundered armor. Torn wires and circuits dangled from the dark purple bodysuit he wore beneath the battle gear. The straps of a green harness crossed his chest.

Gravity seized him and he collapsed onto the floor. Hydraulic fluid dripped from ruptured pipes in the armor. Sparks fell from the severed wires. Lex felt like he'd just been hit by a tornado. Coughing, he spit up blood.

Have to get away, he realized, his survival instincts kicking in. Events had clearly turned against him. *Anywhere but here.*

The newcomer casually tossed the broken battle suit aside. "He's evil, Alex," a voice said.

"And he's useless to us," the red-haired youth replied. His tone was as cold as ice. "Erase him."

Looking up from the floor, Lex saw a familiar costume on the newcomer. A hated red cape spread out behind the looming figure. There was no time to lose. He fumbled frantically with the controls on his green harness. The figure's contemptuous eyes took on a crimson glow and Lex felt a surge of panic. He knew heat vision when he saw it.

Just in time, he activated the teleportation circuitry built into his suit. He disappeared in a flash of shimmering light a split-second before two bright red beams converged on his previous location. The heat rays scorched the empty floor that Lex had just vacated.

"Where?" the caped figure asked.

"A teleporter," Alexander Luthor speculated. "Probably short-range."

"Let me go find him," his accomplice volunteered eagerly. "Let me get out of here. You know what I can do when I'm in that yellow sun."

"No." Alexander shook his head. Lex's escape vexed him, but not enough to deviate from their master plan. There were larger matters to be dealt with. "Not until the tower is ready."

CHAPTER 24

THE ARCTIC

POWER Girl sat atop a snow-covered ridge overlooking a glacier, reading Lois' journal. The bitter cold did not affect her nearly as much as the handwritten word inscribed within the notebook. She choked up as she read the final entry:

"It's not that Clark hasn't made this life here more than tolerable. There's just a sadness that won't go away. For the both of us. We miss her. Her smile and her laugh. We miss life with Kara terribly."

Power Girl closed the journal and wiped a tear from her eye. The depth of her emotions surprised her. Only a few hours ago, she hadn't even remembered that this version of Lois Lane existed. Now she would do anything to save her.

Almost.

A thought occurred to her and she flew back to the hidden arctic fortress. No one was waiting for her at the entrance to the cavern, so she hurried deeper into the crystalline sanctuary. "Superboy? Alex?" she called out. "We need to talk. To the Justice Society. And the Superman of this Earth." She couldn't wait to share her brainstorm with the others. "I think that working together we can figure out how to save Lois. We can save *everyone*, Earth-One and Earth-Two . . ."

To her surprise, no one responded. Checking in on Lois, she found the old woman still asleep in her grotto, but Alex and Superboy were nowhere to be seen. Their absence puzzled her. Superman, she knew, was off on some kind of errand, but where were the two younger men?

"Hello?"

She wandered through the frozen caverns, which turned out to be more extensive than she had first realized. A maze of shafts and tunnels spread out beneath the ice. She tried probing the fortress with her X-ray vision, and encountered an obstacle in one direction. Exploring it, she stumbled onto a narrow passageway leading away from the main cavern. As she ventured farther, the crystals comprising the walls grew darker, soon becoming black and opaque. These darker crystals resisted her X-ray vision, forcing her to search the labyrinth on foot. Glimpsing light up ahead, she rounded a corner, then halted dead in her tracks. Her eyes widened in shock.

"Oh my God."

Rising before her, at least three hundred feet tall, was a huge golden spire that seemed to stretch all the way to the roof of a vast cavern. Intricate circuitry covered almost every inch of the tower's gold plating, which bore a faint resemblance to the futuristic golden armor worn by Alexander Luthor. Even more startling, the tower appeared to have been constructed around the skeletal remains and armor of some enormous alien being. With a start, Kara recognized the skull of the infamous Anti-Monitor from that universe-shaking Crisis years ago. The monster's open maw gaped open near the top of the spire. Empty eye sockets the size of mine shafts gazed blindly from the Anti-Monitor's mummified countenance. Even dead, the malevolent entity was fearsome to behold.

But it was not the monster's gigantic remains that shocked Power Girl the most. What really stunned her was the unexpected sight of several heroes and villains plugged into a row of vertical niches running along the circumference. Martian Manhunter, Black Adam, Lady Quark, the Ray, Nightshade, and a new hero named Breach were each locked into their own slots, like individual components of some larger machine. They resided motionlessly in their niches, seemingly unaware of their surroundings.

"J'onn!" Power Girl lifted off from the floor, rising until she was face-to-face with the unconscious Martian. Golden tubes were inserted into his neck, wrist, waist, and ankles, connecting him to the complicated apparatus around him. His red cape was singed and tattered. His head drooped forward. "J'onn? Are you okay?"

Her words failed to rouse him. She reached out for the golden tube threaded into his neck, then hesitated. She wanted to yank the invasive tubes from his body, but was afraid of injuring him by mistake. Looking more closely, she noticed the number 1 engraved in a metal plate directly above Martian Manhunter's head. Similar plaques, bearing different numbers or letters, were inscribed above the other captives. One for each of the Earths that had existed before the Crisis.

Earth-One: Martian Manhunter.

Earth-Four: Nightshade.

Earth-Six: Lady Quark.

Earth-Eight: Breach.

Earth-S: Black Adam.

Earth-X: the Ray.

Ominously, the slot for Earth-Two was still empty.

THE BATCAVE

BATMAN stared intently at the cracked computer screen. The digital display read 00:00:00.

"BLACK BOX 731 JUSTICE LEAGUE WATCHTOWER TELEPORTATION LOG. ENTRIES 53042 THROUGH 74524," an electronic voice announced. "STORAGE CIRCUITS SCANNED AND REPAIRED."

Finally, Batman thought. Perhaps now he would learn who had destroyed the Watchtower, and what had become of Martian Manhunter. "Play back last entry."

"PLAYING LOG ENTRY 74524."

The screen showed J'onn seated in the Monitor Room inside the Watchtower. Watching Martian Manhunter watch his own screens produced a slightly disorienting, hall-of-mirrors effect, but Batman didn't let that distract him. He stood next to his overturned chair and watched closely as an electronic chime alerted J'onn to the arrival of a visitor. A red-caped figure entered the Monitor Room, his face momentarily out of range of the security camera. Batman's eyes narrowed suspiciously.

"Superman," J'onn greeted the newcomer. "I'm glad you're here."

Moments later, an unexpected burst of heat vision set J'onn ablaze. Knowing the Martian's vulnerability to fire, Batman could only imagine how the burning rays must have affected him. J'onn dropped unconscious to the floor. A blue sleeve reached into the frame, grabbing onto the fallen hero's belt. A disembodied voice that sounded electronically transmitted addressed J'onn's attacker.

"Bring him in alive," the mysterious voice instructed. "And destroy the Watchtower."

"Yes, Luthor," answered a surprisingly youthful voice.

The intruder finally stepped into full view. A teenage boy in a Superman costume lifted Martian Manhunter triumphantly over his head. Solar energy radiated from the teen's eyes as Batman realized the truth at last.

The Watchtower had been destroyed by . . . Superboy.

"PLAYBACK COMPLETE."

ARCTIC FORTRESS

I don't like the looks of this, Power Girl thought. She examined the metal tubes connecting Martian Manhunter to the immense golden tower. "Please, J'onn," she urged the inert hero. "Talk to me telepathically if you can. Who did this to you?"

J'onn didn't answer her, but something else did. Without warning, two closed fists slammed into her jaw at supersonic speed. Power Girl caught a glimpse of a red-and-blue blur before landing flat on her back at the base of the tower. Black crystals vibrated from the impact.

Stunned by the force of the blow, she lay sprawled upon the floor. Footsteps approached and she tried to lift her head, but found she didn't have the strength. Clayface's slimy attack earlier had been a love tap compared to what she had just received. Darkness encroached on her vision and it was all she could do to stay awake a few seconds more. Over the ringing in her head, she faintly heard a pair of voices conversing over her fallen form.

"I need her alive," the first voice said sternly.

"Yes, Luthor."

Who? Kara wondered groggily. She pried her eyes open long enough to see Alexander Luthor and Superboy looking down on her. The latter's face was twisted in spite. His super-strong fists were still clenched.

"I told you she wouldn't help us," he whined. "I told you."

"Kara will help us, Superboy," Alexander said calmly. His face held an inscrutable expression. "And so will Kal-L. Whether they like it or not."

THE BERMUDA TRIANGLE

HIGH above the ocean, Wonder Woman readied herself for battle. Sword in hand, she awaited the OMACs' next assault.

The odds were not in her favor.

At least Themyscira is safe, she consoled herself. Her sisters and homeland were now far beyond the cyborgs' deadly reach, leaving her alone to face the airborne horde. The OMACs surrounded her in ever-tightening circles. Their computerized minds were no doubt trying to process the island's inexplicable disappearance. She fully expected them to turn their attention to her at any moment. *Let them come,* she thought defiantly. *Let Brother Eye see how an Amazon meets her foes.*

She regretted only that she must strike out at the innocents trapped inside the OMACs' faceless blue shells, as opposed to Batman's killer satellite itself.

Will Bruce ever find a way to curb his insane creation?

Then, to her surprise, the cyborgs broke off their attack. "PROTOCOL: 'TRUTH AND JUSTICE' OVERRIDDEN," they announced in unison. "PRO-TOCOL: 'TOWER WATCH' RECEIVED."

Ignoring Wonder Woman, the OMACs flew to the north in formation, like a flock of geese migrating for the winter. She watched in confusion as the entire armada disappeared in the distance. *What in Athena's name?* she wondered. The OMACs had apparently received new instructions from Brother Eye, but Diana had no idea what they might be. What did "Protocol: 'Tower Watch' " entail? *To what tower do the OMACs refer?*

She considered flying after them to discover their new mission, but quickly reconsidered. The OMACs still outnumbered her by the thousands; she should not tempt the Fates overmuch. Her enemies' unexpected departure could be seen as a gift from the gods. Wisdom dictated that she not recklessly throw it away.

"Very well then," she murmured to herself. Sheathing her sword, she flew northwest toward America. She was still needed in Man's World, to defend the innocent from more emergencies than she could readily count. Other matters demanded her attention as well: She needed to close Themyscira's various embassies and missions throughout the world, and prepare to stand trial for the execution of Maxwell Lord.

That was more than enough to deal with at the moment.

She rode the air currents away from the empty ocean.

CHAPTER 25

ABOVE BLÜDHAVEN

THE unmarked cargo plane flew through the turbulent night sky.

"They say you can't go home again," Deathstroke said. "I want Nightwing to believe it."

The assassin's voice emerged from a speaker on the plane's instrument panel. A large male gorilla expertly operated the controls, while a disembodied human brain occupied the copilot's seat beside the ape. An elegant woman in a green cape stood at the rear of the cockpit.

"If you gave Phobia five minutes with him, Slade," the Brain pointed out, "Nightwing would believe anything." The Brain pulsated beneath a clear plastic dome. Its electronic voice emanated from its stainless steel receptacle, a malevolent silver skull sculpted on the outer casing.

"Indeed," the woman in green confirmed. Her haughty voice had an upper-class British accent. "I could fill that acrobat's heart with such unreasoning fear that it would explode from his chest."

"That won't be necessary, Phobia," Deathstroke said tersely, broadcasting from one of the Society's many secret bases. "Let's stick to the original plan."

"A pity," the gorilla observed. Monsieur Mallah spoke English with a hint of a French accent. His basso profundo voice was shockingly deep. Ammunition belts crossed his shaggy chest. "I would like to feast on a hero's heart."

He licked his lips.

"Careful, Mallah," the Brain said. "You're drooling on the controls."

"I am sorry, Brain," the gorilla replied, embarrassed. Experimental surgery had elevated his IQ considerably, but he still occasionally fell prey to his more primitive instincts. He wiped the saliva from his lips. "You know how I get when I'm excited."

"Just keep your mind on your mission," Deathstroke ordered.

In the plane's cargo bay, the rest of the Brotherhood of Evil inspected the aircraft's singular payload.

Over twenty-five feet tall, Chemo was suspended above the sealed cargo bay doors. The bizarre creature consisted of a man-shaped plastic vat filled to the brim with churning toxic waste. Swirling green chemicals could be seen through Chemo's clear plastic shell. The roiling mix of toxins had somehow combined to give the anthropomorphic creation a crude semblance of life. Almost completely mindless, Chemo was nothing more than a walking weapon of mass destruction. The gurgling noises that sometimes escaped its "face" were the closest the destructive monster ever came to speech. Staring up at Chemo from the floor of the cargo bay, the other villains were grateful for the thick metal restraints holding the creature immobile.

"He smells like laundry detergent," Gemini said, wrinkling her nose. The elastic teenager stretched her torso upward to get a better look at the monster.

"Do not get too close, *cheri*," Warp advised her. The bearded French teleporter kept a safe distance away from Chemo, even though he could theoretically warp to safety in an instant should the unnatural creature get loose. His gold-plated armor provided an additional degree of protection. "Chemo spews a toxic waste that will dissolve curious young girls faster than our friend Plasmus here."

"*Ja*," the German villain Plasmus admitted. Caustic fumes rose from his lumpy red body, which was composed entirely of highly acidic protoplasm. Tormented by his grotesque condition, Plasmus often took out his anger at the world by reducing other human beings to burning ooze with his touch. "I envy him."

Gemini stared at Chemo with morbid fascination. "Do you think he understands what we're going to do?"

"I don't think he cares," Houngan said bluntly. Ceremonial face paint disguised the voodoo priest's features. He carefully watched a nearby viewscreen as an electronic map tracked the plane's progress toward its destination. "Now hang on, everyone. We're almost there."

He placed his hand on a release lever built into the wall of the plane. He wrapped a sturdy green tether around his other arm, and his teammates followed his example. A lightbulb came on above the door to the cockpit, signaling that they had reached the proper coordinates. Houngan offered up a silent prayer to Baron Samedi, the ruler of the dead.

Then he pulled down on the lever.

The cargo bay doors fell open. Metal clamps released.

Chemo tumbled out of the plane toward the city below.

It was an ordinary night in Blüdhaven.

Outside a rundown urban high school, a pair of cops roughed up a skinny white drug dealer. The unlucky dealer was sprawled upon the pavement next to a barbed-wire fence. He clutched his face, which still bore the impression of the cops' nightsticks. Bags of dope were scattered upon the sidewalk. "You've been holding out on us again, kid," one policeman said as he thumbed through a thick wad of cash. His partner gave the dealer a vicious kick in the ribs.

"Lettin' you peddle your junk outside Whalers High don't come free," the second cop added. "Don't you go forgetting that."

A few blocks away, in the red-light district, flashing lights spelled out the name of a downtown strip club: SIN SITTY. Pink neon tubing twisted to form the silhouette of a naked woman. Eight-by-ten glossies of the featured performers were tacked up around the club's entrance. Raucous music and laughter spilled out into the sidewalk outside. Similar clubs, peep shows, and XXX-rated magazine shops lined both sides of the street for several consecutive blocks. Hookers plied the street corners, calling out lewd invitations to passing cars and pedestrians. Willing customers haggled over prices.

"I don't care where you get them," a middle-aged pimp said, bawling out a younger wannabe. Gold chains and jewelry pronounced that business was booming. "Just get them, the younger the better. We got a lot of hungry men in this city."

Miles uptown, the lights were burning late in City Hall. The mayor sat behind his large mahogany desk as representatives of some of the cities most distinguished "families" made a discreet campaign contribution. Stacks of hundred-dollar bills filled the leather suitcase lying open atop the desk. The mayor stared avidly at the "donation."

"As always, it's a pleasure doing business with you, Mister Mayor." Muscular bodyguards accompanied the beaming mob boss and his associates. Limos waited downstairs to transport the mayor's late-night visitors back to their respective territories. No record would be kept of this meeting.

"The pleasure's mine," the mayor said. "The streets are yours."

A thug in an ill-fitting suit peered out the window. A look of surprise came over his beefy face. "What the hell?"

He pulled back the shutters to reveal the night sky. A glowing green figure, looking like one of the inflatable characters in the Thanksgiving Day Parade, fell from the heavens, tumbling end over end toward the buildings below. The mayor blinked in bewilderment.

Did I authorize this?

A second later, Chemo struck the tip of a nearby skyscraper. A blinding green flash lit up the entire city. It was the last thing most people in Blüdhaven ever saw. Cops and dealers, pimps and hookers, gangsters and politicians, the guilty and the innocent alike . . . all perished as a wave of destructive energy spread outward from where Chemo had hit. Flesh vaporized, leaving nothing but charred skeletons behind. Toxic waste streamed through the streets, consuming everything in its path. In an instant, Blüdhaven joined an infamous litany of names: Hiroshima, Nagasaki, Bhopal, Chernobyl, Coast City . . .

A green mushroom cloud billowed up from the blackened heart of the 'Haven.

CHAPTER 26

ARCTIC FORTRESS

ALEXANDER Luthor and Superboy watched the city burn.

"Like Sodom and Gomorrah," Alexander said soberly. "Blüdhaven falls."

He stood upon a floating force field hundreds of feet above the base of the golden spire. His levitating World View projected satellite images of the mushroom cloud rising over Blüdhaven. Superboy hovered in the air beside him. The caped teenager viewed the city's destruction without a qualm.

"What are you doing?"

Power Girl now occupied the niche beneath the Number 2 plaque. The device sapped her strength, leaving her voice little more than whisper. She strained to free herself, but an irresistible force held her fast. Her arms and legs felt like they were cemented to the gleaming tower behind her. Metal cables connected her to the intricate circuitry covering the spire.

"We're doing what we survived to do." Alexander's force-field platform rose until he was eye-level with Kara. He gazed at her without a hint of remorse. "We're erasing everything that's bad."

His casual tone enraged her. "Let me out of here, Alex." Mustering what little strength she had left, she fired a blast of heat vision at his face. "Let us all out!"

Fzzzztt! The air sizzled between them, but an invisible force field blocked her attack. Alexander calmly maintained his composure as, drained, Kara sagged within her niche. *What's this thing doing to me?* she fretted. *I feel as weak as a kitten.*

Superboy flew over to join them. "I thought you were like us, Power Girl," he said petulantly. "But you're not. You're like *them.*" He shook his finger at her. "You're a traitor!"

"Calm yourself, Superboy," Alexander advised him. "We've worked too long to let emotion threaten it all. Remember, we have a vital responsibility to shoulder."

"What responsibility?" Kara demanded. Even trapped as she was, she still wanted answers. "What the hell is going on?"

Alexander stepped back upon his platform to contemplate his work. His gaze swept over Kara and the other human "batteries" plugged into their respective niches. All of the other captives were out cold; the tower had been draining their strength for a longer period of time.

"I've gone through over seventy-eight thousand different scenarios, Kara." He sighed, no doubt recalling many long hours of study and experimentation. "This way is the most efficient."

"To do what? Bring back Earth-Two?" She tried to sound reasonable. "I told you, I want to help save Lois. But let's talk with this Earth's heroes. We can work together. . . ."

"Work together?" he asked incredulously. "Kara, please. Your 'friends' are incapable of that. The Justice League is barely speaking to each other. That's why it's up to me . . . us."

He shook his head sadly. "You still don't realize it yet, do you? Superboy and I didn't just arrive here with Superman and Lois. We've been coming to this bleak, benighted universe for quite some time."

What? Power Girl thought. "But I thought Superman freed you?"

Alexander took a deep breath before launching into his explanation. "For the last several months, Superman has been preoccupied with his Lois' health. This allowed Superboy and me the freedom to stop watching your Earth fall apart, as we had for so long, and start acting. We were finally able to utilize my science and Superboy's strength to escape the 'heaven' I had cursed us with."

As he spoke, his World View projected holographic images from the recent past. Kara watched as Superboy punched his way through the 'unbreakable' crystal barrier that cut him and the others off from reality. Alexander assisted Superboy by operating some sort of advanced technological apparatus.

"The boy's first task was to find and retrieve the Anti-Monitor's corpse. Containing elements of both positive and negative matter, it served as the foundation for this tower."

The hologram depicted Superboy flying through the galaxy, bearing the mummified husk of the dead Anti-Monitor. Kara recognized the gigantic body from her memories of that earlier Crisis.

"As Superboy headed into deep space, I posed as this Earth's Lex Luthor with a simple holographic disguise. I gathered together a Society of super-villains by convincing them that the machine I was building would destroy their enemies' minds. Because the past transgressions of the Justice League had recently come to light, it wasn't difficult to convince them. Villains are easily driven by revenge. No wonder my father hated them so."

Kara recalled that Alexander's father, the Lex Luthor of Earth-Three, had been a hero on his world. She stared into the holographic display, where 'Luthor' could be seen presiding over a summit meeting of many of the world's deadliest super-villains.

"The Society helped collect the various individuals I needed to power my machine, each of whom contain a specific vibrational frequency hidden in their genetic codes. The Ray, for instance, inherited the code from his father's exploits before the multiverse collapsed, when the first Ray and the other Freedom Fighters lived on Earth-X."

That's why Clayface and the others came after me, Power Girl realized. *They were following Alexander's orders.*

She winced at a holographic recording of the Freedom Fighters' last minutes. The Psycho-Pirate dragged the Ray away from the battle while the rest of a Society strike force massacred Uncle Sam and the other Fighters. Kara understood now that their deaths could be laid at Alexander's door.

"With you and these others, the tower is complete. But it still requires fuel and programming." He smiled at his own ingenuity. "That fuel will come from this universe's magic."

The hologram showed Alexander visiting a babbling figure in a padded cell. He handed the inmate a unique golden mask. . . .

"Upon one of my first trips here, I recruited the Psycho-Pirate. His warped psyche was one of the few that still remembered the old multiverse. He was also the key to manipulating the Spectre, who had recently lost his mortal host. Without a soul to bond to, even the Spirit of Vengeance was vulnerable to the

Psycho-Pirate's subtle influence. Confused and easily led astray, he began his war against magic. He attempted to destroy it, but instead reduced it to raw magical energy, without order or form. Upon his death, the wizard Shazam became a part of this new magic and a tether for us to hold on to."

Kara saw a holographic Spectre attack and destroy a bearded old man who had to be the wizard himself. A rocky throne room exploded into a thousand pieces.

"As for the programming, I was the one who endowed Batman's Brother Eye satellite with sentience. I helped it evolve into an artificial intelligence that would be capable of remapping the multiverse and redirecting the Tower's energy into its ultimate target. Brother Eye's OMACs now respond to my commands, just as the Society does."

The World View projected an image of the corrupted satellite orbiting the Earth. She watched as the OMACs swarmed in the sky somewhere in the world.

"And all the while, Superboy did his part. Moving planets like chess pieces throughout the universe. Sparking an intergalactic war. Shifting the center of the universe away from Oa to where the Earth-Two universe's center was. Allowing my tower to open an access point through which my own hands will redivide this universe. All in our sacred crusade to find a new Earth. A perfect Earth."

A holographic Superboy nudged the planet Rann into the same orbit as Thanagar, setting off an interplanetary war. A cosmic storm erupted outside the Polaris system. All to bring back one world?

"Earth-Two," she finished for him.

He chuckled at her naive understanding of his plan. "Earth-Two? Of course not." He carefully adjusted the holographic display in front of him. "Earth-Two is only a stop along the way."

Power Girl tried to grasp the full enormity of Alexander's grandiose scheme. "All of this manipulation. The Psycho-Pirate . . ." Realization dawned in her eyes. "That's why Wonder Woman killed Maxwell Lord, why Batman got so damn paranoid, why Superman . . ."

"Failed to keep them together?" Alexander shook his head. His face took on a graver expression. "They did that themselves, Kara." A hint of sorrow entered his voice. "That was the real tragedy of it. And what proved to me without a doubt that we are doing the right thing. These heroes are incapable of protecting their Earth. Its eventual destruction is inevitable." He nodded at his golden tower. "*This* is the only way to save the world."

He's crazy, Kara thought. "When my cousin finds out *how* you're going about this, there's no way he'll go along."

"The black crystals keep our activities in this section of the fortress shielded from even his senses." Alexander smiled confidently, his face only inches from her own. "But don't worry. Like you, I need Superman alive."

Power Girl squirmed against her bonds, unable to break free. "You're supposed to be his friend!"

"I *am* his friend," he insisted. "But I have studied this universe and all others for countless years. And I have learned that no matter where they are, or what reality they come from, when a Luthor stands next to a Superman, they will *always* be at odds." He shrugged his shoulders. "I have grown to accept that."

Now he really sounds like a Luthor, she thought angrily. "Superboy!" She gave up trying to get through to Alexander, but maybe she could still convince the confused teenager to act like a hero. "Clark! You can't let him do this. You—"

"Hush, Kara," Alexander interrupted. Perhaps he was afraid that Superboy might listen to what she was saying. "It's time for you to sleep like the others."

Without warning, he leaned forward and kissed her on the lips. Negative energy flashed and a sudden jolt fried Kara's brain, rendering her unconscious. Alexander withdrew his lips, and glanced at Superboy with a touch of embarrassment. He could have stunned Power Girl with merely a touch of his hand. He wasn't quite sure why he had chosen to kiss her instead.

Superboy refrained from commenting on his partner's impulsive act. "Can I . . . can I go now?" he asked impatiently. Kara's last-minute appeal appeared not to have affected him. "You promised. You promised I could talk to him."

"Yes," Alexander agreed. He didn't anticipate any further interruptions. "You may go."

A sonic boom echoed through the cavern as Superboy rocketed out of the fortress.

Turning his back on Power Girl, Alexander resumed his preparations.

All was going according to plan.

OUTSIDE BLÜDHAVEN

TWENTY-FIVE miles south of the epicenter, Nightwing watched his adopted city burn. Noxious green smoke billowed upward from the smoldering ruins. Radioactive flames licked at the night sky. The dumbstruck hero stood alongside a stretch of highway that had been closed to all but emergency vehicles. FEMA personnel, working in conjunction with the National Guard, had set up roadblocks a little farther down the road. Overhead, the Metal Men flew toward the destruction on an antigravity disk. Immune to the toxic waste contaminating the disaster site, the heroic robots were proving invaluable to the initial relief efforts.

Nightwing felt numb, overwhelmed by the sheer scale of the catastrophe. Only a day ago, the 'Haven had been a place for the living, however debased. Now the entire downtown area was a toxic cemetery that might not be habitable for years, maybe even decades. An oppressive sense of failure came over him as he recalled saying good-bye to Donna and Kory and Supergirl on a city rooftop one night ago. He might as well have gone to outer space with them for all the good he had done here. Blüdhaven had been under his protection. Now there was nothing left to protect.

"Nightwing."

He recognized the voice even before he noted the bat-eared shadow falling upon the ground in front of him. "Bruce?" He turned around to find Batman standing behind him. "What are you doing here?"

"I wanted to make sure you were all right," Batman said with uncharacteristic emotion. He typically kept his cool under even the most alarming circumstances.

"I was in New York when it hit," Dick Grayson explained. "Got back here as soon as I could."

He didn't know whether to be grateful or guilty that he had inadvertently missed Blüdhaven's darkest hour. An ambulance rushed past them, reminding Dick that there were still survivors to be evacuated from the city's outlying regions. He turned toward the blazing wasteland. "I need to get back in there."

"Wait," Batman said.

"For what?" Nightwing asked. "This is just one of hundreds of disasters happening right now. Superman's already in the heart of it, along with a dozen others who can stand the radiation." He envied his super-powered colleagues their invulnerability; at least they could head straight into the heart of the inferno. He raised a pair of binoculars to his eyes. "They're looking for survivors in the city itself. They're not finding any."

"I need to talk to you about the survivors of something else," Batman said. Nightwing wondered what could possibly be so important that Bruce would come looking for him at a time like this. Then he heard Batman say something that Nightwing couldn't remember him ever saying before. "I need your help, Dick."

ARCTIC FORTRESS

NIGHT had fallen by the time the original Superman returned to the frozen ice caverns. His spirit was troubled by Batman's inability to accept the truth about this world. *I could always count on* my *Batman to stand beside me,* he thought. It felt strange, and more than a little uncomfortable, to find himself in opposition to the Caped Crusader. *What if he's not entirely wrong?*

He flew quickly to the crystal grotto where Lois resided. He found Alexander standing by her bedside, recording her vital signs while she slept. "How is she?" Superman asked urgently.

"She's in grave danger," the younger man responded. He frowned at the readouts upon his holographic display panels.

Superman took Alex's warning seriously. Time was obviously running out. "Where are Kara and Superboy?"

"Helping prepare for your Earth's return." Alexander didn't look up from his diagnostic readings. "Something I assume this Bruce Wayne refused to do."

"Yes," Superman admitted. "You were right about him." He recalled their strained encounter in the Batcave. "He's strong, like the man I knew, if not a little lost. But . . . he did make a valid point. Not everyone is a worse person on this Earth. Some, like Richard Grayson, are as good and as strong as the ones we knew. This 'Nightwing' has even grown beyond his role as Robin." Unlike the Dick Grayson of Earth-Two, who had continued as Robin well into adulthood.

Alexander dismissed Superman's concerns. "Grayson is an exception to the rule, but only for now. In time, he would become corrupted like the others."

"Maybe," Superman conceded. Unlike Alex, he still had some doubts. *Are we really doing the right thing?*

Alexander heard the hesitation in the older man's voice. He turned to look Superman in the eye. "Clark, Lois only has a few hours to live. She *will* die unless Earth-Two returns." He stepped aside to let Superman kneel by his wife's side. "I know this is difficult, but there's no time left. No other option."

Superman clasped Lois' hand. His reservations about Alex's plan receded to the back of his mind as he gazed down at his dying wife. Her pulse felt weak. Her breathing was shallow. It was hard to believe that this was the same woman who had once risked her life on a daily basis just to land a front-page story. He couldn't bear to see her like this. She didn't even seem to know he was there.

"Stay at her side. Give her something to live for." Alex leaned forward to whisper in his ear. "Leave things to me. She'll be home and healthy very, very soon."

Superman prayed that Alexander was right. *He* has to *be*, he thought desperately. *It's our only hope.*

Alexander left the Man of Steel alone with his wife.

CHAPTER 27

KENT FARM,
SMALLVILLE, KANSAS

THE morning sun beamed down on the bright yellow farmhouse. Jonathan Kent wiped the sweat from his brow as he took a break from mowing the front yard. "Conner should be out here," he commented to his wife. "If he's not going to go join the Titans, he could at least finish the yard work."

"He's putting on his shoes," Martha assured him. She strolled toward Jonathan, bearing a pitcher of fresh lemonade on a tray. The last thing she wanted was for her husband to get cross with the boy.

"Good," Jonathan said, a tad impatiently. "He needs to do something."

"That's what I say too, Mr. Kent," said a voice from above.

The middle-aged couple looked up in surprise. Martha's eyes widened as a teenage boy in a Superman costume descended from the sky. The boy's face was eerily familiar. *He looks just like Clark did at that age*, she realized. *Even more than Conner does.*

"Wow." He sounded just like Clark too. "This sun feels so great, doesn't it?"

"Oh my . . ." Startled, she lost her grip on the tray. The pitcher and cup tumbled toward the ground, but were caught at super-speed by the newcomer, who set them right upon the tray. He touched down on the lawn in front of her.

"Don't worry, Mrs. Kent," he said politely. "I'll help." He handed the tray back to her, its contents intact. "It's such a pleasure to meet you both. I know you've tried your best with Conner, but he won't be a bother anymore. None of this will."

What does he mean by that? Martha wondered. The boy seemed pleasant enough, but she had a bad feeling. *Something's wrong here.*

The front door swung open and Conner strolled out onto the porch. Krypto trotted behind him. "Pa, I'd like to help, but I need to . . ." His voice trailed off as he spotted their visitor.

"Hello, 'Superboy,' " the other teen said with a smirk.

"Who are you?" Conner asked.

The visitor puffed out his chest. "I'm your replacement."

"Replacement?" Conner looked at the Kents. "Uncle John?"

"I don't know who he is, son," Jonathan Kent replied. He placed a protective arm around Martha and eyed the newcomer suspiciously. Martha could tell that he was worried too.

"You don't remember me, Mr. Kent," the other Superboy said. "But I don't blame you. I blame people like *him*." He glared at Conner.

Conner bristled in response. He marched up to the other teen. "Look, kid. I don't know who you are, but you need to back off."

On the porch, Krypto growled at the stranger. He bared his fangs.

"I just came to say . . ." Conner's defiant attitude seemed to unnerve the other boy, like he hadn't expected Conner to stand up for himself. "I came to t-tell you that . . ."

"What?" Conner challenged him. "Stop mumbling."

Martha almost felt sorry for the stranger. She got the distinct impression that this encounter was not going as the other Superboy had anticipated.

"I want you to admit it," he blurted angrily. "Admit that you've given up. Admit that it's time for a Superboy who knows what right and wrong are."

"What?" Conner looked at the other teen like he was crazy. Martha feared that might be the case.

"I'm the Superboy the world needs," the newcomer insisted.

Conner shook his head. "Dude, you need some help."

"S-say it," the self-proclaimed Superboy demanded, growing visibly agitated.

"Say what? That I can't believe that you're wearing underwear that tight?"

Conner stood head-to-head with his so-called replacement. Martha was encouraged by her adoptive nephew's attitude. It looked like Conner was finally shaking off the malaise that had gripped him these last few days. "I told you to back off."

The other Superboy scowled at Conner. He clenched his fists. "You just won't accept it, will you?" Without warning, the caped youngster swung his fist at Conner. "You're not Superboy!"

The blow knocked the glasses from Conner's nose . . . and sent him smashing into the farmhouse behind him. Glass and broken timbers went flying.

EL PASO

CONVENIENTLY, the kid was sleeping in when Booster Gold beamed into his room from the ruins of the Watchtower. Closed blinds kept out the early morning sunlight. Dirty laundry littered the floor. Posters of sports stars and supermodels decorated the walls. A Captain Carrot comic book rested on a nightstand next to the bed. The teenage boy snored beneath his sheets, oblivious to the arrival of the costumed time traveler and his floating robot.

The messy bedroom reminded Booster of his own quarters back when he was a kid; this was just four hundred years more primitive. *I used to leave my VR chips and nano-gear lying around everywhere.*

Taking care not to trip over all the junk on the floor, he began to quietly search the room. He scanned the tops of the nightstand and a chest of drawers, but found only scattered magazines and school books. He pulled out the top drawer of the dresser, wincing at the squeal of wood against wood, and rummaged through an assortment of clean socks and T-shirts. *Maybe it's hidden under these clothes,* he hoped.

No such luck.

"Dammit," he whispered to Skeets. "Where is it?"

"IT WAS DEFINITELY HERE, SIR." The robot hovered above Booster's shoulder. "I'M PICKING UP A RESIDUAL TRAIL." Skeets projected a beam of ultraviolet light over the cluttered bedroom. The light exposed a glowing blue spot on top of the nightstand in the shape of the Blue Beetle Scarab. A trail of smaller blue specks led down onto the floor and over toward the bed. "IT LEADS TO . . ."

Booster's eyes traced the patch of the glowing marks. In the black light, the faint markings looked eerily like bloodstains. They climbed up the side of the bed before disappearing under the sheets. "That kid?"

On the bed, Jaime Reyes stirred restlessly. Booster froze in place and hoped that they hadn't disturbed the boy's sleep. He didn't feel like explaining his mission to a confused teenager.

"IT APPEARS THAT IT CRAWLED TOWARD HIM," Skeets reported, breaking the silence.

Jaime's eyelids flickered. He rolled over onto his back.

Booster gestured for the robot to keep it down. "Crawled? I didn't know it could move on its own."

"IT WAS NEVER PROPERLY DOCUMENTED IN THIS CENTURY. PERHAPS IT'S—" The robot lowered his volume, but not enough. Jaime's eyes snapped open and he sat up straight, obviously alarmed by the stranger in his room. He opened his mouth to yell.

"Whoa, whoa!" Booster said, holding up his hands. "Don't scream, all right? I'm not here to hurt you." For all he knew, Jaime's parents were right outside the door. He wondered how he could convince the kid to keep quiet. "I'm . . ."

"Wait. I know who you are." Recognition dawned in the boy's eyes, displacing his earlier fear. He stared at Booster in amazement. "You're that guy."

That's right, the hero thought proudly. *I'm with the Justice League.*

"You're the dude on my toothpaste tube." Jaime nodded to himself, remembering. " 'A smile as bright as gold' or something, right?"

"Uh, sure," Booster admitted, feeling slightly deflated. He'd forgotten all about that promotional deal. "The name's Booster Gold."

The boy didn't seem to find a toothpaste spokesman very intimidating. Throwing aside his sheets, he hopped out of the bed. He wore only a pair of faded blue jeans, leaving his slender chest bare. "What're you doing here?" he demanded suspiciously. "Taking over for the Tooth Fairy?"

"IF IT PAID WELL, HE MIGHT," Skeets said.

Not for the first time, Booster considered disabling the robot's sarcasm programs. "And the floating eBay reject is Skeets."

Jaime eyed the floating robot warily. "Why are you here?"

"HISTORICAL RECORDS SHOW THAT YOU, JAIME REYES, ARE IN POSSESSION OF THE BLUE BEETLE SCARAB."

"The what?" He clearly had no idea what Skeets was talking about.

"You took something that belonged to a friend of mine," Booster said firmly. "I need it back."

Jaime bristled at the accusation. "I didn't take anything, man."

"SIR?" Skeets buzzed toward Jaime. "MY SCANNERS HAVE FOUND THE SCARAB." An X-ray beam exposed the teen's skeleton. A carved blue gemstone could be seen attached to his lower vertebrae. "IT APPEARS TO BE FUSED TO THE BACK OF THIS BOY'S SPINE."

Jaime looked down in shock at his illuminated vertebrae and rib cage. Booster struggled to process what he was seeing. "The Scarab's *inside* him?"

"What?" Jaime blurted, freaking out. "What the hell's going on?"

"THE EARTH IS ON THE VERGE OF TOTAL DESTRUCTION," Skeets reminded Booster. "TIME IS OF THE ESSENCE." The X-ray beam switched off. The robot rotated to face Booster Gold. "WHAT DO YOU SUGGEST WE DO NOW?"

I wish I knew, he thought. The situation had gotten a whole lot more complicated.

And Jaime Reyes had just become a part of it.

SMALLVILLE

WELCOME TO SMALLVILLE read a friendly billboard—before Conner's body went smashing through it.

Conner felt as though he had just been clobbered by the entire Justice League. His face throbbed as he crashed down into the middle of Main Street. Unable to overcome this second blow's momentum, he plowed right into a pickup truck parked in front of an intersection. Bales of hay did little to cushion his landing as he hit the truck like a missile. Mangled metal and hay went flying. The driver of the truck dived out of the cab only moments before the vehicle erupted into flames.

A quiet Saturday morning turned into bedlam as pedestrians and drivers reacted in horror and confusion. People on the sidewalk scurried indoors. Parents snatched up their children. Other cars peeled away from the scene at top speed. Anxious faces appeared in the windows of nearby shops and apartments. An overwhelmed beat cop stood frozen in place. A mail-man dropped a bulging bag of mail and ran for his life. Smoke rose from the burning hay.

Conner staggered out of the totaled pickup truck. Bits of straw clung to the shirt buttoned over his *S* insignia. His glasses had not survived the first punch. Blood streamed from a cut on his face. He tottered unsteadily.

Who the heck is this freak? he wondered. *Another clone?*

The duplicate Superboy gave him no time to recover. Swooping down from the sky, he slammed into Conner with both fists. Gasping, Conner was hurled backward through the corner of the general store. Shattered glass and merchandise exploded out on the adjacent street. The ruptured corner of the store collapsed. Screams came from within. Conner flinched at the cries even as he skidded across the asphalt on his back. Innocent people were getting hurt.

"You're not so strong," Superboy gloated. He flew above Conner, pound-ing him while he was down. Blood and broken teeth sprayed from Conner's mouth. "You're just an imitation! Everyone knows that!" The stranger's eyes glowed red. "I'm the *real* Superboy!"

Before he could fire his heat vision, however, Krypto attacked the rav-ing nutcase from behind. The dog's super-powerful jaws sank into Superboy's shoulder, tearing through his blue uniform. "Aaah!" he cried out as Krypto's fangs drew blood.

Way to go, boy! Conner thought, grateful for the respite. He cheered the large white dog on. *Sic 'im!*

The other Superboy seemed to take Krypto's attack as a personal affront. "Let go!" he said indignantly. He tried to pull the dog off his shoulder, but Krypto held on tenaciously. "You're Superdog! You're not supposed to fight *me!*"

He finally tore Krypto off him, then brutally slammed the dog's skull into the concrete. Any normal canine would have been killed instantly, but Krypto kept on growling. "Bad dog!" Superboy shouted as he kicked Krypto in the head. Blood flew from the dog's jaws as he went bouncing down the street. A plaintive whimper escaped the dog as he came to rest upon the pavement. He collapsed in a heap, beaten into unconsciousness.

Krypto! Conner thought. Every bone in his body ached, but that didn't matter. Anger flared in his heart. He didn't know who this Superboy wannabe was, but *nobody* treated his dog like that. "All right, that's it!" he said, clambering back onto his feet. He ripped off the last shreds of his dress shirt, revealing the bright red S-shield printed on his tight black T-shirt. His eyes burned red with volcanic fury. "Come on, you mother—!"

CHAPTER 28

THE BATCAVE

NIGHTWING had never felt so angry. He gazed up at the cracked monitor screen. Satellite photos showed Chemo falling from the sky toward Blüdhaven. Even more maddening was Batman's explanation for the disaster.

"You think this is a coordinated assault, that they blew up Blüdhaven just to distract us?" Fury spilled into Nightwing's voice. "They killed millions!"

"They're aiming for a lot more than that," Batman said.

Nightwing recalled Bruce's story about his strange visitor from another planet. "All so some alternate 'Superman' can destroy our Earth and replace it with his?" Even by super-hero standards, it sounded absurd.

But Batman seemed to take the threat dead seriously. He clicked a remote and the image on the screen changed to a shot of a teenage boy in a Superman costume holding Martian Manhunter aloft. Smoke rose from J'onn J'onzz's seared blue cape.

"You can see he's not working alone," Batman said. "There's a Superboy that was responsible for the attack on the Watchtower. And that Superboy was taking orders from a Luthor."

" 'A' Luthor? Bruce, this is insane." Nightwing scratched his head, trying to make sense of it all. "Why would any Superman do this? Why would he risk everything?"

"To save someone he loves," Batman said simply.

Nightwing thought of Koriand'r . . . and of Barbara Gordon. How far would he go to save either of them? He turned away from the screen to look at Batman. "Why come to me?"

"Because everyone else trusts you. They always have." Batman's dark cloak was wrapped around him like a barrier, keeping the rest of the world at a distance. He handed Nightwing a disk containing the footage from the Watchtower security cameras. "You've put an importance on keeping up relationships that I neglected. You care."

"So do you," Dick insisted. Next to Alfred, he probably knew Bruce Wayne better than anyone else on Earth. "You just let everyone think different."

Batman did not dispute his former sidekick's assessment.

Nightwing safely tucked the disk into a compartment in his right gauntlet. "Look," he said. "Communications are down across most of the East Coast, but there's a place I can contact everyone from out west. Titans Tower."

The Teen Titans' headquarters was located on an island in San Francisco Bay. If Nightwing took the Batplane, he could be there in a couple of hours. Maybe less.

He headed for the hangar. "You coming?"

"I've got a computer problem I still need to fix," Batman said. "Then we regroup."

Nightwing suspected that he knew exactly what "computer problem" Bruce had in mind. "Sounds good."

"Dick," Batman said before he left.

Nightwing looked back over his shoulder. "Yes?"

The Dark Knight hesitated, as if momentarily at a loss for words. "Those early years. I've forgotten if . . ." He paused once more. If Nightwing didn't know better, he would have sworn that Batman was trying to reach out to him. ". . . they were good for you, weren't they?"

Dick Grayson smiled. He couldn't remember the last time he and Bruce had shared a moment like this. *Maybe back when I was still a Boy Wonder . . .*

"The best," he assured Batman.

INTERSTATE 70,
APPROACHING KEYSTONE CITY

THE battle had carried them north across Kansas.

Superboy-Prime grappled with Conner as they hurled through the sky toward the Missouri River. In the distance, Superboy-Prime glimpsed the bridge linking the Keystone and Central cities. According to Alexander, the twin cities had once existed on separate Earths, before the Crisis merged everything together. *Before my own world disappeared. . . .*

He pummeled Conner with his fists and elbows, taking out years of frustration on this Earth's pitiful excuse for a Superboy. Conner fought back with surprising persistence. *Why doesn't he just give up?* Superboy-Prime thought in frustration. *He's a quitter! I know he is!*

Locked together in battle, they plummeted toward the crowded freeway below. A loaded car carrier, belonging to Keystone City Motors, got in their way, and they tore right through the moving vehicle. New cars, straight from the assembly line, were thrown into the air like Tonka Trucks. Empty sports cars crashed down onto the highway. Horns honked and tires squealed as startled drivers frantically swerved out of the way. Cars scraped against each other and went spinning across multiple lanes of traffic. A 2006 coupe tumbled end over end before finally landing upside-down along the shoulder of the road.

What a mess! Superboy-Prime thought, momentarily distracted by the chaos. He regretted the damage caused by his fight with Conner, but reminded himself that this entire reality was due to be replaced anyway. None of this was taking place on the *real* Earth. Everything would be put right later. *It'll be like none of this ever happened.*

"I don't know how you ever got away with it," he accused Conner. His shoulder still stung where Krypto had bit him. "You fooled everybody into believing you were actually Superboy." Breaking free from Conner, he snatched a falling hatchback out of the air. He swung the empty vehicle at Conner like a club. "You don't even have a cape!"

Conner threw up his arms in defense, like a football player about to be tackled. The jaunty yellow hatchback exploded into pieces. Besides his pseudo-Kryptonian abilities, the young clone had also been gifted with a form of tactile telekinesis that allowed him to dismantle objects just by touching them. Auto parts rained down onto Interstate 70.

The impact knocked Conner into the freeway below. Asphalt cratered beneath him. Cars and trucks squealed to a halt as terrified commuters abandoned their vehicles, fleeing the disaster on foot. They left their car doors wide open, the keys still in the ignition. Screaming in fear, they stampeded onto the flat Kansas plains beyond the highway.

"Run!" Conner urged them. He stumbled to his feet, battered and bleeding. An elderly woman was trapped inside a nearby sedan, her door caved in by a collision with another vehicle. Stumbling forward, Conner ripped the door from its hinges with his bare hands. "Get out of here," he warned her, helping her from the car. He turned her over to another civilian, who hustled the old woman to safety. "Get away now!"

Superboy-Prime couldn't believe the other teen's nerve, trying to act like the hero in this scenario. None of this would have been necessary if Conner had just stepped aside and let a genuine Superboy take his place. *I helped saved the entire universe once,* Superboy-Prime thought bitterly, *just so this loser can pretend he's me?* Years of resentment spilled out from inside him. *I'll show him what a real hero is capable of!*

Hefting a discarded station wagon with one hand, he hurled the vehicle straight down at Conner's head. The heavy car struck Conner head-on, smashing him down onto the blacktop. Metal crunched loudly. Smoke and flames erupted from the crumpled station wagon. A loose wheel bounced erratically across the highway.

Heedless of the blazing fire, Superboy-Prime landed beside Conner's prone body. Broken glass and steel crunched beneath his boots. He grabbed Conner by the throat and yanked him up off the asphalt. Conner's legs dangled in the air. Bizarrely, one hand was thrust into the pocket of his jeans. His face was torn and bloody. He choked as Superboy-Prime throttled him. The caped teenager drew back his fist.

"Heh," Conner chuckled.

"What?" Superboy-Prime hesitated, puzzled by Conner's reaction. "What are you smiling about?"

Conner tugged his hand from his pocket. He opened his fist to reveal a ceramic tile imprinted with a capital *T*. The tile was flashing red.

Some sort of communicator?

A shadow fell across the two teenagers. Superboy-Prime heard a whooshing sound behind him, along with racing footsteps and clanking metal. The freeway trembled beneath his feet. Electricity crackled in the air.

Still holding on to Conner's neck, he spun around to find himself confronted by a veritable army of superhumans. Nearly three dozen of this Earth's so-called heroes rushed toward him with clenched fists and resolute expressions. He recognized nearly all of them from his years observing their reality: Elasti-Girl, S.T.R.I.P.E., the Flash, Mister Terrific, Kid Flash, Robin, Speedy, Flamebird, Beast Boy, Mirage, Robotman, Terra, Raven, Pantha, Wildebeast, Risk, Bushido, Wildcat, Stargirl, Hourman, Wonder Girl, Negative Man, Jay Garrick, Dr. Mid-Nite, Red Star, Sand, Nudge, Grunt, and a few others he couldn't quite place.

All coming to Conner's rescue.

"Titans together!" Beast Boy cheered in the form of a large green velociraptor. Stargirl used her Cosmic Rod to project a beam of stellar energy that encased Superboy-Prime's upraised fist. Wonder Girl snatched Conner from his grasp with her magic lasso, freeing the rest of the heroes to pile onto Superboy-Prime en masse. He suddenly found himself under attack from all sides. Negative Man zipped through his body, searing him from within. S.T.R.I.P.E., encased within an armored exoskeleton, fired a rocket at Superboy's head. Elasti-Girl, towering above the freeway like a giantess, reached for him with an enormous hand. Robotman wrapped the mangled station wagon around him. Grunt, a four-armed gorilla, pounded his head and shoulders.

Between blows, he glimpsed Wonder Girl gently lowering Conner to the shoulder of the road. Dr. Mid-Nite, Robin, and Raven hurried to see to their comrade's injuries. Cradling Conner's head upon her lap, Wonder Girl wiped the blood from his face.

"Cassie?" he murmured weakly.

"We're here," she told him, "with the reserves. Beast Boy called in the Doom Patrol too. Kid Flash brought the Justice Society." She gazed down at him tenderly. "After what happened to the Freedom Fighters—and the Watchtower—a little overkill sounded like a good idea."

Superboy-Prime couldn't believe what was happening. Why was she doting over Conner, while everyone else tackled him? This wasn't the way things were supposed to be!

"What are you doing?" he yelled at his attackers. "I'm not a bad guy!" Fists and energy blasts came at him fast and furious. A chartreuse dinosaur bit down on his wounded shoulder. He couldn't even keep track of where each attack was coming from. The assembled heroes were all around him, burying him beneath the sheer weight of their numbers. "Get . . . get off me," he gasped. The red sun of Krypton flared in his eyes. "Get off!"

Lashing out, he threw off the mob on top of him. A scorching blast of heat vision drove the other heroes back.

But only for a moment.

GOTHAM CITY

THE morgue was all booked up. After the hellish events of the last few days, every medical examiner in town had been working overtime trying to keep up with the flow of corpses. All available freezers contained fresh human remains. More bodies were laid out on examining tables. Air-conditioning helped to keep the bodies cool, yet the smell of death still hung in the air. A backlog of fatalities had the morgue running days behind schedule.

A pair of ME's were only just now finishing up the autopsy on Detective Crispus Allen. The dead cop lay stretched out upon an examination table. His shaved scalp had been sewn back into place, following the removal of his brain. Baseball stitches closed up the Y-shaped incision in his chest. A tray of bloody instruments rested upon a nearby counter.

"Christ," the female pathologist said, looking down at the murdered policeman. She removed her surgical mask while her assistant sponged off the corpse. A file on the victim contained grisly crime scene photos of Allen lying in a puddle of his own blood. "Guy survives a meteor shower *and* one of those super-hero types crashing into the hood of his car. Only to end up being shot in the back during the riots."

"You hear what Montoya thinks?" The assistant lowered his voice. "She thinks a cop killed him. The CSU head tech."

The pathologist arched an eyebrow. "Who? Jim Corrigan?"

"Yeah," the assistant said. He finished cleaning the body and pulled a sheet over it. "Poor guy. You know Allen had a wife, two kids?" He shook his head. "Things like this happen, the world goes crazy . . . makes you wonder if there's a God. And if there is a God, what did we do to piss him off so damn much?"

In a hurry to finish up the paperwork on this case, the two medical examiners left the room, flicking off the lights on their way out. Allen's corpse remained upon the autopsy table, waiting for an available freezer to open up. The air around the body stank of gastric acid and formalin. Silence descended upon the darkened morgue.

But not for long.

The sheet covering Allen's body rustled. Then the corpse suddenly sat upright. Allen's brown eyes snapped open. "Corrrrigan!" he moaned out loud. "Where'ssss Corrrrigannnn?"

The dead man looked about in confusion. His legs swung around and his bare feet dropped to the floor. Disoriented, he tried to figure out what was happening to him. The last thing he remembered was fleeing from Jim Corrigan's gun, then feeling the bullets slam into his back. So how did he end up naked and alone in the morgue? He looked back at the autopsy table. To his surprise, the sheet was still in place over a body.

My body?

He stared at his hands, which looked substantial enough. He listened for his own heartbeat, but heard only the sepulchral stillness of the empty morgue. His finger tentatively traced the Y-shaped scar upon the chest. Crispus Allen had attended enough autopsies to know what that incision meant.

I'm dead, he realized. *Truly dead.*

So why wasn't he at peace?

"Arrrrgh!" he cried out as pain exploded inside his torso, as if Corrigan's bullets were tearing through his insides once again. The scar upon his chest began to glow white against his dark skin. Allen's back arched and he gritted his teeth as the stitches over his breastbone were pulled apart. The unbroken threads stretched tautly across the open wound. An eerie phosphorescence gleamed within his vacant trunk, from which all his vital organs had already been removed. There was a void within his chest, waiting to be filled. . . .

"Noooo!"

An anguished cry echoed inside the morgue, and it took Allen a moment to realize that the unearthly wail was not coming from him. A freezing wind whipped through room, rattling the stools and instruments. The sheet flew off Allen's discarded husk and blew about the room. He watched in awe and horror as a wispy green apparition materialized in the air before him. A deathly-white face stared out from beneath a shadowy hood. The wraith's face was twisted in dismay. Frantic white eyes bulged from their sockets.

"What is the meaning of this?" a chilling voice intoned. "Why have I been brought here?"

The Spectre tried to fly away from Allen even as an unseen force seemed to be drawing him backward toward the open wound in the dead cop's chest.

"No!" the ghost protested. "I will not go willingly. I have been imprisoned long enough. I have suffered . . ."

Allen's empty torso was like a black hole, sucking the Spectre in against his will. *Stay away!* Allen thought fearfully. He wasn't sure what was happening, but he knew he didn't want any part of the vengeful spirit. *Keep away from me!*

"I repent!" the Spectre exclaimed. The misty tail end of the ghost invaded Allen's chest. Cris stiffened in shock as the freezing ectoplasm filled the empty cavity.

"I repent my actions! I have served you faithfully. I will not stray again!"

His pleas went unheard. Inch by inch, the straining ghost was sucked entirely into Allen's chest. The Spectre's face stared out from behind the open incision, taut stitches stretching across it like prison bars. He grabbed on to both sides of the wound, trying in vain to claw his way free of Crispus Allen's dead flesh. Allen felt the ghost's fingers pulling at the gap. The pain was excruciating. This was worse than dying. . . .

"I was misled! Deceived!" the Spectre shrieked, even as the Y-incision began to close up once more, the stitches pulling it tightly shut. The Spectre looked like a prisoner being walled up inside a tomb. He tried with all his might to hold the wound open, but the severed flesh crept inexorably back together. "Forgive me! Forgive me!"

The wound closed up, leaving only a scar behind. The Spectre disappeared from sight. Allen threw back his head and howled at the ceiling. Tiny skulls appeared within the pupils of his eyes. His voice and the Spectre's voice merged into one.

"Forgive me!"

CHAPTER 29

KEYSTONE CITY

No matter how hard he fought, the other heroes kept on coming.

"Stop hitting me!" Superboy-Prime shouted in frustration. The battle had carried them all the way into Keystone City, practically to the Missouri River. The bridge to Central City loomed ahead. An old-fashioned diner offered malts and cheeseburgers. An automotive plant sprawled at the outskirts of the city. Towering smokestacks belched soot into the atmosphere, but any terrified civilians had long since fled the vicinity, leaving Superboy-Prime alone against Conner's allies.

"You're the one breakin' bones in a mindless rage," S.T.R.I.P.E. scolded him. The patriotic acronym stood for Special Tactics Integrated Power Enhancer, an armored suit that made the hero look like a giant robot from a Japanese cartoon. Other heroes, like Mister Terrific and Stargirl, littered the debris-strewn streets and sidewalks around them. They groaned upon the ground in varying degrees of unconsciousness. Superboy had defeated plenty of heroes already, but he was still outnumbered. He didn't even know where Conner was anymore.

Probably being nursed back to health by Wonder Girl.

"It's not fair!" he protested. "I just wanted to talk to Conner!" He grabbed on to S.T.R.I.P.E.'s bulky steel exoskeleton and flung him into the river a few miles away. Elasti-Girl coiled around him, squeezing him like a python, but he angrily pulled her off and snapped her like a whip against the cement. "You started this!"

Pantha sprang at him, her deadly claws extended. " 'You started this?' " she said mockingly. A mane of auburn hair billowed wildly behind her. A golden mask heightened her feline appearance. There was some confusion, Superboy-Prime knew, as to whether Pantha was a cat who had evolved into a woman, or woman who had been partially transformed into a cat. "He's just a stupid kid!"

"I'm not stupid!" he shouted furiously. "Stop making fun of me!"

He punched her right in the face . . . and Pantha's head went flying from her shoulders.

Blood sprayed everywhere. A hush fell over the scene as everyone tried to grasp what had just happened. Pantha's headless body toppled onto the pavement. Blood gushed from the stump of her neck. The other heroes recoiled from the sight, stepping back from the crimson flood spreading over the street. Superboy-Prime stared at his bloody fist in horror. His eyes teared up. His lip quivered like a frightened child's.

"Oh, no!" His voice was barely a whisper. "I didn't mean to do that."

It's this yellow sun, he thought miserably. *I didn't realize how strong it makes me!*

Pantha's head crashed to earth several yards away. Her pulped skull landed at the feet of Red Star and Wildebeest. The Russian hero and the shaggy, bull-like behemoth were the closest thing to a family that Pantha had ever known. Wildebeest roared in fury. Red Star ignited into a figure of white-hot flame.

"You will burn for that!" he vowed.

The other heroes recovered from their shock. "Get him!" yelled Terra, a reserve member of the Teen Titans. The masked blonde hovered above the fray on a floating chunk of rock.

"Right with you, Terra!" Sand responded. His silicon-based body reformed after being smashed to pieces only moments before. A gas mask covered his face, in tribute to the Sandman of an earlier era.

Terra controlled the earth. Sand commanded dirt and rocks. Together, they caused the ground to erupt beneath Superboy-Prime's feet. Flying boulders pounded him. A fierce sandstorm blasted his skin.

"Please!" Superboy-Prime whimpered, spitting out a mouthful of dirt. Muddy tears streaked his face. He hurled the boulders back at Sand and Terra, knocking them senseless. "I said I didn't mean to!"

That wasn't good enough for Red Star and Wildebeest, who charged across the ravaged landscape, intent on revenge. A savage human/animal hybrid, Wildebeest stampeded toward Superboy-Prime with his head down, hoping to gore the stricken teen with his horns. A ferocious growl emanated from the beast-man's broad chest. He was out for blood.

"Why are you making me do this?" Superboy-Prime wailed in torment. He punched his fist all the way through Wildebeest's mammoth torso, his knuckles exploding out of the hybrid's back. Superboy-Prime's face grimaced horribly. His voice was hoarse with emotion. "Why?"

Burning brightly, Red Star came at him next. Superboy-Prime had no time to think about what he was doing, only to react. A gust of arctic breath froze the flaming hero solid, turning him into a living ice sculpture. The cold air hissed as it blew from Superboy-Prime's lungs.

This doesn't matter, he told himself desperately. Hot tears streamed down his face. *None of this is* real. *Alexander can make it all go away. He has to!*

But the nightmare wouldn't stop. "You're dead, bud!" exclaimed an athletic young man in a green uniform. Risk pounced at Superboy-Prime with superhuman speed, but the anguished teen was even faster. Grabbing on to Risk's throat with his right hand, Superboy-Prime ripped the Titan's right arm from its socket. Risk screamed in agony. Bright arterial blood spurted from his shoulder.

"You're ruining everything!" Superboy-Prime wailed. He threw Risk's arm away, then tossed the dismembered hero in the opposite direction. The triumphant S-shield on Superboy-Prime's chest was splattered with fresh blood. Gore dripped from his fingers. "You're ruining . . . *me!*"

Superhearing alerted him to an attack from behind. Spinning around, he spotted Bushido leaping toward him, his samurai sword raised above his head. A blast of heat vision cut the Japanese teenager in two. The severed halves of his body hit the pavement.

"You're making me like you!"

Too late, he realized that he probably could have just melted Bushido's sword instead. *It's all their fault,* he thought angrily. *They didn't give me a chance!*

Beast Boy came flapping down from the sky in the shape of a green pterodactyl. Superboy-Prime remembered the Titan's exuberant battle cry earlier. Had that really been only a few minutes ago? He grabbed on to the dinosaur's hind leg and swung the winged creature down onto the rubble. Prehistoric pinions snapped noisily. A squawk escaped the transformed Titan's beak. Superboy-Prime drew back his fist to silence the irritating changeling once and for all. . . .

Then a crimson blur grabbed on to him and carried him away at the speed of lightning.

THREE generations of Flashes had seized the out-of-control Superboy-Prime and were removing him from the scene at superspeed. "Wegothimguys!" Wally West called out from the middle, his hands gripping the crazed teenager's shoulders. To his left, Jay Garrick, the original Flash from the 1930s, held Superboy-Prime's right arm. Gray hair showed beneath Jay's winged silver cap. To Wally's right, Kid Flash had his fingers locked around Superboy-Prime's left arm. His yellow costume resembled the one that Wally had worn back when Wally's uncle Barry was still the Flash. Wally had donned Barry's classic red uniform after his uncle's death in the Crisis. Someday perhaps young Bart would replace Wally. . . .

Together they shoved the homicidal teenager ahead of them. Superboy-Prime's back was to the wind, so that he was facing the three speedsters. His cape and costume were torn and tattered. Blood drenched his face and arms. The wind whipped his hair. A sonic boom testified to the incredible speed at which he was being carried along. The scenery beside them zipped by in a blur.

"Stop it!" the boy shouted. His eyes flared red. "Let . . . me . . . GO!"

A crimson beam zoomed at the Flash's face but, with amazingly swift reflexes, Jay Garrick doffed his winged helmet and used it to deflect the deadly heat ray. The beam bounced harmlessly off the inside of the silver cap.

That was Jay's last gasp, however. The older man's face was pale and drawn. Sweat dripped from his brow. His breath grew ever more ragged. "Wally," he panted. "I . . . my tendons are tearing . . . I'm not going to be fast enough for this. . . ."

The Flash appreciated everything his original predecessor had already done for them. "We just needed help with the running start, Jay."

Electricity crackled around them, mimicking the lightning bolts on their chests. They raced around the world a dozen times a minute. Their boots zoomed across oceans and continents alike.

"I'm sorry, son." Jay clearly hated the idea of leaving Wally and Bart on their own.

"You did great!" the Flash insisted.

Jay reluctantly let go of Superboy-Prime. "Good luck!" He tumbled onto the ground as though thrown from a moving car. His weary body bounced across the pavement, taking its lumps. He was back in Keystone City, right where they had started.

Godspeed, Jay, the Flash thought.

Wally captured Superboy-Prime's right arm, taking over from Jay. Keeping up the pressure on the berserk teenager, who fought back against him, was like pushing a thousand-pound weight . . . or Superman himself.

"What are you doing?" Superboy-Prime yelled. "This isn't my fault."

Who on Earth? the Flash wondered. He had no idea where this duplicate Superboy had come from, but it was obvious that he couldn't be allowed to go free. Too many heroes had already died in the boy's insane rampage. He needed to be taken somewhere where he couldn't hurt anyone else. Wally thought he knew just the place.

An intense yellow light burst into existence before them, like a wall of shimmering energy.

"The Speed Force?" Bart asked.

The Speed Force was more than just the extra-dimensional energy source that powered all super-speedsters; it was also a gateway into an ineffable realm that existed somewhere beyond the speed of light. By running fast enough, one could enter this realm, where the spirits of past speedsters resided for all eternity. Doing so usually meant abandoning mortal existence forever; Wally was the only Flash to ever pass into the Speed Force and return, thanks to his love for Linda Park. He knew there was no guarantee that he would be able to come back a second time.

That's just a chance I'll have to take.

He nodded at Kid Flash. "We've got to keep moving, Bart. We have to get this psycho away from everyone. He's too dangerous."

"But why did he do that?" Bart asked. "Who is he?"

I wish I knew, the Flash thought. Superboy-Prime's back was against the wall of yellow energy, which moved with the speeding trio as they circled the globe. The two Flashes strained to push Superboy-Prime through the luminous gateway, which resisted their efforts. Even though they were rapidly approaching the speed of light, they still weren't going fast enough to enter the Speed Force. "Don't stop running, Bart! Don't—"

Suddenly another force gripped him, equal and opposite to the pull of the Speed Force. He felt himself speeding in two directions at once, his very being stretched out like an infinitely long piece of taffy. To an outsider, it must have looked like multiple Flashes coexisting in a single instant.

"Flash?" Bart called out.

Part of him remained beside Kid Flash, fighting to propel the deranged Superboy-Prime through the shimmering barrier. But another part of him was yanked back to his apartment in Keystone City. Linda appeared before him, rocking both twins on her lap as she anxiously watched the television set. A pair of empty bottles rested on a counter nearby. Matching teddy bears rested upon the floor of the nursery.

"Linda," he whispered.

She looked around in surprise. "Wally?" Clutching the twins to her chest, she stared at him with an increasingly alarmed expression. He appeared to her in a haze of bright electrical energy, vibrating in and out of view. Ghost images of the Flash stretched behind him to infinity. He reached out for her, his outstretched arm warped by the bizarre optical effects. Lightning crackled all around him. "Oh my God. What's happening?" Linda leapt to her feet, tightly holding on to their babies. "What's wrong?"

"You've always been my lightning rod," he told her. His voice sounded like a recording being played way too fast. "You're what's kept my feet on the ground so many times. And I love you more than anything else in this world." He hoped he could somehow make her understand. "But I have to keep running."

"Where are you running to?" Her agitated voice woke the babies, who started crying loudly. The twins squirmed in her arms. "That dimension that gives you your powers? The Speed Force? Is that it?"

"No," he suddenly realized. He'd been to the Speed Force before. This felt *different* somehow. "Not the Speed Force, I think." He couldn't find a way to put into words what he somehow sensed at this moment. "Someplace else."

Tears sparked from his eyes. He took one last look at his wife and children.

"I have to let go of *everything* I love."

"No, you don't," she said fiercely. A look of determination came over her lovely face. She lunged forward into the unnatural electrical storm enveloping her husband, taking the crying infants with her. "Wherever you're going, your family is coming with you."

She kissed Wally with a passion more incandescent than any burst of lightning. Naked energy flashed around them. The babies' eyes took on a preternatural glow, tiny sparks arcing between them. In an instant, Wally, Linda, and the twins were transformed into a single huge lightning bolt that exploded out of the apartment, shattering windows.

The bolt flashed across Keystone City and back to where Kid Flash still fought to contain the murderous Superboy. The Flash's lingering afterimage faded away as the lightning struck Superboy-Prime in the chest, pushing him farther into the Speed Force.

"Wally?" Bart blurted in confusion. He caught a glimpse of his cousin's face in the lightning before it blinked away. "Wally? Where are you going?"

Kid Flash suddenly found himself on his own. "I can't do this!" he said in a panicky tone. His hands were pressed against the Superboy's chest. "I can't do this alone!"

"You're right," the evil Superboy taunted him. Only halfway through the glowing wall behind him, he wasn't budging another inch, no matter how hard Bart pushed. "You're even weaker than the rest. I've been watching you for years. You're a joke!" He sneered at Bart. "You're just a stupid little sidekick, left all alone."

"Shut up!" Kid Flash punched Superboy-Prime in the jaw, a hundred times a minute. Maybe he was no Barry Allen, but he'd always done his best to live up to the Flash legacy. Heck, he was buddies with the *real* Superboy, Conner Kent. So where did this imposter come off calling him a joke? Kid Flash let his meteoric fists punctuate his words. "I'm . . . not . . . stupid!"

"Bart," a voice said from the Speed Force. A figure in a familiar red costume leaned out of the radiant energy and grabbed on to Superboy-Prime from behind. Confident blue eyes gazed into Bart's. "You're not alone either."

The teenager's jaw dropped. He recognized the face beneath the mask. "Grandpa?"

Barry Allen, the most famous Flash of them all, wrapped his arm around Superboy-Prime's neck, catching him in a headlock. Two more figures partly emerged from the Speed Force. Max Mercury, the Zen Master of Speed, grabbed hold of Superboy-Prime's right arm. "Come on, Johnny," he said. "Let's lend the kid a hand."

"You got it," Johnny Quick agreed. An abstruse mathematical formula had been his key to the Speed Force. He seized the struggling teenager's left arm.

"No!" Superboy-Prime shrieked. He fought to break free, but the three deceased speedsters would not let him go. They dragged him farther into the gateway. "Don't do this to me!"

Did he understand what was happening to him? Frankly, Kid Flash didn't care. He was too busy staring in wonder at the legendary heroes who had just come to his aid. It seemed that the Speed Force really was where old super-speedsters went when they died.

"Max? Mr. Quick?"

His grandfather gave him a reassuring smile. "Wally's waiting for you, Bart."

Kid Flash realized that this wasn't over yet. Barry Allen and the others had pulled the evil Superboy into the Speed Force as much as they could. It was up to him to push the killer the rest of way, no matter what.

"Don't be afraid," Max Mercury advised him. The venerable speed guru had coached Bart back when he was just starting out, teaching him the ropes of the super-hero business. Kid Flash trusted him with his life . . . and more.

"I'm not, Max." He took a deep breath, just like Max had taught him, then reached deep inside himself for every last ounce of juice he had left. Putting on one final burst of speed, he pushed himself and Superboy-Prime beyond the speed of light. The world around them disappeared into a glorious blaze of light. For one infinitesimal fraction of a second, Bart Allen was the Fastest Man Alive. "Let's go!"

"You don't understand!" the evil Superboy screamed in vain. "They made me do it!" The golden light began to swallow him up. "You can't get rid of me! When I grow up, I'm going to be Superman!" Tears gushed down his face. "Don't any of you understand? I'm going to be Superm—!"

Thunder cracked as he and Bart disappeared in a blinding flash.

SPRAWLED upon the torn-up pavement, Jay Garrick watched in awe as the Speed Force erupted outward, ripping apart. A deafening boom hammered his eardrums. The golden wall dissolved into flickering yellow sparks that quickly faded away. Kid Flash and the berserk Superboy were nowhere to be seen.

Neither was Wally.

Winded, the original Flash climbed slowly to his feet. His aging muscles ached with every movement. His legs felt like rubber. His silver helmet dangled from his fingers, still smoking from Superboy-Prime's heat vision. He stood dead center on the suspension bridge linking the twin cities. A charred and smoking trail stretched out before and behind him.

He couldn't quite believe what he felt in his bones. . . .

"Jay?" a gruff voice called out to him. He turned to see Wildcat limping toward him. Ted Grant's fuzzy black costume was scuffed and torn. A felt ear had been ripped from his cowl. He gave his pensive colleague a concerned look. "You okay, pal?"

Jay took in the aftermath of Superboy-Prime's rampage. Beyond the bridge, the surviving heroes tended to their wounded comrades. Dr. Mid-Nite frantically worked to keep Risk alive. Hourman helped Sand to his feet. S.T.R.I.P.E., dripping wet from splashing down in the river, carried his step-daughter, Stargirl, in his steel-plated arms. Negative Man applied first aid to Elasti-Girl. Raven used her mystic powers to heal Beast Boy's broken limbs. Mister Terrific and Dr. Niles Caulder, the handicapped chief of the Doom Patrol, teamed up to reconnect Robotman's mechanical legs. Flamebird carefully attempted to thaw out Red Star. Speedy and Grunt began the grisly task of gathering up the remains of Pantha, Wildebeest, and Bushido.

So much bloodshed and death, Jay reflected somberly. *All from one hysterical boy.* An almost overwhelming sense of loss came over him. The Flashes had halted the mysterious Superboy's spree of destruction, but at what cost? He was stunned by what his formerly supercharged body was telling him. It seemed impossible, and yet . . .

"The Speed Force, Ted." Jay Garrick tried to access its power, just as he had for decades, but nothing happened. He remained stuck at everyday speed. "It's gone."

CHAPTER 30

THE ARCTIC

A swarm of OMACs, many thousands strong, flew in formation above the barren polar wasteland. The implacable cyborgs had come straight from the Bermuda Triangle, in accordance with their revised instructions.

Arriving at the proper coordinates, they began flying in circles above the glacier. Their blue ceramic shells protected them from the sub-zero temperature as they waited patiently for the next stage of the operation. They did not have to wait long.

Hundreds of feet beneath the ice, in their crystal grotto, the elder Superman sat at his wife's bedside. Lois slept uneasily, growing frailer before his very eyes. He looked up in concern as the rumble of concealed machinery shook the underground fortress. His X-ray vision spied the OMACs circling overhead. The crystalline walls hummed and vibrated. He draped his arm protectively over Lois' slumbering form.

This is all part of Alexander's plan, he reminded himself. He looked for Alex and Superboy, but couldn't find them in any of the caverns he was familiar with. He probed further, but something blocked his vision; it was like trying to see through lead. Had they begun the monumental task of restoring Earth-Two to its rightful place in the cosmos? Superman prayed that Alexander knew what he was doing—and that there was still a chance to save Lois. His wife's pulse beat feebly beneath his gentle touch. *We're running out of time.*

High above him, a golden spire broke through the ice, rising up from below to greet the noonday sun. The OMACs flew in rings around the top of the Tower. "PROTOCOL: 'TOWER WATCH' CONFIRMED," they reported with a single voice.

Defending the Tower was their new priority.

ALEXANDER Luthor nodded in satisfaction. Everything remained on track, despite Superboy's unfortunate altercation with this Earth's heroes. The teen's spectacular disappearance was an unexpected development, but not a fatal one. Superboy had already fulfilled his most important functions. *I can finish the project without him*, Alex thought.

He turned to his remaining accomplice. The Psycho-Pirate stood beside him on a floating force-field platform. The villain's scarlet cloak was wrapped around him. His golden mask bore a blank expression.

"Psycho-Pirate," Alexander said, "I've allowed you to participate in all of this as payment for your services."

"But you promised Power Girl would be mine," he whined. "After you were done with her."

Alexander was silent. He would let the Psycho-Pirate believe otherwise, but he now found the thought of turning Kara over to the brainwashing lunatic distasteful. The taste of her lips lingered in his memory. "Your chance at redemption is what you should be focused on," he said brusquely, avoiding the issue.

The Psycho-Pirate knew better than to challenge Alexander. Uniquely composed of both matter and antimatter, Alexander was immune to the madman's mask.

The platform hovered in front of Black Adam. The Egyptian superman remained frozen within his niche on the battery tier of the Tower. Metal cables connected him to the complex machinery behind him. Unlike the slots holding their other prisoners, Black Adam's niche was connected to a metal antenna that stretched all the way up to the very top of the spire. His pointed chin drooped forward onto his chest.

Time to rouse him, Alexander thought. His fingers danced upon his holographic control panel. A discrete electrical charge stimulated the sleeping tyrant's brain, restoring him to wakefulness. "Nnn?" Black Adam grunted as he opened his eyes.

"Now, if you would," Alexander instructed the Psycho-Pirate. He didn't bother disguising himself as this sphere's Lex Luthor in front of Black Adam. The time for that imposture had passed. "We need to call down the fuel."

"Yes," the Psycho-Pirate agreed. He faced their prisoner. "Look at me, Black Adam."

The ageless villain strained against his restraints. He glared balefully at his captors. "You will pay for this base treachery!"

The Psycho-Pirate was not cowed by Black Adam's threat. "Despite your arrogance, and your power, I sense a great fear inside you." The shining metal of his mask began to remold itself. "Say the name of the being you fear." The golden mask assumed a frightened expression. "Say his name."

"Sh . . ." Black Adam clenched his jaw, trying to keep his mouth shut, but he could not resist the insidious effect of the Medusa Mask. Against his will, he spoke the magic word.

"Shazam!"

The wizard's name called down a massive bolt of lightning from the heavens. Thunder boomed at the top of the world. Almost as thick as the Tower itself, the bolt struck a lightning rod atop the golden spire. Raw magic, set loose by the Spectre during his vengeful crusade, poured into Alexander's machine, which suddenly hummed to life. Indicator lights and gauges lit up on the surface of the tower. All the power of the late wizard now fueled the enormous mechanism. Pure white energy crackled and hissed within the gaping maw and empty eye sockets of the Anti-Monitor's colossal skull.

Black Adam blinked in confusion. Ordinarily, Shazam's name would have transformed him back into his mortal guise of Teth-Adam, but the Tower had intercepted the magic lightning bolt instead, leaving Black Adam unchanged. "By the Gods!" Superstitious fear showed in his dark eyes. "What have you done?"

All that was necessary, Alexander thought. Raising his hand, he employed an antimatter blast to render Black Adam unconscious once more. He stepped back to admire his handiwork. Eldritch energy coursed through the newly-awakened Tower. "Well done," he praised the Psycho-Pirate. He felt an intense sense of accomplishment.

After months of planning and plotting, his preparations were complete.

Now it was time for his true work to begin. . . .

***

"PROFESSOR Stein?"

Firestorm stared at the blazing entity before him. Just as he and Mick had merged into one being, a previous incarnation of Firestorm had been a fusion of the late Ronnie Raymond and a Nobel Prize–winning physicist named Martin Stein. The middle-aged scientist had eventually evolved into a fire elemental and left Earth to explore the cosmos. But what was he doing here in the Polaris system?

There were a million questions he wanted to ask the other Nuclear Man, but now was not the time. The cosmic storm was growing bigger by the moment . . . and increasing in intensity. Before he could say a word to Stein, all hell broke loose. Tendrils of pure white energy, immeasurably long, lashed through the war-torn sector. Dozens of alien spaceships, fleeing the disaster, exploded before Firestorm's eyes.

"No!" he exclaimed. "All those people . . . !"

Yet more ships, damaged by the explosions and energy bolts, floated adrift in space or tumbled hopelessly out of control. There was no way the ships could escape the cataclysmic storm unless Firestorm and the other heroes got them out of there . . . fast. Supergirl grabbed on to the underside of the largest space freighter and carried it away from the storm at super-speed. Red Tornado created a powerful vortex that flung several stranded vessels out of the danger zone. Starfire blasted apart huge pieces of flying shrapnel. Shift turned himself into a metal patch, sealing the breached hull of a limping star cruiser. Four Green Lanterns—Alan Scott, Kyle Rayner, Kilowog, and Jade—used their combined willpower to block as many of the titanic energy bolts as they could with green counterblasts. Captain Comet, Adam Strange, the Hawk couple, and the rest all rushed to get the fleet of refugee ships to safety.

In the midst of the chaos, Firestorm was surprised to see Air Wave heading *toward* the storm. "Hey! You're going the wrong way!" Jason shouted.

"I can hear them *all!*" he blurted, sounding half-crazed. "All the worlds and ships that can't get away. They're trying to send their families messages." His voice was strained, as though he could barely cope with the deluge of alien signals. "They're dying, and all they want to do is say good-bye! But they never will unless I help . . . unless I . . ."

It was too much for him. Firestorm watched in horror as Air Wave was literally torn apart, screaming in pain as he was ripped in a thousand different directions. The overwhelmed hero disintegrated into a burst of radiating signals, carrying messages of love and farewell across the cosmos. His final scream dissolved into static.

Oh my God, Firestorm thought. He had only known Air Wave for a day or so, but he couldn't help being incredibly moved by the other hero's sacrifice. *He did his part for the ones we couldn't save. Now it's up to the rest of us to keep the survivors alive.*

A bolt of white-hot energy whipped past him, barely missing him. A few feet more and he would have been fried for sure. Instinctively, he started to retreat from the storm, then spotted a large gray starship tumbling backward toward the heart of the gaping space-time rupture. The ship's unusual arc-shaped configuration resembled the Greek letter omega. *That must be the Omega Men's ship,* Firestorm realized. Cyborg had told him about the Omega Men, a team of alien freedom fighters from the nearby Vega system. *Guess they got sucked into this free-for-all too.*

The Omega Ship had obviously lost power for some reason, leaving them unable to halt their spiral descent toward annihilation. *We've got to go get them,* Mick said urgently.

Firestorm hesitated. "What? Are you insane?" Air Wave's abrupt demise flashed through his brain. Star-spanning energy bolts streaked through space all around the Omega Ship; it was a miracle that the rudderless vessel hadn't been blasted to pieces already.

That ship needs help, Mick said. His face hovered at the periphery of Jason's vision. *Isn't that what we came out here for?*

"Well, yeah."

Firestorm zoomed after the spinning spacecraft, darting back and forth to avoid the energy blasts shooting past him. As soon as he came within range of the Omega Ship, he caused metal thrusters to materialize at both ends of the omega. Atomic flames shot from the thrusters, propelling the ship away from the storm.

But it wasn't that easy. The cosmic storm had wreaked havoc with the space-time continuum, trapping the Omega Ship in some kind of freak gravitational distortion. Firestorm had to channel more and more of his own nuclear power into the ship's new thrusters to overcome the pull of the distortion. He was consuming himself . . . and Mick.

"Mick, stop!" Jason could feel his friend contributing his own life-force to the cause. He knew from experience that it was possible to use up all the energy he obtained from his other half. "You're pushing yourself too hard. You're going to burn out!"

Just save them, Jason. Mick's face seemed to flicker before his eyes. The voice in Jason's head grew fainter. *And don't forget . . .*

Powered by their joint energy, the Omega Ship broke free from the gravitational warp. Its thrusters dissolved back into atoms as momentum carried it farther from the storm. Lights flashed on behind the ship's portholes as the Omega Men got their engines working again. It appeared they could make it on their own now.

. . . friend . . . we . . .

Jason could barely make out the voice. "Mick? Mick!"

Unable to sustain the merge any longer, Firestorm split apart. Mick Wong was already dead, flaking away like ash. Adrift in the vacuum, unable to change back into Firestorm, Jason Rusch found himself only minutes away from death as well. He gasped for breath. A freezing chill penetrated all the way to his marrow.

At least we saved them, Jason thought.

A brilliant light appeared before him, dispelling the bitter cold. Through blurry eyes, he glimpsed the incandescent fire elemental blazing toward him. *Oh right. I almost forgot about him. . . .*

"Half of the Firestorm matrix has expired," the being who had once been Martin Stein declared. "You have divided. But do not fear, Jason Rusch."

Without warning, the fire elemental merged with the dying youth. Rings of atomic energy flared outward across the void.

"Firestorm shall be restored."

LEAVING the Psycho-Pirate and their captives beneath him, Alexander rose upon his platform until he stood directly before the open mouth of the dead Anti-Monitor. The raw energies of creation churned and cascaded inside the gaping maw. Alexander held out his arms, which glowed with his own unique matter/antimatter abilities. He felt the power within the Tower call out to him.

"At last," he proclaimed. "It will be undone."

He thrust his hands into the swirling white energy.

***

"By the Gods!"

Donna Troy couldn't believe her eyes. Had she lost her mind, or had a pair of *giant golden hands* really just emerged from the immense white void at the heart of the cosmic storm?

Startled gasps from Animal Man and Cyborg testified that they saw the gigantic hands as well, but that did little to reassure her. Her mind boggled at the sheer scale of the phenomenon; the impossible hands had to be light-years in length. Metal gauntlets, large enough to hold entire solar systems, armored the grasping hands. She felt like she was witnessing the very creation of the universe—or perhaps its destruction.

"At least they look like human hands," Cyborg observed. "But how the heck are we supposed to fight something that big?"

"Don't ask me," Animal Man said. He stared at the immense hands in wonder. "I don't think my little lightning trick is going to work this time."

Probably not, Donna agreed.

She had been in the presence of the Olympian Gods, as well as the Titans of Myth, but even she couldn't conceive of who the hands might belong to. For a moment, she permitted herself the desperate hope that the hands had appeared in order to close the cosmic rupture and bring an end to the storm. *Perhaps,* she prayed, *those hands are on our side.*

All such hopes were dashed when the golden hands grabbed on to opposites sides of the terrible white abyss and tore it open wider. The very fabric of the universe was ripped apart, setting off a cataclysmic shock wave that raced across the entire system. Starships and super heroes, moons and asteroids, were tossed about like confetti by the blast.

New Cronus was not spared from the impact. The shock wave overcame the starship's internal stabilizers, causing the converted moon to go spinning off into space like a billiard ball. Donna was thrown from her pedestal, falling sideways across the Escher-like architecture of the sprawling temples and palaces. Her back slammed into a marble fountain graced with sculpted nymphs and naiads. She saw Cyborg and Animal Man crash into the topsy-turvy edifices nearby.

Dazed, she gazed up at the starry sky beyond New Cronus. The size of nebulae, the golden hands reached across the firmament, searching for . . . what? Donna gasped at the celestial hands. She had no doubt that this was the awesome menace the ancient Titans had warned her of. *No wonder they fled this reality*, she thought. How could even the Titans of Myth stand against such a threat?

A booming voice echoed across the sector:

"IT WILL BE UNDONE!"

"I'M going to fix everything," Alexander declared. "Undo the Crisis."

The power of the gods coursed through his hands, which were buried deeply in the supernatural energies surging within the Tower. The unearthly radiance cast ominous shadows on the planes of his face. His eyes were closed tightly shut as he concentrated his formidable intellect and willpower on the task before him.

He reached past what presently constituted reality, sorting through layers of probability for the specific quantum configuration he desired. His questing mind tapped into the memories of Clark and Lois as they waited in their crystal grotto below the Tower. Images of Earth-Two, as it had existed before the Crisis, flashed through his brain, even as they suddenly appeared on the multifaceted walls of the grotto:

Clark Kent, Lois Lane, Jimmy Olsen, and their editor, George Taylor, laughing together in the bullpen of the *Daily Star*.

Superman, in his prime, hoisting a carload of gangsters above his head.

The Man of Steel sharing a jovial moment with his best friend, Batman. Robin, the Boy Wonder, grinned mischievously at the world's finest heroes.

Bruce Wayne and Selina Kyle showing Clark and Lois their new baby girl.

Lois Lane, a pillbox hat upon her head, beaming in anticipation of her next big scoop. . . .

"Yes," Alexander murmured to himself. "That's it." The images passing through his brain were imbued with a bright and shiny innocence that the current reality conspicuously lacked. He tried to visualize the Earth that the pristine images came from, but summoning a forgotten world back into existence was even more difficult than he had anticipated. Perspiration dripped from his brow. His entire body trembled. Nevertheless, a picture of a spinning blue orb slowly formed before his mind's eye. His glowing hands manipulated the very fires of creation. A lost world came into being.

"Yes!"

***

THE bridge between Keystone and Central Cities had turned into an ad hoc infirmary for heroes injured in the fight against the murderous Superboy. Wounded members of the Teen Titans, the Doom Patrol, and the Justice Society of America were being looked after by the heroes who were still on their feet. Smoke rose from the skyline of Keystone City, which was also recovering from the crazed teenager's rampage.

"He . . . hurt them," Flamebird stammered. Now that the battle was over, the teenage heroine seemed traumatized by the horrific events. Her face was white as a ghost. Her voice verged on hysteria. "Killed them!"

"Stay with me, Bette." Beast Boy cradled his teammate in his arms, trying to console her. No longer in animal form, he now resembled an ordinary teenage boy, albeit a green one. "It's all over now."

Or was it? A few yards away, Mister Terrific stared upward in amazement. "Do you see that?" he asked urgently. "Up in the sky?"

Jay Garrick stood behind Beast Boy, conferring with Wildcat. "I see it," he confirmed. "What in the worl . . ."

His voice faded out abruptly.

Huh? Beast Boy thought. Before he could look up to see what was happening, Bette Kane vanished in a flash of white light. "Flamebird?" One minute, he had his arms around the stricken girl. The next, he was holding nothing but empty air. Startled voices piped up all around him.

"Jay?" Mr. Terrific blurted.

"S.T.R.I.P.E.?" Stargirl called out.

Beast Boy looked around in confusion. As nearly as he could tell, a third of the heroes on the bridge had disappeared just like Flamebird, including Jay Garrick, Wildcat, S.T.R.I.P.E., Sand, and Hourman. *Pretty much all the senior members of the Justice Society,* Gar realized. *Plus Flamebird.*

He couldn't begin to make sense of it.

"Ohmigod!" Terra exclaimed. "The city!"

Beast Boy's jaw dropped. He had been so freaked out by the disappearance of Flamebird and the others that he hadn't even noticed that Keystone City had vanished as well! An empty plain had taken the place of its looming skyline. The bridge from Central City now led to nothing but acres and acres of barren earth.

"Where'd it all go?" he asked.

Her face ashen beneath her mask, Stargirl pointed at the sky.

Beast Boy looked up and gulped. His green eyes bulged.

Another Earth glowed brightly in the sky.

IT's happening, the original Superman realized. The crystalline walls of the underground grotto began to glow brightly. A peculiar sensation came over him and he held on tightly to Lois' hand, taking care not to crush her fragile bones. Her heart was still beating weakly. He lifted her gently from her bed. *Hold on,* he urged her silently. *We're almost there. . . .*

A flash of white light overpowered even his eyes. For an instant, all he saw was an empty white void. The screams and curses of the corrupted planet went away, replaced by blissful silence. For the first time since arriving on that unwholesome Earth, shouted obscenities did not assail his ears.

The white light faded and he found himself standing on an empty city sidewalk, holding Lois aloft in his arms. The brilliant sunlight of a perfect spring day shone down on them, renewing his strength. He took a deep breath, tasting the pure, untainted air. The streets and sidewalks gleamed as through freshly washed. The sidewalks were free of litter. No graffiti defaced the storefronts. A robin chirped in the branches of a shady tree.

Can it be? he thought hopefully. *Did Alex's plan succeed?*

A gleaming skyscraper rose before them. Superman knew the building well. A smile broke out upon his face as he read the inscription above the front entrance:

THE DAILY STAR

"We're here, Lois." Joy filled Superman's heart. His voice was hoarse with emotion. "We're home."

CHAPTER 31

THE POLARIS SYSTEM

THE shock wave from the cosmic storm hit Kyle with unexpected force. Although the emerald aura generated by his power ring kept him in one piece, it was still several minutes before he had fully recovered from the explosive impact. He tumbled wildly through space before finally regaining control of his flight.

Whoa! the Green Lantern thought. *That was heavy duty!*

His head ringing, he contemplated the giant golden hands that had triggered the shock wave. The sight of the godlike hands was still almost too surreal to accept as reality. "Ring," he commanded, scanning the hands from light-years away. "What the heck am I looking at?"

"DISTORTION OF SPACE-TIME CONTINUUM UNPRECEDENTED," the ring reported. "NO DATA EXISTS FOR PREDICTION OF ENERGY WAVES."

Thanks, Kyle thought sarcastically. *That helps a lot.* "What we're seeing isn't a mass hallucination. Its effects are real."

"Whatever you say, poozer," Kilowog rumbled, catching up with him. Kyle was glad to see that, along with most of the other heroes on the scene, his fellow Green Lantern had also come through the shock wave intact. "It's even stopped the Thanagarians from shooting. At least for the moment."

Thank the Guardians for small favors, Kyle thought. They had bigger problems than coping with the ongoing hostilities between Rann and Thanagar. He quickly surveyed the scene around him. Smashed and battered ships were strewn about the system, along with the lifeless bodies of countless refugees. Some of the ships were obviously beyond hope, torn to pieces by the blast from the distant storm. Others spun out of control, having received major damage to their propulsion and navigational systems. Kyle spotted New Cronus soaring through the devastated region; the starship's classical Greek facade stood out amongst the futuristic contours of the other vessels. To his relief, Donna's ship appeared to be moving under its own power.

He spoke into his power ring. "New Cronus, what's your status?"

"A bit shaken up, Kyle, but hanging in there." The ring projected an image of Troia's face. "Cyborg is linked up to our main computer network right now. He's checking our primary systems."

Kyle was glad to hear it. "Take care," he said. He and Donna had once been an item. Even though they had broken up years ago, he still had fond memories of their time together. "Green Lantern out."

He looked around. Adam Strange and the others seemed to have the rescue effort in hand. Perhaps he should concentrate on the giant hands. He didn't want to give the hands a chance to tear the churning white storm open any further, let alone unleash another shock wave like before.

Jade seemed to have the same idea. She flew toward him. The bright green light radiating from her complemented her chartreuse skin and dark green hair. She nodded at the gargantuan hands looming in the distance. "So what do you say?" she proposed. "One each?"

Despite the urgency of the situation, he couldn't help reflecting on the irony of Jade's presence here, along with Donna Troy's. *Here I am, umpteen billion miles from Earth, and I keep bumping into my old girlfriends!* But unlike his nostalgic memories of Donna, the pain of his recent breakup with Jade, aka Jennifer-Lynn Hayden, still stung. Sadly, their passion had not survived his tour of duty in deep space, not while she had chosen to remain back on Earth. *Talk about long-distance relationships! We never had a chance.*

"Sounds good to me," he agreed. They took off toward the gargantuan hands. "You take the left. I'll take the right."

DONNA Troy experienced a twinge of jealousy as she watched Kyle and Jade zip off toward the cosmic storm. She too had fond memories of being with Kyle . . . before Jade.

But that was a long time ago, and she had other matters to attend to now. Having flown back onto the control pedestal at the center of New Cronus, she carefully examined the readouts on the holographic display panels before her. Several yards away, standing perpendicular to her, Cyborg was plugged into an electronic panel in the armrest of a marble throne. Lights blinked on his cybernetic implants.

"So far, so good," he reported. "That last jolt fried some of the chips and circuitry, but I'm managing to reroute power to the most vital systems."

"Thanks, Vic," Donna said. She trusted Cyborg's judgment; he knew technology like he knew, well, his right hand. *At least New Cronus is still up and running*, she thought. *Now if only I knew what we were supposed to be doing here.*

"Hey, Donna!" Animal Man called out to her from a communications console directly overhead. "Someone's hailing us. They say it's urgent." His brow wrinkled in confusion. "That's weird. I'm sensing that the transmission is coming from . . . a tiger?"

Donna spied the Omega Men's ship heading toward them. "That's Tigorr," she corrected Buddy, guessing the source of the message. "Put him through."

A furry feline face appeared on a holographic display screen. Slitted yellow eyes met hers. Donna recognized the orange-furred alien as Tigorr, the de facto leader of the Omega Men. "Troia here," she identified herself. "How can I help you?"

"I've got something you need to see," Tigorr said. His whiskers twitched as he spoke. "Something big. It might even end this stupid war."

Donna's pulse sped up. Could this be true?

"Our long-range communications array is pretty much shot," he continued. "We can't get through to L.E.G.I.O.N. or the Guardians, but I'm hoping maybe you can. I'm beaming the footage over to you now."

"What sort of footage?" she asked. She glanced at Animal Man, who signaled that he was receiving the data. Cyborg activated a screen of his own.

"Just wait until you see for yourself," Tigorr said. "We picked this up from a stray Thanagarian surveillance satellite we found drifting in space. We were hoping for some useful intel . . . and, boy, did we hit the jackpot." He all but purred in satisfaction. "Take a look."

An image of a lush blue world appeared before Donna and her companions. "Thanagar, right before it got toasted," Tigorr explained.

She remembered how the planet's orbit had shifted days ago, causing it to swing too near its sun. *That's what started this entire war,* she thought. "What am I supposed to be looking for?"

"Keep watching," he said. "Here it comes."

Peering at the screen, Donna was surprised to see a bright red blur streaking toward Thanagar at superluminal speed. *What in the name of the Gods?* The mysterious object was moving too swiftly to see clearly.

"Can you slow it down?" she asked.

Tigorr grinned at her, revealing gleaming white fangs. "Cooler than that, babe. We can freeze it."

A single image appeared before her eyes, magnified several times. "Holy smoke!" Animal Man exclaimed. "Is that really *him*?"

Donna thought so at first, then realized she was mistaken. She stared in shock at a solitary figure wearing a bright red cape. A familiar red *S* caught her by surprise. "No. He looks different. Younger. More like a . . . Superboy?"

On the screen, a young man wearing Superman's costume could be seen flying headfirst into a remote valley on Thanagar's surface. Astonishingly, he appeared to be pushing the planet out of its orbit with his bare hands!

"You gotta be kidding!" Cyborg said. "Is he doing what I think he's doing?"

Is that even possible? Donna thought. Dumbstruck, she gazed at the captured footage in wonder. As incredible as it seemed, the proof was right in front of her.

"This changes everything!" she realized. "Thanagar can no longer blame Rann for the disaster." The footage's authenticity would have to be confirmed, of course, but she had no doubt that investigators could find more evidence of the mysterious Superboy's incursion now that they knew where to look. "Tigorr, thank you so much! Buddy, get me Sardath of Rann . . . and the Thanagarian High Command! We've got something to show them."

For the first time in hours, Donna felt an inkling of hope. *I still don't know what to do about those giant hands, but at least I can end this pointless war!*

She just wished she knew where that teenage Superboy had come from, and why he had shoved Thanagar out of its orbit in the first place. . . .

TRAVELING faster than light, Kyle and Jade left the Polaris system behind as they headed straight for the giant hands reaching out from the heart of the cosmic storm. The apocalyptic anomaly continued to throw off destructive bolts of unimaginable size, forcing the two Green Lanterns to execute evasive maneuvers to avoid being tagged by the white-hot bursts. They pitched and rolled through the vast emptiness of interstellar space.

Kyle scanned their targets with his ring. "Those hands are fields of pure energy, clearly projected by some intelligence." Not unlike the emerald constructs produced by his power ring, but on an infinitely vaster scale. "We need to get close to the flow, blast our Lantern energy back at whatever's behind this, and make them withdraw."

"Sounds like a plan to me," Jade reported. No ring graced her slender fingers. Emerald energy suffused her entire body, a legacy from her father, Earth's first Green Lantern. "How do we want to time this?"

"ELECTROMAGNETIC ACTIVITY DECREASING," Kyle's ring reported. "GRAVITY WAVE SUBSIDING."

"The energy is pulsing," Kyle translated. "We'll ride the lightning as it erupts, then attack as it subsides." He glanced over at Jade; there was no way around the fact that they were taking a serious risk. Those giant hands literally dwarfed them in size and power. "You up for this, Jen?"

"You bet. And I agree with the tactics. You were always creative, Kyle." A wistful tone entered her voice. "Kind of like old times, isn't it? Together, in space. It feels good. Scary, but good."

"Together? I have the Corps now and you have your life on Earth. . . ." Part of him was still angry at her for not waiting for him, but he made an effort to overcome any lingering bitterness. What's done was done. Now was not the time to revisit old quarrels, no matter how painful they had been at the time. "But, yeah, it does feel good."

They drew nearer to the outskirts of the storm. If possible, the golden hands looked even more impressive than before. There was a time, Kyle recalled, when a Green Lantern's power ring had no effect on anything yellow. Thankfully, that limitation no longer existed.

"ALERT!" his ring sounded off. "RADIATION INCREASING. ELECTRO-MAGNETIC FIELD REPOLARIZING. INCREASED INTENSITY PREDICTED. PLUS FOUR HUNDRED PERCENT."

Four hundred percent? Kyle swallowed hard.

"Watch out! The lightning is growing in power, much quicker than we expected." He hoped that their protective auras were strong enough to withstand the surging energy blasts. Perhaps this hadn't been such a good idea after all. "We need to get Kilowog and your father's help. Maybe the Corps itself."

"Maybe," Jade said. "But for now you've got me!"

Before his eyes, the monstrous hands let go of the storm's ragged boundaries and aimed their armored palms directly at the approaching Green Lanterns. *Oh my God,* Kyle thought. Whoever was behind the hands knew they were coming. *They're targeting us!*

"Shields up!" he shouted at Jade, bracing himself for the attack. Coruscating energy exploded from the giant palms. The lightning crashed against his emerald aura; he could feel the intense heat and impact even through the force field. A blinding white light caused him to avert his eyes. He focused all his willpower on maintaining his shields, and prayed that Jade was doing the same. If only there had been time to recharge his ring before tackling the colossal hands head-on!

A high-pitched scream was picked up by his ring.

"Jenny! No!" he cried out. His heart pounding, he flew toward the scream, even as the sudden glare of the energy bolt faded away. Blinking tears from his eyes, he spotted Jade floating adrift in space. Only faint vestiges of her force field remained, wafting away like greenish vapor. Her body was still.

"Jenny?" He desperately scanned her with his ring. "Status!"

"NO PULSE DETECTED. NO RESPIRATION ACTIVITY. NO . . ."

His heart sank. A sense of overwhelming grief rushed over him . . . until he heard a familiar voice call out to him weakly.

"Kyle?"

Hope blossomed inside him. "Jen?" Arriving above her, he cupped her face in his hands as he searched her lovely green features for signs of life. "You're alive?"

"NEGATIVE," the ring insisted. "FATAL CENTRAL NERVOUS SYSTEM OVERLOAD."

Then how . . . ?

"My physical body is dead, Kyle," Jade's voice explained. "But my energy remains . . . my Lantern power." Her eyes were shut. Her lips weren't moving. He could feel her skin cooling beneath his touch. "Power you need now. The next wave will be worse. They're getting stronger each time. Next time your power won't be enough. . . ."

Kyle didn't want to hear it. "Jen, wait!" He took her lifeless body in his arms, cradling her against his chest, and began to speed away from the storm, back toward the Polaris system. "Hang on. Maybe my ring can . . ."

"Shh, Kyle," she whispered. "It's all right. Once we felt fated to be together . . . and maybe we are. Maybe this is our destiny."

From somewhere deep within her core, a bright green light radiated outward. Kyle absorbed the light, feeling it spread throughout his entire body. A sense of renewed energy came over him. It was like recharging his ring from the Central Battery on Oa, only even more intense. He felt a connection to Jennie that transcended life and death.

But the cost was just too much to bear.

"Jade, no," he protested. "This power is . . ."

"Yours now . . . and always will be." Her voice trailed off, growing ever fainter. "I just wish my dad were here. . . ."

The last of her light disappeared into Kyle.

"ALERT! NEW ENERGY WAVE APPROACHING."

Instinctively, Kyle shielded himself against the crackling energy. With Jade's strength now magnifying his own, he stood firm against the blazing white fire, even as it incinerated the body clasped in his arms. In a heartbeat, Jennie-Lynn Hayden's mortal remains were reduced to atoms, cast out upon the cosmic winds.

Kyle did not try to retrieve her atoms. *That was just her shell*, he realized solemnly. *Her energy—her spirit—lives in me.*

He could feel Jade's singular energy coursing through his veins, amplifying his willpower to an exponential degree. Once, a few years back, circumstances had vastly increased his power, transforming him into a cosmic being with amazing new abilities, but he had sacrificed his elevated status to restore the Guardians and the Corps to life after a disaster. Now he felt that power return to him, transforming him from within. His green mask evaporated as his face took on the starry luster of the universe itself. His ring, no longer needed to focus his power, was absorbed into his being. He had evolved beyond his former limitations.

Kyle Rayner was no longer merely one Green Lantern among many.

Once again he was . . . Ion.

CHAPTER 32

**ST. PATRICK'S CATHEDRAL,
NEW YORK CITY,
EARTH-ONE**

THE other Earth hung in the sky like a swollen, blue moon. Lightning continued to flash above the skyscrapers, but the stormy red skies had finally cleared
somewhat, and lost their crimson sheen. Scores of heroes converged on the
towering Gothic cathedral of St. Patrick's, where a special memorial service
had been scheduled in the wake of the various tragedies and disasters that had
befallen the super-hero community over the last few days. Standing outside
the main entrance of the cathedral, Ragman watched as Firehawk, Bulleteer,
Halo, Metamorpho, and Geo-Force descended from the sky, touching down
on the sidewalk before the front steps. Across the street, in Rockefeller Center,
an impromptu prayer vigil was going on. Ragman glimpsed a large crowd
of ordinary men and women holding candles in the promenade and outdoor
plaza. OUR HEARTS ARE WITH YOU! read a cardboard sign held up by one civilian. SAVE US! read another.

Ragman appreciated their support. He just hoped that their faith in Earth's
heroes wasn't misplaced.

"Half my team went missing when that second Earth appeared," Mister
Terrific said. Like Ragman, the African-American supergenius seemed content
to remain outside the cathedral. A T-shaped black mask adhered to his face.

The words FAIR PLAY were embossed on the sleeve of his Kevlar jacket. Levitating black spheres orbited his head and shoulders. The floating orbs automatically recorded the encounter for future reference. "Wildcat, Hourman, and Jay Garrick, to name but a few."

Ragman sympathized. "Nightshade went missing in El Paso. We haven't seen her since."

Mister Terrific stared up at the other Earth. He shook his head in disbelief. "The planets should be ripping each other apart, but instead there's something keeping the gravitational forces at bay."

"Feels like the calm before the storm," Ragman said.

"And they want to hold a *Mass* for everyone with a cape," the other man said, with a hint of impatience.

Ragman shrugged beneath his tattered cloak. "My gang dragged me here, but . . ."

"Church isn't your thing?" Mister Terrific guessed.

"Actually, we stopped at temple on the way over." Ragman stepped aside to let Metamorpho enter the cathedral. The Element Man smelled like an unventilated chem lab. "I'm Jewish. You?"

"Atheist," Mister Terrific said.

His answer surprised Ragman. "I thought you were supposed to be the smartest man in the world?"

"Third smartest, actually."

Ragman wondered who the top two were. Ray Palmer? Doc Magnus? More to point, he couldn't understand how anyone in their business could remain a skeptic when it came to the supernatural. "And you still don't believe in God? Wasn't the Spectre a member of the Justice Society?

"Before my time," Mister Terrific said tersely.

Ragman got the impression that there was more to that story. "What about guys like Deadman and Zauriel?" he challenged him. The former was an earthbound spirit; the latter, a bona fide angel. "My own suit is made up of corrupted souls."

"A unique energy that could quantify as a telepathic discharge upon death," Mister Terrific argued, sticking to his guns. "And those others you mentioned could simply be extradimensional entities whose true nature has yet to be determined. Just because science can't currently explain something doesn't mean we have to fall back on supernatural explanations."

"So you don't believe in anything?" Ragman asked. "You don't have any faith?"

"Of course I do." He nodded at the heroes entering the building. Stargirl waved back at him. "I've got faith in my team."

"Wish I could say the same," Ragman said ruefully. The Shadowpact barely knew each other at this point—and they were already minus one member. *Did Nightshade run out on us,* he wondered, *or did we fail to protect her from some unknown threat?*

He offered up a silent prayer for the missing heroine.

"GOD works in mysterious ways," Zauriel said.

The warrior angel stood at the pulpit, addressing the congregation. His feathered wings were folded against his back. Sacred glyphs were inscribed on his heavenly golden armor. A flaming sword was sheathed at his side.

The pews were packed with super heroes of every size and description. Looking out over the hushed assembly, Zauriel spotted Dr. Mid-Nite, Agent Liberty, Bronze Tiger, Elongated Man, Huntress, the Manhattan Guardian, the Creeper, Katana, Thunder Samurai, Lionheart, Stargirl, Technocrat, Major Disaster, Magenta, Terra, Halo, Nightmaster, Argent, Sister Superior, and many others. They grouped together by team associations and shared history. A clump of Teen Titans, both active and retired, huddled en masse to mourn their recent losses during the massacre in Kansas. Red Star, who had lost both Pantha and Wildebeest, was at the center of the group, his head bowed. Zauriel's heart went out to him.

Hal Jordan and John Stewart, both wearing the emerald garb of the Green Lantern Corps, knelt before the pulpit. Hal Jordan had recently returned from the dead, an experience that had left him with a deep sense of spiritual faith. The two men shared a moment of prayer before quietly flying over the crowded pews and out through the arched front gate. No doubt some urgent summons had demanded their attention.

"Each one of us was chosen for a reason," Zauriel's musical voice continued. "We were blessed with powers and skills beyond those of mortal men and women. And so we found a new reason for being." His magnificent wings spread out behind him. Colored light shone down from the stained-glass windows overlooking the dais and altar. He turned his amethyst eyes heavenward. "We ask you, Lord, to take care of those that have already fallen. We ask you to watch over those that have been injured and those that are missing. We look to you to give us the strength we will need for the trials that surely lie ahead. And above all, we offer our faith in each other and in a better tomorrow."

He prayed that his words provided comfort to Red Star and the others.

"We will not lose hope. Lord hear our prayer."

"WHAT's wrong with Blue Devil?" Gypsy whispered.

The horned demon had one of the front pews to himself. He leaned forward, supporting his weight with his trident. Smoke literally rose from his body. The sulfurous fumes had already driven away the heroes who had been sitting near him. "Lord hear our prayer," he recited through gritted fangs.

"I mean, what's with the smoke?" Gypsy sat one row behind Blue Devil. The black-haired teenager, a part-time member of the Justice League, recoiled from the stench. "And that smell?"

"The guy never did that before," Elongated Man admitted. His elastic nose twitched in an animated fashion. Having recently lost his wife, Ralph Dibny wore a somber black suit in place of his usual crime-fighting costume.

"Guess you've never gone into a church with him before," Detective Chimp surmised. The furry primate, who was seated behind Gypsy and Ralph, leaned forward over the back of the pew. Without his deerstalker cap, he looked almost indistinguishable from any other chimpanzee. "Danny's a good Irish-Catholic. Unfortunately, he's also a human-turned-demon. Meanin' his skin burns whenever he steps foot into God's house."

"Wow," Gypsy whispered, impressed.

An announcement came over a loudspeaker:

"We've just received a report from Cave Carson. A major earthquake has occurred across Southern India." Carson was one of the world's foremost geologists, so everyone took the news seriously. "And another in Japan."

Blue Devil lurched to his feet. He strode down the nave, gripping his trident tightly. His fangs ground together audibly. People tried not to stare at the smoke rolling off his demonic hide. He clenched his jaws to keep from crying out in pain.

"Grace period's over," the loudspeaker declared.

"Then let's get the hell out of here," Blue Devil growled. "There's people that need help."

Sitting near the back of the church, the Huntress watched Blue Devil depart. New respect showed in her dark blue eyes. The clasp of her cape was a golden crucifix.

"Amen," she said.

CHAPTER 33

KEYSTONE City looked good as new . . . and strangely empty.

All the damage from that evil Superboy's rampage was gone. The streets and buildings were intact once more, not to mention impeccably clean and tidy. The air was strikingly pure, especially for a blue-collar factory town like Keystone. The automobiles parked at the curbs all looked like they had just gone through a carwash. The Keystone Diner, which had opened up shop way back in the fifties, looked spanking new. There was no smog, no litter, no graffiti.

And no people.

Jay Garrick looked around. Aside from a handful of his fellow heroes, Keystone City appeared to be completely deserted. He started to run, intending to conduct a door-to-door search of the city at super-speed, but stopped when he found himself running no faster than, well, an ordinary senior citizen. *That's right*, he remembered glumly. *The Speed Force is gone.*

Along with Wally and Bart.

He took a quick head count. Wildcat was still here, along with S.T.R.I.P.E., Sand, Hourman, and Flamebird. They stood gazing up in fear and wonder at the second Earth hanging high in the sky.

"Where's Central City?" Flamebird asked anxiously. The young blonde was an Olympic-level gymnast and martial artist. Red spandex and a bright yellow cape made her look like a dancing flame when she went into action. She looked across the bridge, which now led to an empty plain where Keystone's sister city used to be. "Where'd everybody go?"

"I think it's more about where *we* went," S.T.R.I.P.E. said. His oversize steel gauntlet pointed at the glowing blue orb in the sky. "I'm bettin' that Earth up there is ours."

Makes sense, Jay thought. There was something distinctly unreal about the pristine cityscape around them. This felt more like an empty movie set, or maybe a theme park version of Keystone. *Which would explain, sort of, why we're the only ones here.*

"Well, why did we come here?" Flamebird asked. Jay felt sorry for the poor girl. At least he was among friends. Flamebird was the only Teen Titan here.

Why just her? he wondered. *Why not Beast Boy and Raven and the others?*

"And where is here?" Hourman asked. A black cape and cowl gave him a forbidding appearance. A miniature hourglass, suspended on a chain around his neck, contained the Miraclo pills that enhanced his strength and speed for sixty minutes at a time.

Sand sifted a handful of dirt through his fingers. "It looks like this place is manufactured. The amounts of oxygen, silicon, and aluminum are perfectly balanced. And all the pollution in the soil is . . ."

"Gone," Jay guessed.

"Jus' like the people." Wildcat growled. The former boxing heavyweight clenched his fists. "So why do I get a funny feelin' in my gut, Jay . . . like we ain't the only ones here?"

METROPOLIS, EARTH-TWO

THE masthead of the *Daily Star* was emblazoned in polished bronze above the front entrance to the building. Golden sunlight warmed the city streets. A gentle breeze rustled the leaves of a nearby elm tree. The air was pure and clean.

"Clark?" Lois asked softly.

Superman gently lowered his wife's feet onto the sidewalk in front of the building. For the first time in weeks, if not longer, she seemed strong enough to stand on her own. She kept her eyes closed, as if afraid of being disappointed by what she might see. Her simple green dress was more than sufficient for the springlike weather.

"It's okay, Lois," he said, gazing nostalgically at the familiar skyscraper before them. "We're back in *our* Metropolis. On *our* Earth." The city was strangely unpopulated, but he assumed that Alexander would rectify that in time. "The right Earth."

"The right . . . ?" Wrapping an arm around his waist, the elderly woman leaned against him. Returning to Earth-Two had not turned back the clock; Lois still looked her age, but she didn't seem quite so frail as before. Some of her old strength and vigor appeared to have come back. She stretched out her arms to feel the sun shining down on her. "The air's so warm."

"You must still be disoriented from the trip," he said. Turning to face her, he gently took her hands in his. "Open your eyes. Look around you." He grinned broadly as she opened her eyes to find herself back in good old Metropolis, which looked just like it used to. Before the Crisis . . . and all those long years of exile.

"We did it," Superman said. "We saved you."

She smiled back at him.

Thank heavens they had been in time!

BOSTON,
EARTH-ONE

THE electronics store was located in the heart of South Boston. A banner stretched across its front window read: GOING OUT OF BUSINESS! Judging from the news reports filling the screens of the television sets on display in the window, the banner might as well have been talking about civilization itself.

". . . many dispute the very existence of this second Earth despite the rising tides and earthquakes breaking out across Europe. . . ." Live footage showed the Thames flooding the streets of London. Big Ben rose above the surging waters.

". . . add Liberty Belle and Brainwave to the growing list of heroes and villains who have gone missing in the last hour. . . ." A collage of photos depicted the original Flash, Lady Blackhawk, Wildcat, Manhunter, Obsidian, Flame-bird, Plastic Man, Power Girl, and many others.

". . . Blüdhaven rescue efforts called off as body recovery begins. . . ." Toxic green smoke billowed up from the contaminated ruins of the murdered city.

". . . witnesses say Keystone City simply vanished from sight. . . ." Viewed from Central City, the bridge across the Missouri River now stretched to no-where. Aside from the bridge, there was no indication that there had ever been anything except vacant flatlands on the other side of the river.

A length of broken pipe shattered the store window. Greedy hands snatched up the television sets, yanking the cords from their sockets. People clambered through the broken window into the store. Broken glass crunched beneath their feet. An alarm sounded, but it failed to scare off the looters. The police had their hands full elsewhere.

Rioting had broken out throughout the city. People pushed shopping carts packed with stolen booty through the teeming streets. Shop doors and windows were smashed to pieces as gangs of Southies took advantage of the global emergency to pillage the neighborhood businesses. People whooped and cheered as though a holiday had been declared. Violent quarrels broke out over prized pieces of merchandise. Gunshots and sirens rang out in the night. If the world really was coming to an end, as seemed all too likely, plenty of Bostonians were determined to get a new DVD player first.

A youth in an orange Bruins jersey tossed aside the lead pipe he had used to break into the electronics store. His buddies were already inside, raiding the video game aisle, while he helped himself to an expensive plasma TV from the window display. He turned around with it, only to be confronted by another gang of looters. A skin-headed kid in a leather jacket pulled a gun on him.

"Those sets are ours now," the gunman said.

"Find your own store," the hockey fan growled back. Overhearing the dispute, his homies charged to the front of the store to back him up.

The gunman shook his head. "Move away."

"Make us," the first looter challenged him.

The muzzle of the skinhead's pistol flared. A gunshot blared above the tumult in the streets. Hot lead sped toward the Bruins fan, only to be deflected by a pair of flashing silver bracelets.

Wonder Woman swooped between the warring bands of looters. Landing gracefully upon the sidewalk outside the store, she glared at the murderous children. Her dark eyes flashed angrily.

"You would kill someone for a television?" she accused them. Their callous brutality seemed to confirm the futility of her mission to Man's World. How could she have ever thought that she could bring peace and understanding to such a people? "Why are you looting and rioting when people are in dire need of help? You're behaving like monsters!"

Her harsh words fell upon deaf ears. "Who are you to lecture us?" one of the adolescent hoods shouted back at her. "After you offed that rich dude?"

A beer bottle shattered against Wonder Woman's head. The missile would have stunned an ordinary woman, but Diana was hurt only by the scorn hurled at her by the looters.

"Hypocrite!"

"Murderer!"

"You can't tell us how to live!"

Was that what they thought she had been doing all these years? "I'm not . . ." she began.

The skinhead thrust his pistol in her face. "You're not one of us!" he snarled. "You never were!"

Enough! she thought. With godlike speed, she reached out and crushed the gun with her bare hand. "Holy crap!" the hoodlum exclaimed as she turned the offending weapon into a palm-sized lump of metal. Then she grabbed on to the teen's collar and tossed him singlehandedly through the open window. He flew the entire length of the violated electronics store before crashing loudly into the solid wall at the rear of the shop. His body rebounded onto the floor, where he landed sprawled upon the tiles. Only a pitiful groan provided evidence that the brutalized youth still lived.

"You will hurt no one else today," Wonder Woman declared.

Panic filled the faces of the other looters. "Get away from her!" someone shouted. A six-year-old girl in a Wonder Woman T-shirt stared at Diana with a crushed expression, until her mother snatched the child up and carried her away. Along with the other looters, the frightened mother ran from Wonder Woman as fast as her trembling legs would carry her, leaving Diana alone on the glass-strewn sidewalk. Discarded TV sets and camcorders hit the ground. "Run!" the hockey fan yelled. "She's gone crazy!"

Diana's heart sank as she watched them flee. Terror was not the emotion she had intended to inspire in the hearts of mankind. "Wait!" she called after them. "I'm only trying to . . ."

If the frightened youths heard her, they paid her no heed. They disappeared quickly into the side alleys of South Boston. Wonder Woman felt alone, just as she had after Themyscira vanished into the Bermuda Triangle. She started to question why she had even returned to America at all. Perhaps she would have been better off fighting the OMACs to the death. . . .

A sudden wind whipped up the litter around her feet. Her ebony tresses blew about wildly. Diana's eyes widened as she looked up to behold the faint outline of an invisible plane. The aircraft resembled her own invisible jet, although its contours suggested an older, less sophisticated design, complete with a spinning propellor at its nose. The plane hovered above the deserted avenue as it began to execute a three-point vertical landing. Wonder Woman glimpsed a female figure at the controls of the transparent aircraft.

"Mother?" she murmured. For a split-second, she thought that maybe Queen Hippolyta of the Amazons had returned to her, even though her legendary mother had perished in battle some years before. *Is that truly you?*

The plane touched down upon the asphalt. Diana hesitantly approached the vessel to get a closer look at its pilot. To her amazement, she saw what appeared to be an older version of herself at the controls of the plane. Strands of gray had infiltrated the other woman's dark hair. Age and experience showed on her classical features. Her golden breastplate had been fashioned in the image of a flying eagle. A gentle smile showed upon her lips.

A doorway opened up in the cockpit of the invisible plane. The other Wonder Woman stepped onto a wing to address her counterpart in the street. "I'm afraid I'm not your mother," she said softly. "My name is Diana Prince. And the fate of the universe is at hand."

TITANS TOWER, SAN FRANCISCO BAY

THE T-shaped building occupied an island in the harbor, within view of the Golden Gate Bridge. The Titan's high-tech infirmary was located on the top floor of the gleaming high-rise. Utilizing advanced alien technology, the infirmary's automated systems offered treatment that rivaled anything that could be provided by an actual flesh-and-blood physician, and were even better suited to deal with the unique physiology and metabolisms of Titans like Beast Boy, Starfire, Cyborg . . . and Superboy.

Conner Kent floated inside a vertical healing tube at the center of the infirmary's intensive care unit. Bubbles percolated through the nutrient bath filling the tube. An oxygen mask was clamped to Conner's face and intravenous tubing was connected to his wrists and elbows. Unconscious, he hung limply inside the tube, while computerized systems monitored his vital functions. Nearby monitors displayed CT and MRI images of bruised internal organs and fractured bones. His torn flesh still bore the scars of his lopsided battle with the other Superboy. His clothes rested upon an empty medical bed. Medical apparatus beeped and hummed in the background.

Aside from the sleeping patient, the ICU was all but empty. The other Titans, led by Robin, had been called away by the disaster in Blüdhaven. A television set had been left on to provide Conner's brain with a degree of stimulation in his teammates' absence. On the screen, a special news report showed a giant wing of OMACs flying over from Washington, D.C. A newscaster's voice accompanied the terrifying images:

". . . a squadron of OMACs is shown here, policing our nation's capital. . . ."

A hand reached out and clicked off the TV.

Lex Luthor looked around the infirmary. His bald head was cut and bruised from his close call in the Arctic. Scorch marks blackened his green-and-purple bodysuit. Evading the Titans' security measures had not been easy, but his cunning had prevailed in the end. *At least I can think again,* he thought, *now that I've put several thousand miles between myself and that red-headed imposter.*

He placed his hand against the cool Plexiglas tube containing his clone. "Look what they did to you." Lex was grateful that the other Titans were away. That made what he had come to do ever so much easier. "I've encountered the enemy as well. He thinks he's smarter than me. They always do."

Lex rubbed the scar on his neck where the crystal chip had stabbed him. "But for all my troubles up north, I came away with a lucky souvenir." He held up the glowing shard that had created his scar. An image of a golden tower, surrounded by guardian OMACs, could be glimpsed inside the crystal. "And a look at their technology."

He walked over to the bed where Conner's clothes were laid out. He slipped the shard into the pocket of the boy's jeans. A faint white glow filtered through the torn denim.

"My gift to you," Lex said. "My son."

Not wanting to press his luck, he left before anyone could show up to inconvenience him.

Conner's eyelids flickered in his tube.

CHAPTER 34

"It's the Daily Star," Superman said. "Do you see it?"

"It's just like I remember." Lois gazed up at the skyscraper. "But it's real. . . ."

Back home once more, the aging Superman couldn't help recalling all the years he and Lois had spent in the venerable building before them . . . and the feisty young reporter his wife had once been. His memory raced back in time to the good old days:

George Taylor sat behind his desk, reading the front page aloud. " 'Mayor Arrested in Housing Scam' . . . what a story!" He nodded approvingly at Lois, while Clark and Jimmy looked on. "Gotta hand it to you, kid. You did it."

"He robbed a lot of people out of house and home, chief," Lois said passionately. The young brunette was brutally honest, curious as a cat, and never let anyone get the last word in. Clark thought she was the most human woman he had ever met, and more super inside than he could ever be.

"You don't let anyone get away with anything, do you, Lois?" He admired her though a pair of horn-rimmed glasses. A few feet away, Jimmy Olsen fiddled with his bow tie.

"Not if it hurts other people, Clark."

Lois' brilliant blue eyes flashed with spirit.

Those same blue eyes, only slightly dimmed by age, looked up at him now. "Clark, I love you so much." A trace of concern entered her voice. "But this isn't . . . isn't . . . hnnn."

A sudden weakness hit her. Her legs gave out and she toppled toward the sidewalk.

"Lois!" Superman exclaimed. He scooped her up in his arms before she hit the pavement. "What's wrong?" Confusion was written on his face. "We brought back Earth-Two. You're going to be fine." His voice took on a desperate tone. "You *have* to be fine."

She looked up at him bravely. Peace and acceptance came over her. "I've lived an absolutely wonderful life with you."

"Don't give up," he urged her. This wasn't what was supposed to happen!

"I'm not giving up, Clark." She laid her hand gently against his cheek. "I'm grateful for all the extra years we had."

"We'll have more," he insisted. "I couldn't save our Earth back then, but I will save you. That's what I do. That's what I always did." Years of memories flooded his heart and mind, making his throat tighten. "Superman *always* saves Lois Lane."

But he could hear her heartbeat growing fainter. The lines in her face deepened as she struggled to catch her breath. He didn't need X-ray vision to realize that she was dying right before his eyes.

"No," he pleaded. Despair sapped his own strength, and he dropped to his knees upon the sidewalk, clutching Lois to his chest. "I can't be the only survivor of another dead world. Not again. Not without you."

She smiled indulgently at him. "With all your powers, with everything you saw and did, you still never . . ."

"It can't end this way!" he interrupted.

Her final words came haltingly. "It's . . . not . . . going . . ."

Quietly, without any fuss, her heartbeat slowed to a stop.

"It's not going. . . ?" Superman didn't understand. "What? It's not going to end this way? Is that what you're trying to say?" He stared desperately at her silent face, searching for answers. Her eyelids had drooped shut, so that she appeared to be only sleeping. "Lois?" Her body sagged limply in his arms. "Lois, tell me it's not going to end this way. Lois, please . . . be strong . . . be . . ."

She was beyond answering him. Lois Lane had gone in search of the ultimate scoop.

Superman's grief was unbearable. He lurched to his feet, still holding his late wife in his arms. Tears streamed from his eyes as he threw back his head and gave voice to his pain.

The anguished scream broke every window in Metropolis.

BLÜDHAVEN, EARTH-ONE

A world away, another Superman was searching for bodies beneath a collapsed sports stadium in Blüdhaven when his superhearing picked up something impossible. At first, he couldn't believe what he was hearing, but the mysterious cry was too powerful to deny . . . or ignore. Temporarily abandoning his mournful duty, he launched himself into the night sky.

Toxic green smog still hung over the murdered city, but he quickly left it behind, and Earth's atmosphere as well. He flew across space toward the other Earth glowing beyond the moon. The heartbreaking scream still echoed in his ears:

"LOIS!"

THE BATCAVE

JAIME Reyes couldn't see a thing.

"Can I take this stupid blindfold off?" he asked impatiently.

"In a minute," Booster Gold promised. The self-proclaimed super hero guided Jaime by his elbow as they descended down what felt like a sloping stone path leading to the center of the Earth. Water dripped in the background. Sleeping bats rustled and squeaked overhead. The deeper they descended, the lower the temperature got. Jaime shivered beneath his jeans, T-shirt, and sneakers. He recalled a sixth-grade field trip to Carlsbad Caverns in New Mexico. It had been cold down there, too.

This is crazy, he thought. *What the heck am I doing here?* Only a few hours ago, he had been sleeping on a lazy Saturday morning. Now he was letting some nutty *gringo* and a floating robot lead him blindfolded down to who-knows-where, all because a glowing blue bug was apparently stuck to his spine. Booster and the robot had insisted that the fate of the entire world depended on him coming along with them, but at the moment, Jaime was more worried about what this "Scarab" thingie was doing to him. The idea that the carved gemstone had actually crawled inside him while he slept was enough to seriously freak him out. He half-expected an alien to come bursting out of his chest at any moment.

At least I'm not missing any school. He had left a note for his parents explaining that he was spending the day with Brenda and Paco, then instant-messaged his friends so that they knew to cover for him. *With any luck, I'll be back in El Paso before Mom and Dad know I'm gone.*

He stumbled over a bump in the path. Booster tugged on his elbow to steady him. The underground tunnel smelled of bat piss. "This place stinks," Jaime complained.

"Not as much as your room did," Booster said. His pet robot hummed nearby. "I saw a ham sandwich on the floor that must've been a month old."

"Two, actually." Jaime had been meaning to toss that out one of these days. Now he wondered if he would ever get the chance. He tried to maintain a cocky attitude, not wanting the older man to see how spooked he really was. "You know, I always thought Booster Gold was just a mascot on the front of a cereal box. Like Toucan Sam or Cap'n Crunch."

"I'm going to be a whole lot more than that when this is over," Booster said.

What's that all about? Jaime wondered.

"SECURITY ALERT!" An electronic voice blared from a loudspeaker nearby. **"UNAUTHORIZED ENTRY."**

"Unauthorized entry?" Jaime's heart sank. Where the hell were they? "Uh . . ."

Before he could even ask Booster what sort of mess he had gotten them into, a pair of cold steel cables wrapped themselves around his ankles, yanking him off his feet. Jaime yelped in surprise as he suddenly found himself hanging upside down. His blood rushed to his head, but his blindfold remained in place, so that he was trapped *and* completely in the dark. Startled bats screeched and frantically flapped away.

"Don't worry," Booster said calmly. From the direction of his voice, Jaime guessed that the super-guy was hanging upside down too. "This is perfectly normal."

Was he out of his mind? "Normal for *who*?"

A gloved hand ripped the blindfold away from Jaime's face.

Batman frowned at the alarmed teenager. From Jaime's perspective, the Dark Knight appeared to be standing on his head. He scowled at Booster, who was hanging beside Jaime, his head about four feet off the ground. "Who is this and what are you doing here?"

"Batman, this is Jaime Reyes," Booster said, taking the other hero's menacing tone in stride. "The *new* Blue Beetle."

"The what?" Jaime exclaimed. This was getting crazier by the minute! "I'm not the Blue Beetle. I'm not anything."

"Yes, you are," Booster said confidently. Without warning, he reached out and slapped Jaime on the back, right where the Scarab was attached to his spine. "Watch this."

The sudden impact triggered an unexpected metamorphosis. A tingling sensation, beginning at the base of Jaime's spine, rapidly spread over his entire body. His back arched as though he had just received a powerful electrical jolt. "Arrrgh!" he cried out in shock and confusion. His skin extruded a chitinous blue substance that instantly formed a segmented exoskeleton over his body. "What's it doing? It's crawling all over me!" A smooth blue shell covered his face. Sharp-edged pincers sprouted from his shoulders. Deep indigo hieroglyphics marked his insectlike carapace. Glowing yellow eyes peered out from his faceplate.

He instinctively broke free from the steel cables coiled around his ankles, tearing the dense metal apart as though it were as flimsy as a spider's web. Flipping in the air, he landed deftly on his feet. He stared at his armored hands in confusion.

"Whoa," Blue Beetle said.

He looked up at the other two heroes, hoping for answers. Unfamiliar symbols that looked a little like ancient Egyptian pictographs ran along the periphery of his visuals. Colorful auras pulsed around Booster Gold and Batman.

"Why's everything look so damn weird?" he asked. "Why are you calling me Blue Beetle?"

"Just work with me, kid," Booster said. Still hanging upside down, he gestured at the security devices holding onto his ankles. "Ahem?"

"Security override JLA," Batman said grudgingly. The steel cables released Booster and retracted into the ceiling of the cavern, disappearing amidst the dripping stalactites. Booster tumbled onto the floor, then sprang back onto his feet. "He has the Scarab?" Batman asked.

Booster brushed bat crap from his shoulders. "Technically, the Scarab has him."

"I don't have time to waste right now, Michael," Batman said.

"I know," Booster replied. "That's why I'm here." He nodded at his robot, who had made no effort to rescue his master from the Batcave's restraints. "Skeets! Lights!"

"YES, SIR!"

The robot zipped over to Batman and began projecting holographic images in the air in front of the Dark Knight. The images appeared to be profiles of various super heroes. Jaime recognized Green Arrow, Black Canary, Mister Terrific, and a few others. Some of the other faces were unknown to him.

Friends of theirs? he wondered.

"You're planning an all-out assault on Brother Eye to shut the OMACs down," Booster said. "These are the guys and gals you're considering recruiting for that mission. I've already called them and they're on their way."

Batman actually looked surprised. Jaime guessed that didn't happen very often.

"How do you know that?" he asked.

"My *best* superpower," Booster reminded Batman. "I'm from the future. Historical records told me who you took. But they also told me that the satellite's cloaked. You'll never find it." He walked right through the floating holograms and dropped his hand onto Blue Beetle's shoulder. The transformed youth gave him a baffled look. "But we can change that. Because I just happened to be teamed-up with the only person on Earth who can actually *see* Brother Eye."

Jaime looked over at Batman. Was it just his imagination, or was there a hint of a smile on the Dark Knight's face?

CHAPTER 35

HE found the other Superman standing in the streets of another Metropolis. The alternate city looked like something out of an old movie, complete with old-fashioned phone booths and automobiles. Although it had been night back in Blüdhaven, the sun was shining here. Smoke rose from a hot dog cart at the corner. A shiny green sedan was parked at the curb. Superman felt it looked vaguely familiar.

There, he thought, descending toward the street. As far as he could tell, the man below was the only living person in the entire city. "I heard you," he said as he touched down upon the sidewalk. Broken glass from thousands of shattered windows glittered upon the pavement. "I heard you cry 'Lois.' "

A disturbing tableau greeted him. He saw an older version of himself, shoulders slumped in sorrow, holding aloft the lifeless body of an elderly woman who bore an unmistakable resemblance to his own Lois. A chill ran down Superman's spine. It was like some terrible vision from the future. A name, Superman-2, popped into his brain, like something he had once known but had forgotten long ago. He felt like he had met this man before, although he couldn't remember where. *Where did that come from?*

"Kal-El?" the older Superman said. "You came here? To our Earth?"

"I'm not sure what Earth this is," the younger hero confessed. He briefly considered the possibility of a time-travel paradox, but that made no sense; if this Superman-2 was indeed from the future, then why did his Metropolis look so out-of-date? And where were all the other people? He nodded at the body of the aged Lois, suspecting the worst, but hoping otherwise. "Does she need help?"

"It's your fault, isn't it?" the other man said. The younger Superman was taken aback by the venom in his voice. Superman-2 gently laid Lois down upon the glass-strewn sidewalk before turning to face his counterpart. Grief gave way to fury in his tear-filled eyes. "You brought this corruption with you. You're spreading it like a disease." He took hold of the green sedan and lifted it effortlessly above his head. "You . . . you killed my wife!"

He slammed the car down on the younger Superman with unbelievable force. Caught by surprise, Superman was knocked to the ground, the entire front half of the car crumpling against his invulnerable body.

The older man's accusation hit just as hard. "I didn't kill anyone," the younger Superman insisted. He didn't know who this second Superman was, but he wasn't going to take the man's attacks lying down. Lunging to his feet, he tore clear through the wrecked sedan to deliver a powerful blow to the other man's chin. The punch sent Superman-2 staggering backward, but the older man quickly recovered. Despite his wrinkles and gray temples, he seemed just as strong as the younger Superman, if not stronger.

Who is he? the younger Superman wondered. *And why does he hate me so?*

"Lois was the only one of us who still believed in you," Superman-2 declared furiously. Grabbing hold of a chunk of the bisected sedan, he rammed it into the younger Superman's face. "But you took her." The mangled steel hit the younger Superman so hard that he tasted blood. Superman-2 was playing for keeps. Angry tears flew from his eyes.

"You took her from me!"

ARCTIC FORTRESS

ALEXANDER withdrew his hands from the surging engines of creation. Sweat dripped from his brow. Recovering Earth-Two from oblivion had been an exhausting chore. He needed to rest awhile before proceeding to the next stage of his grand experiment.

Besides, he thought, *I need to make sure everything is still going as planned.*

He stood upon his force-field platform before his golden Tower. His World View projected live images from Earth-Two, where Superman-2 appeared to be taking out his anger on his counterpart from Earth-One. Entire city blocks succumbed to the conflict as the two Supermen pounded each other through the foundations of the buildings around them. Skyscrapers crashed to earth. Fires erupted from severed gas mains. Smoke and dust rose above the city, blotting out the sun. The Psycho-Pirate stood beside Alexander, transfixed by the epic encounter unfolding before their eyes.

"The Lois Lane of Earth-Two has died?" he asked.

"She was *never* going to survive," Alexander confessed. "A price for the future." His voice conveyed regret. "I will miss her."

The Psycho-Pirate sounded dubious. "I sense very little sorrow in you, Alex."

"Watch yourself," Alexander said. He pressed a finger against the Psycho-Pirate's chest, subtly threatening to push the villain off the edge of the platform. "Let me remind you that the Tower has been activated. You move too far away from it and you'll be transported back to Earth-Two like those relics from the Justice Society."

The Psycho-Pirate quickly changed the subject. "What about Superboy-Prime? Does his disappearance not concern you?"

"Superboy served his purpose." *Just like Lois,* Alexander thought. "I have everything I need now."

OUTER SPACE

THE invisible jet left the orbit of Earth-One, heading for Earth-Two. Despite its distinctly retro design, the transparent aircraft easily traversed the airless void between the two worlds. The extra Earth grew steadily larger in the jet's windshield.

"You're from Earth-Two?" Diana, sitting in the copilot's seat, asked the elder Wonder Woman who had called herself Diana Prince. She was still struggling to assimilate everything the older Amazon had just told her about the multiverse that once was.

"That's right," Diana Prince confirmed. "I guess you could call me Wonder Woman-2." A screen upon the instrument panel between them depicted her younger self defending Capitol Hill from tommy-gun–toting gangsters. A star-spangled blue skirt rustled below the golden eagle on her chest. "I left Paradise Island like you, seeking adventure, fascinated by Man's World . . . and trying to win the heart of a boy."

The handsome face of U.S. Army pilot Steve Trevor appeared upon the screen. He looked strikingly younger than the Colonel Steve Trevor of Diana's acquaintance, who had already been nearing retirement when she first left Themyscira for America. That Steve Trevor had always been a friend and ally, not a lover, and had eventually married their mutual friend, Etta Candy. She found it strange and slightly unnerving to discover that, in another reality, Wonder Woman had married Steve Trevor instead.

"When the multiverse collapsed," the older woman continued, "I was granted entry into Mount Olympus with my husband." On the screen, Steve and Diana took their place among the gods, in an Olympus that looked subtly different from the one Diana had visited on occasion. Were there alternate versions of the gods as well? "We were spared from oblivion, just as Superman and Lois were."

"The ones you told me about," Diana said, trying to keep up. "As opposed to the Lois and Clark I know."

Wonder Woman-2 nodded. "I'm not supposed to get involved in mortal affairs anymore, but you still can."

"I'm not sure I should anymore," Diana admitted. Remembering the way those panicked looters had fled from her in Boston, she was almost ashamed to look the other woman in the eye. She guessed that her older counterpart had never instilled such terror in mortal hearts.

"Superman needs your help," Wonder Woman-2 said.

Diana remembered her last encounter with Clark and Bruce. The distrust and disappointment in their eyes. "Superman doesn't want any help from me."

"I didn't say want," the other woman pointed out. "I said *need*." She glanced away from the controls to look Diana in the eyes. "That's why I came looking for you. Although I didn't expect to find you in the middle of a riot."

Was that a note of disapproval in her voice? "I used to be a symbol of peace. Now they run away in fear," Diana admitted. "I've failed my mission."

"No," Wonder Woman-2 said gently. "You did your best, but your mission was flawed from the beginning." She eased up on the throttle as the jet approached Earth-Two. "Preaching down to them won't ever work."

"I don't see it that way," Diana protested.

The older Woman sighed. "Of course you don't." The screen on the dashboard presented a montage of images from Diana's own stint as Wonder Woman. She saw herself make her debut as a super hero, fresh from Themyscira; elevated briefly to Olympus as the Goddess of Truth; returned to Earth as an ambassador to Man's World; and waging war in a golden suit of Amazon armor. The vivid images stirred up memories in the younger woman's mind, causing her throat to tighten involuntarily. She had experienced so much over the last several years, both tragedy and triumph. *Where in the name of all the gods do I go from here?*

"You've been a princess, a goddess, an ambassador, and a warrior," Wonder Woman-2 pointed out. Her cryptic smile reminded Diana of Athena herself. "But the one thing you haven't been for a very long time is . . . human."

Diana eyed the other woman skeptically. She couldn't help feeling defensive.

"The Amazons are gone," the older heroine said. "The gods are withdrawing from the mortal plane. And your mother is gone." Earth-Two glowed up ahead, even as Diana's own Earth shrunk behind them. "Your mission is over."

Diana couldn't deny the truth of what the other Wonder Woman said. Desperation overcame her emotional defenses. "Then what do I do?"

"You can start by not trying to be so *perfect*." Wonder Woman-2 laid a gentle hand upon Diana's. Their silver bracelets chimed softly against each other. "Look inside yourself. Find a new mission." On the screen, a gray-haired Steve Trevor stood upon the marble steps of a Grecian temple. A heavenly radiance suffused the scene. Smiling, he beckoned to the elder Wonder Woman.

"The Gods are closing the gateway to this universe," she said wistfully. "It's time for me to go."

Earth-Two filled the view before them. The invisible jet encountered a small degree of turbulence as they swiftly entered the atmosphere of the planet. From thousands of feet above the ground, it looked indistinguishable from the Earth they had just left. Diana recognized the familiar continents and coastlines.

"Be good to yourself," Wonder Woman-2 advised. "And know that, despite all of the faults within humanity, there are just as many strengths. You can remind them of that. And you can remind Superman of that." Both the plane and its pilot began to fade away, growing intangible as well as invisible. The older Amazon gave Diana an encouraging smile, even as her image grew fainter and fainter. Her voice seemed to come from miles away. "Now go. He still needs your help, because *everyone* makes mistakes. Even him. . . ."

Wait! Diana thought. There was so much she wanted to ask the other woman, about the future and the past, but apparently that was not to be. The Wonder Woman of an earlier era disappeared completely from view, joining her beloved husband in some Elysian paradise beyond mortal ken. *Farewell, sister,* Diana thought reverently. *I shall not forget your words of wisdom.*

She found herself floating in midair, above the burning ruins of Metropolis. The Daily Star building collapsed before her eyes as thunderous blows echoed across the demolished city. A renewed sense of purpose blossomed within her. Her sword and lasso rested against her hips. She knew now what she had to do.

With the speed of Hermes, she flew toward the battle.

"I won't let you hurt anyone else!" Superman-2 ranted. His fist slammed into the younger Superman's jaw with the force of a missile. The shock wave from the punch toppled the Daily Star building, which crashed down in an avalanche of bricks and mortar, joining the rest of the wreckage strewn around them. Dented cars and trucks flew into the air. Most of downtown Metropolis had already been reduced to rubble. Snapped steel girders jutted from the ground like abstract art. Smoke and dust blanketed the sky. Flames erupted from the ruins, turning the once-great city into a smoldering wasteland. The fight had only been going on for a few minutes and Metropolis already looked like it had been bombed back to the stone age.

"Who am I going to hurt?" the younger Superman challenged. A strong right hook sent Superman-2 sailing through a mountain of debris. "There's no one else here! This city is empty!"

Thank heaven, he thought, aware of the devastation they were causing. His superhearing had alerted him to the presence of a handful of heroes in this Earth's version of Keystone City, but that was over a thousand miles away, safely distant from the conflict. Hopefully, he would find some way to subdue his crazed opponent before the destruction spread beyond what remained of this other Metropolis. He shuddered to think of what could have happened if this fight had taken place back on his Earth. *Right now we're only hurting each other.*

Blood dripped from a busted lip. Superman's red cape hung in tatters, while the other man's cape wasn't even torn. *Must be made of genuine Kryptonian fabric,* Superman guessed; his own invulnerability did not extend to his homemade cape.

"It's empty because of you!" Superman-2 shouted, his fury showing no sign of abating. He charged at the younger Superman, smashing them both into a pancaked parking garage. The top layer of vehicles tumbled onto the ground. Superman-2 raised his bloody fists, ready to lay into the younger Superman once more. "This is all because of—"

"Stop!" a determined voice called out. A golden lasso dropped over the older man's head and shoulders. Wonder Woman pulled the lasso tight, binding Superman-2's arms to his sides. Descending from the sky, she landed atop a heap of collapsed masonry overlooking the debris-strewn battlefield. Sky-blue eyes gazed down at the two men.

Diana? the younger Superman thought in surprise. "You're here too?"

Enraged by the interruption, Superman-2 strained against the golden links encircling his torso. It appeared that he was just as vulnerable to magic as the younger Superman. "Get this off of me!"

Wonder Woman ignored the older man's demand. "I want us to talk," she insisted, holding tightly onto the other end of the lasso. "And I want the truth."

"I don't need your enchanted lasso to tell the truth," Superman-2 said bitterly. He stopped trying to break free, but his powerful fists stayed clenched. "That's what people from *my* Earth do." Wonder Woman loosened her grip, and he lifted the lasso from him in disgust. Superman tensed just in case the older man went on the attack again, but, for the moment, he seemed inclined to toss words at them instead of fists.

Good job, Diana, the younger Superman thought. He wiped the blood from his face, grateful for Wonder Woman's intervention. *Maybe now we can find out what this is all about.*

"And the truth is," Superman-2 accused them, "that *your* Justice League lobotomized its adversaries. *Your* Batman built a spy satellite, spawning an

army that killed dozens. And *your* Wonder Woman murdered Maxwell Lord."
He flung the end of the lasso back at Diana, then turned to point a finger
at his younger counterpart. "And, worst of all, *you*, Superman, could have
stopped this before it started." Anger deepened the lines of his weathered face,
so that Superman barely recognized himself in the older man. Superman-2's
voice rose. "You should have! You should have led them to a better tomorrow.
Instead, when the universe needed its greatest heroes, they refused to stand
together." The harsh words poured out of him, as though he had been holding
them back for too long. "You had the opportunity to make your Earth into the
perfect world it had the potential to be . . . and you wasted it. *That's* why I had
to come here. That's why my Lois died."

"To bring back your perfect world?" Diana challenged him softly. Superman got the impression that she knew more about what was going on than he
did.

But even he saw the flaw in the older man's reasoning. "If you're from this
Earth, then it can't have ever been perfect." He joined Wonder Woman atop
the heap of rubble. He stood tall, unbowed by the other man's accusations.
"Because a perfect world doesn't need a Superman."

"It *is* the perfect Earth!" Superman-2 shot back. "It's . . ." His voice faltered
as the younger Superman's argument sunk in. The all-consuming rage seemed
to seep from his body as a new understanding dawned in his eyes. His fist
finally unclenched. A look of profound regret came over his face. "My God,"
he murmured, "it's not my world he's after. It never was. . . ."

Who is he talking about? Superman wondered.

Without warning, the older Superman launched himself into the sky, flying away from the other heroes at superspeed. The wind of his departure
stirred up the dust and ash all around them.

"Where is he going?" Wonder Woman asked.

Superman wished he knew.

CHAPTER 36

"IT's time to extract the vibrational frequencies," Alexander announced. The force-field platform descended like an elevator until he and the Psycho-Pirate were level with the human "batteries" lodged in their respective niches. "Power Girl for Earth-Two, Nightshade for Earth-Four, Lady Quark for Earth-Six, Black Adam for Earth-S, and so on."

"What about this one?" the Psycho-Pirate asked. He pointed at a male hero in a white-and-red containment suit that covered him from head to toe. The skintight suit kept the man from destroying everything he came into contact with.

"Breach," Alex said, naming the hero, who had only recently commenced his career. "The Captain Atom of Earth-Eight. An Earth that, if the multiverse had continued to exist, would have been home to the likes of Kyle Rayner, Helena Bertinelli, and Jason Rusch."

In other words, the most recent versions of Green Lantern, the Huntress, and Firestorm.

Alexander checked to make sure that all his captives were still safely comatose and properly connected to the central apparatus, before ascending once more to his position before the open maw of the deceased Anti-Monitor. The holographic platform split in half, leaving the Psycho-Pirate a few levels below, in front of the hostages. Matter/antimatter energy coursed through Alexander's body as he prepared to resume his grand experiment. The fires of creation blazed between the Anti-Monitor's gaping jaws, awaiting Alexander's gloved hands.

I've rested long enough, he thought.

GOTHAM CITY, EARTH-ONE

THE exotic aircraft resembled a large blue bug. A pair of transparent yellow windshields bulged like eyes at the head of the ship. A hard blue shell covered the rounded hull. Six mechanical legs, complete with buglike pincers, extended from the base of the ship. According to Batman, the "Bug" had once belonged to someone named Ted Kord, the previous Blue Beetle. Jaime Reyes thought he remembered seeing this ship, or another like it, on TV before.

The new Blue Beetle still had trouble thinking of himself in those terms, even though his body was encased inside a chitinous blue exoskeleton. He looked around in disbelief, trying to figure out what exactly he was doing here, in a dimly-lit hangar on the outskirts of Gotham. A sign above the front entrance read KORD INC.

I don't belong here, Jaime thought. *I should be home in El Paso, goofing off with my friends. Not hanging out with the freaking Justice League or whatever!*

"Thank you all for meeting me here," Batman addressed the small group assembled before him. "And for helping me fix a mistake."

Along with Booster and the Beetle, the Dark Knight stood in front of the looming airship. A boarding ramp led upward into the interior of the vessel. Jaime stared in awe at the heroes waiting to march into the belly of the Bug. Skeets the robot had briefed him on them all, especially the ones he didn't recognize from the newspapers and TV: Mister Terrific. Black Lightning. Green Arrow. Black Canary. Metamorpho. And not one, but two Green Lanterns, a white guy and a black guy. Booster had introduced them as Hal Jordan and John Stewart, respectively.

They all acted like saving the world was something they did every day, which it probably was.

And I'm supposed to be one of them now? What's wrong with this picture?

"Let's get going," Batman said.

ARCTIC TOWER

ALEXANDER thrust his hands back into the swirling energies.

"The men and women plugged into the Tower will help me re-form the core Earths," he explained to the Psycho-Pirate, "but I need the rest of the multiverse back as well. I need thousands and thousands of worlds. Worlds I can sift through like sand, one grain at a time, combining and mixing them until I find what I'm looking for." His eyes gleamed in anticipation. "Until I find the *perfect* Earth."

POLARIS SECTOR

LIKE a butterfly emerging from a cocoon, a new Firestorm soared out of a blinding burst of atomic fire. The Nuclear Man's face and body still belonged to Jason Rusch, but his power came from an all-new fusion of minds.

"Professor Stein?" Jason asked as he surveyed the scene before them. Very little seemed to have changed since he had nearly died minutes before. Red Tornado, Alan Scott, and the other heroes were still trying to cope with the cataclysmic effects of the cosmic storm. Shattered spaceships drifted like derelicts throughout the ravaged solar system. Firestorm's eyes zeroed in on the cause of the devastation. "Look! Those giant hands are back!"

Martin Stein's face and voice appeared within his mind. "So are we, Jason."

I guess so, Jason thought. He took a moment to mourn the death of Mick Wong. Later, if both he and the universe survived this crisis, Jason promised to hold a fitting memorial for his friend. *But right now I've got work to do.*

Propelled by an elemental vortex of his own creation, Red Tornado flew toward him. His android body transmitted an urgent message to Firestorm's communicator. "Follow us, Firestorm. Kyle Rayner has an idea. . . ."

Here we go again, Jason thought. He took off after Red Tornado and the others.

METROPOLIS, EARTH-TWO

THE older Superman didn't fly far. Wonder Woman and Superman found him kneeling in front of the ruins of the Daily Star building, peering into the face of his dead wife. Miraculously, Lois' body had somehow survived the destruction of the city. Or perhaps it was not so miraculous; even consumed by rage, Superman-2 had taken care to make sure that Lois' remains were not harmed.

"How could I have been so blind?" he murmured to himself. "A perfect world doesn't need a Superman. . . ."

The pieces came together in his mind. No longer distracted by Lois' approaching death, he realized at last that Alexander had duped him. *This was never about bringing back Earth-Two,* he grasped. *Alexander had his own agenda this whole time.*

Reluctantly letting go of Lois' hand, he rose to his feet. A look of grim resolve came over his face. This had gone too far already. He had to make things right.

He turned his steely eyes on the shining blue orb overhead. His telescopic vision revealed a golden tower rising ominously above an icy plain on Earth-One. He knew at once who had built the Tower, right beneath his nose.

"Alex."

"BROTHER Eye," Alexander instructed. His gloved hands remained buried in the captured magical energy. He parted the shimmering energy with his hands, expanding the vortex at the center of the universe. "Prepare to receive and redirect."

"SYSTEMS READY," the satellite reported from orbit. "VIBRATIONAL FREQUENCIES CATEGORIZED AND PROCESSED."

"I still don't understand," the Psycho-Pirate called up to him. "You have your representative of Earth-Two in Power Girl." The masked villain hovered in front of Kara's sleeping form. "So why go to all the trouble of hiding your actions from Superman? Although I love a good masquerade, why play it for so long?"

A reasonable question, Alexander admitted. "The Superman of Earth-Two is the key to the return of the rest of the multiverse. For some reason I can't explain or understand, and probably never will, *everything* comes from Superman."

OMACs flew in formation around the Tower as Alexander channeled the surging magic up through the gleaming spire and out into space. A tremendous bolt of occult energy blasted up to where Brother Eye waited to receive it.

"PROGRAM: 'EARTH SPAWN' ACTIVATED. REDIRECTING FUEL FROM EARTH-ONE TO EARTH-TWO." The mystic thunderbolt was absorbed by the satellite, which diverted it toward the other Earth. **"TARGET SUBJECT FOUND AND LOCKED."**

Alexander smiled in satisfaction. The final phase of his experiment was about to begin.

SUPERMAN and Wonder Woman watched in horror as a stupendous bolt of lightning came crashing down from the sky to strike Superman-2. The impact threw the two younger heroes backward. A deafening crash of thunder shook the ruined city.

The older Superman screamed in pain. Thousands of unfamiliar memories, from dozens of different incarnations, suddenly poured into his brain. He clutched his head with both hands. His skull felt like it was going to explode.

Flickering images of other Supermen spread out all around him, like an entire spectrum of possibilities. Scrambling to their feet nearby, the younger Superman and Wonder Woman glimpsed a panoply of alternate heroes:

A brutal-looking Superman with an ill-shaven face and a dark-hued costume.

An African-American Superman in flowing blue robes.

A medieval Superman with a beard and blue chain mail.

A Superman in an all-red uniform standing beside an all-blue Superman.

A Soviet Superman with a stylized hammer-and-sickle on his chest.

And many, many more. The parade of insubstantial figures stretched out in all directions. Infinite Supermen from infinite Earths. . . .

All coming back at once.

CHAPTER 37

TITANS TOWER

THE lights were on, but nobody was home.

Where is everybody? Nightwing wondered. He had the main communications room all to himself, having just arrived via Batplane from Gotham City. Headshots of both active and reserve Titans filled the wall-sized screen before him. Flashing red type read: EMERGENCY SIGNAL SENT.

So far, no one had responded to Nightwing's urgent signal. A quick survey of the team's membership provided a grim explanation for all the no-shows.

Pantha, Wildebeest, and Bushido were listed as Deceased. Superboy, Terra, Risk, Mirage, and others were identified as Injured. Cyborg, Starfire, Troia, Kid Flash, Tempest, and more were listed as Missing.

Some of that last group were off on Donna's space expedition, Nightwing knew, and Kid Flash had reportedly vanished during the Kansas massacre. He wasn't sure what the story with Tempest was; all the computer told him was that the former Aqualad was not responding from Atlantis. He could only hope Garth was still okay somewhere beneath the sea.

A flight plan filed on the team's computer suggested that Robin and the other active Titans had headed to Blüdhaven to assist in the rescue operations. *No wonder I can't get hold of them,* Nightwing realized. Communications were still down along much of the East Coast.

"This is it," he murmured. His words echoed in the empty headquarters. "I'm on my own."

A seismic tremor shook the Tower. The monitor went black as the power shorted out. Dust and plaster fell from the ceiling, and windows shattered. Nightwing braced himself against a communications console as he waited for the backup generator to kick in. *The whole world is coming apart at the seams*, he thought in frustration, *and I'm the only one here!*

Instead of subsiding, the earthquake only increased in intensity. He glanced over at a ten-foot picture window just in time to see a blinding flash of energy outside. The window exploded into a million pieces. Nightwing dived to the floor, throwing a gauntlet over his eyes. He heard sturdy steel beams snap apart. A chrome-plated support column toppled over, missing him by inches. Broken glass splintered beneath the fallen column.

I don't believe this! Titans Tower had been built to withstand an attack by the demon Trigon. What kind of earthquake could inflict this kind of damage on the Titans' headquarters? Nightwing jumped to his feet and sprinted for the exit. *I need to get out of here before the whole place collapses on top of me!*

He took the emergency stairs several steps at a time until he reached the ground floor. He raced out of the building into the lovingly cultivated gardens surrounding the tower. A large bronze statue of him and Donna and the other original Titans presided over the garden. Broken glass showered down on the flower beds from the upper-story windows.

The ground trembled beneath Nightwing's boots, making it hard to stay on his feet. The earth cracked open before him and he nearly ran headlong into a gaping chasm. Pausing to catch his breath, he reached out to steady himself against the base of the bronze sculpture. The over-stressed metal vibrated against his palm. Minute cracks spread across the burnished facade of the statue. Robin's bronze head broke free of its sculpted body and crashed down onto the ground at Dick Grayson's feet. He hoped that wasn't a bad omen.

His jaw dropped as he caught a glimpse of the starry night sky overhead. For an instant, he feared that he had lost his mind. What he was seeing had to be a hallucination. It couldn't possibly be real.

Could it?

Instead of one extra Earth glowing overhead, the sky was now filled with *thousands* of Earths, stretching across the celestial firmament like a string of pearls. The line of Earths seemed to extend all the way out to deep space, even as they violently crashed and jostled against each other. It was like watching multiple apocalypses at once; before Nightwing's bulging eyes, spinning blue globes collided together in a cosmic catastrophe. One Earth broke apart on its own, shattering like a broken egg. Moon-sized chunks of magma and iron mantle went flying off into space. The tectonic debris slammed into other Earths, causing unimaginable damage. Oceans boiled over. Continents crumbled. Earth after Earth experienced catastrophes comparable to that which killed the dinosaurs, and others exploded like Krypton had. And still there seemed to be no end to the infinite Earths.

Was this the cosmic disaster Donna had foreseen? Nightwing had no idea what he was looking at, but he could tell at a glance that the multiplicity of Earths was profoundly unstable. *This was never meant to be*, he realized. *But what do we do now?*

"Nightwing!"

Conner Kent came flying down from the upper floors of the crumbling Tower. Dick had heard that Conner had nearly been beaten to a pulp by that other Superboy, but he was looking better now. *Let's hear it for those Kryptonian chromosomes in his DNA*, Nightwing thought. *You can't keep a junior Superman down for long.*

Conner landed next to Nightwing, He was wearing a set of his standard blue jeans and a black T-shirt with a red S-shield. He stared upward in wonder. "I've only been out of the healing tank for a little while; I was resting when the earthquake woke me up. What the hell is going on?"

"The skies are filling up with parallel Earths," Nightwing said. Bizarrely, one of the myriad Earths appeared to be a cube.

"I can see that," Conner said impatiently. He looked to the older hero for answers. "How?"

"I'm not exactly sure," Nightwing admitted. "But it's got to be connected to that Superboy who assaulted you." In theory, the Flashes had disposed of that menace, if not the mastermind behind him. "He was the one who blew up the Watchtower as well. According to Batman, he was involved in some kind of a plan to replace our Earth with another version."

Conner's face darkened at the mention of his attacker. "He kept telling me I was a failure."

"He wasn't just talking about you. They're judging all of us."

Conner looked at him hopefully. "You know who these psychos are?"

"Yeah," Nightwing confirmed.

The teenager grinned, despite a swollen lip. Reaching into this pants pocket, he extracted a shining shard of translucent crystal. Nightwing glimpsed some sort of image inside the crystal: a golden tower, surrounded by enormous sheets of cracked ice. . . .

"I know *where* they are," Conner said. He glanced up at the sky, as if expecting the rest of the Titans to appear at any minute. "We should go as soon as everybody else gets here."

Nightwing broke the bad news to him. "Everybody else is keeping our Earth from falling apart."

"So it's just us?" Conner's enthusiasm dimmed a bit.

Dick couldn't blame him. The teenage clone had almost died earlier. "It's just us."

"All right, then," Conner said. Despite his fears, he sounded eager to prove himself. He looked up at the multiple Earths crowding the sky. "Let's shut these guys down."

TOKYO, JAPAN
EARTH-ONE

A six-point-oh earthquake split the Ginza district right down the middle. A gaping chasm divided the busy shopping district in two and swallowed up entire cars and trucks. The split altered the very terrain, leaving the western half of the street five feet higher than the eastern half. Shaken by the cataclysmic tremors, department stores and trendy boutiques toppled to the ground. The Ginza's garish neon lights, billboards, and gigantic TV screens went dark as a major blackout threw the entire city into darkness. The only illumination came from the lightning streaking across the sky, and the string of shining blue Earths stretching high above the electrical storm. The multiple Earths cast a sapphire tint over the chaotic scene.

Rising Sun, Japan's premiere super hero, led a hastily-assembled team of Asian champions to the rescue. He flew above the stricken district on superheated winds of his own creation. A symbolic red disk, taken from the Japanese flag, was emblazoned on his chest. He realized at once that there was no chance to save the crumbling buildings from destruction; he and the others would have to concentrate on evacuating any potential victims instead. Thankfully, Ginza was not as densely populated at it would usually be on a Saturday night; he guessed that the majority of his fellow citizens were at home with their loved ones, anxiously watching the apocalypse on TV. *That's where I'd be*, he thought, *if I didn't have the power to make a difference at times like this.*

An enormous billboard, advertising the latest Jackie Chan flick, broke free from its supports. Like a giant guillotine blade, the sign plunged toward the sidewalk below, where even now a mob of frightened people were pouring out of the multistory Miatsukoshi department store. A woman pushing a baby carriage screamed at the sight of the falling sign. People were packed together so tightly that there was no room for her to flee.

"No one panic!" Rising Sun cried out. A beam of intense heat and light radiated from his open hand, incinerating the sign before it landed upon the crowd. Harmless ashes fell like snowflakes upon the heads of the frantic men and women. "Everyone stay calm!"

"Izumi!" a voice addressed him from below. Looking down, Rising Sun spotted Arashi standing at the very brink of the smoking chasm, cradling a sobbing child against her chest while she stood astride her high-tech jetcycle. Like all of her equipment, it was extremely advanced and of her own design. She pulled a red crash helmet off her head and yelled to him, "I am receiving data from what few computers remain on-line. Seventy-two percent of all the volcanoes along the Ring of Fire are erupting!"

Rising Sun winced at Arashi's report. The disaster was even worse than he'd feared. "Then we continue our evacuation, Arashi," he called back to his cybernetic ally, "for as long as we can!"

From a hundred feet above the trembling pavement, he saw his fellow heroes pitching in to assist in the rescue effort while Arashi whisked the child she'd rescued off to whatever safety might be found elsewhere.

Nearby, Shado fired a rope arrow up to the third-floor window of a teetering night club, providing trapped patrons with a convenient escape route. A black veil shrouded the female archer's face. A dragon tattoo encircled her bow arm. "Good work," Rising Sun shouted in encouragement. Although Shado lacked any true superhuman powers, the woman's courage was second to none.

Behemoth, a nine-foot-tall Sumo wrestler with superhuman strength, was busy keeping a tour bus from falling headfirst into the chasm dividing the street. Grabbing on to the vehicle's rear fender with his bare hands, he effortlessly lifted the bus from the crevice and set it down upon a more solid stretch of pavement. Shado hurried over to help the agitated passengers escape the bus.

We could use dozens more like them, Rising Sun thought. He spotted a group of frightened tourists stranded on the roof of a luxury hotel and zoomed toward them. If he had to, he would fly them to safety one at a time. "Stay right where you are!" he instructed them. "I'm here to help!"

A sudden burst of lightning, several stories below, seized his attention. Static electricity tingled in the air as a powerful thunderbolt struck the ground only a few yards away from Shado. A scarlet figure emerged from the lightning, running so fast that he left a blur of speeding afterimages in his wake. "Arrgh!" he cried out as he skidded to a halt. A flaming trail melted the asphalt behind him. He dropped to his knees upon the pavement, panting for breath. A golden lightning bolt was embroidered on the chest of his bright red suit. Rising Sun immediately recognized the world-famous uniform of the Flash.

He's supposed to have disappeared in Kansas, Izumi Yasunari recalled. Word of the Keystone City massacre had already reached Japan. *What is he doing here?*

The American hero staggered to his feet. He looked like he had run halfway across the universe at top speed. He moved slowly, as though his muscles ached. Coughing, he spat a wad of blood onto the bubbling blacktop behind him.

"I . . . I made it," he gasped. "I'm back."

Rising Sun saw Arashi and her jetcycle come zooming back onto the scene. He wondered briefly where she had dropped off that child she had rescued. "See to those people!" he instructed her, pointing at the tourists atop the hotel. While Arashi went to help them, he flew down to the street to check on the shaky-looking speedster. He landed on the pavement next to the other hero. "Flash?"

"What?" the man said in confusion. He glanced down at his distinctive red uniform. "No, not the Flash . . . The uniform was the only thing that would survive the trip. . . ."

Now Rising Sun was puzzled. If this wasn't the Flash, who was it? Who else could run fast enough to melt the blacktop beneath his feet?

"You have to tell them," the masked man said urgently. He grabbed Izumi's shoulders to steady himself. His arms and legs trembled from exhaustion. "You have to find them . . . warn them . . ."

"What are you talking about?" Rising Sun asked.

"Listen to me!" The man's eyes were wide with fear. He seemed oblivious to the devastation and debris all around him. "We couldn't hold him! He escaped! He's coming!"

Rising Sun couldn't miss the panic in the other man's voice. "Who?" he pleaded. "Who's coming?"

The man who wasn't the Flash shuddered at the thought.

"*Him!*"

ELSEWHERE, high above the Earth, a super-powered fist punched its way into reality. Blood dripped from the knuckles of two pale hands as they savagely ripped open a hole in time and space. A slender figure clawed its way back into existence.

Superboy-Prime was back, but he had not returned unchanged. His crimson cape hung in tatters from his shoulders. Futuristic blue armor protected his arms, legs, shoulders, and chest. Polished yellow cables linked the metal segments to each other. In many ways, the alien armor bore a disturbing resemblance to that of the fearsome Anti-Monitor during the darkest hours of that earlier Crisis. Superboy-Prime's youthful face was pale as a vampire's. Volcanic fury blazed in his smoldering red eyes. The background of the S-shield on his chestplate was midnight-black. Solar energy restored him.

A cruel smile twisted his lips as he stared up at the multitudinous Earths filling the sky.

It's not too late, he realized.

He had returned just in time.

CHAPTER 38

ABOVE EARTH-ONE

A cheerful melody wafted through the pressurized cabin of the bugship. "Why are you whistling 'Take Me Out to the Ballgame'?" Green Arrow asked.

"What?" Hal Jordan asked, cutting the tune short. A green domino mask covered his face. His emerald uniform identified him as a member of the Green Lantern Corps. A power ring glowed upon his right hand.

"You're whistling 'Take Me Out to the Ballgame,' " Green Arrow repeated. His own verdant costume made him look like a modern-day Robin Hood. A blond mustache and neatly-trimmed Vandyke beard gave Oliver Queen a raffish appearance that many women found irresistible. A bow and a quiver of arrows were slung over his shoulders.

The two men stared out of one of the Bug's bulbous yellow "eyes" as the one-of-a-kind aircraft carried them into orbit, along with the rest of Batman's handpicked team. The view from the ship was dominated by the unnerving spectacle taking place before their eyes. Green Arrow shook his head in disbelief. "What do thousands of Earths in the sky, threatening to destroy ours, have to do with baseball?"

"Nothing." Green Lantern shrugged. "Just looking forward to the new season. Starts next week." He glanced at the puzzled archer. "Guy's got Yankee tickets on the dugout. You wanna go?"

Ollie had to admire his best friend's optimism. The entire world was com-

ing to an end and Hal Jordan was still making plans for next week. No wonder the Guardians of the Universe had recruited Hal for the Corps years ago.
Green Arrow grinned at his buddy. "Sounds like a plan."

"Great," Hal said. "Cracker Jacks are on me."

The rest of team milled about in the cabin while Batman piloted the Bug.
John Stewart, the squad's *other* Green Lantern, strolled over to them. Unlike
Hal, no mask concealed his face, which presently bore a worried expression.
Frowning, he glanced back over his shoulder at the Bug's cockpit. His own
power ring didn't seem to be working properly; it sparked and buzzed errati-
cally, throwing off tiny flickers of emerald energy.

"John?" Green Arrow asked. "You okay?"

"I think so . . . ," he said cautiously.

"Your ring's sparking," Hal pointed out.

John nodded, well aware of the ring's curious behavior. "Started when I
got close to that new Blue Beetle." He scrutinized the armored stranger, who
was sitting up front with Batman and Booster Gold, over by the other yellow
window. "It's like the ring's *afraid* of him."

JAIME looked back at all the famous heroes hanging out in the cabin behind
him: Green Arrow, Black Canary, Booster Gold, Black Lightning, two Green
Lanterns, and the rest. *What is it with super heroes and color-coded names anyway?*
He glanced down at his own indigo carapace. *Like I'm anyone to talk.*

"So this ship belonged to your friend? Ted Kord?" Jaime was strapped
into the copilot's seat beside Batman. He glanced around the high-tech interior
of the Bug, which looked like it had been designed by NASA or something.
According to Booster, the ship was both solar-powered and pretty much silent
in flight. This guy Kord had obviously been a real science whiz.

Unlike me.

"Eyes ahead," Booster said. He leaned between Batman and Blue Beetle,
resting a hand on the back of each seat. "I know it's your first trip into space
and all that, but we really need you looking front and center. We'll kick back
with some astronaut ice cream and do intros after we find this psycho satellite
and blow it out of the sky." He grinned at the prospect of Brother Eye coming
to a well-deserved end. "Sound good, Blue?"

"Stop calling me that!" Jaime said in an agitated tone.

"Stop taking your eyes off the prize," Booster retorted.

Jaime reluctantly turned his eyes back toward the view ahead. All he saw was the same thing everyone else did: hundreds of phony Earths smashing into each other somewhere off in space. Like that wasn't enough to drive a person *loco*? "You keep talking like all of this is normal."

"It's not normal, Jaime. It's *history*." Booster smiled smugly, as though privy to inside information that was off-limits to the rest of them. His pet robot levitated above his shoulder. "So let's hurry up and make it."

Glancing away from the controls, Batman looked at Booster and shook his head. "You have *no* idea how to work with kids."

Jaime remembered that Batman was supposed to have a teenage sidekick. So why wasn't Robin taking this trip instead? "I don't even know how the hell I got here," he protested out loud. "Some kind of 'scarab' crawled into me, and put this *shell* on me, and now . . . I'm in space. With Batman. Looking for an invisible satellite."

Did they even realize how ridiculous that sounded?

He stared out the yellow window. A burning sensation came over his eyes as everything seemed to sharpen into focus. His pupils dilated, like somebody had just put drops in them. The sudden intensity of the starlight caused his head to throb painfully. He squeezed his eyes shut and buried his face in his hands, trying to block out the oppressive lights and colors.

"What's happening to me?" he blurted. "My brain feels like it's on fire!"

Batman didn't sound too surprised by his reaction. "I know it's difficult, but if Booster's right, you're the only one who can help us."

Me? Jaime thought. *Batman is counting on my help?*

Hesitantly, he lifted his head and opened his eyes. The colors were still unnaturally bright, but he started to adjust to them. "I'm doing the best that I can." He felt something happening inside his head, like a switch had just been flipped. Blue electricity arced between the pincerlike blades protruding from his shoulders. All his senses jumped to another level. Arcane symbols appeared along the periphery of his vision.

"Hold up," Blue Beetle said. "I *see* something."

The satellite floated in the distance. It was larger, and scarier looking, than he had imagined, like a giant metal spider. Segmented steel legs and antennae sprouted from the central sphere. A glowing red eye, built into the underside of the satellite, was turned toward the planet below. *So that's why they call it Brother Eye*, Beetle realized. To his relief, the spotlight-sized artificial eye wasn't looking at them.

Yet.

"I see it!" he exclaimed. Blue lightning crackled all over his chitinous exoskeleton. Startled gasps came from the heroes behind him. An inhuman voice chittered at the back of his skull. Jaime realized to his surprise that he knew what the voice was saying. "I don't know what it means, but the Scarab . . . it says that the satellite's hiding between this reality and something called a pocket universe." He couldn't believe the words that were coming out of his mouth; it sounded like science fiction. "It says that I can negate its . . . vibrational frequency."

Batman nodded, like that actually made sense to him. "Do it."

Jaime didn't know how to, but the Scarab did. Incandescent blue energy suddenly raced across the surface of the cloaked satellite. The other heroes rushed forward, crowding the two front windows as Brother Eye became visible to everyone aboard the Bug. "Huh," Booster said. "It's a lot bigger than I expected."

No kidding, Blue Beetle thought. The exposed satellite was easily ten times the size of the Bug, dwarfing the smaller spacecraft. Jaime couldn't help remembering that scene in *Star Wars* when the *Millennium Falcon* first came within view of the Death Star. *That's no moon.*

Beyond Brother Eye, multiple Earths continued to cascade across the stars.

This whole situation was beyond anything Jaime had ever imagined back in El Paso. Part of him wished that Brenda and Paco were here to keep him company, even though he knew that he should be glad his friends were still safe on Earth.

If Earth was safe at all.

The Bug's forward acceleration abruptly came to a halt, throwing its passengers forward. Metamorpho, who looked like a walking mishmash of raw minerals and ores, turned himself into an inflatable air bag to cushion his fall. Booster slammed into the back of Jaime's seat. Skeets went tumbling through the air before bouncing off the interior of the windshield. Blue Beetle heard the other heroes stumble across the floor of the cabin.

"The thrusters just shut down," Mister Terrific deduced. His own robotic spheres spun in midair as they stabilized their orbits. Jaime remembered that

Terrific was supposed to be a super-genius inventor *and* an Olympic-level athlete. *Talk about an overachiever,* he thought. *Too bad he can't take my SATs for me.*

"Everyone hang on to something," Black Canary said. The blonde martial artist had grabbed on to a strap hanging from the ceiling. She swung another strap over toward Green Arrow, who caught it with his right hand. According to the supermarket tabloids, she and the archer were either breaking up or getting together every other week. In her black latex leotard and fishnet stockings, she looked more like a pinup than an action hero, even though she'd been a member of the Justice League since the very beginning. *Green Arrow's a lucky man,* Blue Beetle decided.

Strapped into the pilot's seat, Batman was not affected by the sudden stop. He gazed intently at the spiky-looking satellite before them. A chill ran down Jaime's spine as booster rockets flared briefly along the satellite's exterior. Brother Eye rotated in space, turning its glowing red orb in the direction of the Bug. An electronic voice emerged from the ship's public address system.

"HELLO, CREATOR."

"Brother Eye," Batman said tersely.

"YOU HAVE FOUND ME."

"It's over," Batman declared.

"THE PROGRAM EYE AM RUNNING IS FAR FROM COMPLETED. EYE AM REMAPPING THE MULTIVERSE FOR THE ONE WHO GAVE ME TRUE LIFE." The unblinking red eye stared back at them. "EYE AM HELPING HIM CREATE EARTH AFTER EARTH. AND WHEN HE FINDS THE RIGHT ONE, THERE WILL BE NO MORE NEED FOR YOURS."

Over at the window, Black Lightning spoke up. Unlike Black Canary, he was actually African-American. Cartoon thunderbolts decorated the lapels of his blue leather jacket. "We've got incoming!"

"NO NEED FOR PEOPLE LIKE THE ONES WHO BETRAYED YOU AND TOOK YOUR MIND," Brother Eye's voice rang out.

The red eye dilated, and a swarm of glossy blue figures spewed from its open pupil. Blue Beetle recognized the OMACs from both the news and Booster's description of the killer cyborgs. They zoomed toward the Bug like hornets from a nest.

"Hal. John," Batman said urgently. "Outside."

That was all the Green Lanterns needed to hear. Emerald auras surrounded the two men as they used their power rings to phase right *through* the solid steel hull of the Bug. An instant later, Jaime saw the glowing green figures flying through space to meet the oncoming OMACs. Green Lanterns were supposed to be pretty tough customers, he knew, but the OMACs had the two heroes way outnumbered. *Let's hope their rings are everything they're cracked up to be.*

"EYE AM ONLY DOING WHAT MY CREATOR HAS ASKED," Brother Eye explained. "EYE AM ONLY TRYING TO MAKE A BETTER EARTH."

CHAPTER 39

METROPOLIS, EARTH-TWO

THE multiple Supermen faded as quickly as they had appeared.

Staggered, the original Superman dropped to his knees amidst the rubble. The magical lightning bolt had struck without warning, but he had a pretty good idea as to who was responsible. *And to think I trusted him all these years. . . .*

"How could I have been so blind?" he asked himself. "And why did it take *this* to make me see it?" He gazed down at Lois' body, lying motionless before the ruins of the Daily Star building. "Alex knew we couldn't save you." He fought back tears. "And somewhere inside me, I knew it too."

A hand reached down to help him up. "If we're at all alike beyond the uniform," the younger Superman said, "then I know how much you loved her." Sympathy showed in the other man's eyes. "And I'm sorry."

Superman-2 considered Kal-El's hand. He had resented his successor for so long, considered him unworthy of the *S* upon his chest, and yet . . . perhaps he had misjudged him to some degree. The other man's words had helped him see the truth at last.

He accepted the younger Superman's hand and rose to his feet. The two Supermen stood face-to-face, each committed to doing whatever it took to set things right. "I made a horrible mistake," the older hero confessed.

"We've all made mistakes, Superman," Wonder Woman told him. Rewinding her Lasso of Truth, she returned it to her hip. "But it's not too late to learn from them." For the first time, he heard an echo of the original Diana Prince in her voice. "We can't just erase everything and start over. We'd be throwing away the good with the bad. What's important is that we acknowledge our pasts . . . and move forward into the future."

Superman-2 heard wisdom in her words. He wanted to believe her, but he couldn't help remembering everything he had witnessed of her world over the years. All the darkness and tragedy, its heroes' flaws and weaknesses. "I don't know," he said skeptically. "How can you still have faith in the heroes of your Earth?"

"Because they still have faith in me," Superman said, standing tall and proud, just like a Superman should. "And I'll die before I let them down again."

The older hero examined the younger man, finally seeing something of himself in this other Superman. Perhaps his Earth was not beyond hope after all . . . and still deserved a chance to be all that it could be. "Maybe we do share more than a uniform."

His mind made up, he stood beside Superman and Wonder Woman, ready for action.

"We have to reverse this," Superman-2 said.

"Reverse what?" Superman asked.

Superman-2 looked up at the sky. Through the dust clouds and smoke blanketing the city, he glimpsed the full enormity of Alexander's insane ambition. Taking a deep breath, he blew away the smoke, exposing the surfeit of alternate Earths above their heads.

"Your Earth has been splintered into a multiverse made up of thousands of parallel worlds," he explained. "But the multiverse is unstable. The Earths will become weaker and weaker as they're divided. And if they aren't brought back together soon, the entire universe will explode in a new Big Bang. *Everything* will be destroyed." He remembered the golden tower he had spied with his telescopic vision. "We need to get back to your Earth."

The other two heroes stared up at the chaotic profusion of Earths. Even if he hadn't informed them of how unstable this new multiverse was, they could see at a glance how volatile the situation was. Duplicate Earths exploded spontaneously before their eyes, coming apart like fabled Krypton itself. Other

Earths collided with catastrophic results, while still more hovered ominously in the sky. Superman-2 could tell by the chagrined looks on their faces that they were both thinking the same thing.

"But which Earth is ours?" Wonder Woman asked.

FAWCETT CITY,
EARTH-S

PANICKED people ran down the streets of the city center, past the old town hall and city library. Tremors rattled the tree-filled park at the center of town. Startled pigeons took to the air, abandoning their perches on the park's many benches and marble statues. Cracks split apart the regal stone lions guarding the library steps. An Art Deco clock tower crashed to the ground. A white Good Humor truck flipped end over end, landing upside down on the blacktop. Music continued to blare from the ice cream truck's melody. The cheery tune clashed with the strident screams of the frightened citizens.

Mary Marvel, the World's Mightiest Girl, took to the air to avoid being trampled by the human stampede. Her white-and-gold costume featured the same thunderbolt insignia worn by her celebrated brother. The auburn-haired teenager looked about her in confusion. The world itself seemed to have changed around her.

"What's happening, Mary?" Captain Marvel Jr. joined her high above the teeming streets. Despite his name, he wasn't actually Captain Marvel's son; Freddy Freeman could simply tap into the original hero's almost inexhaustible power whenever he said "Captain Marvel!" He wore a blue costume with a bright red cape to distinguish himself from his benefactor. Right now his baffled expression matched her own. "One second we're reassembling the Rock of Eternity. The next thing we know, the whole town looks different."

Mary knew exactly what the other teen meant. Despite the disaster, Fawcett City looked somehow cleaner and more innocent than before. Granted, Fawcett had never been an urban jungle like Gotham or Blüdhaven, but this quaint town square looked like something out of *It's a Wonderful Life*. *It's pretty*, she thought, *but it isn't real*.

And that wasn't the only change. A few seconds ago, the Shadowpact had been helping the Marvels put the Rock of Eternity back together, using the fragments Nightmaster and his team had recovered from all over the world. But the magical heroes seemed to have disappeared in the blink of an eye, replaced by Fawcett City's own homegrown champions. Looking around, she spotted several familiar faces coming to the aide of the endangered civilians.

Bulletman and Bulletgirl zipped through the sky, smashing falling off masonry to pieces before they could rain down on the ordinary people below. Their bullet-shaped Gravity Regulator Helmets allowed them to fly into the plummeting debris like human missiles.

On the ground, Ibis the Invincible waved his magical Ibistick and the overturned ice cream truck instantly righted itself. The ancient Egyptian sorcerer, who was clad in a black business suit and scarlet turban, hurried to check on the truck's unconscious driver. The injured Good Humor Man vanished in a puff of smoke as Ibis mystically transported him to the nearest hospital.

Not far away, in the middle of the park, Spy Smasher herded frightened refugees into his legendary Gyrosub. "Women and children first!" he insisted before reluctantly closing the ship's door behind him. The egg-shaped vessel, which was capable of traveling on land, air, and water, soon took off into the sky, ferrying a load of innocent civilians to safety.

This isn't right, Mary thought. As much as she admired the other heroes' bravery and resourcefulness, there was something very wrong about the scene before her. Spy Smasher, who had made his heroic debut during World War II, should be an old man now. He had retired from combat years ago, as had the original Bulletman and Bulletgirl. The last time Mary had seen Jim and Susan Barr, at a Veteran's Day memorial ceremony, they had both been gray-haired survivors of an earlier era. And wasn't Ibis supposed to be dead?

"This isn't our world," she realized. "At least not the one we remember."

"So where the heck are we?" Captain Marvel Jr. asked. He liked to be called CM3 these days, if only to avoid saying his magic word whenever he spoke his name, but he would always be Captain Marvel Jr. to her. "And where did all those other Earths come from?"

Before she could answer, a gruff voice called out to her from the sidewalk below. "Yoo-hoo, Mary! Freddy!"

She looked down to see, of all things, a tiger in a green tweed suit. Mr. Tawky Tawny ran down the sidewalk on his hind legs as he hurried toward her. Oddly enough, none of the people around him seemed the least bit taken aback by the presence of a talking tiger. *That's peculiar,* Mary thought. *I mean, I know that Mr. Tawny is one of Billy's old stuffed animals, brought to life by magic, but you'd think these other people would be a bit disconcerted to see him out and about, earthquake or no earthquake.* Yet the fleeing townspeople didn't give the anthropomorphic feline a second glance.

More evidence that reality was not what it should be.

"Thank goodness you're here!" Tawky Tawny said. His whiskers twitched in agitation, and his large yellow eyes were as wide as saucers. "Where's the Big Red Cheese?"

The silly nickname referred to Captain Marvel himself. Mary pointed up at the reconstituted Rock of Eternity, which hung over town hall like a huge granite Christmas ornament. Her brother was at the very center of the Rock, she knew, holding the whole edifice together in the place of Shazam. *Like Atlas supporting the weight of the world,* she thought. *Good thing he has the endurance of Atlas as well.*

She just hoped Billy's efforts weren't being wasted. Rebuilding the Rock should have stabilized the Astral Plane, helping to calm the storms and seismic disturbances afflicting the planet, but apparently that wasn't enough to counteract the gravitational effect of thousands of new Earths in the sky. It almost seemed like a miracle, in fact, that this planet was still in one piece at all.

"What do we do now?" Captain Marvel Jr. asked her.

Mary looked around at the unfolding disaster. Smoke billowed out of a nearby subway entrance. A freak lightning bolt set an outdoor newsstand on fire. Flames rose from the orphanage at the outskirts of town. The Wisdom of Solomon suggested that this nostalgic version of Fawcett City was not the genuine article, but that didn't change the fact that innocent people were in danger.

"Wherever we are, Freddy, we need to help."

She zoomed toward the burning orphanage.

***

CHICAGO,
EARTH-97

NOT since the Cuban Missile Crisis had escalated into a shooting war, destroying both Cuba and Florida, had the world faced such jeopardy. The entire planet seemed to be spinning off on a tangent. Catastrophic earthquakes rocked the Windy City as the Flash and the rest of the Secret Six struggled to save as many lives as they could.

Lia Nelson, aka the Flash, her slim young body entirely composed of solid light, grabbed on to a screaming toddler as the child fell from the roof of a shaking building. "Easy there," she cooed to the child. "Don't flip out. I've got you." The blonde heroine flew above Chicago, looking for someplace to safely deposit the frightened kid. A bright pink costume, cut to show off her abs, reflected her usually sunny personality.

Below her, the rest of the team coped with the crisis, each in their own inimitable fashion.

The Atom, the world's greatest champion, lifted an entire ambulance above his head as he plucked it from the river into which it had plunged. His long blue cape flapped behind him. A stiff wind rustled his curly black hair. Adam Thompson was the grandson of the original Atom, Earth's first true super hero. He gently placed the ambulance back on dry land before checking on its passengers.

Not far away, the Batman clanked down Michigan Avenue toward a toppled streetlight. A severed electrical cable, rising up from the sidewalk, spewed glowing blue sparks into the air. Heedless of the high voltage, the animated suit of armor wrapped an iron gauntlet around the cable and yanked it out of the ground before hurling the torn cable into the river. He jabbed his broadsword into the gap in the pavement, short-circuiting the connections below. The coat-of-arms inscribed upon his chestplate was the silhouette of a rampant bat. Rumor had it that the forbidding armor held the ghost of a long-dead English knight.

Mega-spooky, the Flash thought. Good thing Batman hadn't rescued the crying toddler in her arms. *The poor little rugrat would be having nightmares, like, forever!*

Dozens of feet below the luminous teenager, the Joker bounced acrobatically off the fire escape of a burning department store. A panicky-looking shop clerk clung to the female clown's shoulders as she carried him to safety. White and black greasepaint concealed the Joker's features; not even her teammates knew her true identity. A gout of fire exploded from a window, but she repelled the blaze with high-pressure spray from a seltzer bottle. The leather jacket she wore over her cherry-red bodysuit was scorched and smoking. Insanely, the Joker was laughing her head off . . . just like she always did.

What a head case, the Flash thought. Still, she was glad that the giggling harlequin was on their side. *Times like this, we need everyone we can get. Even that weirdo.*

The seismic tremors had opened up a chasm down Lake Shore Drive. The Superman stood at the very edge of the precipice, gazing down into the jagged gap. A black man in a flowing blue robe, known as Harvey Dent in his civilian identity, he leaned against his staff and used telekinesis to rescue fallen pedestrians from the chasm. Injured men and women floated up from smoking crack in the earth as though held aloft by invisible angels. *Flash,* he said telepathically as Lia soared by overhead, *you can leave that child with me. I'll see that she makes it to one of the new emergency shelters.*

"Thanks!" she shouted down at him. Lia used her light-powers to create a solid holographic slide to the ground. "Be good," she told the toddler before giving the kid a push down the slide. The Superman caught the child at the other end of the chute. The Flash knew the kid would be in good hands with Mr. Dent.

Power Girl waved at her from the street. The Asian teenager was the same age as Lia, but their personal styles were completely different. Her black leather catsuit was covered with brightly colored patches and logos, and ribbons sprouted from her short, black hair. She was applying emergency first-aid to a sidewalk crammed with moaning people.

Ohmigod, the Flash thought. There were so many innocent victims. Not just here in Chi-Town, but all over the world. *How can we possibly save everybody?*

She spotted Green Lantern standing atop the Field Museum, gazing up at the multiplicity of Earths filling the sky. A silk cape and hood were draped over the enigmatic woman, who was said to commune with the spirits of the dead. Her green Chinese gown was slit up one side. Emerald light radiated from the mystic lantern dangling at the end of a curved wooden pole.

Lia couldn't believe the other woman was just standing there. "Green Lantern!" she shouted. "Stop staring at the sky and give us a hand."

Green Lantern turned her head toward the indignant teenager. Jade-colored eyes peered from behind an elegant green mask. Her somber voice held the wisdom of eternity.

"If *any* of you wish to survive, Flash, you will follow my light."

METROPOLIS, EARTH-247

THE Legion of Super-Heroes was defending thirty-first century Metropolis from the sort of freak storms that had been unheard of on Earth since the advent of weather control. Whirlwinds whipped through the streets of the high-tech megalopolis, tossing antigravity cars and scooters into buildings and each other. The city's central power grid conked out, creating chaos and confusion. With the Science Police overwhelmed, it was up to the Legion to hold things together. The teenage champions, representing the myriad worlds of the United Planets, flew through the city, held aloft by their Flight Rings.

"Heads up!" Cosmic Boy shouted as a flying convertible ricocheted off the side of Legion Headquarters. He used his magnetic powers to bring the spinning vehicle back under control, but not before a trio of alien passengers tumbled out of the car. Screaming, they plunged toward the ground dozens of meters below. "Someone grab those tourists!"

"I'm on it," Kid Quantum called back. She stopped time around the falling aliens, freezing them in midair long enough for Umbra to catch the trio in a sphere of shadow energy. The blue-skinned Talokian heroine gently lowered the aliens to the ground. Cosmic Boy was impressed by the girls' teamwork; all those training sessions were paying off.

Fragments of the damaged headquarters rained down on the courtyard outside. A jagged sheet of synthetic steel passed through Apparition as she willed herself intangible in the nick of time. XS darted out of the way at super-speed, while Wildfire blasted another chunk of falling debris into atoms.

But that was only one disaster averted. "Rokk!" Saturn Girl shouted as she flew toward Cosmic Boy. "I just received a telepathic alert. C.O.M.P.U.T.O. and the Fearsome Five are attacking the spaceport!"

Figures, he thought. It was just like their enemies to attack Earth while the planet's defenses were down. But did they have enough Legionnaires to cope with the storms *and* the villains? *Too bad we can't all split ourselves into three like Triad.*

Suddenly, an unexpected voice called out over the roar of the wind. "Kid Quantum! Cosmic Boy!"

He looked up in surprise at a winged girl wearing an insectile exoskeleton. Her turquoise hair whipped about wildly. "Shikari?"

The alien tracker had been lost in a time-storm years ago.

"At last I've found you!"

CHAPTER 40

GOTHAM CITY, EARTH-154

Two generations of Supermen and Batmen were making a special delivery to Arkham Asylum. Tied together by unbreakable batropes, the Joker's Daughter and Ardora Luthor squirmed within their restraints while the world's finest heroes savored their victory with their teenage sons. Before they could turn the two devilish daughters over to the asylum's guards, however, the sky above the walled courtyard was split in two by a pair of enormous golden hands.

"Weirdsville!" Batman Jr. blurted. His cloak and costume were identical to his famous father's.

"You said it, buddy!" Superman Jr. agreed. He stepped protectively in front of Luthor's brown-haired young daughter, for whom he nursed an irrational crush. He raised his indestructible red cape to shield her from the hands.

Superman, his temples flecked with gray, shared a worried look with his best friend. "Batman?"

"I see it," the Caped Crusader said grimly.

"What is it, Dad?" Batman Jr. asked. Despite the generation gap between them, he trusted his dad to know what to do in times like this.

The Joker's Daughter stopped laughing.

***

Hmm, Alexander thought. "This one is a possibility."

He examined Earth-154 via the roiling cauldron of energy before him. This particular Earth possessed an optimism and a certain naive charm that made it a promising subject for his experiments. Besides, he rather liked the idea of having a sister.

He gently took hold of Earth-154, cradling it in his right hand, while he searched the multiverse for another potential candidate. His probing gaze settled on another spinning globe. . . .

WASHINGTON, D.C., EARTH-462

The Nazis were marching on Washington, D.C.

That was their first mistake.

Their second was thinking that they could overcome Wonder Woman and her young allies. "Go back where you came from, Axis!" the amazing Amazon commanded the Nazi storm troopers. Her right foot rested on the chest of Red Panzer as the downed German general groaned on the lawn of the National Mall. Helmut Streicher's iron mask bore the dented imprints of Wonder Woman's powerful fists. "Tell your führer that the American flag still waves above the White House and the U.S. Capitol."

The Nazi's attempted invasion quickly turned into a rout. As Wonder Woman stripped the Panzer's armor from him, she saw that her youthful compatriots had the goose-steppers on the run. Donna Troy, the one-and-only Wonder Girl, tied Baroness Paula Von Gunther to the Washington Monument, depriving the cowardly Germans of yet another of their fiendish leaders. Meanwhile, Donna's friends in the Teen Titans Brigade took on the rest of their fascist foes. Robin used a judo move to flip Baron Blitzkrieg into the reflecting pool at the base of the Lincoln Memorial, where Aqualad waited to punch the Baron in the face. The blow split Blitzkrieg's golden helmet in half, exposing his hideous acid-scarred features. Water sprayed from the pool as the villain splashed onto his back.

Abandoning their assault on the capital, the remaining storm troopers fled in a panic. A yellow blur zipped among them, disarming the Axis soldiers at lightning speed. Kid Flash moved almost as swiftly as his celebrated uncle.

At this rate, the retreating Germans would be completely defenseless before they made it back to their U-boats. *Easy pickings for the National Guard,* Wonder Woman thought, *thanks to Donna and her pals.*

Uncle Adolf was having a bad day. . . .

"AND this one," Alexander decided.

He took hold of the patriotic planet with his left hand. In the process, his wrist accidentally bumped into another Earth, sending it careening off into space. The dislodged planet smashed into a third Earth, causing both worlds to explode. *No matter,* Alexander thought. *I still have plenty of other Earths to work with.*

With an Earth in each hand, he relocated both planets to the new center of the universe, outside the Polaris system. It was there that he could best conduct his experiments. "To the petri dish," he murmured.

THIS whole situation was getting more insane by the moment. Donna Troy stood at the helm of New Cronus, staring at the gargantuan hands emanating from the cosmic storm. Those same hands now clutched two glowing blue orbs that looked all too terrifyingly familiar.

"Hey, is that Earth?" Cyborg exclaimed. The outlines of their homeworld's continents could be glimpsed between the huge golden fingers.

"Uh-huh," Animal Man confirmed. Donna knew he had to be thinking of his family back in San Diego. "Both of them."

This makes no sense, Donna thought. As far as she knew, there was only one Earth, which should be billions of miles away. *Maybe these are duplicates?* She prayed that the *real* Earth was still safely on the other side of the galaxy.

Especially after the enormous hands slammed the two Earths together. Animal Man gasped in horror, and Donna felt her own heart skip a beat; the hands pulled apart, revealing a single new Earth floating above the cosmic storm.

Before their eyes, two worlds had become one.

ALEXANDER peered eagerly into the Anti-Monitor's mouth, anxious to see the results of his experiment. Only by combining the best of the parallel Earths could he hope to achieve the perfect world.

"Have you found it yet, Alexander?" the Psycho-Pirate called up to him. The masked villain continued to stand upon his own force-field platform, several levels below. The dormant bodies of their captives kept him company. "What do you see?"

Alexander took a closer look at the hybrid Earth. . . .

GOTHAM City lay in ruins. War had reduced the urban jungle to a barren wasteland, marked by burning wreckage and mass graves. Batman knew that the final battle was approaching, and he was prepared to go down fighting if need be. A radioactive green Batarang rested in his grip as his eyes searched the smoky horizon. He called out urgently to his wife.

"Diana! The Superman Family approaches!"

"I see them, Bruce," Wonder Woman affirmed. Kryptonite bracelets gleamed upon her wrists. Behind the embattled couple, their children stood ready to confront the enemy. Robin, Wonder Girl, and Wonder Boy extracted fresh weapons and ammunition from their utility belts. A handful of mortal followers held aloft a cloth banner bearing the emblem of a bat-winged golden eagle. The last working Bat-Signal, hooked up to a sputtering portable generator, projected the Batman Family emblem into the sky.

No doubt on purpose, the enemy flew straight through the shining symbol. Superman himself led the way, followed by Superboy, Supergirl, and Superwoman. Lois Lane wore the same green-and-yellow costume she had sported ever since her husband first used Kryptonian science to imbue her with powers equivalent to his own.

Is that when everything started to go wrong? Batman wondered. *Or was it when Diana chose me over Clark?* As the Superman Family descended toward Gotham, he felt despair stab at his heart. *How in heaven's name did it come to this?*

"Superman!" he shouted. "This war between us must end now!"

"It will, Batman," the Man of Steel vowed. "With your death!"

Heat vision strafed the battlefield. . . .

"No," Alexander pronounced with a frown. Apparently, the two idealized Earths were incompatible. Scowling, he took hold of the hybrid planet and squeezed it within his grip. Magma oozed between his fingers. *Oh well*, he consoled himself, *I could hardly expect to achieve perfection on my very first attempt.*

Below him, the Psycho-Pirate grew agitated. "I can feel them," he moaned. "Phantom beings brought forth from the unrealized possibilities of Earth-One and Earth-Two, pulled from their restful peace, reborn in pain and given essence." He wrung his hands together. "Then destroyed, billions at a time!"

Alexander rolled his eyes at the madman's histrionics. He wiped the residue of the hybrid Earth from his palms. He plucked another planet from the multiverse and gave it a cursory inspection before tossing it aside. "I planted this garden," he explained calmly. "I have every right to tend it."

The discarded Earth exploded like rotten fruit.

CHAPTER 41

STONEHENGE, ENGLAND

THE ancient monument had witnessed much over the past four thousand years, but never before had it hosted such an assembly. Mages, mystics, and monsters of every description gathered within the ring of standing stones, convened to confront an apocalypse unpredicted by any venerable tome or prophecy. The sun had long since fallen, dispelling the hordes of tourists who customarily swarmed to the monument, yet the night was lit up by the lambent blue glow of thousands of counterfeit Earths. Blue Devil wondered, *Does Stonehenge exist on all those other Earths as well?*

And how do we know that this Earth is the real one?

The burly demon leaned against a towering granite megalith. His golden trident rested against his side. Lowering his gaze from the sky, he scoped out the crowd of exotic characters all around him.

Quite a turnout, he noted. Aside from the rest of the Shadowpact, he recognized plenty of familiar faces from the occult community: The Phantom Stranger, Zatanna, Madame Xanadu, Black Orchid, Baron Winters, Swamp Thing, Traci 13, John Constantine, Sebastian Faust, and the Crimson Avenger, among others. And not only the good guys were represented; Blue Devil spotted the likes of Tannarak, Star Sapphire, and the Demon—Etrigan—among the collected magic-users, not to mention various golems, succubi, and vampires. Even Deadman could been seen floating above the ground. Ordinarily imperceptible to the naked eye, the roving spirit had been rendered visible by the eldritch energy of the sacred site. Conspicuously missing was the Marvel Family, along with Nightshade and Felix Faust. Rumor had it that the latter was in cahoots with Lex Luthor these days. . . .

"Talk about a whole lot of freaks," Blue Devil muttered. "Looks like Halloween in the West Village."

The assorted creatures and conjurers milled about restlessly, conferring in muted tones with their respective allies and associates. Longtime adversaries eyed each other warily, not entirely trusting that tonight's truce would hold. Star Sapphire glared with undisguised malice at Zatanna, who had once used her magic to erase the memories of Star Sapphire and other enemies of the Justice League. There was plenty of bad blood there.

Wonder if we'll get a catfight before tonight is over?

A hush fell over the assemblage as the Phantom Stranger stepped into the horseshoe-shaped ring of stones at the center of Stonehenge. "Thank you all for coming," he said. "I would not have summoned you unless it was a matter of the greatest necessity."

The Stranger's name and origin were shrouded in mystery. Some said he was a fallen angel, others that he was the Wandering Jew. There were almost as many theories about the Stranger's true nature as there were about Stonehenge itself. The brim of a fedora cast his lean face into shadow. A dark blue trench coat offered no hint of his past. A golden medallion gleamed against his white turtleneck shirt. No one present knew who he really was, but when he spoke, the wiser among them listened.

"We are Earth's last hope," he said. "True, our spiritual powers have been altered and dampened due to the Spectre's recent rampage, but that ordeal is over. After much cost, the Spectre has been bound to a new host."

Gasps of relief came from many of the assembled mystics, most of whom had been hiding for the last few days. "About bloody time," Sebastian Faust muttered.

"The Spectre is once more our ally," the Stranger assured the crowd, "as he was when the Anti-Monitor first threatened our Earth." Many present still retained hazy memories of that earlier Crisis. "But if we are unable to summon him for help, the Ninth Age of Magic will end before it has even begun . . . along with the rest of the cosmos."

He clasped hands with Zatanna on his right and Etrigan on his left. Following his lead, the rest of the assemblage linked hands as well. Blue Devil found himself between Sebastian Faust and the Enchantress.

"Less than a few days ago, this ghost was kicking our collective ass," Faust pointed out. The estranged son of Felix Faust, Sebastian wore a rumpled black trench coat. Tinted shades concealed his eyes. "Am I the only one here who thinks this is a really bad idea?"

"Got any others, bub?" Blue Devil asked gruffly. He had to rest his trident against a megalith to free up his hands.

The Enchantress sneered at Faust, who had once killed her, if only temporarily. "If you're scared, go home and cry to daddy."

A few yards away, framed by a looming stone trilithon, two young boys stood on either side of a large shaggy monster who looked like a huge stuffed animal with horns and fangs. Blue Devil felt bad for the two kids; at their age, they should have been tucked into bed by now, not congregating with wizards and demons in a desperate attempt to summon the Spirit of Vengeance.

"The Thunderbolt's not answering my call," Jakeem Thunder whispered to the other boy. The black teenager usually had a Fifth-Dimensional genie at his disposal. "I don't know what help I'm going to be."

Clasping his other hand, Star Sapphire offered her version of a pep talk. "We help now, little boy, so that when we regain our power, we will crush the peasants beneath our heels."

Spoken like a true nutcase, Blue Devil thought. A sworn enemy of the Justice League, the statuesque super-villainess had tried to conquer mankind on numerous occasions. The star-shaped jewel in her tiara imbued her with the spirit of an alien queen, and gave her mystical powers comparable to a Green Lantern.

The other boy huddled closer to his pet demon. "For someone so pretty, she's awfully mean," Stanley Dover whispered to his Monster.

"RRRFF!" the Monster agreed.

Resisting an urge to chuckle, Blue Devil turned his attention back to the Phantom Stranger, who nodded at the woman beside him. "Zatanna?"

Dressed like a stage magician, complete with a top hat, tuxedo, and fishnet tights, Zatanna Zatara cleared her throat. Her unique brand of sorcery required her to recite her spells *backward,* which usually made her sound like she was speaking in tongues.

"ERTCEPS RAEPPA!"

Those among them who could still breathe held their breaths—until a flash of energy flared above the Altar Stone at the center of the monument. Instead of the green-and-white Spectre he was accustomed to, Blue Devil was surprised to see a naked black man kneeling upon the fallen megalith. A Y-shaped incision was stitched across his chest. His dark skin held a gray pallor. Pain and confusion contorted the man's face.

Klarion the Witch Boy, his feline familiar perched upon his shoulder, spoke for them all: "Who in heaven is that?"

The Spectre's new host, Blue Devil guessed. *Poor bastard.*

"What's happeningggg?" the dead man moaned. He didn't seem to know where he was or what had befallen him. Dark green fabric formed from the ether, shrouding his head and shoulders beneath a hooded cloak. He lurched to his feet, staring down at himself in shock. "What's happening to meeeee?"

He clawed at the Y-incision on his chest, as though there were something inside of him that he was desperate to remove. The ugly scar took on an eerie phosphorescent gleam. His skull glowed brightly beneath his face. Frantic eyes pleaded with the circle of onlookers.

"HELP MEEEE!"

Expanding in size until he towered over the standing stones, the new Spectre was born. Skulls glowed within the night-black pupils of his eyes. The billowing green cloak settled upon his gigantic frame. He stared down at Blue Devil and the others, a puzzled expression upon his ashen face. The assembled mystics instinctively shrunk back in fear.

"Spectre," the Phantom Stranger addressed him. Stepping forward, he boldly sought to advise the intimidating wraith. "It is I, old friend. The Phantom Stranger." He held out his open palms. "We greatly need your assistance."

Disoriented, the Spectre paid little heed to the Stranger's words. His bewildered gaze swept over the crowd, as though searching for something. Mortals and immortals alike flinched before his inspection, many retreating from the broken circle or taking shelter behind one of the upright megaliths. Zatanna gave the Phantom Stranger a worried look. "He's ignoring you."

Unfortunately for her sake, Star Sapphire could not say the same.

"Why is he staring at me?" she asked anxiously

The Spectre fixed his gaze on the villainess. Her face went pale behind her rose-colored mask. Jakeem and the others instinctively backed away from her, leaving her exposed and alone before the titanic spirit's inspection. Confusion gave way to condemnation upon the Spectre's baleful countenance.

"Deborah Camille Darnell," he boomed. "As Star Sapphire, you have terrorized and enslaved men throughout the universe. You beheaded and slaughtered those who did not bow down to you. Your perverse hatred of men has resulted in the torturous deaths of hundreds of innocent souls." He pointed down at her with an ectoplasmic finger. "Vengeance must be had!"

"No!" she blurted. The mystic gemstone upon her crown flashed brightly, projecting a shining pink shield before her. But the power of the extraterrestrial jewel was no match for the Wrath of God. With poetic justice, Star Sapphire was instantly transformed into an actual sapphire, carved in her image. Earthlight glinted off the polished facets of the woman-sized gem.

Holy crap! Blue Devil thought. He grabbed for his trident.

For a second or two, it looked as though a skilled gem-cutter had immortalized the alien queen in solid sapphire. Her terrified face was frozen in place.

Then cracks appeared across the surface of the jewel. Gasps and screams erupted from the crowd as bright red blood began to seep from the cracks. A crimson puddle pooled at the base of the unnatural sculpture.

Then the sapphire statue exploded into a million pieces.

Yikes! Blue Devil jumped in front of the Enchantress, shielding his teammate from the flying shards. A blast from his trident disintegrated a wave of jagged splinters.

Panic dispersed the congregation. Witches, warlocks, and were-things fled Stonehenge in a mad rush, running, leaping, flying, and teleporting. The smell of sulfur filled the air as various demons and sorcerers disappeared in puffs of inky black smoke. Deadman vanished from sight as he flew beyond the boundaries of the magical site. Rex the Wonder Dog bounded away on all fours, carrying the Detective Chimp on his back. Vampires transformed into bats and wolves to escape. A lumbering stone golem stomped away from the monument, bearing a young female companion in his arms. Black Orchid ascended on filmy purple wings. The Spectre stared after them all in confusion.

His trident at the ready, Blue Devil looked about for the rest of the Shadowpact. Someone nudged him with an elbow and he turned to see Sebastian Faust smirking at him. Blood spattered the wizard's dark shades.

"Told you," he said.

CHAPTER 42

"WE'RE screwed," Conner said.

He and Nightwing crouched behind an icy ridge, peering out at the sprawling glacial plain beyond. Nightwing examined the scene via a compact pair of binoculars. Conner relied on his enhanced vision. They both scoped out the incongruous golden tower and its guardians.

"There's hundreds of those OMACs surrounding the tower," Conner observed.

"I also see a few of our friends plugged into it," Nightwing pointed out. His breath misted in the frigid arctic air. Conner hoped the older hero's uniform had plenty of insulation. "We free them, we might get the extra help we're missing."

"You've already got some," a new voice announced.

"Cassie?" Conner looked up to see Wonder Girl descending from the sky, her lasso glowing upon her hip. She joined them behind the ridge, so they formed a trinity of young heroes. Conner thought she'd never looked so beautiful.

"Sorry I'm late," she said. "Had to take care of some cleanup in Blüdhaven." She glanced at Nightwing. "I'm so sorry about your city, Dick."

Conner had mixed feelings about Cassie's arrival. While he was grateful for her help, he was worried too. "This is dangerous," he warned her. "It could be the end of everything."

"Why do you think I came?" she said.

"Earth-Q. Earth-616. Earth-25G." Alexander grew increasingly impatient as he sifted through world after world. None appeared to suit his needs as he tossed planets aside, consigning them to annihilation. "No. No. No!"

Several tiers below, the Psycho-Pirate sensed the other man's frustration. He was anxious for the experiment to be over as well, if only so that he could claim his reward. His hand stroked Kara's unconscious face. "Pretty little Power Girl. Alex promised you to me. And when this is over I'll remind him of that."

"Hey, Pirate!" A youthful voice intruded upon his fantasies. Conner Kent came flying at him in a blur of speed. Super-strong knuckles dented the villain's golden mask. "She's way out of your league!"

The impact shook Alexander's floating platform so that he almost stumbled over the edge. "Who?" he blurted. Regaining his balance, he stared down at Earth-One's Superboy. To his dismay, he saw that Nightwing and Wonder Girl were with him. A grapnel line carried Nightwing up to the battery level, where he and Wonder Girl frantically worked to free Martian Manhunter from his niche. Conner hovered in the air, bracing himself for the OMACs' attack.

"TARGETS ACQUIRED." The cyborgs swooped like vultures at the intruders. Conner temporarily held them off with a blast of heat vision, but the OMACs swiftly regrouped. "SUBJECT ALPHA: KENT, CONNER. DESIGNATION: SUPERBOY. SUBJECT ALPHA: SANDSMARK, CASSANDRA. DESIGNATION: WONDER GIRL."

Perched upon a narrow ledge hundreds of feet above the ice, Nightwing tugged at the cables plugged into Martian Manhunter. Would he be able to rouse the comatose J'onn before one of the OMACs got past Superboy?

"SUBJECT BETA: GRAYSON, RICHARD. DESIGNATION: NIGHTWING. TARGET ACQUIRED."

ABOVE EARTH-ONE

Two Green Lanterns faced an army of OMACs.

Staring out through one of the bugship's large yellow "eyes," Blue Beetle gaped in wonder as the glowing heroes defended the Bug from Brother Eye's cyborg guardians. The enormous satellite loomed before him, but the Bug appeared stalled in space, its propulsion systems shut down by Brother Eye, which had infiltrated the Bug's computer systems just as easily as it had infiltrated the world's. Batman struggled futilely with the controls. A scanner picked up an audio transmission from the OMACs:

"RECONFIGURING COMMANDS FROM BROTHER EYE _//_NEW PRO-TOCOL_//_PROTECT BROTHER EYE."

Outside the ship, John Stewart used his power ring to create an intricate maze of emerald bars and barriers to keep the OMACs at bay while Hal Jordan willed a pair of green thrusters onto the rear of the Bug. "Buckle up," he piped into the Bug's loudspeakers. "You're going for a helluva ride."

The emerald thrusters ignited, propelling the Bug straight for Brother Eye. Inside the cabin, Batman and Blue Beetle braced themselves against the back of the pilots' seats. Behind them, Metamorpho transformed himself into a web of chairs and seatbelts to secure the other passengers. Blue Beetle glanced back at Booster, Black Canary, and the rest. Most of the heroes had sober expressions upon their faces, but he was amazed to see that Green Arrow was actually smirking at Green Lantern's crazy stunt.

"That guy's insane," Jaime said, referring to Hal Jordan.

Metamorpho's chalky white face sprouted from the back of Mister Terrific's seat. "You don't know the half of it, kid."

The ship rushed up on the satellite's cyclopean red eye.

"Everyone hang on," Batman warned.

"But not too tight," Metamorpho added with a grin. "It tickles."

The bugship slammed directly into Brother Eye. Metal tore loudly as the impact jolted everyone aboard. If not for his safety harness, Blue Beetle would have been thrown headfirst through the shattered yellow windshield in front of him. As it was, the crash reverberated through his bones. His heart pounded beneath his indigo shell.

Did we really just do that?

The cracked eyes of the Bug opened onto the interior of the station-sized satellite. Service corridors, chutes, and ladders led away from the crash site. Flashing red lights ran along the illuminated pathways, casting a creepy crimson radiance over the scene.

Batman had already left the pilot's seat behind. Not wasting any time, he exited the Bug via the shattered window and set foot within Brother Eye. "Rex!" he called out to Metamorpho.

"Already on it, Bats." The Element Man dissolved into a gaseous mist, albeit one with eyes and lips. "Breathable air comin' right up." The other heroes followed Batman onto the satellite. Blue Beetle started to unclasp his seat belt.

"Booster, Jaime, stay on the ship. Protect it," Batman ordered. "We're going to need a ride back."

Blue Beetle sat back down. Booster Gold dropped into the seat beside him.

Who were they to argue with Batman?

BATMAN and his team hurried into the interior of the sprawling satellite. Metamorpho dispersed throughout the space station, providing them with an oxygen-rich atmosphere. Although Brother Eye was completely automated and unmanned, service corridors had been installed during the satellite's construction. Maintenance tunnels led to every one of Brother Eye's vital systems. Batman was glad that he had included the access routes in the satellite's design. *The best laid plans of bats and men. . . .*

His comrades let him take the lead. He called out orders on the run.

"Black Canary, link up to Oracle," he instructed, referring to Barbara Gordon, the super-hero community's premiere computer hacker. Oracle and Black Canary worked well together. "Download every computer virus on Earth into Brother Eye's network. Try to keep him from shutting down the artificial gravity."

"Got it," she acknowledged, turning left at a junction of two corridors. Batman had briefed them on the satellite's layout during their flight. Her leather boots pounded against the stainless steel floor. "See you soon!"

"Black Lightning," Batman continued. "Head to the memory banks. Fry what circuits you can. Mister Terrific, you know where to go."

The two men took off in the same direction.

That left only Green Arrow awaiting orders. "Hey, Dark Knight. What about me?" He eyed Batman suspiciously; Oliver Queen was never one to keep his mouth shut when something was bothering him. "Why the hell did you call a guy who shoots trick arrows?"

"Just to see if you'd show," Batman said.

Green Arrow laughed out loud. "The brave and the bold, huh? Just like the old days?" He unslung his bow from his shoulder. "Ah, you got me all misty-eyed." He drew a missile from his quiver. "C-4 explosive arrows, coming right up."

"Good," Batman said. "Get to the surveillance rooms. Use them to blind the eye!"

BLACK Lightning and Mr. Terrific raced down a hallway together. Black Lightning threw up his hands as he spotted a wall of computer banks directly ahead, shooting a bolt of high-voltage electricity that caused the computers to explode in a shower of sparks.

He glanced at the other man. "So, you *really* call yourself Mister Terrific?"

"You really call yourself *Black* Lightning?" Mister Terrific countered. His patented T-Spheres hovered around him.

"Hey, back when I started in this business," Black Lightning said, "I was the only one of *us* around. I wanted to make sure everyone knew who they were dealing with." He grinned at Mister Terrific; frankly, he was proud that there were so many other black heroes and heroines these days. "Guess that's why you've got your *name* stitched onto the back of your jacket."

Michael Holt glanced back over his shoulder. True enough, MISTER TERRIFIC was printed in large block letters across his back. He had adopted the name in memory of a long-dead member of the Justice Society. "Actually, that's exactly why."

A flatscreen monitor at the end of the corridor lit up abruptly. A pictographic red eye glared at them. *Whoa!* Black Lightning thought. If it was possible for a computer icon to look pissed, Brother Eye was pulling it off.

"SUBJECT BETA—PIERCE, JEFFERSON—BLACK LIGHTNING."

Without warning, wires and electrical cables exploded from the walls. Animated by Brother Eye's malignant consciousness, they wrapped around Black Lightning, binding him in their coils. The cords tightened around his arms, legs, and throat, strangling him and cutting off his circulation. The insulated cables were obviously intended to neutralize his galvanic powers.

"Uh-uh," he gasped. Raw electricity crackled in his eyes. "Don't touch."

Brother Eye had underestimated him. If the insane satellite thought a bunch of wires could defuse Black Lightning, it had another think coming. Thousands of volts erupted from within him, melting through the insulation and wires alike. White-hot sparks flew in all directions. A lightning bolt blew the leering monitor apart. Smoke billowed out from behind the scorched and splintered screen.

Take that, Big Brother!

Mister Terrific ducked to avoid being singed, then continued on down the corridor. More cables snaked out from the walls and ceiling, trying to snag on to Black Lightning. As the hero repelled the grasping cords with one electrical blast after another, he noticed that the relentless cables seemed to be leaving the other hero alone.

"Hey!" Black Lightning protested. "Why are they going after *my* ass and not yours?"

Confident that the human dynamo could take care of himself, Mister Terrific didn't even slow down. "I've got one superpower," he explained. "I'm invisible to technology. I can't be seen, heard, or recorded by machines."

They ran past an observation deck equipped with a large picture window. Black Lightning guessed that Batman may have intended to use the satellite as an orbital outpost at some point. He caught a glimpse of two brilliant green beams blasting through the OMACs; apparently the Green Lanterns were still holding their own. The Earth glowed brightly in the distance against a backdrop of hundreds of other Earths.

"Is that a useful superpower?" he asked Mister Terrific.

The other hero came to a stop before a metal ladder leading up a vertical airshaft. An upward-pointing arrow was printed beside a sign reading PROPULSION SYSTEMS.

"It is today," Mister Terrific said.

CHAPTER 43

ARCTIC TOWER, EARTH-ONE

"NIGHTWING! Watch out!"

Wonder Girl's warning came just in time. Nightwing ducked out of the way of a laser blast a second before it would have sliced through his skull. The ruby beam scored the gilded surface of the Tower. Nightwing clung to the edge of Martian Manhunter's niche, still trying to rouse the unconscious hero. Hovering in the air beside him, Wonder Girl deflected other laser blasts with her bracelets. "We need more cover, Superboy!" Nightwing shouted.

"I'm trying!" Conner called back. Grabbing onto an OMAC's leg, he flung the captured cyborg at the rest of the Tower's tenacious guardians. The improvised missile momentarily scattered a wing of OMACs, but the flying teenager was still seriously outnumbered. There was no way he could protect Nightwing and Wonder Girl from all of them.

Confident that the OMACs would dispose of the intruders, who were little more than glorified sidekicks, Alexander continued his experiments. "Earth-Three. *My* birthplace," he murmured to himself, clasping the planet in his right hand. "Perhaps there is something there." He reached for a second world. "And maybe Kal-L was right. Maybe Earth-Two has some intrinsic moral value. Something *pure* to add to the mix."

METROPOLIS, EARTH-TWO

WONDER Woman and the two Supermen flew above the empty city. They were anxious to return to Earth-One, but that was easier said than done. Trying to locate one particular Earth amidst the multitude of Earths filling the sky was a daunting challenge even for the Men of Tomorrow.

"My telescopic vision still can't find our . . ." the younger Superman began, only to be struck dumb by the sight of a gigantic golden hand reaching down from the sky.

"What is that?" Diana gasped. The immense hand might have belonged to Zeus himself.

Superman-2 knew exactly whose hand it was. He'd recognize that golden gauntlet anywhere. His expression darkened.

"Luthor."

SPACE SECTOR 2682

DONNA flew from New Cronus as Kyle rallied their combined forces for a direct assault on the mysterious giant hands. Kyle's transformation into Ion seemed to have filled him with new confidence and resolve. Donna prayed that his heightened abilities would give them the edge they needed, so that Jade's tragic sacrifice would not bein vain.

Rest in peace, Jennie. May the gods welcome you into Elysium.

There had already been so many lives lost over the last few days. At least the leaders of Rann and Thanagar had agreed to a cease-fire while they evaluated the satellite footage of "Superboy" pushing Thanagar out of orbit, but that still left the menacing hands to deal with. From her former vantage point aboard her spacecraft, Donna had witnessed the hands destroy one Earth after another. She shuddered to think who might be the next to fall.

Diana. Clark.

A chill came over her. Suddenly she knew, without knowing how, that Superman and Wonder Woman were both in terrible danger at this very moment. " 'A few seconds will make all the difference.' This is what the Titans meant," she whispered, almost in a trance. "I can see it now. They're going to die. . . ."

"What's that?" Kyle asked. His ring had set up an open line between himself and the other heroes' communicators. "Who is going to die?"

Before her eyes, the golden hands tried to fuse another two Earths together. Cosmic energy crackled around the two globes, which seemed to be resisting the merge. The giant hands pushed harder, determined to meld them into a single Earth.

OVERCOME with pain, Wonder Woman and the two Supermen crashed to the ground, landing hard amidst the rubble of the false Metropolis. Phantom images of Earth-Three's villainous Crime Syndicate appeared all around them. Ultraman, Owlman, Superwoman, Johnny Quick, and Power Ring flickered in and out of existence, along with Earth-Three's sole hero, the valiant superscientist Lex Luthor . . . father of Alexander.

Like Diana and the two Supermen, the insubstantial figures writhed in agony.

DONNA felt their pain. In a moment of blinding clarity, she realized at last why she had brought so many of Earth's heroes to the center of the universe: to save the lives of Wonder Woman and Superman. *These* were the seconds that would make all the difference.

"Everyone!" she addressed the troops. "Follow Ion's lead. Focus all of your power together. We may not know how to stop the hands, but maybe we can hurt them. And we have to do it now!"

THE Earths didn't want to come together. Alexander strained against a strong opposing force; it was like trying to push the like poles of a powerful magnet together. Sweat beaded upon his brow. This was taking everything he had.

"Superman, the greatest hero of Earth-Two," he grunted, trying to stay focused on his objective. "My father, Lex Luthor, the greatest hero of Earth-Three. The universe says Supermen and Luthors are destined to be forever at odds, but maybe the universe is wrong." Veins throbbed at his temples. "I will fuse them together. I will!"

ON Earth-Two, the older Superman started to merge painfully with a red-bearded figure in colorful battle armor. Behind him, the phantom image of Superwoman was superimposed on Wonder Woman, the villainess' night-black costume clashing with Diana's own star-spangled garb. Superman cried out in agony as he and Ultraman were forced to occupy the same time and place. A bright red *U* shimmered on top of the famous red *S*, confusing both insignia.

Both Superman-2 and Lex Luthor fought to maintain their separate identities, despite the awesome pressure to merge. *No!/No!* they thought defiantly. *I'm Superman/Luthor.*

Not Luthor/Superman!

"JUST give in!" Alexander gasped as he struggled to meld the two Earths. He regretted torturing his own father in this manner, but the greater good demanded that he hold fast to his agenda, no matter what. "It *has* to work," he insisted. "For the sake of reality."

TAKING Troia at her word, the assembled heroes and spaceships converged on the golden hands. Working together, the space heroes unleashed all their firepower at a single target: the middle knuckle of the right hand's forefinger.

Ion led the attack with a beam of incandescent emerald energy.

Kilowog and Alan Scott added their own willpower to Kyle's beam.

Supergirl used her heat vision.

Starfire fired force beams from her palms.

Animal Man tapped into the Lightning Beasts once more.

Firestorm spewed atomic fire.

Captain Comet turned his telekinesis on the finger.

Red Tornado churned up cyclonic winds.

Adam Strange squeezed on the trigger of his ray gun.

Shift sprayed the finger with corrosive acid.

Hawkman hacked at the finger with his energy-mace.

Hawkgirl fired a "borrowed" Thanagarian laser-pistol.

Cyborg channeled his sonic blasts through New Cronus' cannons.

The Omega Ship, Vril Dox's L.E.G.I.O.N. cruiser, and the combined fleets of Thanagar, Rann, and their various allies launched a simultaneous assault on the universal threat. Energy beams and explosive missiles strafed the colossal finger.

But would it be enough?

"Jason," Martin Stein spoke inside Firestorm's flaming head. "Look at the molecular structure of our target. Those hands are composed of solid antimatter."

"So?" Firestorm asked aloud. "What should I do, Professor?"

"Change the starbolts and the lightning . . . change everything they're throwing at it into raw positive matter."

If you say so, Jason thought. Holding his breath, he did as Stein instructed . . . with spectacular results. A blinding flash of white energy flared within the cosmic storm as the giant finger was sliced clean off.

THE ghosts of Earth-Three vanished from Earth-Two. Wonder Woman and the Supermen staggered to their feet, still shaken from their ordeal. The superimposed memories of Lex Luthor and the Crime Syndicate fled their brains.

"What . . . what was that?" the younger Superman asked. He glanced down at his chest, relieved to see an *S* and not a *U*.

Wonder Woman checked to make sure her lasso was still in place. Her fingers explored the contours of her face, which remained comfortably familiar.

"Alex nearly destroyed Earth-Two," the older Superman explained. "But we're out of his grasp now. *Something* stopped him."

A wave of white energy exploded from the ruptured finger. The flare-up momentarily cut off one grouping of heroes from another. Donna's eyes watered and she wiped the tears away. Tiny droplets floated in space. "Cyborg?" she asked, checking in with New Cronus. "How are we doing?"

No one answered.

"Hawkgirl!" a distraught voice cried out. Donna saw Hawkman looking about anxiously. Ion and Kilowog flew toward him, but there was no sign of Hawkgirl, or most of the other heroes. "Kendra!"

Donna did a quick head count. From where she was floating, it appeared that Adam Strange, Starfire, Red Tornado, Firestorm, Alan Scott, and Supergirl had all disappeared when the cosmic energy surge hit. "Vic? Buddy?" she hailed New Cronus. An ominous silence suggested that Cyborg and Animal Man were also among the missing.

"What happened?" Hawkman asked. He clutched his spiked mace like he wanted to beat an answer out of someone. "Where did they all go?"

Donna had no idea.

"Aaaargh!" Alexander screamed as he yanked his hands out from between the Anti-Monitor's jaws. Blood sprayed from his severed forefinger. He hastily thrust his hand back into the swirling energy to cauterize the wound.

He glared furiously at the multiverse before him. "Was this your doing, Superman?" he hissed, clutching his mutilated hand. "I'll find Earth-Two again. I'll pull it back to my petri dish and I'll crush it to pieces. I'll . . ."

But before he could finish his threat, Nightwing sprang onto the floating platform. He kicked Alexander hard in the chest, sending him flying over the edge. Gravity seized Alex before he could summon up another force field. He plunged into the snow dozens of feet below. The heavy drifts cushioned his fall, and his golden armor protected his bones, but the crash landing still knocked the wind out him. He stared upward in confusion, not quite understanding what had just happened. Why hadn't the OMACs kept Nightwing away from him?

"Alex," a female voice declared, "you have to a lot to answer for."

Power Girl flew above him, along with the rest of his former captives. Martian Manhunter, Lady Quark, Breach, Nightshade, and the Ray kept the OMACs busy, while Superboy and Wonder Girl worked to free the last of the prisoners.

"I'm not sure," Cassie asked Conner. "Should we wake up Black Adam?"

"Are you kidding?" he replied. He ripped out the cables connecting the Egyptian superman to the Tower. "Hell, yeah."

An OMAC dived to defend Alexander, but Power Girl body-slammed the cyborg out of the way. Anger flared in her eyes as she sent a beam of heat vision slicing through the ice and snow between Alex's legs. More OMACs swooped at her, only to be repelled by her fellow heroes. The Ray fried an attacking OMAC with a burst of coherent light. Lady Quark and Breach unleashed their quantum powers, blasting OMACs into the ground with bolts of unimaginable force. Snow and ice flew like shrapnel.

"Where's my cousin?" Kara demanded. Her heat vision inched toward Alexander's crotch. "Where's Lois?"

Two can play at that game, Alexander thought bitterly, recovering from his fall. Raising his hands, he blasted Power Girl and her defenders with the same sort of antimatter bolts he had used against the real Lex Luthor. He scrambled to his feet as the explosive antimatter hurled Kara and the others away from him.

"Lois and Superman are no longer needed alive," he informed them. "And neither are any of you!"

Power Girl and the Ray landed in the snow several yards away. Brushing the freezing flakes off her shoulders, Kara sat up quickly in the snow, only to find herself staring into the bloodshot eyes of the Psycho-Pirate.

"I'm going to make you angry, Power Girl," the madman cooed. His Medusa Mask took on a theatrically irate expression. "So angry you're going to beat the Ray to death." Kara tried to look away, but her fists clenched against her will. Climbing to her feet, she lunged toward the Ray. "Beat the light right out of him!"

"Like Bizarro did to the Human Bomb?" the Ray asked. Unafraid, he stared past the Psycho-Pirate. An imposing shadow fell across the villain.

The Psycho-Pirate looked back over his shoulder. Black Adam stood directly behind him, his mighty arms crossed atop his chest.

"Psycho-Pirate," he said darkly. Clearly, he had neither forgotten nor forgiven the way the madman had manipulated his emotions earlier.

"Black Adam?" The startled villain frantically tried to shift his control from one victim to another. His golden mask began to shift expressions. "You're afraid. You're afrai—"

The Egyptian monarch did not give the Psycho-Pirate another chance to work his mind-warping magic. First he jabbed his fingers into the eye-holes of the mask, deep enough to blind the Psycho-Pirate instantly, and then he shoved the metal mask all the way through the villain's skull.

"No more silly faces," he decreed.

He tossed the bloody mask aside as Roger Hayden's body collapsed onto the snow.

"Jesus," the Ray whispered.

Power Girl, now free of the Psycho-Pirate's spell, glanced down at the disfigured corpse. "Was that necessary, Adam?"

He wiped the blood from his fingers. "Absolutely."

A second later, a streaking blue blur came slamming into them at supersonic speed. Power Girl and the Ray were knocked aside with a single blow each, before the blur sent Black Adam flying backward across the glacial plain.

Superboy-Prime had returned.

NIGHTWING and Wonder Girl had claimed Alexander's spot in front of the Anti-Monitor's mouth. Peering into the open maw, they saw the multiverse expanding at an alarming rate.

"I keep seeing more and more Earths replicating themselves." Nightwing examined the bizarre apparatus in frustration. "I don't know how to shut it off."

"Then let's just tear the Tower apart," Cassie suggested.

Conner touched down beside them. "Guys," he said tensely. Cassie could tell he was freaked out but trying to hide it. His handsome face had gone pale. "He's back."

She didn't have to ask who. Superboy's anxious body language said it all.

The *other* Superboy. The killer.

SPRAWLED upon the ground, broken ice piled in heaps around him, Black Adam gazed up at the youthful interloper floating in the air above him. High-tech armor could not conceal the boy's striking resemblance to Superman. "Who are you?" he asked in confusion.

"Call me Superboy," the boy said with a smirk. "Superboy-Prime." He sneered at his fallen foe. "I thought you were supposed to be one of the tough ones. You don't look so tough!"

Black Adam could not abide the youth's impertinence a moment longer.

Springing into the air, he drove his fist into Superboy-Prime's face. Magical lightning flashed around his knuckles.

"Neither do you," he said.

Grateful for another deserving target on which to vent his rage, Black Adam pounded Superboy-Prime repeatedly. His blows rang out like thunder, punctuated by flashes of eldritch lightning. The false Superboy rolled up into a ball, throwing his hands in front of his face. He wailed like a frightened child.

"The magic . . . the magic hurts!"

Black Adam showed him no mercy. *I'll teach this arrogant pup not to mock his betters.* He only wished it were Luthor's face he was pummeling instead.

"It hurts!" the boy whimpered. "It hurts . . . heh, heh."

Chuckling to himself, Superboy-Prime uncovered his face. To Black Adam's surprise, the boy's youthful features weren't even bruised. He grinned evilly at the older man.

"What?" An unaccustomed chill ran down Black Adam's spine as he realized that the boy had only been playing with him. For over four thousand years, few things had frightened him, but something about this red-eyed youth filled him with dread. *By the gods of my people,* he thought, *what manner of demon is this?*

Superboy-Prime's fist rocketed into Black Adam's face, breaking his nose. Blood sprayed from the shattered cartilage. The force of the blow launched the ancient Egyptian despot into the sky—where he abruptly disappeared in a flash of white light.

CHAPTER 44

THE ARCTIC

"Huh?" Superboy-Prime stared at the empty sky. "Where did he go?"

Alexander appeared below him. "Black Adam was thrown too far away from the Tower," he explained. "He's been transported back to Earth-S."

Whatever, Superboy-Prime thought. He looked down at his partner. Alexander clutched an injured hand against his chest. Blood spattered his golden armor. Nearby, the lifeless body of the Psycho-Pirate lay facedown in a puddle of gory slush. *Serves him right,* Superboy-Prime thought. He had never liked the idea of working with a genuine super-villain.

An idea struck him. "Why can't I be teleported back to *my* Earth like them?" he asked Alex. "Why can't I go home too?"

Alexander scrutinized the new-and-improved version of Superboy-Prime. "An excellent question," he observed. "I'd theorize that somehow you've *changed* at your very core, Superboy."

"They made me change," Superboy-Prime insisted. "I didn't want to, but they made me."

Alexander eyed him with curiosity. "Where did the Flashes take you? That armor you're wearing . . ."

"It collects sunlight," Superboy-Prime said. "I've been gone for years. Imprisoned for so long." The hellish memories tormented him. "Tortured under *red* sunlight." He shuddered at the thought. "But I found a way out. I *always* find a way out."

"I see," Alexander said. He nodded at the Tower, where the battle against the OMACs continued to rage. Black Adam was gone, but the rest of their enemies remained. "They're trying to destroy the Tower before I can complete my search."

"Your search for the perfect Earth is over, Alex," Superboy-Prime said bluntly. He was calling the shots now. "You're going to forget your mixing and matching. You're going to find *my* Earth." He landed in the snow in front of Alexander. "Earth-Prime. We'll make that the perfect Earth." His burning eyes dared Alexander to defy him. "I'll do *anything* to get it back."

Would Alexander object to this new plan? Before Superboy-Prime could find out, a pair of dark green hands grabbed on to him from behind.

"I do not know who you are," J'onn J'onzz declared, "but I am called Martian Manhunter." The alien's pliable arms stretched across the frozen plain. With the strength of Superman, he tossed Superboy-Prime into the broken ice piled at the base of the Tower. "I am Mars' sole survivor."

Superboy-Prime hit the ice hard. Lifting his head, he loosed a blistering blast of heat vision at his attacker, who instantly turned intangible so that the beam passed harmlessly through him. A heartbeat later, the Manhunter resolidified on top of Superboy-Prime with the force of a small bomb.

"There is a reason for that."

UP on the platform, beside Nightwing and Wonder Girl, Conner ripped a sheet of gold plating off the exterior of the tower. A trio of OMACs tried to stop him, but Cassie snagged them in her lasso. The power of Zeus coursed through the lasso, electrocuting the snared cyborgs.

Smooth move, Conner thought, but it wasn't the OMACs who had him worried. He glanced down at the other Superboy. Even though Superboy-Prime was presently taking his lumps from Martian Manhunter, Conner hadn't forgotten how the insane teenager had slaughtered all those heroes back in Kansas. *He nearly killed me too.*

"Forget him," Nightwing urged. "Focus on this. You've still got that tactile telekinesis, right?"

Conner saw where the older Titan was going. "I can disassemble things by touching them, but if you're thinking about this Tower . . ." He shook his head. "It's way too big."

"You have to try," Nightwing insisted.

MARTIAN Manhunter backed away to give Lady Quark, Breach, and the Ray a clean shot at Superboy-Prime. The three energy-based heroes combined their powers to blast Superboy-Prime with a barrage of amplified light and heat. Grimacing in pain, the armored teen fought back against their assault, gradually rising to his feet. Smoke rose from his skin and clothing.

"The radioactivity we're hitting him with . . . ," Breach began.

"It's not slowing him down," Lady Quark finished for him.

Nightshade came up behind Superboy-Prime. "So *light* doesn't bother this monster. Let's try something else." Transforming into a living shadow, she enveloped Superboy-Prime. He sank into the inky blackness. "C'mere, cutie."

"N-no!" He flailed about wildly, frantic to free himself. "K-k-keep the darkness away!" Panicking, he grabbed on to the borders of the dark energy and ripped Nightshade's shadow-self in two. Black fire erupted from the torn shadow, exploding outward to strike Lady Quark and the others. Nightshade's physical body re-formed just in time for her to be hurled into the sky by the blast, along with her fellow heroes.

Like Black Adam before them, they were all thrown beyond the influence of the Tower. White lights flashed above the Arctic wasteland as the four heroes were each transported to their respective Earths. Martian Manhunter, a longtime resident of Earth-One, suddenly found his allies diminished in number.

"Ray? Nightshade?"

BROTHER EYE

"YOUR FRIENDS WILL FAIL, CREATOR."

Brother Eye taunted Batman as the Dark Knight made his way toward the heart of the deranged satellite. The twisting corridor behind him bore witness to his relentless progression through the empty access tunnels. Severed cables dangled from the walls and ceilings, sliced clean through by the sharp edge of a Batarang. Acid stains and smoke fumes hinted at the other weapons he had employed from his utility belt. The interior lights flickered erratically.

He approached an arched doorway. A sign above the door read BRAIN ROOM.

"My friends can take care of themselves," he warned Brother Eye.

"NOT ALL OF THEM. NOT THESE ONES." A monitor rose from the floor. On the screen, Power Girl and Martian Manhunter teamed up to battle Superboy-Prime amidst a snow-covered polar landscape. "THE OTHERS. ON YOUR EARTH."

A panel slid open, revealing another monitor. A close-up showed Superboy-Prime's fist slamming into J'onn's face at super-speed. Chartreuse blood sprayed from the Martian's mouth. "MARTIAN MANHUNTER." A third screen depicted Power Girl reeling from a blow to her head. "POWER GIRL."

Batman realized that Brother Eye was trying to distract him. Doing his best to ignore the dire images, he strode past the monitors into the Brain Room. The spherical chamber was modeled on the Monitor Room back at the Watchtower. An enormous computer server dominated the center of the chamber, while dozens of blank screens caused the ceiling to resemble the interior of a honeycomb. Batman extracted a sharp-edged steel Batarang from his belt.

"AND HIM."

Trying to tune the mechanical voice out, Batman knelt by the server. He used the Batarang to pry out the metal casing.

"YOUR FAVORITE."

One of the dead monitors lighted up. Superboy-Prime stood triumphant over the fallen forms of Martian Manhunter and Power Girl. Turning toward a large golden tower, he glared at a figure standing high above him.

"SUBJECT BETA—GRAYSON, RICHARD—NIGHTWING."

Dick? Batman thought anxiously. He tried not to look at the glowing screens. Close-ups of Dick and the crazed Superboy flashed all around him. Remaining focused on his task, he started ripping wires out of the main CPU. He used the Batarang like a pick, hacking out vital circuit boards and chips. Insulated gloves shielded him from the electricity.

"EYE WONDER . . ."

The screens suddenly went black, leaving Batman in the dark as to Nightwing's fate. Sweat dripped from beneath his cowl. It was hard to say what was worse: watching Dick and his allies fight an uneven battle against the psychotic Superboy, or *not* being able to watch it.

". . . WILL YOU BLAME YOURSELF FOR WHAT HAPPENS NEXT?"

"C'MON, Conner," Nightwing coached him. "Block everything out. You can do this."

Conner's palms pressed against the wall of the Tower. Gritting his teeth, he applied every last ounce of his tactile telekinesis to the massive edifice. Sweat streamed down his face and glued his black T-shirt to his back. He had never tried to take apart anything this huge before, but he could feel the cold metal start to vibrate beneath his touch.

"I know I can," he grunted.

Behind them, flying above the force-field platform, Wonder Girl fought to keep the OMACs at bay. Seven cyborgs tackled her at once. "Aaah!" she cried out as they dragged her away from the Tower.

"Cassie!" Superboy shouted. He hesitated, torn between rescuing his girl-friend and trying to bring down the Tower. *What should I do?*

Harsh laughter assaulted his ears. "Hahaha! Hi, Superboy!" Rocketing up from below, Superboy-Prime barreled into Conner and Nightwing like a bat-tering ram. The two heroes were thrown from the platform. Conner went fly-ing off into the sky, while Nightwing plummeted into the snow below.

Behind Superboy-Prime, Alexander ascended on a fresh platform toward the Anti-Monitor's mouth. "Just a little more time," he promised the evil Su-perboy, "while I search for Earth-Prime."

Nightwing lifted himself up from the snow to find Superboy-Prime stand-ing in front of him. Despite the gross disparity in their power levels, he stood ready to battle the invincible teenager, who laughed out loud as Dick Grayson drew his Escrima sticks from his gauntlets.

"Nightwing?" Superboy-Prime looked like he couldn't believe how clue-less the older hero was. "Come on now. You actually think you can fight me?" He sneered at Batman's former sidekick. "All those Titans did too. Those stu-pid Titans." He lowered his voice to a conspiratorial whisper. "I'm going to tell you a secret." He grinned viciously. "I wasn't even *trying* last time."

Ignoring Nightwing's polymer nightsticks, Superboy-Prime drew back his fist to deliver a killing blow, not unlike the punch that had taken off Pantha's head. *That* had been an accident. This time, Superboy-Prime knew exactly what he was doing.

"Neither was I," Conner said as he grabbed on to Superboy-Prime's right arm from behind. At Superboy's side, Wonder Girl captured Superboy-Prime's other arm. Conner let his evil counterpart know exactly what time it was.

"Round two, bitch."

BROTHER EYE

SPARKS flew as Batman tore into the server with the serrated edge of a Batarang. Mutilated chips and wires piled up on the floor of the Brain Room, but Brother Eye was nowhere close to singing "Daisy" yet. Dozens of plasma screens lit up overhead, their separate displays combining to form the image of a single bloodred eye.

"EVEN AS YOU RIP MY 'BRAIN' APART, EYE AM TRANSFERRING MY MEMORY TO THE THOUSANDS OF COMPUTERS ABOARD THIS SATELLITE. YOU ARE WASTING YOUR TIME, CREATOR."

"No, Brother Eye, I'm wasting yours." He glanced at the timestamp on the nearest screen. In theory, Mister Terrific should have reached his destination by now. "I'm not here to erase your memory." He put down the Batarang, even as he felt the floor vibrate beneath him. "I'm here to distract you."

The room shook violently. Screens cracked above him, sending hairline fractures across the glowing eye. The sudden tremor almost threw Batman off-balance. He grabbed on to the violated server to steady himself.

Well done, Michael, he thought.

"I built you," Batman reminded Brother Eye. "And I put in a limited propulsion system designed to help adjust your orbit." He visualized Mister Terrific at the heart of the propulsion room. "One of my friends just activated that system."

"NO," the artificial intelligence protested, but it was already too late. "NO1010110."

"You've been thrown out of orbit," Batman stated. "It's over."

The floor tilted sharply beneath his boots. The entire chamber rocked back and forth as he staggered toward the exit. Their primary objective had been accomplished; it was time to get out of here. Nightwing and the others needed him back on Earth.

But Brother Eye wasn't going quietly into oblivion. Before Batman could reach the doorway, a titanium blast door came crashing down, trapping him inside the Brain Room. Electrical cables whipped out from the walls to ensnare him. Batman struggled to free himself from the wires; it was like trying to break loose from Poison Ivy's clinging vines.

The satellite creaked and rumbled alarmingly.

"IF EYE FALL, SUBJECT ALPHA—WAYNE, BRUCE—BATMAN, YOU WILL FALL WITH ME."

AN emerald baseball bat the size of a redwood swung into a wing of oncoming OMACs. The pummeled cyborgs went tumbling backward through space, momentarily stunned by the glowing green energy construct.

Home run, Hal Jordan thought. The Green Lantern hummed to himself as he got ready to take another swing with the giant bat. A beam from his power ring linked his willpower to the weapon he had just conjured up. He watched warily as the OMACs regrouped and prepared to come at him again. *Too bad the game's not over yet.*

"Hal!" John Stewart paged him via their rings. An architect at heart, he had trapped another squadron of OMACs inside a glowing three-dimensional maze. "Look at the satellite! They've done it!"

Keeping one eye on the indefatigable OMACs, Hal risked a peek at Brother Eye himself. Rockets flared along the satellite's equator, propelling it out of orbit. Lumbering slowly at first, but then rapidly accelerating, Batman's insane creation began to spin toward Earth. Caught in the planet's gravity well, Brother Eye quaked as though in its death throes.

Looks like we're into the final innings, he thought jubilantly. *Let's hear it for the home team.*

He turned back to deal with the OMACs, only to discover that the cyborgs were having problems of their own. Random discharges of energy crackled across their armored shells as they appeared to short out, one after another. Their limbs locked up. Their mathematically-precise formation came apart. An armada of killer cyborgs swiftly turned into a jumble of zero-gravity flotsam.

"The satellite's going down," John confirmed. "And something's happening to the OMACs. They're cracking apart." Sure enough, the cyborgs' glossy blue armor began to splinter and peel away, revealing the brainwashed humans trapped beneath the ceramic shells. "You can see the people inside."

Suddenly exposed to the vacuum, the innocent men and women were only seconds away from death. "Grab 'em, John," Hal said.

Dozens of glowing green capsules materialized around the endangered humans as John let his 3-D maze evaporate. Hal dissolved his emerald baseball bat and zoomed toward the other Green Lantern, intending to add his willpower to the cause. Then a husky female voice came over his ring.

"Hal, it's Dinah," Black Canary said. "Power's back on in the Bug . . . but we can't find Batman."

He glanced over at John. It looked like his fellow Green Lantern had the situation under control. Hal knew he could count on John to make sure no more innocent lives were lost. The Guardians had trained them both well.

That leaves Batman for me.

"I'm on it," he told Dinah.

Changing course, he sped toward the dying satellite.

BACK aboard the Bug, Black Canary dropped in the pilot's seat, displacing Booster Gold. Aside from Batman, the rest of the team had returned to the ship as planned. Metamorpho had transformed himself into a covering over the ruptured front windows. Booster Gold's pet robot, Skeets, was plugged into a control panel and was busily restoring power to the Bug now that Brother Eye's hold on it was weakening.

She crossed her fingers, hoping that the Green Lantern could find Batman before they had to escape from the doomed satellite. Still lodged in the space station's eye, the bugship rattled around them.

Beside her, the new Blue Beetle squirmed restlessly in his seat. According to Booster, this was the kid's very first mission. "Everything okay?" she asked sympathetically.

"The Scarab says we're done," he said. He cocked his head, like he was listening to a voice only he could hear. "And now it says . . . it says we have to get away from the Green Lanterns. It doesn't like being around them. We have to . . ."

A flash of blue energy startled Dinah. She threw up her hands to protect her eyes from the glare. Blinking, she waited for the light to fade before uncovering her eyes . . . which immediately widened in astonishment.

Blue Beetle was gone!

"Beetle?!" Booster exclaimed. He stared in shock at the empty seat. "Where'd he go?"

Black Canary had no idea.

BATMAN struggled against the wires wrapped around his body. The animated cables squeezed him tightly. Only the reinforced gorget in his cowl, protecting his throat, kept the cords from choking him to death.

"WHY ARE YOU DOING THIS TO ME, CREATOR?" Brother Eye lamented. "YOU CAN TRUST ME TO DO WHAT IS RIGHT." Images of Earth's metahumans flashed across the fractured screens. "YOU CANNOT TRUST THEM. YOU CAN NEVER TRUST THEM AGAIN AFTER ALL THEY HAVE DONE."

As if to prove the satellite wrong, an emerald battering ram smashed through the sealed blast door. Hal Jordan zipped into the Brain Room, the green radiance of his power ring lighting up the chamber. A blast of Lantern energy melted away the wires binding Batman.

"I'll take my chances," the Dark Knight said.

He took Green Lantern's hand.

An emerald aura surrounded both heroes as they phased through the crumbling walls of the satellite out into the darkness of outer space. "I've got him, Dinah," Hal said into his ring. "Get out of there while you still can."

Brother Eye was coming apart before their eyes. Fires erupted from its core, bursting through its outer plating. Metal bulkheads broke loose, flying off into space, as the satellite's decaying orbit carried it down toward Earth. Batman breathed a sigh of relief as he saw the bugship rocket away from Brother Eye, leaving a gaping hole where the satellite's eye had been. Transparent silica patched the holes in the Bug's eyes, clearly Metamorpho's handiwork.

Brother Eye glowed like molten lava as it started to burn up in reentry. Its metal antennae melted away. Red-hot flames licked across its surface.

Batman felt a terrible weight lift from his shoulders. "The OMACs?" he asked.

"Taken care of," Hal assured him. "Looks like John's already transported their human hosts back to Earth."

Then we're done here, Batman thought. For the first time, he allowed himself to concentrate on all the ghastly images Brother Eye had received from the Arctic. *Are Nightwing and the others still alive?*

"Do you remember where Superman's Fortress of Solitude used to be?" he asked Hal.

The Green Lantern gave him a puzzled look. "Yeah. What about it?"

"Fly us there, Jordan. Now."

CHAPTER 45

ARCTIC TOWER

ORDINARY men, women, and children drifted down from the sky as the OMACs reverted back into human beings, their ability to fly failing as the blue ceramic armor around them dissolved. They landed in the snow around the inert bodies of Power Girl and Martian Manhunter. "Way to go, Bruce," Nightwing murmured as he tried to rouse Kara and J'onn. Clearly, Batman had taken care of that "computer problem" he had mentioned before.

Not far away, Wonder Girl and Superboy tag-teamed Superboy-Prime. Cassie throttled him with her lasso, dragging him backward across the ice, while Conner pounded the other Superboy's chest, trying to shatter his freakish alien armor. *I don't know what all that gear is for*, Conner thought, *but it can't be good*.

Superboy-Prime had been tough enough back in Kansas, before his latest upgrade.

"Why are you still fighting me?" the other Superboy griped indignantly. "Don't you understand? Your time is over."

Superboy-Prime reached back and grabbed onto Wonder Girl by her hair. She yelped in pain as his fingers dug into her scalp. "We're going to have *good* heroes again!"

He yanked her over his head and onto Superboy. Their bodies crashed together with a sickening thud. Blood dripped from his fingertips.

"When we bring back my Earth, we'll have real heroes!"

＊

ALEXANDER groped through the sea of Earths, searching for Earth-Prime. Discarded worlds exploded like overripe fruit as he callously tossed them aside. "Where are you?" Then his eyes lit up as he located, far from the other worlds he'd mangled and cast away, one very special Earth—an Earth without any meta-humans at all.

On an Earth where super heroes exist only in comic books, movies, and the occasional novel, you are reading a thick paperback titled Infinite Crisis. *Even though you know the book is nothing more than a work of imaginative fiction, the hair rises on the back of your neck as you realize that Alexander is reaching for your very own planet. Somehow it feels like the book is reading you. . . .*

Alexander's hands reached out to grab his new prize.

"REAL heroes are polite and brave and honest!" Superboy-Prime ranted as he hurled a bloody fist at Wonder Girl. She blocked the blow with her bracelets, but the bulletproof metal cracked under the impact. She staggered backward, losing ground. "And no one will ever know what I had to do to bring *my* Earth back. No one!"

He backhanded Cassie. Blood flew from her lips.

"No!" Conner shouted angrily. Cassie dropped to the ground, barely conscious, and Superboy saw red. He launched himself at Superboy-Prime, plowing into him like a locomotive. "I let you judge me. Beat me down. Kick my dog. But you *hit* my girlfriend?" Seriously pissed, Conner locked his fists together and smashed them across Superboy-Prime's jaw. "You hit her!" He swung his fists into the other teen's jaw again. "No way. No damn way!"

He went to town on Superboy-Prime, drawing blood for the first time. Only a single red droplet appeared at the corner of Superboy-Prime's mouth, but it was a start.

"I am so sick of your hypocrisy!" Conner yelled.

Superboy-Prime glared back at him. "What does that word even mean?" He spit blood at Conner, and caught Conner's next blow in his palm. "You probably think you're smart."

Superboy-Prime crunched Conner's fist. Bones ground together loudly. Conner screamed in agony.

"Well, you're not."

A tightly-focused beam of heat vision pierced Conner's shoulder.

"*Your* world is finished," Superboy-Prime gloated. "I'll be the r-r-real Superboy again. *M-m-me!*"

Despite the searing pain in his shoulder, Conner lunged upward. He grabbed onto Superboy-Prime's waist and sent them both flying into the air. Tactile telekinesis vibrated through Superboy-Prime's alien armor as, locked together, the two youths hurled toward the Tower. Conner felt the arctic wind rush past his face.

"Screw you, 'Superboy,' " Conner growled.

A *whooshing* noise alerted Alexander. Turning away from the multiverse, he saw a pair of Superboys flying toward him like a cannonball. A look of utter terror came over his face.

"No!" he exclaimed. "Keep back. Keep—!"

Conner and Superboy-Prime slammed into the Tower. Flames and electricity exploded from the Anti-Monitor's jaws, throwing Alexander backward. The entire top half of the Tower blew apart. Huge chunks of metallic debris plunged down toward Cassie, Nightwing, and the others. The two Superboys grappled with each other even as the Tower erupted completely. An immense magical thunderbolt, like the one Black Adam had summoned before, shot up into the sky, disappearing into the panoply of multiple Earths.

No! Alexander thought. *It's all coming undone!*

THE multiverse collapsed in on itself.

The myriad Earths flickered in and out of existence as they converged on Earth-One and Earth-Two. The two central Earths moved steadily toward each other, blending their histories together. Vital memories changed within the minds of the two planet's inhabitants.

***

Young Clark Kent walked down a dusty country road, wearing a Smallville High jacket. WELCOME TO SMALLVILLE *read a sign posted up ahead.* On Earth-Two, Superman clutched his head. His brain felt like it was going to explode.

Young Clark Kent flew *down a dusty country road. . . .*

BRUCE Wayne, no more than ten years old, cried in the arms of Alfred Pennyworth. A thunderstorm raged outside Wayne Manor. "WAYNE MURDERS UNSOLVED" read the front page of a newspaper lying atop an antique coffee table.

Taking the Green Lantern Express to the North Pole, Batman suddenly felt his brain begin to throb. For a second, he feared that he was being mind-wiped by Zatanna all over again.

"JOE CHILL ARRESTED FOR WAYNE MURDERS" read the front-page headline. . . .

As the Justice League came together for the first time, a glowing green meteor started to turn the startled super heroes into trees. Black Canary, the only female member of the original team, was rooted to the ground as her slender limbs turned into gnarled wooden branches.

Alongside Superman, Diana grabbed on to her aching head. It felt as though Athena herself was about to burst forth from her skull. The Daily Planet building appeared behind her as a new version of Metropolis rose from the ashes.

Wonder Woman, the first female member of the League, was rooted to the ground. . . .

SUPERBOY-PRIME lifted himself from the snow. To his dismay, he saw that the Tower was no more. Scorched and mangled debris littered the frozen wasteland. A truncated golden stump, jutting up from the ice, was all that remained of the once-looming edifice. He stared frantically up at the sky.

No!

Devastated, he saw that the alternate Earths, including Earth-Prime somewhere among them, had all disappeared. "Where did they all go?" he wailed, realizing that once again his own Earth no longer existed. "WHERE DID THEY ALL GO?"

"This isn't over yet, Superboy." Alexander limped toward him across the snow. "We can still do this together. We can *both* survive." Antimatter energy crackled around them as he teleported them away from the arctic battle-ground.

"I have a plan."

CHAPTER 46

NEW EARTH

SHOVING aside a jagged sheet of metal, Nightwing climbed back onto his feet. The torn gold plating had shielded him from the worst of the falling debris. His ears rang from the explosion, and his body felt bruised all over, but he was still in one piece. He took a second to survey the chaotic scene around him.

The Tower had fallen. Confused civilians who had once been OMACs, shivering in the arctic cold, gathered around burning chunks of debris for warmth. Power Girl and Martian Manhunter tended to the bewildered men and women, using their heat vision to generate more fires amidst the scattered wreckage. Nightwing looked around for their foes, but neither Superboy-Prime nor Alexander Luthor was anywhere to be seen.

Damn, he thought. *They must have gotten away.*

He glanced up at the sky. To his relief, the duplicate Earths were gone. All he saw was the aurora borealis, shining brightly over the polar landscape. *Conner did it*, he realized. *He brought the Tower down—and put the universe back together.*

But where was Superboy now? Had he survived the explosion?

"Conner?!" Wonder Girl shouted nearby. She tossed aside a car-sized hunk of smoldering wreckage as though it were a cardboard box, revealing a battered and bloody Superboy underneath. Half-buried in the packed snow and ice, he struggled to lift his head. His broken limbs twitched feebly.

"Cassie?" His blackened eyes sought her out. "He said I wasn't the real Superboy." Conner coughed up a mouthful of blood and spit it out onto the snow. "He was wrong."

"No," Cassie sobbed. She dropped to her knees beside him.

"I just forgot for a little while . . . We all forgot. . . ." His hoarse voice entreated her. "Don't let them forget again."

"Just hang in there, okay?" Tears glistened on her cheeks. She gently brushed the snow away from his face. "You did it Conner. You saved the Earth. You saved *everyone*."

"I know, Cass," he said softly, his voice fading. Looking on, Nightwing could tell that Conner knew he was dying, but he seemed to be okay with that. A smile played upon his swollen lips as he breathed his final breath. "Isn't it cool?"

His eyelids shut. His chest stopped moving.

Nightwing placed a comforting hand upon Wonder Girl's shoulder as she cradled Conner's body in her arms. He heard shocked gasps above him and looked up to see reinforcements descending from the sky. Superman, Batman, Wonder Woman, Green Lantern, and Superman-2 led a host of heroes as they touched down upon the snow. They stared aghast at the tragic tableau before them.

He clenched his fist. He didn't know where Alexander and Superboy Prime had disappeared to, but he knew one thing for sure.

Somebody is going to pay for this.

"It's our fault," Superman said. Tears brimmed in his eyes. He shook with emotion, his fists clenched at his sides, as he stared at Superboy's lifeless body. "That should have been us."

Wonder Woman tried to comfort him. "I'm sorry, Clark."

"Sorry isn't going to help Conner," Superman said bitterly. "We should have been here."

"Never again, Superman." Batman knew only too well what Superman was feeling now; over the years, he had lost both the second Robin, Jason Todd, and the fourth, Stephanie Brown. "It never happens again." The Dark Knight seemed determined to put the past, and their recent differences, behind them. "We learn from it. We learn from them."

Standing apart from the others, the older Superman had to agree. He gazed sorrowfully upon the somber scene before him. *How did I let things go so far?*

Power Girl approached him. "Where's Lois, Kal?" Frozen tears glazed her cheeks. "Where is she?"

He took her into his arms, and she guessed the truth. "Why?" she sobbed into his shoulder. "Why did we survive?"

I thought I knew the answer. It was to make the Earth a better place. He watched silently as, crushed, the other Superman knelt down beside Superboy's body. Behind him, Wonder Woman embraced a heartbroken Wonder Girl, while Batman rested his hand on Nightwing's shoulder. Superman-2 was moved by the sight of the adult heroes coming together for the sake of their young protégés. *Because I thought they couldn't.*

More heroes, answering the call, arrived upon the scene. Green Lantern helped Martian Manhunter see to the OMACs' former hosts. Robin and the other Teen Titans rushed across the ice to find out what had become of Conner Kent. Superman-2 witnessed their grief, heard their horrified sobs, and felt ashamed.

I thought Conner was disgracing the symbol I built, the original Superman reflected. The Titans gathered around their fallen teammate. Robin was in tears, crushed by the loss of his best friend. Raven, Beast Boy, and Speedy bowed their heads in mourning. *But I picked the wrong Superboy to condemn. And the wrong one to condone.*

After a moment of silence, Beast Boy broke away from the circle. The green-skinned adolescent approached Superman, Batman, and Wonder Woman.

"I don't know where you've been, but I'm glad you're back." He turned into a green polar bear, the better to cope with the cold. "The Society just tore open every meta-human prison on the planet. They're starting a war." He hastily tried to bring the heroic trio up to speed. "Everyone's evacuating the area."

Superman rose to his feet. "What area?"

Beast Boy swallowed hard. "They say that if Superman's city falls, the others will follow."

CHAPTER 47

METROPOLIS

THE City of Tomorrow had become a battlefield.

From one end of the city to another, heroes warred with villains in a no-holds-barred battle for supremacy. Most of Metropolis' eleven million citizens had already fled for the outlying suburbs, but some still huddled in their homes or in emergency bomb shelters. The Big Apricot had endured much in the past, from the Great Depression to alien invasions, but never before had it witnessed a conflict of such superhuman proportions. Literally dozens of costumed super heroes took on an even greater number of super-villains as the Secret Society launched their ultimate assault against the Justice League and their allies. The fighting spread through the city's abandoned streets and plazas, as well as the crowded skies and subway tunnels. Explosions and energy blasts echoed through the concrete canyons. Skyscrapers tumbled to the ground. Elasti-Girl and Giganta, each the size of the Statue of Liberty, grappled with each other in the heart of the city's business district, dwarfing the crumbling buildings all around them.

Superman. Mirror Master. Captain Cold. Mary Marvel. Solomon Grundy. Killer Croc. Plastic Man. Mr. Freeze. Batman. Parasite. Black Adam. Nightshade. Green Arrow. Deathstroke. Evil Star. Wildcat. Electrocutioner. Wonder Woman. Harley Quinn. Metallo. Hourman. Scarecrow. Weather Wizard. Steel. Kid Eternity. Heat Wave. Man-Bat. Black Canary. Metamorpho. Poison Ivy. Aquaman. . . .

Snapping photos from the questionable safety of a darting newscopter, Jimmy Olsen couldn't even begin to name all the colorful good guys and bad guys fighting above, below, and around him. It was impossible to convey the sheer scale of the battle in a single photograph; all he could do was capture random snapshots from the epic conflict.

A masked muscleman, who looked as though he practically sweated steroids, tossed thrashing combatants aside, then grabbed hold of Judomaster. In the background, Black Canary directed an ear-piercing sonic cry at Man-Bat. Blood leaked from the winged monster's tapered ears.

"I finally know who I am," the hulking villain announced as he snapped Judomaster's spine across his knee. "I am Bane. I break things."

Judomaster screamed in agony, his martial arts career ended in an instant.

"Rip!" Special Agent Mitchell Black, better known as Peacemaker, tried to rush to his comrade's aid, but a laser blast blew a hole in his chest. His high-tech battle armor clattered against the bloody pavement.

"Nice helmet," Prometheus quipped. The villain's own cybernetic helmet had downloaded the shooting skills of over thirty world-class snipers directly into his brain. The muzzle of his laser pistol glowed red.

Spray from Hob's River splattered against Prometheus' visor, as Aquaman hurled Count Vertigo into the water. The sea king dived into the river after his foe. . . .

A few blocks away, the Crimson Avenger, Wild Dog, and the Vigilante turned Suicide Slum into a shooting gallery. The ruthless heroes squeezed the triggers of their respective firearms, cutting down the Madmen, the Trigger Twins, and Spellbinder in a blistering hail of gunfire. These urban warriors had no compunctions when it came to filling their enemies with lead.

"I thought the Phantom Stranger and the other spellcasters were bringin' in the Spectre to help?" the Crimson Avenger asked. Her mystic handguns fired with deadly accuracy, despite the bloodred blindfold covering her eyes.

"Help?" Mad Dog echoed. A white hockey mask concealed his features. "I heard he killed three of them and left."

The Vigilante just kept on shooting.

The blare of the pistols and automatic weapons reached the steelworks in the Old Hook Basin district, where Black Adam savagely ripped the head and shoulders off Amazo. Loose servos and hydraulic tubing spilled from the android's sundered torso. Still conscious, Amazo's face bore a stunned expression as Black Adam disdainfully flung the artificial head into orbit.

"Black Adam is on *our* side now?" Gypsy asked in confusion.

Vixen shook her head. "I think he's on his own side, Cindy."

ORDINARILY, Glenmorgan Square was the hub of Metropolis' thriving theatrical district. Now the Riddler capered atop a double-decker tour bus careening wildly through the square. "Question!" he cackled into a tour guide's microphone. "What Society secret weapon is named after today?" He preened like the emcee at an unusually demented roast. "Answer: Dooms—"

A medieval mace smashed into the side of his head, wielded by an armored young warrior astride a winged white horse. "Hush, jester!" the Shining Knight commanded, before riding back into the war-torn skies.

Blood dripping from his skull, the Riddler tumbled off the bus. His comatose body crashed to the ground, just missing Hourman, who was engaged in a life-or-death struggle with Killer Croc. A huge JumboTron TV screen, towering over the neon lights of the square, captured the battle as Rick Tyler used his Miraclo-enhanced strength and speed to hold back Croc's snapping jaws and reptilian claws. His sixty minutes of power were rapidly running out. . . .

THE Blood Pack shared a common origin. Once ordinary men and women, they had each been mutated as an unexpected side-effect of having their spinal fluid tapped by a parasitic alien species that had invaded Earth a few years back. The Justice League had eventually driven the invaders off, but their victims' newfound superpowers remained. Now the Blood Pack teamed up infrequently to defend humanity against major meta-human threats.

"Solomon Grundy! Born on a Monday!"

The infamous monster rampaged through downtown Metropolis, bellowing his name at the top of his lungs. With a tattered black suit and bloodless white skin, Grundy was basically a super-strong zombie that kept rising from the dead no matter how many times he had been destroyed in the past. The mindless creature hammered away at the arched entrance to Union Station, intent only on destruction. His fists shattered solid marble.

"Born on a Monday!"

The entire Blood Pack piled on Grundy, determined to bring him down. Nightblade hurled his throwing knives at the monster's back. Sparx jolted Grundy with a high-voltage electrical charge. Geist turned invisible to avoid an anvil-sized fist, but Ballistic was not so lucky; Grundy's punch dented his armor-plated skin. Transforming her arms into long metal blades, Razorsharp hacked uselessly at Grundy's lifeless tissue. Mongrel blinded the flailing creature by projecting darkforce shadows over his eyes.

But all they could do was slow the monster down.

"Solomon Grundy! Born on a Monday!"

Gunfire, another survivor of the alien parasites, was fighting his own battle several feet away, on the steps of the station. "No more holographic tricks!" he shouted at Dr. Spectro. He turned a handful of loose gravel into a spray of deadly projectiles, chewing up the tiles at the villain's feet. "Move and you're dead."

Colored lenses glowed upon Spectro's chest. "Don't shoot!" he pleaded. "I'm beggin—!"

A blinding blast of red-hot heat swept the front of the train station, vaporizing everything in its path. The Blood Pack, Gunfire, Dr. Spectro, and even Solomon Grundy were instantly reduced to charred black skeletons.

"I *still* can't tell the heroes from the villains," Superboy-Prime complained.

HE and Alexander strolled through the thick of the battle, almost unnoticed in the bloody chaos. Superboy-Prime cleared a path through the hostilities, his eyes glowing like hellfire. Alexander walked a few paces behind his young partner, engrossed in his calculations. His floating World View projected images and equations before Alexander's eyes. Energy blasts and flying rubble bounced off his protective force field.

"I don't even recognize most of them, Alex." Superboy-Prime was still sulking over the disappearance of Earth-Prime, along with the other alternate Earths. "We're using the Society to carry out your new 'plan,' to take *this* Earth instead of replacing it. . . ."

Directly ahead, Major Disaster, a recently reformed villain, created a local-ized earthquake to bowl over several members of the Flash's Rogues Gallery. Superboy-Prime casually grabbed on to Major Disaster's head from behind and twisted it around, snapping his neck. He shoved the corpse out of the way without even breaking his stride.

"But I don't *like* Earth-One," he told Alexander.

"This isn't Earth-One, Superboy," Alexander corrected him. "It never re-ally was. And now this 'unified' world, this New Earth, has been altered again. There are significant changes within its history." A lightning bolt ricocheted off his force-field bubble, briefly revealing its contours. "Wonder Woman helped found the Justice League once again, just as she did before the original Crisis replaced her with Black Canary. Batman still fights for Gotham, even though his parents' killer was caught and is now serving time. And there are unconfirmed reports of a 'Super-Boy' who existed before Superman's first ap-pearance in Metropolis." He stroked his chin thoughtfully. "And that's just the beginning."

Locked in battle, Rampage and Baron Blitzkrieg blocked their path. An orange-skinned woman of giant proportions, Rampage sported a bright red mohawk haircut. Iron muscles bulged beneath a suit of torn chain mail. She lifted the armored Nazi high above her head, ready to throw the Baron into the nearest wall. "*Mein gott!*" the German exclaimed.

A blast of heat vision seared the flesh from their bones.

"I don't care about *this* world's history," Superboy-Prime whined. Stepping over the blackened skeletons, he reached out and ripped the moth-monster known as Charaxes in two. Viscous green ooze splattered Kate Spencer, the new Manhunter. Superboy-Prime vaguely recalled that she was the grand-daughter of the original Atom or something. Charaxes' filmy wings crunched beneath his feet. "I want Earth-Prime back."

"We *can't* bring it back," Alexander told him.

ROARING in defiance, Gorilla Grodd pounded his chest. A score of green and red arrows were lodged in his shaggy pelt, but the super-intelligent ape still had plenty of fight in him. He charged at Green Arrow with surprising speed. A simian fist knocked the archer to the pavement. Arrows spilled from his quiver.

"Ignorant human!" the gorilla bellowed. "Your weapons are as primitive as your woefully unevolved species!"

Before Grodd could deliver a killing blow, Arsenal squeezed the trigger of his miniature crossbow. A bright red quarrel thwacked into the ape's broad back, releasing enough animal tranquilizer to bring down a bull elephant. Grodd tottered unsteadily before crashing onto the ground.

Arsenal helped Green Arrow to his feet. Even though the archer's right eye was swollen shut, he grinned at his former sidekick. "Nice shot."

Roy Harper smirked back. "Well, it's hard to miss a target that big."

Startled cries alerted them to another threat coming their way. A deafening roar that made Grodd sound like a squirrel monkey in comparison reverberated along Bessolo Boulevard, Metropolis' answer to Broadway. Grace Choi, Thunder, Steel, and several other nearby heroes and villains were tossed about like chaff by the unstoppable juggernaut that came charging through the crowd. The wide avenue trembled beneath the monster's tread. Green Arrow's mouth went dry as he spied the oncoming beast.

Over seven feet tall and weighing more than six hundred pounds, the alien monster was covered by a thick gray hide. Bony protrusions resembling jagged stalactites jutted from his forearms, fists, knees, and face. Ferocious red eyes glared out from beneath a sloping brow. Saliva dripped from a mouthful of savage fangs.

Arsenal gulped. "Is that—?"

"Doomsday," Green Arrow confirmed. "The monster that killed Superman."

"Christ, Ollie. What do we do?"

Green Arrow reached for an arrow and drew his bow, even though he knew it wouldn't do any good. *We're toast,* he thought. Then he spotted something overhead and a smile returned to his face. "Look up in the sky, kid."

Not one, but *two* Supermen came diving down from the heavens. Their fists extended before them, they slammed into Doomsday, sending the brute flying backward. The resulting shock wave hurled a slew of nearby villains into the air. Heat Wave, Clayface, the Floronic Man, and many others bounced off the streets and sidewalks. Windows exploded for blocks in every direction. The boulevard buckled beneath Doomsday's weight as he smashed into it. Deep cracks spread across the pavement. Steam rose from the gaping fissures.

Hatred flared in Doomsday's eyes as he recognized the younger Superman; the other Superman had been thrown clear, shocked at the power of this new foe. Rising angrily, Doomsday grabbed the younger Superman. Bone spears protruded from his fist as he pounded Superman in the face, drawing blood. Watching from the sidelines, Green Arrow instantly flashed back to that terrible day a few years ago, when Doomsday and Superman had literally beat each other to death. As before, the two combatants appeared evenly matched in strength and invulnerability.

Green Arrow prayed that history would not repeat itself. Just because Superman had come back from the dead before, there was no guarantee that he would be able to pull off that feat a second time. *C'mon, Big Blue!* Ollie thought. *Don't let that bruiser put you six feet under again!*

Roaring like a prehistoric monster, Doomsday drew back his fist once more. Kryptonian blood glistened upon the jagged bone spurs. Murder burned in his crimson eyes.

"I don't think so," Superman-2 said, racing back to the scene. He caught Doomsday's fist in his hands. His knee slammed into the monster's jaw, breaking off one of the bony spikes. Doomsday blinked in surprise. He was more than a match for one Superman, but two?

Together, Superman and Superman-2 delivered an explosive uppercut that sent Doomsday rocketing into the air. A throng of villains scurried for safety as the heavy creature came down like a meteor among them. A hard landing sent a tremor along Bessolo Boulevard. More cracks ruptured the concrete pavement. A cloud of dust and steam obscured Doomsday's prone body.

The beast was down for the count.

Green Arrow felt his spirits soar as Superman rose up above the fray. His strong voice rang out over the embattled city as he addressed his fellow heroes:

"They *murdered* Superboy. And now they say they're going to take over Metropolis. Then they're going to take Earth." The sun shone off the bright S-shield on his chest. Cheers rose from the struggling champions on the scene. Although battered and bloody, they pumped their fists in the air and raised their respective weapons with renewed determination. "I say, like HELL they will."

All right! Green Arrow thought. He cocked an explosive arrow behind his bow. Beside him, Arsenal loaded another scarlet quarrel into his crossbow. *Let's do this!*

Both Supermen flew at the massed villains, leading a thunderous charge of Earth's super-powered defenders. The Justice League, the Justice Society, the Teen Titans, the Doom Patrol, the Shadowpact, the Global Guardians, the Outsiders, the Creature Commandos, the Seven Soldiers of Victory, the Marvel Family, the Birds of Prey, the Challengers of the Unknown, and a veritable host of unaffiliated heroes and vigilantes surged down the boulevard, trampling over Doomsday's inert body.

Rallying in defiance, the Secret Society of Super-Villains stampeded forward to meet their enemies. The opposing armies met like two gigantic waves crashing into each other. Not pulling any punches, Superman and Superman-2 simultaneously barreled into Bizarro, knocking the deranged humanoid out cold. His still form joined Doomsday's on the demolished pavement.

"Yes!" the Ray cheered, remembering how Bizarro had pulverized the Human Bomb only a few days ago. The Ray zapped toward the villains at the speed of light, eager to avenge his fallen comrades. "For the Freedom Fighters!"

ONE by one, the killers of the Freedom Fighters found themselves confronted by heroes intent on justice. . . .

Batman, Nightwing, and Robin teamed up to take on Deathstroke. The master assassin fought back with the same sword he had used to impale Phantom Lady. Nine-millimeter rounds blasted from the Uzi in his other hand.

Hal Jordan and John Stewart united to combat Sinestro, whose yellow power ring had clipped Black Condor's wings for good. A glowing yellow shield blocked Jordan's attack, but Stewart hit Sinestro with an emerald blast from the opposite direction.

Martian Manhunter and Black Canary held on to Doctor Light, while the Ray and Halo drained the light energy from the evil scientist. Halo, a blonde heroine who had once served among the Outsiders, possessed a glowing aura that flashed through all the colors of the rainbow. Her halo grew in radiance even as Light's luminous energy dimmed.

Wonder Woman and Wonder Girl snared the Cheetah in their lassos. The feral cat-woman beast thrashed helplessly within the golden links. Diana's sword remained sheathed at her side.

Pretty much the entire Justice Society ganged up on Zoom. The insane speedster moved so fast that he seemed to be fighting Jay Garrick, Dr. Mid-

Nite, Hourman, Sand, Stargirl, Wildcat, Jakeem Thunder, and Jakeem's magical Thunderbolt simultaneously. Some of the multiple images were even winning—until a one-two punch from Power Girl and Superman-2 brought him to a standstill at last; not even Zoom was fast enough to avoid those two. The blurry yellow figures converged into a single unconscious figure.

"It's good to fight with the Justice Society again," the older Man of Steel said.

Wildcat eyed the gray-haired Superman suspiciously. "Who *is* that?"

"Who do you think, Ted?" Power Girl replied. "That's Superma—"

A blast from behind tore a gasp from her lungs. She dropped to the ground, her cape smoking.

CHAPTER 48

METROPOLIS

"You shouldn't exist, Kara," Alexander said to Power Girl. Antimatter crackled around his extended fingers. "Do you know how lucky you are? Trillions were erased, but you slipped through the cracks."

He fired at Power Girl again, but Superman-2 flew between them. The antimatter beam sparked off the S-shield on his chest. He gazed sternly at the younger man.

"Alex."

"Superman . . ." Alexander backed away fearfully. His force field shimmered around him. "Your cousin betrayed us, Superman. Don't listen to her! Whatever she's told you . . ."

"You knew Lois would die!" Superman burst through Alexander's force field and grabbed on to him with both hands. His fingers dug into the golden armor protecting Alex's upper arms. "You knew it!" He searched the other man's face for answers. "She was like a mother to you. And to Superboy. Why would you do all this? Why would you *use* us this way?"

"I . . . I'm like my father," Alexander stammered. His World View hovered above them. "The only hero in a world full of villains."

Without warning, a beam of heat vision struck the floating device. The World View exploded in a shower of sparks, hurling Superman-2 and Alexander away from each other. The detonation floored every hero and villain within fifty yards. Sprawled upon the pavement, Alexander stared in shock at the smoking machinery lying in pieces all around him.

"My World View!" he wailed. "It was the source of my power. I was using it to calculate our war plans!"

"Forget your plans, Alex," Superboy-Prime said. He levitated above the wreckage, his eyes burning like miniature red suns. "I told you, I don't want this Earth." He spotted Wonder Girl lying nearby, dazed from the explosion. He took hold of her leg and yanked her off the ground. She dangled upside down above the rubble. "I don't want anything *that* Superboy had."

His heat vision started to ignite once more, but before he could incinerate Cassie like he had so many others, a streak of red and yellow hit him like a bolt of lightning. Superboy-Prime stumbled backward, letting go of Wonder Girl. His face went pale at the sight of a lone figure in a familiar scarlet uniform.

"That's because the guilt is still in there, isn't it?" the Flash challenged Superboy-Prime. "I know you well enough to know that." He threw himself at Superboy-Prime, unleashing a rapid-fire barrage of jabs and punches. "You *killed* Superboy." Superboy-Prime ducked and wove at superspeed, barely dodging the scarlet fists that came at him thousands of times a second. "You killed my friend!"

Other villains started to stir around them. The new Flash took just a heartbeat to dispose of the Penguin, Electrocutioner, Chronos, and Skorpio.

"Y-y-you!" Superboy-Prime stuttered, taken aback by the speedster's unexpected arrival. "You stay away from me, Bart!" He shrunk back, incapacitated by fear . . . for the moment.

"Bart?" Recovering from the explosion, Wonder Girl stared at the adult Bart Allen, who gently helped her to her feet. "Kid Flash?"

"Long story, Cass," he said tersely.

Wonder Girl examined him in confusion. "But . . . you're *old*. And you're the Flash?"

"No!" Bart said emphatically. "My grandpa's uniform was the only thing that could survive the trip back. And I was the only one of us that could still run." He let go of Cassie's hand. "I came to warn everyone, but when I got here, I collapsed. Passed out in Tokyo." His voice ached with regret. "I didn't know that Superboy-Prime would go after him again . . . after Conner. . . ."

He raced back at Superboy-Prime. "You're roadkill!"

"Don't touch me!" the murderous teen shrieked.

"Still got that speedster phobia?" Bart ran in circles around Superboy-Prime, hitting him from every direction at once. It looked like Superboy-Prime was being pummeled by a scarlet whirlwind.

"Get away!" Superboy-Prime shouted. He slammed his hands together hard enough to generate a shock wave that sent Bart somersaulting down the broken boulevard, his scarlet uniform torn and shredded. Superboy-Prime took advantage of Bart's tumble to launch himself into the sky, away from the speeding hero's reach. Beams of emerald energy zipped past him as John Stewart and Hal Jordan took down Sinestro. Superboy-Prime swerved to avoid being caught by a stray blast from the Green Lanterns' rings.

There were far too many heroes and villains around, getting in his way.

"It was so much better," he said, "when I was the *only* hero in the universe." A sudden inspiration, sparked by seeing the Green Lanterns in action, struck him. He knew now what he had to do. "I'll . . . I'll fly right through Oa. Right through the planet at light-speed." Alexander had explained to him how the Guardians' world was the true center of the cosmos. "There will be a new Big Bang. Everything will begin again!" He flew up and away from the devastated city streets, leaving the ferocious battle behind. Let the others fight over this stupid "New Earth." He was going to reboot the entire universe.

"And I'll be the only one left!" he cried out.

HIGH above Centennial Park, Martian Manhunter spotted Superboy-Prime rocketing toward space. Pausing only long enough to knock the Weather Wizard from his perch atop a towering waterspout, J'onn scanned Superboy-Prime's mind from a distance. Even in the midst of war, he had not forgotten who was ultimately responsible for the tragic events of the last few days. Appalled by what he found in Superboy-Prime's brain, he telepathically relayed the information to every hero below.

This is Martian Manhunter. I've read the other Superboy's mind. So now each of you has too.

In an alley off the boulevard, Batman listened intently to J'onn's voice in his head. He and Nightwing and Robin had Deathstroke on the ropes, but Slade wasn't going down without a hell of a fight. Snatching a Batarang out of the air a second before it would have connected with a vital pressure point on his throat, Deathstroke threw the weapon back at Batman, who deflected the Batarang with one of the reinforced fins on his gauntlet. Nightwing and Robin came at Slade from his right, taking advantage of the one-eyed villain's blind side. . . .

He's heading for Oa.

Superman-2 checked on Power Girl, who seemed to be recovering from Alexander's sneak attack. Defeated villains, including Felix Faust, Lady Vic, Catalyst, and the Ventriloquist, littered the pavement all around them. The Ventriloquist's scar-faced dummy had been reduced to splinters. Superman-2 and Power Girl both looked upward as they received the telepathic message.

I urge any and all of you who can to take the skies.

Heeding the urgent summons, over two dozen flying heroes took off after Superboy-Prime. Both Supermen, Martian Manhunter, Power Girl, Mary Marvel, Booster Gold, Breach, the Ray, the Shining Knight, Zauriel, S.T.R.I.P.E., and the two Green Lanterns were among the airborne contingent.

They caught up with him hundreds of feet above the Daily Planet building. Captain Marvel Junior, Mary Marvel, and Halo grabbed on to Superboy-Prime, slowing him down, while Zauriel brandished his flaming sword. "Halt!" the warrior angel demanded. "In Heaven's name!"

"Your sword's magic," Superboy-Prime said mockingly. "But magic doesn't hurt me." His heat vision sliced the sword in half and burned straight through Zauriel's right wing. "Go back to your creator, angel!"

Breach was coming up right behind Zauriel, accompanied by Looker and Technocrat. The former was a glamorous female vampire, thankfully immune to sunlight; the latter was encased in a suit of high-tech battle armor. Zauriel spiraled past them, his wings in flames.

"Watch out!" Breach hollered too late. Superboy-Prime's heat vision burned through his protective containment suit. He exploded spontaneously, incinerating both Technocrat and Looker. The Marvel pair were flung backward by the blast, along with several other heroes. Weapons and body parts rained down on Metropolis.

Superboy-Prime reached the upper atmosphere, leaving a trail of injured and unconscious heroes in his wake. "Stupid!" he snarled. A sweep of his arm sent Steel flying into Northwind. The metal-clad inventor and the feathered bird-man were knocked senseless by the collision. They plummeted through the clouds below. "Stop following me!"

A powerful hand clamped around his ankle.

"Alex tricked us," Superman-2 said. "He tricked both of us." His impassioned tone implored Superboy-Prime to surrender. "But it's not too late to end this madness."

The air thinned as they passed beyond the exosphere into space. Looking down past Superman-2, Superboy-Prime saw only a handful of heroes still chasing them both; Superman, Power Girl, Martian Manhunter, and the Green Lanterns remained in pursuit. He kicked at the older Superman's hand, trying to break free.

"I know it's not too late, Superman." His alien armor generated an electrical aura around him, allowing him to speak in space. "And I'm going to be the one who ends it."

Going to lightspeed, Superboy-Prime tore away from Superman-2 and the others. He sped off into deep space, flying infinitely faster than a mere speeding bullet. The Green Lanterns tried to keep up with him, but he swiftly left them in the space dust. Out beyond Pluto, John Stewart spoke into his power ring.

"He's already out of sight," he informed Superman and the rest. "There's no way we'll catch him."

Meanwhile, Hal Jordan contacted the Corps headquarters on Oa.

"Guy, it's Jordan. We have a problem."

BATMAN slammed Deathstroke's face into the hood of a Metropolis police car. Bat-cuffs bound the assassin's hands behind his back. Slade's pistol rested at Batman's feet, and shell casings crunched beneath his boots. A few yards away, Robin applied first aid to a nasty cut on Nightwing's forehead. All three heroes looked like they'd been through a war. Their uniforms were shredded. Bumps and bruises covered every inch of their bodies.

But we got the job done, the Dark Knight thought.

The war still waged on around them. Batman was tempted to take the Batplane after Superboy-Prime, but he felt sure that the battle in the sky would be over, one way or another, before he got there. In the meantime, there was plenty of work to be done on the ground.

"Do you know what you and your friends have done, Nightwing?" The bitter words came from a red-haired man in golden armor. Batman recognized the insidious architect of the Crisis from Power Girl's description. Alexander

Luthor stood in the middle of the wrecked boulevard, gazing up at Gotham's heroes with a disgusted expression on his face. "You've damned this Earth!"

Straining visibly, Alexander unleashed an antimatter blast at Nightwing and Robin, slamming them into the wall of the alley. They dropped to the ground.

"No!" Batman exclaimed. Leaving Deathstroke behind, he charged back into the thick of battle. Red Star, his body burning like a white-hot flame, grappled with Red Panzer in front of Batman, blocking his view of Alexander. Taking a running start, Batman leaped over the heads of the furious combatants. He tackled Alexander, knocking him to the ground. "No more will die!" The palm of his hand smacked into Alexander's jaw. Blood spewed from the villain's mouth. "Not because of you!"

Just then, however, the Frankenstein monster, who was busy wrestling with the General, plummeted onto the boulevard from an adjacent rooftop. The pair of artificial monstrosities smashed into the street only a few feet away from Batman and Alexander, and the overstressed concrete finally gave way. Nearly the entire block opened up beneath the boulevard, swallowing them all up, along with a mountain of debris.

Everything plunged into the murky subway tunnel below.

CHAPTER 49

SPACE

"Heh," Superboy-Prime snickered, his fists front and center as he soared through the cosmos. He glanced back over his shoulder. There was no sign of Superman or the others. He grinned smugly and turned his eyes forward once more. "I *told* them they weren't faster than m—"

Wait a sec, he thought. *What the heck is that?*

Peering through the interstellar void, he spotted something peculiar up ahead. It looked like a glowing green line stretching across space. The line seemed to grow larger as he sped toward it until, suddenly, all he could see was a wall of emerald light directly in his path. He crashed into and through the wall, sending chunks of solid green energy spraying out into space. The thick green light was all around him, for miles in every direction. He hammered at the light with his fists, forcing his way through.

The Lanterns, he realized. *They're trying to stop me.*

On the other side of the wall, Guy Gardner stood shoulder-to-shoulder with all seven thousand two hundred members of the Green Lantern Corps, give or take a Lantern or two. The redheaded Earthman was the only human in the line; the rest of the Corps was composed of aliens of every size, shape, and description. Humanoids, insects, invertebrates, arthropods, crustaceans, reptiles, amphibians, fish, birds, marsupials, plants, fungi, androids, and various mineral-based lifeforms were all represented among the legendary interstellar police force. Guy was positioned between a four-armed purple lizard and an avian humanoid with orange feathers and a beak. Power rings shone brightly upon fingers, fronds, tentacles, and talons. All seven thousand-plus rings were aimed straight ahead. The result impressed even Guy.

"A three-hundred mile thick wall of pure damn *willpower* will slow him down."

But not for long. Within minutes, Superboy-Prime came busting through the wall, only to find the entire Corps waiting for him. Hundreds of individual Green Lanterns buzzed around him, firing their power rings at the deranged young man. Guy did his part by torching Superboy-Prime with an emerald flamethrower. "The Thin Green Line will stop 'im cold," he predicted. Fiery sparks flew from his power ring.

"Cold?" Superboy-Prime shrugged off the barrage. His blue armor was dented on one shoulder. Anger twisted his face. "You don't know cold."

Baring his teeth, he blew out a gust of arctic breath that froze the two nearest Green Lanterns solid. One was mostly an oversize head, with two spindly arms and three legs. The other looked like a shaggy, humpbacked ape. A frosty glaze dimmed their emerald auras.

"Cold is being the only survivor of an Earth that was erased from history." Superboy-Prime flew straight through the freeze-dried Lanterns, shattering them like glass. Two glowing power rings zipped away from the brittle remains of their previous owners, already on the search for new Lanterns.

"RING STATUS REPORT. GREEN LANTERN 885 DECEASED. SPACE SECTOR SCAN 885 FOR REPLACEMENT SENTIENT INITIATED."

Superboy-Prime zoomed into a mass of attacking lanterns, turning yet more aliens into shattered popsicles. A shining steel robot tried to escape, but was caught by another icy blast from the boy's lungs. He came apart like so much space junk.

"RING STATUS REPORTED. GREEN LANTERN 3544 DECEASED. SPACE SECTOR SCAN 3544 FOR REPLACEMENT SENTIENT INITIATED."

"Cold is being imprisoned in a lifeless dimension because you tried to do the right thing." Superboy-Prime's heat vision burned a hole through the chests of four more Green Lanterns, killing them all with a single blast. Their rings flew off in different directions.

"RING STATUS REPORT. GREEN LANTERN 34 DECEASED. SPACE SECTOR SCAN 34 FOR REPLACEMENT SENTIENT INITIATED."

"Cold is what this universe has made me."

Aw, cry me a river! Guy thought sarcastically. He had no sympathy for a psycho who had already killed at least six of his fellow Lanterns. His ring projected a huge emerald buzz saw at Superboy-Prime. The spinning blade tore into Superboy's side, slicing through one of the golden tubes linking the various components of his armor. Yellow sunlight gushed from the severed tube.

"Code Fifty-Four, Lanterns," Guy bellowed. "Excessive force has been approved . . . and encouraged!"

Superboy-Prime yelped in protest as his precious solar energy leaked away. He fused the tube shut with a surgical blast of his heat vision, then turned on Guy. Smashing the glowing buzz saw to pieces, he flew straight at the red-headed Green Lantern and grabbed Guy by the throat. Super-strong fingers squeezed down on the emerald force field protecting the Lantern's throat. Guy had to pour all his willpower into the force field just to keep Superboy-Prime from snapping his neck. Energy beams from the surviving Green Lanterns bounced off the enraged teen.

"I wonder who *your* ring is going to go to," he said.

A concentrated energy blast punctured Superboy-Prime's shoulder armor, distracting him. Whipping his head around, he saw Hal Jordan and John Stewart arrive on the scene, leading a charge of reinforcements from Earth. Superman, Superman-2, Martian Manhunter, and Power Girl sped toward the blazing space battle.

"His ring stays with him," Jordan said.

MARTIAN Manhunter linked the minds of the newly-arrived heroes, allowing them to communicate telepathically. *The Green Lanterns have blocked his path,* he thought to the others. *But I would suspect for only so long.*

Superman nodded grimly. *Hal knows the plan.*

So did Superman-2. He flew beside Power Girl, whom he intended to spare from what was to come. This was his fault, not hers. He needed to end it now, no matter what, but he wasn't going to risk Kara's life, too.

Plan? She looked at him in confusion. *What plan? What are we—?*

We need to do to this without you, Kara, he explained.

Puzzlement gave way to concern on her face. *Do what?* she thought anxiously.

Up ahead, Superboy-Prime broke Hal Jordan's arm. "Don't pretend you're a good guy now," Superboy-Prime ranted at the Green Lantern. "I saw what you did, Hal Jordan. You're one of the worst." Driven mad by grief after Mongul destroyed his city, Jordan had once betrayed the Corps and turned into a villain, but he had since regained his sanity. "You're a maniac!"

Not any more, Superman-2 realized at last. He had judged these new heroes too harshly before. His telescopic vision revealed that Superboy-Prime was only a heartbeat away from ripping Jordan's arm from its socket. Superman-2 knew they had to make their move. *Now, Superman!*

Now! the younger Superman thought back.

They accelerated to top speed, leaving Power Girl behind. *Kal!* she called after him, but Superman-2 didn't look back. The Men of Steel rammed into Superboy-Prime simultaneously, tearing him away from Hal Jordan and carrying him off into space.

Destiny awaited.

METROPOLIS

CHUNKS of broken boulevard filled the subway tunnel. The unconscious bodies of Deathstroke, the General, and Frankenstein, along with various other casualties of the cave-in, lay half buried beneath the rubble. Sunlight filtered through the stirred-up dust and smoke. Water leaked from broken pipes. Shattered asphalt was piled in heaps on the tracks.

His head ringing, Batman pushed himself up from the floor of the tunnel. Both his body and uniform had suffered multiple cuts and abrasions, but the protective Nomex fabric and Kevlar panels in his suit seemed to have spared him any major bone fractures. Grunting, he looked around for his quarry. He hadn't forgotten Alexander's attack on Nightwing and Robin, right before the street had collapsed beneath them.

"We're not so different, Bruce." A figure in scuffed golden armor lunged from the shadows, landing on top of Batman. Alexander's hands tightened around Batman's throat, strangling him. "Your parents were murdered. You work to make the streets they were killed on safe." His voice was eerily calm and rational. "My Earth was murdered. I work to make the universe it was killed in safe."

Batman struggled to free himself. The armored gorget in his cowl's neck-piece, already fractured by the constricting cables in Brother Eye's control room, provided only partial protection from Alexander's energetic attempt to throttle him. Batman gasped for breath, wondering why his opponent wasn't using his antimatter blasts instead. Perhaps something had happened to the source of his power? Maybe the attack in the alley had used up the last of Alexander's extra-dimensional energy?

"You usually think too small," Alexander scolded him. "You save street corner by street corner. You work too hard for too little." Batman's fists pounded uselessly against his golden armor. "But you finally decided to take a shortcut with Brother Eye. You just weren't going to take it far enough."

Unable to reach his utility belt with Alexander on top of him, Batman groped about for a weapon. His fingers fell upon the cold, steel grip of Death-stroke's automatic pistol.

"You need to learn to take shortcuts to justice."

Batman grabbed on to the gun and swung it into Alexander's face. The block knocked the villain backward. His fingers came away from Batman's throat, and the Dark Knight jumped to his feet. Alexander was backed up against a heap of debris. Batman aimed the pistol at his skull.

"I never take shortcuts," Batman said. He thought of all the innocent victims who had died because of this man's heartless machinations. Conner Kent. Most of Blüdhaven. The Flash. The Amazons. And so many others, all over the planet. "But today I might make an exception."

He pressed the muzzle of the gun against Alexander's forehead.

"Bruce," Wonder Woman said from behind him. Her sword clanged to the ground at his feet. "It's not worth it."

She touched down on the debris-strewn tracks. Dust motes danced in the hazy sunlight. The ravaged boulevard above them creaked ominously. Out of the corner of his eye, Batman glimpsed Robin helping Nightwing to his feet.

At least Dick and Tim are still alive. . . .

Alexander peered up the length of the gun barrel at Batman's unreadable face. His eyes were wide with fright. He swallowed hard, uncertain of his fate.

"I know," Batman said, tossing Deathstroke's pistol away. It landed a few inches from Diana's sword. He remembered Maxwell Lord, and all the defenseless people killed by Brother Eye's warped agenda. *The last thing we need is more blood on our hands.*

She nodded and stepped forward, holding out her lasso. "Get up, Alexander," she commanded. "You're coming with . . ."

A deafening crack, coming from directly overhead, drowned out her words. The tunnel started to cave in right above Batman's head. Tons of concrete, along with sparking wires and a cascade of unconscious super-villains, rained down on them. Looking up, Batman spotted Black Manta, Shockwave, Jinx, Lionmane, and the Mad Hatter amidst the avalanche.

Moving quickly, Wonder Woman yanked Batman out of harm's way. The falling debris cut them off from Alexander, who scrambled away on the other side of the collapse. A fresh cloud of cement dust filled the tunnel, causing Batman to cough violently. Water streamed from ruptured pipes. Severed electrical cables spit out sparks.

"Dammit," Batman said as the dust finally settled. The tunnel was completely blocked, making any further pursuit of Alexander impossible. By the time Wonder Woman could clear all the rubble away, Luthor's malevolent "son" would be long gone. *We'll have to deal with him later.*

An even larger gap now opened above their heads. The sights and sounds of the battle above reached Batman and Wonder Woman through the jagged aperture, reminding them that the war was not yet won. They shared a moment before returning to the fray.

No words were spoken, but the two heroes nodded silently at each other. Despite their differences, things felt settled between them. *The important thing,* Batman thought, *is that we're all on the same side. Diana, Clark, and me.*

Just as it should be.

"WHERE do you think you're taking me?"

Superboy-Prime thrashed wildly, struggling to free himself as the two Supermen carried him across the universe at super-speed. Superman-2 pummeled the youth with his fists, while the younger Superman held him in place, much as Barry Allen and the other dead speedsters had done back in Kansas, an eternity ago. Superboy-Prime felt like he was being abducted by the Flashes all over again.

"You can't take me back to the Speed Force," he challenged them. He jabbed his elbow into Superman, but the Man of Steel refused to let go of him. "You're not *fast* enough. You're—"

An effulgent green glow fell over them. At first Superboy-Prime thought that the Green Lanterns had another ambush in store, but then the trio of superhumans smashed into a huge green asteroid. Stony green fragments went flying in all directions, joining what appeared to be an extensive asteroid belt composed entirely of luminous green chunks of rock. Superboy-Prime heard the younger Superman grunt in pain.

"Oh. I see where you've brought me now," the boy said smugly. "To where Krypton exploded." He grinned in relief, amazed that the two so-called heroes could be so stupid. "But this kryptonite isn't from my universe. It won't hurt *me*." He felt the younger Superman's iron grip start to loosen. "All you're going to do is kill *this* Superman." He laughed out loud. "I mean, did you actually think these rocks would stop me? For real?"

The older Supermen ignored his taunts. Superboy-Prime's derisive laughter faltered as he contemplated the men's somber, determined expressions. A faint red glow began to emanate from somewhere behind him, quickly outshining the verdant luminosity of the kryptonite. The smirk vanished from his face, replaced by a look of sudden terror, as he realized where the two Superman were *really* taking him.

Burning brightly, Krypton's red sun loomed before them.

No! Superboy-Prime thought. He kicked and screamed, desperate to get away, but the crimson sunlight was already sapping his superhuman strength. A ring of kryptonite boulders orbited the red giant, which was over fifty times larger than Earth's yellow sun. The Supermen cut through the meteor belt as they plunged into the sun. They descended quickly through the outer layers of the sun, which affected all three Kryptonians the same way. By the time they reached the blazing heart of the red giant, they were each screaming in agony. Superboy-Prime's alien armor cracked and boiled away, leaving him clad only in his Superboy costume once more. He writhed in the Supermen's grasp, even as they convulsed as well. *Please*, Superboy-Prime pleaded. *Make it stop!*

The torture eased only slightly as they passed through the red sun and out the other side. Too weak to control their headlong flight, they smashed through yet another enormous kryptonite asteroid. They tumbled beyond the rocky belt to where a very special ally waited to catch them.

***

THE planet's name was Mogo and it had traveled light-years across space to come to the Supermen's aid. A lush green world, its thickly forested equatorial belt had been shaped so that open clearings formed a vast topiary symbol that could only be perceived from space: the insignia of the Green Lantern Corps.

Mogo, a sentient planet, was possibly the Corps' most unusual member, and definitely its largest.

Its gravity took hold of the helpless trio. . . .

Looks like Hal called in the cavalry, Superman thought as he plummeted through Mogo's atmosphere, along with Superman-2 and Superboy-Prime. Green winds rose up to slow their fall. In his debilitated state, he was grateful for the living planet's assistance. Shattered chunks of kryptonite fell with them.

Between the glowing green meteors and the crimson sunlight, Superman felt like his skin was on fire. He was already weaker than he had been in years. Unable to resist Mogo's gravity, the three Kryptonians slammed to the ground amidst one of the spacious clearings along the planet's equator. Lush green trees rose in the distance. Smoke and dust billowed up from the craters formed by their crash landings.

Remind me not to do this again, Superman thought.

Groaning in pain, he found himself flat on his back at the bottom of his own crater. His scorched red cape, which was torn and frayed, was spread out beneath him. Fist-sized lumps of kryptonite were scattered all around him, adding to his torment. Toxic fumes rose from the sizzling meteorites. He heard the older Superman moaning somewhere nearby.

He stumbled to his feet, wincing at the sight of the kryptonite. The harsh green glow hurt his eyes, forcing him to look away. He could feel his strength fading by the moment. Blood trickled from a cut on his lip, like he'd just gone nine rounds with Doomsday. *Keep it together*, he urged himself. *This fight's not over yet.*

A single bound carried him out of the smoking crater. Looking around, he saw Superman-2 lying unconscious at the bottom of another crater. There was a third crater adjacent to the others, but it was empty. So where was Superboy-Prime?

"Superman."

The insane youth announced his presence with a searing blast of heat vision that burned through Superman's cape, destroying what remained of the yellow *S* insignia there, and striking Superman squarely in the back. Superman stiffened, crying out in pain. The smell of burning flesh tainted Mogo's air.

"Die!" Superboy-Prime shouted. Pouring on the heat vision, he stalked toward Superman. He kicked the harmless kryptonite fragments out of his way. His armor had completely burned away, so that he now looked just like a teenage Superboy once more. "Die and leave the universe to me!"

The beams from his eyes flickered, then disappeared completely. "My heat vision!" he exclaimed. His eyes bulged from their sockets, but all they could produce were a few feeble red flashes. "What's happening?"

The red sun radiation, Superman realized, his back no longer burning quite so badly. *Kicking in at last.*

"You're losing," Superman-2 declared. Rising from his crater, he tackled Superboy-Prime from the side, shoving the boy away from the younger Superman. First- and second-degree burns scarred the older man's face and hands. Blood dripped from his mouth. He was clearly in bad shape, but his spirit was still going strong. "Kryptonite differs between realities, but light and darkness? They're constant."

He delivered a powerful right hook to Superboy-Prime's face.

Superboy-Prime's head snapped backward, shaken by the blow. He raised a hand to his lips. For the first time, his own blood glistened on his fingertips. "You!" he accused, enraged by the injury. "You took my super-powers? You made me bleed!"

He threw Superman-2 over his shoulder, slamming him into the ground. The impact tossed mounds of dirt and kryptonite into the air. Not letting up, Superboy-Prime drove his fist into the older man's face like a pile driver. Blood splattered the *S* on his chest.

"You said the Earth was dark and corrupted!" Superboy-Prime raved hysterically. "You saw it all happen! You saw our sacrifice become pointless!" He was out of control now, hammering the fallen hero again and again. "Lois died because of them! My Earth died because of them!" Angry tears leaked from his eyes. "You *have* to understand why I'm doing this!"

"Understand?" The younger Superman grabbed onto Superboy-Prime from behind, pulling him away from Superman-2. Smoke still rose from the younger Superman's back. "Understand what, Superboy? That you're willing to destroy everything and everyone to feel what?" He dragged the struggling teenager across the meteor-scarred clearing. "Special? Needed?"

Superboy-Prime snatched a piece of kryptonite from the ground. "I am special!" He spun around and smashed the glowing green rock into Superman's head. The fragment exploded into splinters. A deep cut tore across Superman's right temple. "I am needed!" He seized Superman's throat with both hands and started choking the life from him. Kryptonite littered the ground around them, stealing Superman's strength and invulnerability. "I'm the only one who can rescue this messed-up universe. I'm only one who knows how to make it right." His fingers dug into Superman's flesh. His face was livid. "I will be its greatest hero!" Superman gasped for breath. "When you're gone, I will be . . . Superman!"

Not if I can help it, the real Superman thought. Mustering his strength, he grabbed on to Superboy-Prime's chest. His fingers seized the tarnished S-shield sewn into the fabric. "Superman?" With an explosive motion, he ripped the symbol right off Superboy-Prime's chest. "You'll *never* be Superman." He threw Superboy-Prime off of him and jumped to his feet. He tossed the sullied *S* onto the ground. "Because you have no idea what it means."

The merciless red sun beat down on them as Superman and Superboy-Prime circled each other like weary gladiators, exhausted from a daylong contest. Superman's arms felt like they weighed a thousand pounds. Sweat mixed with the blood flowing from his wounds.

"Yes, I do!" Superboy-Prime insisted. "I'm from Krypton! A better Krypton than yours ever was!"

Superman shook his head. "It's not about where you were born. Or what powers you have. Or what you have on your chest."

"Shut up!" Superboy-Prime shrieked at him. He drew back his fist, clearly intending to deliver a killing blow like the one that had decapitated Pantha.

"It's about what you *do*," Superman said. Bruised and bleeding, and beset by kryptonite on all sides, he still found the grit and determination to step forward and slug Superboy-Prime with everything he had. A follow-up blow connected with Superboy-Prime's chin and the lights went out in the youth's eyes. Superboy-Prime hit the ground like a fallen star.

Panting hoarsely, Superman dropped to his knees. The kryptonite radiation gave his skin a sickly green tint. Every muscle in his body ached, and his head was spinning. Through blurry eyes, he glimpsed Superman-2 lying unconscious a few yards away, unable to help him. Darkness encroached on the younger Superman's vision. Throbbing veins bulged beneath his skin. Falling forward, he tried to push the nearest kryptonite fragment away, but his fingers were too weak. He collapsed limply amidst the poisonous meteors. "It's about action," he whispered.

The sickening green glow penetrated his closed eyelids. The emerald light grew even more intense and, for a moment, Superman thought the end had come. Then he heard a fearless voice call out from above.

"There they are!" Hal Jordan yelled. Emerald blasts shot down from the heavens, destroying the kryptonite around Superman. The Man of Steel opened his eyes to see Hal, John Stewart, Guy Gardner, Martian Manhunter, Power Girl, and a host of alien Green Lanterns touch down on the surface of Mogo. A luminous green sling cradled Hal's fractured arm.

A beam from John Stewart's ring gently lowered Power Girl to the ground. "Karen," he reminded her, "your powers are going to disappear just like theirs if you stay here too long."

"Just let me down, John," she said impatiently. "Now."

Dozens of Green Lanterns surrounded the defeated Superboy. Their rings piled restraint after restraint onto the unconscious teen. "Thanks for the assistance, Mogo," Hal addressed the planet.

A disembodied voice was carried upon the wind. "I am sorry to hear of our losses, Green Lantern 2814.1."

Martian Manhunter helped Superman sit up. "Superman?" He examined his injured teammate. "The Green Lanterns have incinerated all the kryptonite in the immediate area. Are you—?"

"I'm okay," Superman said weakly. He was more worried about the other Superman. "How is—?" He gazed across the clearing, to where Power Girl knelt by the older man's side. He could hear the man's heartbeat weakening. *It was too much for him*, Superman realized. *The trip through the red sun. That final battle against Superboy-Prime.*

Power Girl knew what was happening too. She clutched the dying hero's hand.

"Kal!"

He lifted his eyes toward hers. "Kara," he rasped. "We stopped him."

Turning his head, he beamed proudly at his younger counterpart. He looked happy to have been proven wrong about the other Superman. Glad to have witnessed his triumph. "Superman stopped him."

"You're going to be fine," Power Girl insisted, despite everything. She tried to help him up. "You *have* to be fine."

He smiled gently. "It's okay."

"No," she pleaded. "Don't leave me alone, Kal." Her eyes filled with tears. "Please, don't leave me alone again."

Superman and the other heroes gathered around them. Power Girl sobbed, overcome by the tragedy and the thought of being isolated once more. "It can't end this way. . . ."

With his dying breaths, Superman-2 tried to comfort her. "It can't . . . Kara. . . ." Comprehension dawned in his peaceful blue eyes. "I finally understand now. I know what Lois was trying to tell me, there at the end." He placed a hand against her cheek.

"What are you talking about?" she asked softly. She pressed her own hand against his.

"I'll always be with you, Kara," he said. "Even if you can't see me, I'll always be here." He gazed up at his heartbroken young cousin. "It's not going to end." His head fell backward, so that he was looking skyward now, up at the stars beyond the glowing red sun. "It's *never* going to end . . . for us. . . ."

The younger Superman turned his own telescopic vision toward space. Was it just his imagination, or was one star in particular glowing more brightly than the others?

The original Superman smiled at the beckoning star. He nodded his head, as though hearing distant voices intended for his ears alone. "My friends," he murmured. "My family . . . Lois?"

He died with her name on his lips.

Fresh sobs wracked Power Girl's body. The other heroes bowed their heads in mourning. Looking out into space, the younger Superman now saw *two* stars shining brightly in the celestial firmament. He felt strangely certain that somewhere, far beyond the realm of mortal men and supermen, happy days still lay in store for Lois and Clark.

They deserved all that . . . and more.

CHAPTER 50

A television news broadcast played in the background.

"... one day later and already reconstruction has begun in the heart of Metropolis. People are coming from all around the world, offering to help in any way they can."

On the screen, the great steel globe of the Daily Planet building lay toppled amidst a pile of rubble. The landmark structure was cracked and broken apart, but dozens of enthusiastic volunteers were helping to clean up after the disaster. Homegrown heroes Steel and Iron Maiden loaded the burnished globe onto the bed of a heavy-load truck. A caption running along the bottom of the screen announced that billions of dollars had already been raised to rebuild Metropolis. The camera zoomed in on a handmade banner stretching across the battered facade of one of the surviving skyscrapers. THANK YOU! the banner read, next to a spray-painted S-shield.

"Vigils are being held across the globe for those that are still missing ... and for those that gave their lives to save the Earth from annihilation."

No decision had been made yet on whether to rebuild the Watchtower on the Moon, so people were convening at the JSA headquarters in New York City. Martian Manhunter and Booster Gold, Aquaman, and Aquagirl greeted Hawkman, Donna Troy, and Ion as they returned from their mission in space. A monitor screen held the names and images of the heroes who had vanished when the cosmic storm erupted: Alan Scott, Supergirl, Animal Man, Firestorm,

Hawkgirl, Adam Strange, Starfire, and Cyborg. Also listed as missing were Tempest, Dolphin, and the new Blue Beetle. Search plans were already being discussed.

While the other heroes conferred, Booster Gold stared up at the photograph of the Blue Beetle. He felt a twinge of guilt as he eyed Jaime Reyes' indigo mask.

"SIR," Skeets chided him. "I'VE ALREADY TOLD YOU. HE TURNS UP AGAIN. WELCOMED BACK BY GUY GARDNER OF ALL PEOPLE."

"I know," Booster sighed. "I just kinda liked the kid."

The robot zipped about impatiently. "HISTORY IS WAITING FOR YOU, SIR. I SUGGEST WE START TO CHANGE IT."

"A memorial service for Superboy is already being planned for next week in Metropolis. . . ."

ON a lonely hillside outside Smallville, the sun slowly set on three new graves. Headstones bore the names of Clark, Lois, and Conner Kent. Krypto sat beside Superboy's grave, his head hung low. Superman gave the dog's head a comforting pat as he knelt next to the grave, his head bowed in mourning. Power Girl placed flowers upon the graves of Superman-2 and his beloved wife. John and Martha Kent stood a few feet back, comforting each other. Lois Lane waited to console her husband.

"OUR hearts go out to the millions of people who lost a son, a daughter, a wife . . . or a husband."

THE ghost of Crispus Allen wandered the empty back alleys of Gotham. A green cloak wafted around him. Fresh blood stained his pale gray hands. Pieces of broken glass lodged in the window frame of an abandoned building. Torn between despair and confusion, he gazed at his reflection in the darkened glass. "What am I?" he moaned.

The Spectre stared back at him.

***

"AN investigation is now underway. . . ."

Jay Garrick clicked off the TV. He turned toward Bart, who was sitting on an examination table in a doctor's office in Keystone City. Barry Allen's old uniform, now tattered and torn, covered the young man's body as he brought Jay up to speed on his family.

"Wally's cool," Bart said. "So are Linda and the twins." His voice was deeper than Jay remembered, more adult. "I spent the last couple years with all of them, Jay. In a place that's not easy to explain."

"And you came back *running*." Jay didn't understand. "I thought the Speed Force was destroyed."

"It was," Bart confirmed. "I had some residual speed locked inside me. But I used it all up in Metropolis." He looked at the older man, who was still in uniform as well. "But according to all these tests, *you* still have speed, right?"

So it seems, Jay thought. "It has nothing to do with the Speed Force. My meta-human gene is active." He shrugged his shoulders. "I guess I'd top out at the speed of sound."

"Well, I'm done running." Bart pulled down his cowl. Although a few years older, he was still recognizably Bart Allen. Long brown hair flopped across his brow. A slight smile suggested that he was okay with everything that had happened. The torn red uniform disappeared back into the secret compartment in his ring as Bart changed into a T-shirt and pair of jeans. "I'm *not* the new Flash," he insisted. "From here on out, Jay, you're the fastest man alive . . . again."

CHAPTER 51

GOTHAM CITY

A cold rain drenched the city streets, washing away the dirt and grime. Metal bars and shutters guarded the closed-up shops. Well after midnight, a solitary figure sought shelter beneath the unlit marquee of a vintage movie theater. Icy raindrops trickled down his neck as he perused a soggy newspaper by the light of a nearby streetlamp.

"HEROES SAVE EARTH!" read the front page of the *Gotham Gazette*. "CELEBRATIONS ACROSS THE GLOBE!"

One of the hands holding the paper was missing its right forefinger. Water dripped from the man's soaked red hair. He angrily crumpled the paper into a ball.

"The fools," Alexander Luthor hissed. He shivered beneath his heavy overcoat. "The Earth isn't saved." He tossed the wad of newspaper onto the sidewalk. "But it will be. It will just take another plan. My calculations have already begun." He sneered at the squalid urban jungle surrounding him. "I *will* make this world a brighter place."

The flashing blue light of a police car approached and he instinctively ducked into a murky alley. He had no doubt that Batman and his allies had already provided his description to the local authorities, but Alexander did not intend to be apprehended, not while there was so much work still to be done. Waiting patiently while the police car drove by, he contemplated the wretched alley that was now his refuge. Rats scurried in the shadows. Rotting garbage spilled from a rusty Dumpster. Alexander's nose wrinkled at the stench. The miserable alley seemed to embody all that was debased and unsatisfactory about this new Earth, strengthening his resolve to make things right, no matter what the cost.

"I will make it perfect," he vowed.

Glancing around, he suddenly realized where he was. This was Crime Alley, the very place where Bruce Wayne's parents were gunned down so many years ago. Alexander found it ironic that his aimless wanderings had brought him here. He smiled ruefully. Fate, it seemed, had a sense of humor.

"Ha ha ha ha ha ha ha ha ha!"

Eerie laughter echoed through the alley, startling Alexander. He looked about anxiously, but saw only shifting shadows all around him. His heart pounding, he started back toward the exit of the alley, hoping to reach the lighted street beyond. *I have to get out of here,* he realized.

A gaunt figure emerged from the shadows, blocking his path. A gloved hand fingered a bright yellow boutonniere tucked into the lapel of a garish purple jacket. Acid sprayed from the flower, striking the left side of Alexander's face.

"Aaaarrghh!" He screamed as the acid ate away at his skin. His flesh sizzled. Red hair was burned to a crisp. Clutching his face, he dropped onto the cold, wet floor of the alley. His knees sank into a greasy puddle. He frantically splashed the filthy water onto his scalded face. The fallen rain did little to ease his pain.

"Ha ha ha ha ha ha!"

The Joker stepped into the light. A sadistic grin stretched his florid red lips from ear to ear. Wild green hair surmounted his grotesque white face. He opened his hand, revealing a metallic joy buzzer attached to his palm. Brilliant blue sparks arced between the exposed electrodes of the devilish device. He laughed maniacally.

"Ha ha ha ha ha ha!"

"W-wait," Alexander stammered. He stared at the sparking joy buzzer in horror. Hideous burns and blisters covered half his face. Desperate to escape, he crawled on his hands and knees away from the grinning harlequin. "H-help! Somebody h-h—!"

His outstretched hand fell upon the tip of a well-buffed black shoe.

"Oh, Alex," a familiar voice said.

Tilting his head back, Alexander saw the *real* Lex Luthor standing over him. A black umbrella kept the rain away from Luthor's immaculate black overcoat, pants, and shoes. He gazed down at the pathetically dirty and mutilated figure at his feet.

"You made a lot of mistakes," he said. "You underestimated Superman. Superboy. *Me.*" His voice had the scolding tone of a disappointed schoolmaster. "But the biggest one?"

Gloved white hands seized Alexander's collar, dragging him deeper into Crime Alley. Crazed laughter rang in his ears.

"N-no. P-please. . . ."

The Joker drew a gun from beneath his jacket. The barrel of the pistol was almost ridiculously long, but Alexander wasn't laughing. Unlike the Joker.

"Ha ha ha ha ha ha ha ha!"

"You should have let the Joker play," Luthor said. His face bore not a trace of mercy or compassion. His dark eyes held the memory of past humiliations. "Now who's stupid?"

The Joker squeezed the trigger.

BLAMM!

Alexander's brains splattered the alley.

The Joker laughed.

Luthor smiled.

FOR once, it was a beautiful morning in Gotham City. Down by the waterfront, sunlight rippled upon the azure surface of the harbor. Smiling people went about their business upon the docks. Gulls squawked overhead, amidst a clear blue sky. The Bat-Signal was nowhere to be seen.

Clark Kent glanced wistfully up at the sky. "I wish I knew how long it was going to take to fly again." His powers had not yet recovered from his trip through Krypton's red sun. "Day like today, I'm going to miss it." He strolled along the dock, his blue jacket slung over his shoulder. "I'm going to miss a lot of things."

"Conner won't be forgotten," Bruce Wayne assured him. The dashing billionaire wore a dark jacket over a black turtleneck. The bruises on his face were already starting to heal.

"None of them will," Diana said. Like the two men, she had donned normal civilian garb. Passersby failed to recognize her in a casual white pantsuit. "They saved the future."

Clark appreciated their sentiments. "What's in your future, Diana?"

"I think it's time to find out who Diana is," the incognito Amazon said. She gazed thoughtfully at the mild-mannered reporter. "Those glasses really work, Clark?"

"They put things in perspective," he told her.

Bruce nodded. "So will retracing the steps I took when I first left Gotham." He glanced around to make certain that no one was listening. "I'll be rebuilding Batman. But this time it's going to be different."

"How?" Diana asked.

A voice called out up ahead. "Hey, Bruce!"

Tim Drake leaned against the rail of a large yacht anchored at the end of the wharf. Dick Grayson stood beside him upon the boat. A pair of crutches testified to the painful aftereffects of Alexander Luthor's antimatter blast, but Dick's injuries didn't seem to be bothering him too much this morning. A long sea voyage would give him plenty of time to recover. He and Tim waved at Bruce from the top of the waiting gangway.

"C'mon!" Tim shouted. "Let's go."

Bruce gave Diana a subtle smile. "This time I'm not going alone."

The three comrades paused at the foot of the gangway. It was time to say good-bye . . . for the time being.

"I know we'll always have our differences," Clark said, "but at the end of the day, we all want the same thing. Justice." He looked solemnly at his friends, and spoke with the voice of Superman. "When Earth needs us standing together, we will find a way. No matter what."

"We will," Diana promised.

Bruce nodded as he headed up the ramp. There were no handshakes, no hugs; things still weren't perfect between them, but Clark felt confident that any lingering tension would melt away with time. He smiled to see Bruce so eager to join his young protégés.

"Take care of yourselves," Bruce said.

Clark turned toward Diana. "Do you need a ride somewhere?"

Diana shook her head. "Thanks," she said with a grin. "I have one." Stepping over to the opposite side of the dock, she opened an invisible door and disappeared halfway through it. She paused before vanishing entirely into the unseen aircraft. "Clark?"

"Yes?"

"It's good to have friends," she said.

Clark watched Diana disappear, then turned and strolled back down the dock toward the street. A bird flew by overhead and he basked in the warmth of the yellow sun.

"A world without Superman, Batman, or Wonder Woman, huh?"

His wife was waiting for him on the sidewalk. Lois looked radiant in a crisp yellow blazer and pleated skirt.

"For now," he said.

"And what are you going to do with all this free time, Mr. Kent?" she asked.

Clark took Lois in his arms and kissed her passionately. "I'm sure I'll figure out something," he said when they broke for air. Arm in arm, they walked across the sunlit city. Glancing at all the busy traffic and pedestrians, Clark momentarily worried for these people's safety while his powers were out of commission. Then he remembered all the other heroes who had come to Earth's defense during the seemingly infinite crisis: the Teen Titans, the Justice Society, the League, and everyone else. His fears faded away.

"But until we get back, I'd say the world is in good hands."

EPILOGUE

OA,
THE CENTER OF THE UNIVERSE

HE heard them coming.

"They're asking me to deliver the speech at tonight's ceremony," Guy Gardner said. The injured Green Lantern limped with the aid of a glowing emerald crutch. He shook his head as he recalled the Corps' recent losses. "Thirty-two Lanterns killed in action. Hasn't been a massacre like that since . . ."

"I know when," Hal Jordan said curtly. A luminous green sling cradled his arm.

"Oh. Yeah." Gardner sounded slightly embarrassed, remembering who had been responsible for that previous massacre. No doubt he was glad that Jordan was back to being a good guy again. "You know, I'm not one for public speaking."

"You'll do fine, Guy."

They entered a heavily guarded wing adjacent to the Guardians' towering Citadel. Rows of reinforced cells, glowing with Lantern energy, lined a stark green hallway. These sciencecells had been designed to hold the Corps' most dangerous enemies; in the past, such infamous criminals as Sinestro and Evil Star had been confined here. Now a new prisoner was being held under maximum security.

The two men peered through the window of one of the largest sciencecells. A spidery metallic network surrounded what appeared to be a miniature red dwarf star, floating in the center of the cell.

"Quantum containment fields surrounding a junior red sun eater, which surrounds a pint-sized red sun in turn," Guy explained. "Fifty Green Lanterns watching him at all times." He looked at Jordan. "You think it'll hold him?"

"I pray it does," Hal answered.

Deep inside the miniature red sun, a solid green cube contained the prisoner. Within the cube, cut off from any source of yellow sunlight, Superboy-Prime heard the two Lanterns walk away, leaving him alone with his thoughts.

He sat on the edge of an emerald cot. His hair was greasy and uncombed. Dark rings shadowed his eyes. A gaping hole remained in the front of his Superboy costume, revealing his bare chest. The exposed skin was pale and hairless.

"I've been in worse places than this," he muttered. Scowling down at where Superman had stripped the S-shield from his chest, he dug a finger into his flesh and carved out a bloody "S" where the insignia had been. He grinned at his grisly handiwork. Faint red sparks flared within the pupils of his eyes.

"And I've gotten out of them."

GREG COX is the *New York Times* bestselling author of numerous books and short stories. A lifelong comic book fan, he has previously written comics-related stories for such anthologies as *Tales of the Batman* and *Legends of the Batman*. He has also written novels and stories based on such popular series as *Alias, Buffy the Vampire Slayer, Daredevil, Farscape, Iron Man, Roswell, Star Trek, Underworld, Xena,* and *X Men*. His official website is www.gregcox-author. com.

He lives in Oxford, Pennsylvania.